MORE
THAN
Nothing

MORE
THAN
Nothing

SOPHIE
HAMILTON

 Montlake

Text copyright © 2025 by Sophie Hamilton

Published by Montlake, Seattle

www.apub.com

Amazon, the Amazon logo, and Montlake are trademarks of Amazon.com, Inc., or its affiliates.

EU Product Safety contact:
Amazon Publishing, Amazon Media EU S.à r.l.
38, avenue John F. Kennedy, L-1855 Luxembourg
amazonpublishing-gpsr@amazon.com

ISBN-13: 9781662531316
eISBN: 9781662531323

Cover design by Allyse Karam
Cover images: © Creative Travel Projects / Shutterstock;
© Douglas Sacha / Getty Images

Printed in the United States of America

*For anyone who has ever been made
to feel less than.
You are endlessly and uniquely more than.*

Chapter 1
Elenie

"Best place in town for breakfast if you can put up with being served by scum." The bristles of Chief Roberts' porn-star mustache rippled with familiar contempt. It had an entity of its own which was often mesmerizing, but today it made barely a blip on Elenie's radar. She was too busy casting furtive glances at the hot stranger on the opposite side of the table.

Pulling the notepad from her apron pocket, she smoothed her face into a blank mask and hoped the spring on her hair clip would last to the end of her shift. She could feel it weakening; a few sun-lightened strands of hair tickled her neck where they'd escaped.

"Hello, gentlemen. D'you know what you'd like to order?" Her stomach pitched and flipped, and she objected on principle. Elenie couldn't afford to be a pitch-or-flip kind of person. Sweeping the stray curls behind one ear with the end of her pen, she waited.

All coiled energy and loose limbs, the chief's breakfast companion had an intense, angular face and espresso-dark hair. His graphite gray tactical pants and polo shirt were casual but immaculate—America's Next Top Model in the latest Police Issue Workwear catalogue. He was magnetic. Compelling. She could swear the air crackled around him. Something about the way he watched her made Elenie feel like she had been dropped into deep water from a great height.

And his forearms. Bronzed skin, corded muscles, strong, lean, capable. Don't start her on the forearms or she'd be fangirling like a sixteen-year-old.

She swallowed. Eager to keep as low a profile as possible, Elenie made sure her own appearance whispered, "Nothing to see here": bistro apron tied over knee-length skirt, burgundy short-sleeved shirt, scuffed sneakers. Uniform faded but clean, nude lips and minimal makeup. But however hard she tried, it was impossible to slide under the radar of the police chief's disdain.

"Elenie Dax." A mix of derision and disgust coated her name on his lips. Elenie resisted the urge to squirm, but it was tough. The diner's bustle and babble continued around her, mingling with the country music station she'd tuned into at opening time. "One fifth of Pine Springs' biggest vermin problem. As you'll find out."

Low on charm, light on team-playing skills and manners, Chief Roberts was a bullfrog of a man. Always curt, he usually stopped shy of blatant offense, but not today. Not in this company. Drumming stubby fingers on the table, his puffed-out chest pulling the buttons tight across the front of his shirt, Roberts was bursting to make some kind of an impression on his new buddy.

"I can give you a couple more minutes if you're not quite ready?" Elenie could feel her ears turning red and hot. Her eyes on her notepad, she channeled professional efficiency through every inch of her body, armor and shield clanking securely into place. She reminded herself that she dealt with people like the chief every day. She could write a thesis on jackasses.

"No need. I'll have the pancakes and black cherries, please." Mr. Sexy Forearms had a voice as rough as sand on marble. She felt it like fingertips down her spine.

"Same," growled Roberts. "With a side of bacon and coffee. And make sure it's hot. Don't leave our plates sitting on the counter."

"Of course. *Grozna si kato salata.*" To take the only petty revenge she could, Elenie fell back on her favorite form of stress relief, sliding in a foreign insult she hoped she'd get away with—unless the hot stranger was Bulgarian, of course, but it didn't look likely.

Roberts drew wiry eyebrows together. "No, just the pancakes. If I wanted salad, I'd have asked for it."

His companion made no comment.

Bulgarian for the win. So satisfying.

"Coffee for you too, sir?" It took everything she had not to stammer.

"I'll have a hot tea, please. With milk." One side of his mouth lifted in a half-smile. He should carry a license for that. She allowed herself to catch his eye for less than a second (no more, in case her notepad combusted) and met a shrewd and shuttered gaze.

Well, what do you know? Other people have armor too.

"Coming right up."

Tearing the order from her pad, Elenie clipped it beside the kitchen hatch and grabbed the next selection of plated breakfasts from the counter. Handing them out to a couple with two small children, she noticed another of the booths had filled while she was busy, and stifled a groan.

What fresh hell was this? Not only did she have Chief Roberts to deal with this morning but her stepbrothers too.

Tyson and Dean lounged bonelessly on the padded bench seats either side of a corner table. A brunette in a shaggy yellow jacket that made her look like Big Bird pressed up against Ty, and one of their more cretinous friends, Vince, made up the foursome. Watching Vince pretend to snort three crystal lines of white sugar through a straw, Elenie estimated he'd be behind bars within six months.

"Friends and relatives." She kept her voice flat and low. "What can I get you today?"

Tyson, eldest stepbrother, moron and bane of her life—twenty-five to Elenie's twenty-seven—was a mixture of stupid and nasty that often exploded into violence. A recent barbershop visit had left him with a severe buzz cut at odds with the facial hair he'd left to grow into a short, patchy beard. Elenie eyed the tattoo of a death moth which spread down one side of his neck and disappeared into the grubby collar of his t-shirt. More ink lay beneath it, some better crafted than others. She dreamed of the day he'd come home with a spelling mistake in his latest creation, which no one in their house would notice but her. Not as tall as he'd like to be, Tyson made up for it in attitude. He thought he was a ten. She'd give him a two and a half at best.

Wincing at his loud and guttural sniff, Elenie chewed on her pen, well aware Ty was keeping her waiting just to be a dick. The diner was busy; he knew she was under pressure.

"Get us a Coke float and three chocolate milkshakes," he grunted finally.

A quick sweep of the room told her no one was listening, and Elenie couldn't resist messing with him. "I'll need to see your ID to check you're old enough to order those."

Dean and Vince looked confused; the brunette frowned.

Wow, this table has the collective smarts of a chicken nugget.

Tyson's eyes flared. "Just do your fucking job, Elephant."

"I'll be right on that, Typhoid," she murmured, giving him the fakest of smiles as she turned from the table.

Same shit, different day.

Some shifts felt so much harder than others. It wasn't even mid-morning and Elenie wanted to throw up her hands and surrender. Every time a customer held their purse tighter and gave her a suspicious side-eye, stiffed her on a tip, ignored her, snapped at her, or even moved their small child closer, it chipped away another fragment of her self-worth. Four years of this job would be enough to break anyone's spirit.

One day, things would be different.

One day, she'd slide into a booth, in her own clothes and with well-rested feet. She'd place her order with another waitress. She'd sit with friends and a partner who looked at her like she lit up his world. Like he couldn't take a proper breath without her nearby. Like . . . well, like the heroes in her favorite romance books. Who didn't exist.

Simple dreams. Impossible dreams.

And if I'm going after the impossible, make it him, please. The sexy stranger. Cool, calm, and charcoal-wrapped in gray.

It was a particular form of torture to have him listen, missing nothing, while Chief Roberts talked to her like a diseased possum. Elenie squeezed the mugs, pancakes, and bacon onto a tray and dragged her attention back to the present, wondering for the millionth time if her miserable boss would ever convince a second waitress to last more than a week.

"Here we are, gentlemen."

Roberts didn't bother to acknowledge her. He continued his monologue—something riveting to do with budgets—around a mouthful of bacon, stuffed into his mouth the moment the plate was laid in front of him. Manners of a pig, potbelly of a wild boar.

Mr. Sexy Forearms was a different beast entirely, radiating powerful wild-panther vibes. Fluid, alert, and contained. When he leaned back from the table to give Elenie space to finish unloading the tray, her hand brushed so close to his arm that her pulse took a little jump shot.

"Thank you." His smile was another small lift of his lips, but it was friendly. Surprising enough to make her pause, handsome

5

enough to make her stare. His eyes, so dark it was hard to make out the pupils, studied and evaluated until Elenie felt way too exposed.

His face wasn't perfect. It was a little too drawn, hollowed around the cheekbones. The fine line of a well-healed scar ran just below the curve of his jaw, yanking him by the collar out of "Aftershave Ad" territory and into "I've Seen Some Things In My Time." His nose wasn't quite straight either. Maybe he'd broken it at some point, maybe it had always been that way. Maybe she should stop staring at him now.

Elenie poured the chief's coffee and moved away. Going from table to table, order to order, she made herself focus on the work, her surroundings, the customers—and was successful, to a point.

At the counter, Brody McAlpine, owner of the local gun and rod shop, gossiped with Nathan Reyes from the liquor store. Neither looked her in the eye as she delivered their breakfast sandwiches; unsurprising, as both had little reason for a favorable opinion of Elenie's family. Peggy Winterburn held court at a table of older ladies, complaining about the unnecessary power of her neighbor's security light. And, just inside the door, a gaggle of teenagers with a free first period took on caffeine to fuel their day at Pine Springs High.

Diner 43 was, as the chief said, the best place in town for breakfast.

Ringing up another check, Elenie saw that someone from the local business guild had dropped off a small pile of flyers for their gala dinner, so she shuffled them into a neat stack by the cash register. Taking two from the top and grabbing some clear tape from beneath the counter, she fixed one to the wall next to the coffee machine and took the other to the entrance. Taping it to the inside of the glass, she pulled open the door to check it was straight.

Expertly dodging the foot that Dean stuck out to trip her on her way back, she elbowed him in the head without breaking her stride. Younger than Tyson, Dean was softer in looks than his brother and Elenie found him marginally less irritating. But he upheld the family tradition of making consistently bad choices because he was slow on the uptake, hadn't been taught any better, and had friends who were all losers.

As she cleared her stepbrothers' table, hoping to encourage them to leave, Tyson flicked out his hand, catching the underside of the tray. The four tall glasses rocked and tumbled, a spray of ice cream and chocolate milkshake remnants showering Elenie from chin to waist and soaking her shirt. The float glass rolled over the edge and smashed on the floor.

Delia's head popped through the serving hatch, habitual glare in place.

Thanks for the concern—I'm fine! Globby droplets of vanilla dripped from Elenie's forearm.

Ty studied the puddle by her feet. "That's a health and safety hazard, sis. I'd get onto that if I was you."

Her toes curling inside her sneakers, she fought the urge to hit him smack in the face with the tray, walk her sticky feet through the door of the diner, and never come back. Instead, face impassive but throat tight, Elenie fetched a dustpan and a cloth to clear up the mess, suffering a roomful of eyes on her back as she swept and wiped. When a pair of black lace-up boots appeared at the edge of the broken glass wasteland, her eyelids fluttered closed for a brief, strength-seeking moment.

"Can I help you?" Hands filled with the wreckage from the floor, she tilted her chin to look up at the hot stranger—a long, long way up, into a face of shadows and angles.

Lean, but muscular, his trim, strong frame filled out his uniform like it was bespoke. She had a ridiculous urge to poke her finger into his stomach just to test how much give there was. She would bet on meeting a solid wall of resistance.

Elenie kept her finger to herself.

"I'd like to pay when you have a minute."

"Of course. Let me just get rid of this glass."

He gave her a brief nod and swept eyes as tough as black granite over her stepbrothers and their friends. They fixed on Dean, who stared blankly back from under his beanie.

"You'll want to hand over the cash you took from the next table." Flat and uncompromising, the man's suggestion was not a request.

Elenie stood up, dumped the dustpan and its contents onto the tabletop, and thrust out her hand. Pulling a crumpled bill from his pocket, Dean slapped it into her palm with a shrug.

Behind the counter, she busied herself at the cash register. Mr. Sexy Forearms slid a card from his wallet, his stare never wavering from her face, and the dry tinder inside Elenie's chest threatened to smolder and burn.

Get a grip, girl. He's in uniform, therefore he's dangerous. Out of bounds. Not. For. You.

She wished with all her heart that she was someone else.

"Roman Martinez! I heard you were in town." Dragged back to earth, Elenie watched Nathan Reyes reach out and the two men clasped hands. "Where've you been working?"

"Detroit PD. Homicide division." The words sounded forced on the hot stranger's lips.

"You're not just visiting either, by the looks of it?" Eyes alight with interest, Nathan gestured to his uniform.

"I'll be taking over from Chief Roberts at the end of the week."

Oh, dear God. That was both the answer to Elenie's prayers and a huge complication, all rolled into one.

"This guy. Best cleanup hitter Pine Springs High ever had!" Nathan said, turning to fill in Brody McAlpine with a broad grin.

"No one could touch us when Martinez was on the baseball field. We all thought he was headed for the big leagues."

The new chief smiled but Elenie noticed his fingers had clenched around the credit card in his palm. Ignoring Nathan's comment, he gave Brody a polite chin lift. "Pretty sure I recognize your face, sir. It's good to see you again."

The three exchanged a few more words while Elenie rang up the check. Heart as heavy as a bowling ball, fingers slippery with milkshake on the buttons of the card reader, she tried to pretend she wasn't an unholy mess of chocolate flavoring and ice cream and just did her job.

So, she'd been humiliated in front of the mouthwatering Roman Martinez, former Golden Boy of Pine Springs High. What did that even matter?

He'd find out soon enough why the Daxes didn't feature on the Christmas card list of anyone from the local PD.

Chapter 2
Roman

The emergency call came through just after two a.m.

Instinct had Roman up and dragging on his clothes before he'd finished the conversation with Chief Roberts. He rang his new deputy, Dougie Taggart, from the SUV, collecting him on his way, and pulled up behind the ambulance outside the Masons' house less than ten minutes later. There was no sign of the chief himself as yet.

More than a dozen young people loitered anxiously in small groups. It looked as if others might have left. Two boys were attempting to gather the numerous bottles and cans tossed all over the front yard. A bonfire, lit in an old trash can on the grass, was still smoldering but on its way out. As Roman and Dougie jogged up the path, no one was brave enough to catch their eye.

"You stay out here," Roman instructed. "Start taking names and statements. I don't want anyone else to leave without giving you their details. Tell Roberts I'm inside when he gets here." He headed for the front door. A blond girl, pale and shaky, stepped back as he strode in. "Don't go home without seeing my deputy," he told her. "Where are they?"

She gestured toward a huge kitchen-diner off the hallway.

Bypassing a large central island surrounded by white glossy cabinets, Roman took a chokehold on his focus when it threatened to desert him. His chest felt too hot, his fingers too cold, but he swept his eyes over the scene, taking mental photographs he'd review later.

Two paramedics were kneeling on the floor, a teenage girl lying on the tiles between them. She wore a short lilac dress and her legs were bare. Her shoes were nowhere to be seen, toenails unpainted. Drawing closer, he could see an intubation tube had been inserted into her airway. One of the medics was rhythmically squeezing a bag to push air into her lungs, while the other monitored her vital signs.

Three girls sobbed in each other's arms, their cries covered by the music still belting out from speakers hidden somewhere in the room. A couple of boys hovered uncertainly, clearly torn between comforting the girls and watching what was happening on the floor.

"What's your name?" Roman asked the kid nearest to him, relieved to hear his voice sounded normal.

"Charlie Randall, sir." The boy's eyes darted left and right.

"Whose party is it, Charlie?"

"It's mine. Mine and my brother's." A taller guy, definitely older, appeared in the doorway. Gray-faced with shock, he met Roman's eyes with gritty courage. "I'm Kai. Kai Mason. This is my parents' house."

"Turn the music off, Kai. Then take your friends outside and get them to give their names to my deputy or Chief Roberts. You'll need to stick around and wait for me. I want to speak to you myself."

In the relative silence that followed, Roman crouched next to the girl on the floor and studied her face. He recognized the signs in front of him. Overdoses were a dime a dozen in Detroit, but he hadn't expected to see one here so soon. "What have we got?"

"Millie Westlake. Seventeen years old. We took the call at 01:35 and arrived at 01:47. The patient's vomited twice but was seizing and unconscious when we got here. Pupils constricted, skin and lips are blue. Someone made the call when she went from slurring her words to not being able to speak. We've administered one dose of naloxone and she's stable for now, but we need to move her."

The paramedic stood and wheeled a collapsible recovery stretcher closer to the girl. Roman moved to her feet and, between the three of them, they lifted her onto it. Pulling up the side bars, they raised the stretcher, letting the legs unfold, and locked it into place.

"No other casualties?"

"Not that we've seen."

Millie Westlake's dress had no pockets. He'd need to track down any jacket, coat, or purse she might have brought to the party.

"You're good to go." Roman watched them wheel the stretcher swiftly out of the kitchen, his heart pounding beneath the breast pocket of his shirt. Sweat dampened the hair at the nape of his neck.

When he'd left Pine Springs twelve years ago, he hadn't been chasing thrills or excitement necessarily. Sure, he'd had plenty of ambition and drive, but he'd mostly wanted the opportunity to make a difference. In the intervening years, he'd often wondered if he had made any difference at all. More recently, Roman had barely even been surviving. So close to the edge he was in danger of falling, he'd had no option but to accept this temporary transfer.

Still stalked by the oily, soul-staining shadow of homicide policing, he prayed that Millie Westlake and this case wouldn't destroy his already shaky foundations. Curling his hands into fists as he strode through the house, Roman went in search of the chief and any witnesses.

* * *

Interviews and paperwork dominated his team's working hours for the next two days straight. Chief Roberts was more than happy for Roman to take the lead on a case that would clearly run beyond the term of his last few days in office.

As he read over the lab report with Dougie, a movement in the parking lot outside his window caught Roman's eye. He frowned and squinted against the bright blue of the afternoon sky. It was Elenie Dax. The waitress from the diner and a member of the family Chief Roberts clearly despised.

Leaning against one of the trees that flanked the path, head turned in the direction of the station, she appeared to be waiting.

Roman dragged his attention back to the matter at hand.

"As we guessed, what Millie thought was pure MDMA had been laced with fentanyl." He swiveled his screen to face his deputy.

"Cheap, easy to get hold of, and dangerous," Dougie murmured as he scanned the details. "Bet she didn't count on taking that kind of a risk when she decided to try getting high. Her friends have closed ranks. They're not naming the source of the drugs, or they genuinely don't know."

Roman grunted.

They'd established that Mr. and Mrs. Mason had gone out of state to visit family, taking their two youngest children but leaving the older two at home. It was the perfect opportunity to throw a party. Millie Westlake's closest friends admitted she'd scored some MDMA, seemingly intent on gaining enough false courage to approach a girl she had feelings for. There were no other drugs in Millie's purse when Dougie eventually tracked it down. Although both friends swore blind she hadn't done it before—to their knowledge, at least—the teenager had taken the pill halfway through the evening and within twenty minutes was struggling to breathe.

Recovering slowly in hospital, after forty-eight hours on a mechanical ventilator, Millie—a tall, solid basketball player—owed her survival to a hefty dose of luck and her own general fitness.

"Chief Roberts swears all narcotics in Pine Springs trace back to the Dax family," Dougie volunteered.

Roman took another glance out of the window. "Without evidence to link them to the supply, that gets us nowhere."

The paperwork trail on the Daxes was extensive and revealing. He'd made a point of looking them up. Shoplifting charges, intimidation, arson, car theft, regular alcohol-fueled punchups—and, yes, rumors of drug dealing, as Dougie said. Only a few minor convictions had made it all the way through the system, but every member of the family had come to the attention of the local police force more times than Roman could count.

Every one of them bar Elenie Dax, who was still loitering at the back of the parking lot.

Dougie spread his hands. "We've had a steady increase in thefts of farm chemicals, drugs at the high school, counterfeit cash. Roberts swears it only started after the Daxes moved into town. I don't know if that's true, but Frank Dax's name comes up every single time. Only problem is that no one will give evidence against him. People won't turn on their neighbor if they think that neighbor will burn down their fucking house. He's been untouchable so far."

Millie's panicked parents were still glued to her bedside; it would be another day or so before the girl would be well enough to interview. Would she tell them where the drugs had come from? Or would she be too scared to talk?

Roman had thought he'd left this kind of policing back in Detroit.

An image—*the image*—took his breath as it rose behind swiftly closed eyelids. Swallowing hard, he fought to keep his heart rate steady, even as the blood tingled in his ears and set a tremor running through his fingers.

He would not think. He would not remember.

Battling to keep his thoughts from showing on his face, Roman tugged at his shirt collar. None of his officers knew that he'd taken on this new role under pressure; he needed it to stay that way. He hadn't even come clean to his family or friends that his return had a time limit. Being forced by his superiors to take a twelve-month secondment for his mental health wasn't something he wanted to shout from the rooftops.

He had one year to prove to his captain that he'd got his head straight, and he'd be in with a fighting chance of making lieutenant on his return to the city.

"Thanks, Doug. Carry on logging the statements for now and we'll work out our next step."

When his deputy left the office, Roman turned back to the window with a ragged sigh, suppressing the surge of unease threatening to rise.

The vast, chaotic layout of the Detroit PD had afforded no outside views, only a shared desk with his partner and the hot, heavy scent of too many bodies in an under-ventilated space. This window, looking out onto trees—and yes, the small parking lot, too—was a big tick in the small-town policing box. Being able to see the sky made Roman feel like he could breathe.

Elenie Dax was still there, and he seized on the distraction with relief. Over the next ten minutes, he studied her as she checked her watch, straightened her ponytail, pulled at a leaf, shredded the leaf, dropped the leaf.

What was she doing?

And why did Roman feel so invested?

He knew this town. It remained as familiar to him, as easy a fit, as his favorite sweatshirt. He knew the town fair was coming up soon. He could predict the stalls that would be there. He knew the Pine Springs History Museum was closed more than it was open. He knew Peggy Winterburn was a troublesome gossip and Ray Parker's gruff exterior hid a kind heart. He knew there would be cardboard sledding and chocolate galore at the Downtown Winter Carnival in January. He was even pretty sure the local teenagers still necked at the lakeside off Starling Road.

Yet he'd felt out of step with the situation in Diner 43. An audience of one, stumbling in partway through the second act of a story he had yet to make sense of. Watching Elenie Dax maintain her composure in the face of Roberts' belligerence, his respect for the outgoing police chief had dropped from low to non-existent, disintegrated by the latter's shitty attitude and the quiet dignity of the waitress with the smoky gray eyes. Now he was beginning to wonder if he'd backed the wrong horse.

The front door of the police station was pushed open and Chief Roberts plowed a path to his Subaru Outback, loosening his belt a notch as he neared the car. Elenie ducked into the treeline. Roman checked his watch; it was 2:45 p.m. Roberts, embracing his apathy in the last couple of days before retirement, had decided to go home early.

With the dust still settling from the Subaru's tires, Elenie Dax stepped out of the trees and headed for the main doors. Curiosity had Roman pushing back his chair.

She stood in front of Maggie at the front desk, the low hum of their voices masked by the flick-flack of the ceiling fan. Her hair caught the sunlight, natural streaks of red licking like flames through her mahogany ponytail.

"I can handle this, Maggie," he said.

Elenie's shoulders stiffened. "It's just a lost property issue. No big deal." Her voice was husky, the professional reserve she'd shown in the diner edged out by wary discomfort.

16

"Follow me and I'll take the details." Roman gestured toward his office and ignored Maggie's raised eyebrows that were expressing doubt at his form-filling abilities.

Elenie took a few steps backward. "Um, maybe later would be—"

"No time like the present when you've waited this long." He gave a fractional nod toward the parking lot and headed back along the short corridor without waiting for a reply.

It was a quiet afternoon, with only three of them on duty besides Maggie, now Roberts had gone home. Weaving between the desks in the open office, Roman frowned at the subdued atmosphere. It felt more like a courtroom in session than a hub of activity. He skirted Dougie, who had trapped a phone between his chin and shoulder and was scrawling notes he'd probably struggle to read later. Officer Forsberg glanced away from her monitor and caught his eye. "D'you need me, sir?"

"No, we're good, thanks, Kristina." Roman waved Elenie into his office and half closed the door. "So, how can I help?"

She stepped forward and opened her fist, dangling a jeweled cuff bracelet from her fingers. It was bright, gaudy, and obviously expensive. Laying it carefully on his desk, she prodded it into a straight line of sparkling white and yellow stones.

"I didn't steal it." Elenie's watchful eyes were cautious, her body tight. She looked like a flight risk.

"Obviously not or I doubt you'd have brought it here." He kept his tone reasonable, his words level. "Please, take a seat."

She eyed the nearest chair with suspicion but did as he asked. Roman settled himself behind his desk.

"It was on the floor in the restroom of the diner. I found it this morning and Delia told me to bring it here. I'd have come sooner but we were busy."

This time, he caught a defensive tone. Elenie Dax was like a cryptic crossword or a Magic Eye picture—complicated, confusing. Nothing clear at first glance. She rubbed her nose and examined her surroundings. Roman kept his eyes on her, familiar enough with his new office to know what she could see.

The noticeboard on one wall, laden with leaflets and pieces of paper, some new, some yellow and curling at the corners. A wastebasket, full to the top, next to his desk. The lower drawer of the filing cabinet he'd left ajar. Two outdoor jackets of differing weights hooked to the back of the door; he didn't know whose they were. Some mess was his own, he'd be the first to admit it. But the space he'd inherited had been untidy when he got here. It didn't bother him much. He could put up with anything for twelve months.

When he reached for a pen on the desk, Elenie's eyes skittered back to his face. She smoothed restless hands over a crease in the front of her skirt, frowning at the bracelet. "It was so rammed this morning, I can't narrow down who might have lost it. But I can tell you everyone I remember who came in."

"Right," he said. "Let's take those details then."

Over the next ten minutes, Elenie gave him a list of names, singling out anybody flashy or vulgar enough to own a bracelet of this type. He wrote quickly with occasional prompts, admiring her eye for detail and the concise delivery of information. She'd make a great witness.

As soon as they were done, Elenie bounced to her feet like a prisoner granted parole. He thought she'd leave immediately but she paused in the doorway and turned back to face him. Roman could read little in her expression. She had a poker face to rival the best he'd seen.

Elenie cleared her throat. "I heard about Millie Westlake."

He stood up behind his desk, pushed his hands deep into his pockets, and said nothing, waiting for her to continue.

"Do you know any more about what happened?" She searched his face and there was an added intensity to her voice that hadn't been there before.

"I can't give any details about an ongoing investigation," he repeated by rote. "Why do you ask?"

Elenie looked away. "No reason. I used to babysit Millie, that's all. I wondered if there was any news."

"Not that I can release." Roman let the silence sit to see if she'd say anything else, but instead she took a step over the threshold. He stopped her before she could leave. "The other morning in the diner with Chief Roberts . . . He was aggressive. There wasn't any need for that."

Elenie halted with one hand on the doorframe. A few moments ticked by. Her fingers traced a raised crack in the paintwork. "He was just saying what everyone thinks. My family is trash. And by default, so am I. You'll find that out soon enough if you haven't already." Her poise was remarkable.

"What did you say to him? I didn't recognize the language."

Elenie's mouth twitched and there was something about the unexpected mischief in the miniscule movement that rattled Roman's senses. It felt like touching his tongue to a battery.

"You caught that, huh? I told him he's as ugly as salad. It's my favorite Bulgarian insult." And she ducked out of the room before he could say anything else.

Chapter 3
Elenie

She knew. She just knew that Frank was involved at some level. And all Elenie could think about was Millie—the seven-year-old she'd babysat for, baking messy, uneven cupcakes, and the seventeen-year-old, fitting on the floor in the death throes of a house party.

Tyson had dealt drugs all the way through school. Weed at first and then, after it was legalized, anything else he could get his hands on. Or anything Frank passed his way. Dean dabbled here and there, too. Yet another reason Elenie had found it impossible to make friends over the years.

"Hi, I'm Elenie! I'd invite you to my house but, honestly, it's a shithole. Oh, and sorry my stepbrother pushed drugs on your little sister, and my mother had a drunken shouting match with your mother at the general store. But on the plus side, my stepdad hasn't set fire to anything this week."

Yeah, on the whole, it was easier to find her friends inside the covers of a book.

Just the thought that someone under her own roof might have been responsible for Millie Westlake's overdose had Elenie's stomach in knots. Even reading wasn't cutting it tonight. She turned the pages of the romance she'd borrowed from the library, trying to get lost in the yearning, but the hero was blond and a bit of an asshole, and her concentration was shot to ribbons.

"Want to watch a movie?"

She blinked at her mother standing in the doorway of the living room. Moments of connection between them were so rare that the offer took a minute for Elenie to compute. "Sounds good." It sounded great.

They picked out a romcom and made themselves comfortable. Elenie swung her legs over the arm of the chair, noting new stains on the fabric and a cigarette burn she could fit her finger into. She submerged herself in the first half of the movie. They didn't talk, but the silence was peaceful.

Her mother poured herself a vodka and Coke, and Elenie wondered if it was her first one of the day. Athena stretched out on the couch, long legs easily filling the space. Both taller and thinner than her daughter, she had been choosing alcohol or weed over food for as long as Elenie could remember. The worst times came when she lost herself in something harder.

She hadn't always been Athena; her mother had been born plain Vivian. Apparently, she'd hated her life and enjoyed a lot of men—not something anyone wants to hear about their mom. Athena delighted in her decision to reinvent herself and change her name, as if it made her a role model of some sort. Elenie struggled to remember any occasion when Athena had taken the same pleasure in parenthood. Maybe if she'd been an easier baby or a cuter kid, things might have been different.

Isolated evenings like this were a huge part of why Elenie stayed in this godawful house, caught in the limbo land of being too old to still live at home, too broke to live elsewhere, and desperate enough for some kind—any kind—of relationship with her mother to put off working out a solution.

Sometimes she was ashamed of her childish need to prove Athena loved her.

"Have you heard about Millie Westlake?" The words escaped her before she'd fully decided whether or not to ask.

"The overdose kid?" Her mother took another long gulp of her drink. "Yeah, Frank told me."

Elenie's stomach roiled. "Her mom taught me at PS High. Millie's the one I used to babysit." Athena made a noise that might have been an acknowledgment, her eyes still on the screen. "No one else in Pine Springs would've let me look after their goldfish, let alone a child."

"She liked you."

Elenie's skin felt too tight, her thoughts too abrasive. "They're a nice family."

That made Athena drag her eyes from the screen. "Didn't stay in touch, though, did they? Not after you left school. You've always thought a bit of smarts makes a person better than the rest, but it doesn't. Being clever, having clever parents, hasn't done the Westlake kid any good, has it?"

"Everyone makes mistakes."

"Isn't that the truth." Athena reached for the vodka bottle on the carpet and uncapped it. This time, she didn't bother with the Coke.

Elenie had been new to Pine Springs and a withdrawn fifteen-year-old when Mrs. Westlake recognized her love of learning, spotting the form of escape it had been for a teenager with an unsettled home life. Young Elenie had hoovered up facts, devoured books, and absorbed languages, trivia, and history like a sponge. The more random the better. She still did. And Mrs. Westlake had encouraged her where she could.

Babysitting Millie and her brother was a sporadic but golden opportunity until the contact with Elenie's former teacher dwindled. She'd envied their family life so much at the time. It was painful to think of the turmoil the Westlakes must be going through right now.

They watched the rest of the movie without talking. When it finished, Athena scrolled lazily on her phone and Elenie reached for her book. She'd only bothered saving for a phone once, losing it within a week to a light-fingered stepbrother. It hadn't seemed worth the effort a second time. Money was too hard to come by. She had no friends to keep in touch with anyway, and no desire for instant access to everyone else's perfect lives on social media.

The room lit up with headlights from the driveway. Minutes later, the front door opened and closed, and male voices filled the hall. Years of experience gave Elenie the ability to instantly judge the levels of alcohol, temper, and threat from the first words she heard; this seemed like a promising night. Frank was laughing, a low, raspy chuckle. Dean babbled, high and happy, his sentences falling over each other. Strutting into the room, Tyson stripped off his t-shirt and the overwhelming smell of gasoline permeated the air.

"Fun evening, boys?" Athena tipped up her face, Frank's kiss landing squarely on her mouth.

"Enlightening." He took the glass from her hand and swallowed a slug of vodka before she snatched it back. Lifting Athena's feet from the end of the couch, Frank slumped on the cushions with a grunt and pulled her legs across his lap. "Get me a drink, Dean!" he yelled in the direction of the kitchen, where her stepbrother rifled noisily through the cupboards.

Ty, still bare-chested, sat on the floor in front of Elenie, his back against the armchair. Her eyes began to water. "Jeez, Ty— you stink."

"I love the smell of gas." His grin was a little unhinged. His eyes glittered, pupils huge. "I'll have a beer, too, Dean!"

"Where have you been?" She didn't even know if she wanted to know.

23

"Out."

Dean sloped into the living room, holding three uncapped bottles. Ty took a long drag from one, let out an enormous belch, and snickered. Athena poured herself another vodka and Elenie decided to make a move. The quiet of her room seemed appealing right now, the draw of her mother's company fading.

"Seems the Westlake girl's blown her chances of a basketball scholarship." Frank's voice held an undertone of gloating. His heavyset chest tightened as he raised his beer to his mouth. Elenie felt the loaded look he exchanged with Tyson like icy fingers on the back of her neck. "So much further to fall when you're all high and mighty." He leaned his head against the couch, the picture of relaxation, and glanced at her out of the corner of his eyes. She knew he hadn't forgotten her link to the Westlake family. His words were a poke at them and a poke at her, too.

This was Frank all over. Contained but mouthy, throwing out observations like poisoned breadcrumbs. Stirring and provoking—especially her. He'd been doing it for years, ever since he married Athena when Elenie was eight. He got his kicks from pushing her, winding her up, intimidating her where he could. She'd grown used to tuning him out wherever possible and never rising to his taunts. It was really the only way.

"I'm tired. Think I'll head upstairs." Elenie swiped her book from the arm of the chair. Before she'd reached the door, Tyson had taken the seat. "I enjoyed the movie, Mom."

Athena didn't answer but Frank raised his bottle in a mock salute. A dark realization washed through Elenie, tingling the hair on her head and settling on her chest with the weight of a Corny keg. It didn't matter how she wrapped it up or how much she tried to deny it. This, bottom line, was what her family did.

They set fire to things and nearly killed teenagers.

Chapter 4
Roman

Less than twenty-four hours later, there was positive news on the lost-and-found jewelry.

As Roman headed for his SUV to check out a tripped alarm at the mayor's office, Maggie stopped him at the front desk. Handing over a couple of messages, she said she'd made it to number six on the list he'd given her before reaching Elfrida Alberty, the relieved owner of the bracelet.

"Mrs. Alberty grabbed a coffee with an old neighbor to kick off a day busier than a church fan in August. She retraced most of her steps but forgot about the coffee, so didn't think to call the diner. No doubt we'd have seen her in here today but there's no need now."

"Great." He flicked through his messages as she chatted on.

"The Albertys are Pine Springs' social bigwigs. There's barely a committee one or other of them aren't involved with. Elfrida was gushing with gratitude until I mentioned Elenie Dax's name and then she couldn't get off the phone fast enough."

Roman leaned a shoulder against the doorframe. "But Elenie hasn't been in trouble. I checked her record and it's clean. What's Mrs. Alberty got against her?"

Maggie snorted, her lips forming two tight lines. "That girl's been in here more times than a cold virus. Just because she hasn't been charged, it doesn't make her Barbie."

"Wouldn't there be something on her record if Chief Roberts brought her in for questioning? There's plenty on her dad and her brothers. Even Mrs. Dax. But nothing on Elenie Dax."

"Stepdad," said Maggie. "And stepbrothers. I've heard Elenie was a kid when Frank married her mother. They've lived in town for ten years or so. Maybe longer." They must have literally moved into Pine Springs as Roman headed out. Maggie picked up a pile of forms from her desk and shot him a look over the top of her glasses. "I've only worked here a couple of months but I'm already aware that our files are neither comprehensive nor orderly. What *should* have been documented is not necessarily the same as what *has* been documented." Maggie sniffed and turned back to her papers.

By mid-morning, the alarm had been easily dealt with and Mayor Magellan's ego successfully soothed by the personal attention of the new police chief. Magellan was a decent sort. Roman was happy to give up a little of his time to lay the foundations for a good relationship going forward.

Heading back to the station along Main Street, he turned his car into the parking lot of the general store and grabbed his wallet. As the only member of the team who drank tea—going against the unwritten rules of every cop shop in the US, it would seem—he was sure as hell no one else would have stocked up on teabags.

The argument had already started before Roman pushed through the front door.

"I'm only here for milk. We've run out at the diner." He recognized Elenie's voice a second before he saw her.

"Give me my fucking card or I'll snap your dirty, thieving hands right off your body," growled a slim, wiry man with a bushy red beard and a denim shirt. He was crowding her up against the door of an upright fridge, veins raised at his temples. Elenie dangled a large carton of milk from each hand. She looked tired.

"Move back, please, sir. I'll be the one to decide if there's any snapping." Roman stepped close enough to Red Beard to force the other man to take a step away. There wasn't much room between the shelves at the back of the store as it was, and they formed an uncomfortable triangle in the tight space. "What seems to be the problem?"

"This little bitch swiped my card out of my pocket. I had it a minute ago and now I don't. And she was right behind me by the fridges."

Elenie lifted her hands, deliberately sloshing the cartons of milk like funky tambourines. "And how do you think I took it out of your pocket—with my teeth?" Her sarcasm was biting, her face scornful.

"She has a point, sir." Roman suppressed a smile.

"She's a fucking Dax. She could probably lift a wallet with her toes if she wanted. You're new here. You have no idea."

Roman opened his mouth to make a suggestion, but Elenie beat him to it. Thrusting the milk cartons onto the nearest shelf, she gestured down the length of her body with both hands. "My shirt and skirt don't have any pockets. There's nowhere to put anything apart from my hoodie." Embarrassment warring with frustration on her face, Elenie slipped her arms out of the top and held it out to him. "Please check the pockets."

Roman slid a hand into each pocket in turn, then handed it back to her. "Nothing," he confirmed.

Red Beard scoffed. "Could have put it anywhere! What about your shoes?"

Without comment, she kicked off her sneakers and held them upside down.

"Socks?"

"That won't be necessary." Roman called a halt to any further disrobing.

"CJ? You still here?" Three heads swiveled at the yell from the teenager behind the store counter.

"I'm here." It seemed Red Beard had a name.

"You've left your card in the machine."

There was a moment of silence. Roman gestured toward the cash register with the slight raise of one eyebrow. "I suggest you collect it and go, sir."

Running an irritable hand through his beard, CJ pushed past Elenie and sloped off in the direction of the counter, muttering to himself as he disappeared around one of the shelving units. Elenie bent to push her feet back into her Converse, well-worn and faded, the tongues creased and handkerchief-thin. She retied discolored laces and shoved her arms through the sleeves of her hoodie. "Thanks."

"No problem." Beneath the unmistakable top notes of diner food, she smelled of something citrusy and appealing. It disrupted Roman's train of thought and there was a strained silence before he remembered his conversation with Maggie. "By the way, the bracelet belonged to Elfrida Alberty. She was on your list."

Elenie straightened the cuff of one sleeve. "Well, I'm glad she's gotten it back. I guess I won't hold my breath for a thank you. Like most people around here, she has me pegged for a thief." Her words were flippant, her eyes resigned. He searched for bitterness but didn't find it.

"I suppose everyone is different, but until I know otherwise, I prefer to make up my own mind." The urge to show he wasn't "most people" came from Roman's gut.

Elenie tipped her chin to search his face. She looked genuinely taken aback. He was close enough to see the flecks, like speckles on a bird's egg, in the gray of her irises, and wondered what it would take for her to look at him with less suspicion. Then he wondered why he cared.

Roman rattled his keys against the palm of his hand. "Don't forget your milk," he reminded her gruffly and strode away in search of teabags. By the time he got to the counter to pay, Elenie was gone.

He returned to the station to find a report on his desk. A truck had been torched on a property just out of town.

* * *

So, this could be interesting.

Roman pressed his finger to the bell on one side of the front door and kept it there, Dougie a solid presence at his shoulder. His first ring had gone unanswered, and so had the knock he'd followed it up with, but there was no doubt someone was home. Rap lyrics and a thrumming beat, angry and intense, rained like tickertape from an open upstairs window. Running his gaze over the front yard, he took in the ratty American flag hoisted on a pole alongside the driveway, patchy grass that wasn't quite a lawn, and a three-legged plastic table lying at a tilt against the house. The timber sidings were rotten low down, paint flaking on the weather-damaged boards. Cigarette ends littered the porch steps, scattered around his feet.

He knew from his inquiries that Frank Dax ran a business providing freelance security—a broad term which, to Roman, sounded like muscle for hire. His sons worked with him. Police records also showed that Frank drove an almost new, high-end Dodge Ram truck, at odds with the unloved property in front of him.

The front door opened. A tall, thin woman leaned against the frame, barefoot and mid-yawn. An oversized, orange t-shirt skirted her thighs, an incongruously huge pair of sunglasses perched on her nose. It was possible she also wore shorts but, if she did—and he hoped she did—he couldn't see them.

Athena Dax. Elenie's mother.

She wasn't as fresh-faced as she looked at first glance, and there were lines around her lips that added a tight twist to her mouth. Dyed a vibrant shade of red, her loose, straggly hair would have benefited from either a wash or a brush.

Athena took off the shades slowly in a move Roman suspected she may have practiced in front of a mirror. Her shrewd gaze skipped from him to Dougie and back again, while he assessed her in return. Though he found some similarity in the shape of her face and the neatness of her nose, nothing else reminded him of Elenie. Athena was sharper, more jaded, less natural.

Roman pulled out a perfunctory smile along with his badge. "My name is Chief Martinez. This is Deputy Officer Taggart. We'd like to speak to Frank, please."

"Looks like someone's expanded the budget for the Pine Springs PD." Her eyes, beneath the layers of makeup, flickered with interest.

"Is he here?"

"Why would you need to know?"

Apparently, they were both going to avoid each other's questions.

"You're a definite improvement on the last one." Athena gave a flirty eyebrow raise. "I've heard a lot about you already. Have your ears been burning?" She leaned forward to trace slim fingers over the emblem on his chest. Dougie gave a strangled cough as Roman took a step backward out of her reach, repelled by the calculated move and her empty eyes. In an instant, she switched from predatory to bored. "Frank's out back, in the garage."

"Thank you."

Athena closed the door on them as they walked around the side of the house.

"I think she likes you," Dougie muttered out of one side of his mouth, humor dancing in his voice. "Sorry for third-wheeling."

Roman huffed in answer.

Good-natured and uncomplicated, it was impossible not to warm to Dougie. He was also a little immature and lacking in some of the solid basic training Chief Roberts should have drilled into him, but he knew the town well and was universally liked. That mattered in a place as small as Pine Springs. Every bit of inside knowledge was a head start, every smooth relationship a bonus in a close-knit community of just 2,446 residents. Roman was keen to encourage him to step up his game and take more responsibility within the team.

They followed the sound of male voices. Just as they reached the garage, a meaty hand pushed one of the doors open from the inside and Frank Dax emerged into the sunshine. He fixed Roman and Dougie with an unruffled half-smile, wiping oily hands on a rag that looked unlikely to make them any cleaner. Trailing behind—always the bridesmaid, never the bride—came Tyson, who closed the garage door firmly at a nod from his dad.

Roman did the formal introductions for a second time.

"How can I help you, Chief?" Frank Dax folded his arms loosely across a broad-barreled chest. A simple gold chain was just visible around his wide neck beneath the collar of a black polo shirt.

"At just after eleven p.m. last night, Ray Parker's truck was torched on his driveway." Roman studied Frank's face for any kind of tell. "We received a report of a disagreement in the Rusty Barrel two nights ago between yourself and Mr. Parker, so we wanted your take on the situation."

Frank's smile didn't waver but it also didn't reach his eyes. He gave a careless shrug. "I can't help you. I had a few words with Parker over something and nothing. Don't even remember what about now. And last night, I was here with the family. We watched a movie."

"There are multiple witnesses to the fight in the bar," Roman recounted, "and three separate people heard you harassing Ray again in the parking lot. Sounds like more than a few words."

Frank sighed. "I might have said some things I'm not proud of but I came home and put it behind me." He rolled one shoulder as if to loosen a tight muscle. "Shame about Parker's truck. I hope you find out who did it."

Roman let the loaded silence grow heavy as he took a moment to size up the older man. Frank Dax might have been carrying a little more weight than was good for him but he was far from out of shape. Close-cropped hair liberally sprinkled with gray, his thick eyebrows framed hooded eyes over a wide nose, narrow lips, and stubble. Faded tattoos ran from his wrists up each arm, twisted chains weaving between a melted clockface, skulls, and sea creatures.

Masking his personal feelings, legs planted, Roman was keenly aware his own six feet and two inches gave him a towering edge over the far shorter duo. "Mind if I take a look inside your garage?"

It was worth a try.

"Well, now, I'd like to say yes." Frank's voice was placid. "But a man's home is his castle and, unless you have a warrant, I think I'll pass on this occasion." He turned to thread a thick chain through the double handles of the garage doors, pushing the shackle of a large padlock into place to hold the links. "It's been nice to meet you, Chief. Always happy to welcome someone new in town."

A vein pulsed in Tyson's temple, even as he grinned. He was finding it harder to stand still than his father, control less securely mastered under the surface of his skin.

There was nothing more to be achieved here for now. "Thank you for your time. I like to put a face to a name." Roman made to turn away but halted at the last minute. "What was the movie?" He aimed the question at Tyson.

"Huh?"

"What movie did you watch last night?"

Tyson's mouth flapped as the question caught him by surprise. There were clearly zero options running through his brain. Roman felt more than saw Dougie fight to suppress a smirk.

"Sleepless in Seattle." All three of them turned to look at Frank. "Interesting choice."

Frank Dax held Roman's stare in a silent pissing contest. All that could be heard for several long seconds was the sound of Ty's feet fidgeting on the gravel. Then Frank gave a wide smile and spread his beefy hands. "What can I say? It's a classic and I'm a softy." His eyes, glinting with the hint of a challenge, said differently.

Roman and Dougie headed for the SUV. As they pulled off the driveway, an image of Elenie's shuttered face swam into Roman's mind and he frowned at the nasty taste in his mouth. After meeting both Frank and Athena, the reason why the Daxes were held in such universal contempt was becoming much clearer.

Chapter 5
Elenie

The next few days grew warmer and warmer, the gentle heat blissfully welcome after a capricious Michigan spring. With no need for long sleeves, Elenie enjoyed the brush of the light afternoon breeze against her bare arms and the sun on her back.

The track through the trees was a shortcut that trimmed her commute to work by twenty minutes, as it bypassed a far longer loop of road that wound up the hill. It was a steep climb on the walk home but, apart from when it was very hot or excessively wet, Elenie tackled the path to and from town twice a day, most days of the week.

She gave the patrol car parked at the bottom of the track a wary second glance, her shoulders loosening when she found it to be empty. Heading up the cool tree-covered path, she watched her step on the root-threaded ground; it was uneven but not slippery. She let her mind empty and her thoughts wander as she walked. The peace was welcome. This time to relax after the rush of the diner and before she reached home was precious, especially when she never knew what the evening might bring.

Rounding a bend, more than halfway up the hill, her feet slowed at the sight of Dougie Taggart, local police deputy, hunched on the ground at the base of a tree. He swore colorfully and fluently, his rasping words becoming clearer as Elenie drew closer—angry yet somehow unthreatening. He sounded more like a popular high school teacher having a terrible day than a scarily pissed officer of the law.

Caution had Elenie checking around, hoping to find someone else to step in and take charge, but that was stupid. She maybe crossed paths with another person on this track twice a month, which made seeing the deputy all the more of a surprise.

"You alright, sir?"

When Taggart raised his head, skin pallid, mouth twisted in pain, Elenie's stomach swooped up toward her throat. She smothered a curse of her own. He wasn't alright. Jogging the last couple of yards, she dropped to her knees in the dirt beside him.

The deputy was gripping the top of one thigh with both hands, sweat running down the sides of his face, while blood oozed between his fingers. "Fucking Renner kids caught me with a BB gun. My leg's on fire but I don't think the pellet's hit anything major. Fucking little fuckers." He blew out a shaky breath, dirty blond hair plastered against his damp forehead. "I'll get up in a minute. Just need a moment."

"Let me look." Elenie pried his hands away from his leg. The wound wasn't pumping, but it didn't look pretty. Fresh blood, saturating the material surrounding the jagged tear in his pants, seeped steadily as the pressure was lifted.

"Car's at the bottom of the hill—left my cell and radio in it. I was chasing a stray. What a dumbass. You got a phone?" He eyed her lack of a purse or jacket.

"No, sorry."

Taggart closed his eyes and leaned back against the tree, looking impossibly young and surprisingly vulnerable. Less of an intimidating authority figure and more just a man of her own age needing help. Elenie looked down at her clothes. The skirt and polo shirt gave her nothing to work with for a bandage, and she wasn't carrying anything else with her. The deputy's short-sleeved shirt and pants were no help either.

Checking his eyes were still shut, she half turned away from him. Elenie pulled her arms swiftly through her bra straps and unhooked the back clasp. She sighed internally at the loss of one of her only two bras before tugging the thin scrap of cotton out through the left sleeve of her top.

The irony of stripping off her underwear in the present company didn't escape her, given that her main aim in life was to avoid the attention of the Pine Springs PD. But Dougie Taggart gave off no leery vibes—and Elenie was an expert at spotting them. Plus, not only was he oblivious to the surreptitious maneuver, she was also one hundred percent sure she could take him in a fight right now, with one carefully applied finger to the thigh.

Slipping off her sneakers, she removed both short, white socks and laid them together to form a pad, gently moving Dougie's hands away as he opened his eyes. "Press this over the top, sir." When she wrapped her bra around his leg, he flushed but didn't comment. "I need to pull this tight but you can swear all you like. I'll have heard it before."

She did. And he did. And she had. But the wound was soon carefully bound by the sock/bra bandage, and this time they both let out a ragged breath.

"Think you can try to stand on it?"

"We'll soon find out." The deputy's voice was grim but determined.

"I'm Elenie," she told him, for something to say, as she reached out both hands. It was all she could do to pull him to his feet.

"I know who you are."

Of course he did.

The walk back down the hillside was a slow one. The deputy leaned heavily on Elenie's shoulder. It was a strange experience to be so physically close to someone she didn't know. Her skin prickled with self-consciousness and she could feel her neck growing warm and damp. But the small kernel of pleasure that spread from her chest at the sensation of being needed overpowered the awkwardness. If her support helped Officer Taggart get down this track, she would let him use her for a crutch without complaint.

"The chief will give me so much shit for leaving my radio in the car. I don't blame him either. I'll probably be given every crappy callout until I retire."

"What kind of crappy callouts are there?" Elenie asked, steering him around an overhanging branch. She regretted the question as soon as it left her mouth. Her family were likely responsible for most of them.

"Jarvis Wheelwright's late-night bacon thieves." Dougie dragged air in through his nose.

"Hold on—bacon theft? Is that even a thing?"

Sweat beaded on the deputy's top lip. "Sure is. Jarvis gets wasted every Saturday, comes home with the munchies, and then calls us on a Sunday morning, moaning that his bacon's been stolen."

Elenie gave a strained laugh. "Cheese is the most frequently stolen food in the world," she told him. "There was a car chase in New Zealand—I forget when—after a couple stole a whole load of Cheddar off a train and the thieves chucked lumps of cheese out of the car window at the cops while they tried to escape."

Dougie limped on. "Absolutely not true."

"Absolutely is."

The deputy looked at her sideways. "You're funny, you know that?"

"Funny ha-ha or funny peculiar?" Apparently, bonding over a gunshot wound did away with the need to stand on ceremony.

"Maybe a bit of both."

They stopped briefly to check her bra wasn't slipping and to let him catch his breath. The white cotton was stained pink and Elenie's shoulder screamed from supporting his weight. "Not far now. You doing OK?" He nodded and they set off again. "The Renner kids will be dying a death right now. If they know they winged you."

He swiped the back of a bloody hand across his face. "I hope they are, the little shits. And they definitely know they got me because I yelled like a stuck pig."

Elenie couldn't help a snicker at the deputy's honesty. "How did it happen, anyway?"

"Target practice, I think. Or they were shooting at road signs. Or maybe, just fucking shooting—I don't know." He stumbled, but Elenie propped him up.

"Come on, you've got this," she coaxed. "I can see the car. Tell me about the stray you were chasing. I haven't seen a dog on this path before."

It took them another ten minutes to reach the patrol car, and by the time they got there Elenie was drained. She sank to the ground, listening to Taggart radio for assistance. Her breath sawed in and out of her chest; her polo shirt was soaked with sweat. She'd waved goodbye to any chance of ticking her uniform over another day without a wash. A few loose curls were stuck to her neck and smears of dust and blood marked her hands and clothes. She was a mess.

The deputy slid onto the tufted grass by her side in the small patch of shade. "The chief's on his way."

"Which one?"

"The new chief. Roberts has gone. He'll be in Clearwater, Florida, by now, terrorizing the tuna."

Hurrah to the gods of all that is merciful. Even so, it was time to beat a strategic retreat. In a minute. In just a minute.

Elenie leaned her head against the car. Her arms and legs felt like soggy straws. "You're so much heavier than you look."

"Rude. Maybe you're just a weakling."

"Hey, I carry trays for a living. And the good old residents of Pine Springs can eat their own weight in waffles. I have muscles."

"Sure you do, Noodle Arms."

"*Ashrab mah al-bahr.*"

"I beg your pardon?"

"It's Arabic. It means, 'Go drink seawater.'" Elenie's smile slipped; she was gripped with a momentary panic that she'd overstepped the mark. What happened to thinking these things, rather than voicing them? She'd obviously shed her restraint along with her bra. *Remember, he is a police officer, not a friend.* "I didn't mean that," Elenie mumbled, uncomfortable all over again. She pushed herself to her feet, wrapping her arms around her chest. "I'd better go."

The young deputy stared up at her, a pained grin pulling at one side of his mouth. "Thanks, Elenie." He looked exhausted, battered, but not offended, and relief eased her breath.

The sound of tires on asphalt disturbed the momentary silence. Roman Martinez parked his Ford Interceptor behind Dougie's patrol car and killed the engine. Backing up as his long legs descended from the SUV, Elenie kicked herself for not leaving sooner.

Martinez spared her a quick glance and a nod. He dropped to the ground by Taggart's side, jaw tight, placing a first aid kit beside him in the dirt.

"What—?"

"Elenie's bra." Dougie managed a grin.

A thousand volts punched Elenie in the sternum as those raven eyes shot to her face and down to her chest, before Martinez dragged them straight back up again, his shadowed, narrow face instantly mortified. Elenie shrugged and colored, blood sizzling in her veins like water on a hotplate.

"Not sure you'll want it back." His voice was gruff and he didn't look at her again, but his hands moved gently as he cut through the elastic with a sharp pair of scissors. Dougie blew out a long breath and Elenie tried not to wince as the two ends of her bra fell into the dust. Swiftly and efficiently, the chief peeled away the bloodied socks, sliced a rough, rectangular opening in Dougie's pants, cleaned and redressed the wound. He bound it neatly with a fresh bandage far better suited for the job than her tatty cotton underwear.

"You're lucky the blood loss is no worse. The flow's already slowing."

"Yeah, feeling really lucky right now." Dougie, white-lipped and clammy, managed a tight-throated chuckle.

"I'm using the term loosely." Martinez smiled, and Elenie couldn't help but notice how it transformed his serious face, lighting the hollows and relaxing his jaw. "You're lucky it was a BB gun and that your pants took some of the impact."

"If I was really lucky, it would have missed me," Dougie groused.

"Either way, it's time to get you some expert help. We'll take my car. I'll get someone to collect yours later." Martinez climbed to his feet, reaching down to clasp the deputy's hand. When Dougie's feet slid on the sandy soil, Elenie stepped forward, and between them they pulled him upright and helped him hobble around to the passenger door. "I can drop you in town and have someone give you a ride home?" he suggested.

She was shaking her head before Martinez had finished. In no scenario whatsoever would she be placing her dust-covered, sweaty backside voluntarily in a police vehicle, no matter how much her internal voice groaned at the thought of the return trek up the hillside. "I'm fine. I can walk. Just go and get him sorted."

"Yes, I need me some drugs and a pizza the size of my head—not necessarily in that order. It's been a bitch of a day!" Dougie leaned across to shout through the driver's window.

Elenie exchanged a look with Martinez; amusement skittered between them like a tentative touching of fingers. Finding it almost impossible to keep her thoughts straight under the focus of his full attention, she stepped back. "I'll leave him with you then."

He gave her a brief smile as he wrenched open the door. Elenie tried and failed to look away as his biceps bunched and rippled beneath the short sleeves of his shirt. Muffling a swoony sigh, she lectured herself on the benefits of keeping it real. This skyscraper of masculine perfection had already been exposed to her pathetic excuse for a bra and, undoubtedly, the arrest record of her entire family. On their first meeting, she'd been called scum and covered in vanilla ice cream and chocolate milkshake. For their third, she'd been accused of theft. And now, wearing a sexy mixture of perspiration, blood, and grime, she was ogling his muscles as if she had a fighting chance of ever being able to touch them.

In your dreams, Noodle Arms.

Dougie Taggart shot her a warm and weary grin as they cruised away. He raised his hand and Elenie nodded. She didn't bother watching until they were out of sight; she had a long walk home and a ton of laundry to do.

Chapter 6

Roman

"I come bearing gifts." Roman held up takeout coffee and two wrapped Italian subs as Dougie opened the front door of his apartment.

"Thank fuck for that. There's nothing to eat in the house and I'm starving!" His deputy limped into the open-plan kitchen, pulling himself onto a bar stool in a pool of sunshine which lit him up like an actor onstage.

Sliding one sub over the counter, Roman peeled the paper from the other and took a huge bite. He'd just finished an early shift, missing lunch thanks to an abandoned car which had turned out to have blown a tire. "How's the leg?"

"Sore but it could be worse. Itches like a bastard now and then—usually when I'm trying to sleep." Dougie took a long drag of his coffee with a happy sigh. Relaxed and comfortable in cargo shorts and a college tee, he looked in far better shape than when Roman had driven him to the hospital.

After Dougie's girlfriend, Summer, arrived, sickly green and worried, he'd headed straight to the Renner farm. Thinking he'd come to arrest them—"Believe me, I'm still considering it," Roman told them with every bit of ferocious gravitas he could summon—the youngsters had broken down immediately.

"We didn't know he was there!" Thirteen-year-old Sadie's chin trembled. "I never meant to hit him. My shot clipped the boundary sign by our fence and it went off at an angle!" Her younger brother looked petrified.

Roman lit into them about gun safety, hammering home without mercy exactly how much worse the outcome could have been. He was pretty convinced neither of them would ever pick up a gun again, BB or otherwise. Dougie was declining to press charges but Roman had put the kids on community work for the whole summer with the grateful and remorseful support of their parents—litter picking, graffiti removal, and painting fences. Anything he could think of, basically. They would be his go-to mini-slaves for as long as it took them to learn from the experience.

Chatting as they ate, he and Dougie caught up on the latest news from the station. Despite the best efforts of his other two officers, further inquiries into the torching of Ray Parker's truck had come to nothing, since proof of an argument was not enough to link Frank Dax to arson.

"And Millie Westlake?" Dougie asked.

"She's out of hospital but she's given us nothing on who sold her the pills. Says it wasn't someone she knew. Her description is vague as hell—sounds like she straight up googled 'drug dealer' images for the details. Her parents are protective and she's far from strong right now, so I'm not inclined to push any harder at this stage. But I've circulated the lab reports to see if we get any hits on busts with the same chemical balance."

"If the drugs came from Dax—or someone like him—anyone around here would be terrified of ratting on him."

"If the drugs came from him, I'll find out. He's been treading a fine line for long enough and I think he's balancing right on the edge of it. I'm not Chief Roberts. I have no intention of sitting back and letting Dax ruin other people's lives so that he can trade in for his next new truck." Finishing his last mouthful, Roman stretched his legs out beneath the breakfast bar and propped an elbow on the counter. "Which leads me to Elenie. Tell me what you know."

Dougie ran his palm over the light shading of stubble on his cheek. "Um, about something in particular?"

Picking a crumb off the front of his shirt, Roman licked it from his thumb. "Yeah, I want to know when she's been in the station, what for, and why there are no details of her on file."

Dougie's eyebrows lifted. "There must be. Chief Roberts brought her in at least once a month. There was always something going down. Much like the rest of the family. Always in trouble of some sort."

"Like what?" pushed Roman.

"Well, he used to pick her up if he wanted to press her for information, lean on her a little." Dougie shifted awkwardly on his stool. "There were a couple of times when Roberts said the local kids were scoring pills from a white girl at the Daxes' end of town. The description matched. He was convinced it was her."

"I can't find that lead anywhere either. Neither can Maggie. No statements in support of it. No witnesses in any cases who point in the direction of Elenie Dax. I'm beginning to think this was personal. It looks to me like harassment." Roman scrubbed away the agitation that had settled at the back of his neck. "Tell me, what do you think?"

An uncomfortable flush crept above Dougie's collar. "Damn. You could be right at that. It never felt quite . . . I just let it go because I wasn't sure. And he was impossible to question. The station was run more like a dictatorship before you turned up. It didn't feel like a team." He glanced up toward the ceiling. "There was this one time when Roberts brought her in with cuffs on. Said he had some questions 'as usual.' He implied it was something serious. He put her in the cells for a bit while he prepared the paperwork—shit, or *said* he was preparing the paperwork. I knew she was in there but when I did the rounds and checked on her half an hour later, he'd left the cuffs on. Elenie was still sitting there with her hands behind her back." Dougie took a big gulp of coffee, hunching his shoulders. "I took them straight off and I thought she'd lay into me. But she just said, 'Thank you' in that calm voice of hers. When I asked him about it, he brushed me off. Told me she tried to scratch him when he removed them so he cuffed her again until she cooled down." Silence stretched between them. Dougie examined the last bite of his sub before putting it into his mouth. "I've never had a proper conversation with her before I got shot. Seems to keep a really low profile outside of the diner, but Elenie's pretty sparky when she gets chatting. She made me laugh."

And just like that, Roman felt an unexpected pang of envy for the man who'd taken a pellet in his thigh. He wiped it away with an internal volley of curses directed at Chief Asshole Roberts and his inflexible, lazy judgments.

"When I look at our setup through your eyes, I'm embarrassed." Dougie grimaced, picking at the edge of the dressing on his thigh. "We're spread too thin here. Disorganized and underfunded. Frank Dax knows it. He's made it work to his benefit. All Roberts wanted was an easy path to retirement. He wasn't going to rock any boats or risk reprisals. I like working in a small town and protecting local people, but we have issues that aren't excused by a lack of money or equipment. It's training and leadership we need to get us back on track."

Roman drained his coffee. Dougie wasn't aware his role was a temporary one; none of the officers knew. Roman hadn't expected to feel guilty about it. Part of him itched to get stuck in and make a difference. He knew he had the experience to instigate some key changes in the Pine Springs PD. Another part warned himself not to get too entrenched.

"We can tackle it together," he said, careful about promising too much. "I'll be reviewing policies, procedures, and training. And I'll welcome any input from the team."

By unspoken agreement, they changed the subject for the remainder of his visit, and the tension gradually eased as they discussed Dougie's return to work.

"I'd better head out. Milo invited himself over to my place after work. I've a ton of stuff to get done first that I should have sorted at the weekend." Climbing to his feet, Roman screwed up the takeout wrappers and dumped them in the trash, already looking forward to an evening shooting the breeze with his old school friend.

"Yeah, I heard already. Summer's going over to watch a movie with Caitlyn while he's at yours." Dougie's girlfriend was good friends with Milo's wife. "Thanks for the food, Chief. If you wanna make this a regular arrangement until I'm back, there'll be no complaints from me." Irrepressibly buoyant, his deputy wasn't above pushing his luck.

"I've got better things to do than doorstep you takeout for the next ten days," Roman grumbled, heading for the door.

But all he could picture as he drove home was Elenie Dax's slim wrists locked inside the steel grip of Chief Roberts' handcuffs. And it pissed him off.

* * *

It was hard to get his head around the fact that his best friend—cocky, droll, and fearless—was married and about to be a father. Lounging on the couch, they propped their feet on the low, battered chest which currently served as a coffee table, Roman's functional black socks side by side with Milo's mismatched stripes. The second quarter of a basketball game provided background noise, and they kept half an eye on the action as they relaxed.

"It's good to have you back, bro." Milo held up his beer.

Roman tilted his own bottle to clink them together. "It's good to be back."

There hadn't been much time to catch up with friends over the past few years, and he'd missed the familiar connections. Trips home from Detroit had been rare and brief. Returning to life in Pine Springs felt like easing himself into a bath filled with water at the perfect temperature. Unexpectedly soothing, instantly comfortable.

Gradually, Roman's muscles were unwinding, his chest loosening. His stomach no longer rolled and clenched with stress and exhaustion every fucking morning when his eyes opened—just maybe every other day now. In the three weeks since he'd been back, he was beginning to sleep better, eat more regularly, breathe more deeply. He'd underestimated the effect of coming home. If he could fast-track his recovery over the coming months, this secondment year would fly by and he'd be back on his plotted career path before he knew it.

Milo gave him a nudge. "Is Zena planning to visit or have you two definitely parted ways?"

"We've ended it for good. She won't be visiting." Taking a swallow of his beer, Roman let his head drop onto the couch cushions behind him. "Honestly, we'd been struggling for a while. She told me I'm cold, dull, and 'emotionally unavailable.'"

Milo winced into the neck of his bottle.

"She was right, up to a point," Roman admitted. "I think I've lost the part of me that was fun. I've forgotten how to relax and let go." They drank in silence for a moment. He watched the breeze move the branches of the pines outside the huge living room window, narrow branches twisting like tendons flexing on an athlete. "Maybe being back here will help. It's good to get out of the city."

Roman hadn't believed his luck at finding this place for rent, positioned just on the town border, nestled in woodland. The A-frame cabin was peaceful and secluded—everything his basic apartment in Detroit wasn't. While his few pieces of furniture looked sparse in the rambling space, he didn't need much more right now.

"I wouldn't take the word of someone with a name like a German Shepherd dog as gospel." Milo elbowed him. "Caitlyn wasn't a fan."

Roman grimaced at the memory of two strained dinner dates in the city, when the conversation had flowed like lumpy gravy and the warmth had hovered somewhere on the "blizzard in deep winter" scale.

"We suited each other for a while." He tried to be generous. "She was ambitious. I was ambitious. Neither of us had much time to spare. She didn't need a lot of attention from me."

"That's a good reason to choose a gecko for a pet. Not a fiancée," Milo said, raising an eyebrow. "And you've never been dull. Dorky, maybe, with dubious fashion choices and embarrassing celebrity crushes. But at least your batting average used to make up for it."

Roman snorted. "That was you with the dubious fashion. You're mixing me up with yourself."

"I'm not the one whose jeans were more rips than material. Your mother nearly had a heart attack every time you walked up Main Street with your boxers on show."

"That feels like a lifetime ago."

"You were the best at creative pranking, too." The corner of Milo's mouth quirked. "Remember the time we filled Principal Skellingthorpe's convertible with table tennis balls?"

Roman's lips lifted. "Oh, yeah. That was fun."

"We even put them in the glove compartment and trunk. It cost me all my lawnmowing money for a month, buying those."

"My favorite was the food dye in his wiper fluid," Roman said with a contented sigh.

"We were little shits."

"D'you think he ever knew it was us?"

Milo grinned the wide, contagious grin that made him look fourteen years old again. "Oh, he knew. Poor guy just couldn't prove it. Probably why he retired as soon as we left. We wore him out."

Chapter 7
Elenie

It was a five-minute walk to the library and the sidewalks were quiet.

Pine Springs was rarely buzzing. The town didn't attract tourists, other than those passing through. But somehow Diner 43 stayed busy, due to a lack of competition from anywhere other than the single coffee shop, next to the hardware store. Main Street wasn't so much of a street as a row of buildings, with a gas station at the top end (which charged more than the one a couple of exits down the highway) and the library—Elenie's home from home—at the other, next to the fire station. In between, there was a bank, post office, pharmacy and a small handful of businesses that made life comfortable for the townspeople.

She'd asked after a job at the library more times than she cared to remember, but they were never hiring. Or never hiring a Dax, more likely. The head librarian—Elfrida Alberty's daughter, Josephine—had even turned down her offer of doing volunteer work.

Pushing open the large wooden door, Elenie stepped inside. She slid her backpack from her shoulder, unzipped the main compartment, and returned a couple of books. The only other person in evidence was a young woman with an enviable mass of long dark hair, sitting at a nearby table. She had her nose buried in a book and was scribbling notes on a pad resting alongside. Elenie craned her neck but couldn't read the title.

It was so peaceful in here. No sound except the rise and fall of indistinct voices drifting in the air from across the room, one lower than the other, both hushed.

Elenie checked out the "New In" section, found nothing she hadn't already read and crossed to the "Crime and Mystery" shelves. Sometimes a well-written police procedural could make even her own life seem mainstream.

"Hit me with your best plot twist," she muttered to herself, her head at an angle to read the spines.

"That's a brave request."

Elenie startled.

"My English teacher in tenth grade said it's the unexpected that changes our lives. No idea why those words stuck with me when so much else didn't. I must have been concentrating that day." Roman Martinez leaned casually against the end of the bookshelf, his legs crossed at the ankle. He tossed his car keys from hand to hand, toned arms flexing under rolled-up shirtsleeves, and Elenie straightened. The whole unnerving picture was too delicious to view on a tilt.

"It's a good quote," she said, surprised at how measured her voice sounded. "Makes the unexpected more inviting somehow."

"It does." He studied her in silence.

Well, this wasn't awkward at all. Elenie tried not to chew her lip as she automatically scanned the area for an audience and came up empty.

She had yet to decide what she thought of the new chief of police, other than him being the most beautiful man she'd ever seen. And possibly the most dangerous, too. But looks could be deceiving, and the jury was still out on whether the former Golden Boy would be an improvement on Chief Roberts in the long run.

"I came in to see Miss Alberty, but I'm glad I spotted you. We need to speak." Martinez straightened, and in a handful of fluid strides, he was towering above her.

"Why?" Elenie couldn't keep the worry from her question. His face seemed to soften a little, but it was hard to tell, backlit as he was by the afternoon sun streaming in through the windows.

"You're not in trouble. It won't take long. Do you mind if we sit?" He gestured to a worn leather couch nearby.

Elenie gave another quick glance side to side but couldn't think of a legitimate reason to refuse. "OK."

Uniform impeccable, tanned and lean, a pair of sunglasses tucked into a breast pocket, Martinez dazzled her. As he had done every time she'd seen him. Elenie sat down carefully at one end of the couch, tugging at her skirt to cover her thighs. He took a seat as well, leaving as much space between them as the furniture allowed. A dozen possible reasons why he might be wanting a few moments of her time ran through her mind. None of them good.

"I think I owe you an apology." He looked around at the rows of shelves.

"Oh?" Internally, she cuffed herself around the head for her pathetic conversational skills but surprise had stolen her words.

"I'm still familiarizing myself with my team and everything that's gone on in the time I've been away. That's going to take a while. Most of it doesn't concern you."

Elenie tipped her head to look at him, enjoying the chance to study the distinctive lines of his face, the incongruous imperfection of that narrow scar (a fight? An accident? Broken glass?), while he focused on something else. The breeze from an overhead fan ruffled his hair and Elenie itched to do it instead. Thick and messy, it fell where it wanted, unwaxed, soft and appealing. He smelled undefinably appetizing—of warmth, the outdoors, soap, and himself. His pheromones tapped her pheromones on the shoulder and asked if they'd like to dance.

When he turned and caught her staring, his eyes were too black to read. "What's not OK though is what I'm hearing about you. What I'm finding out about how you've been treated by Chief Roberts." She opened her mouth and closed it again, completely taken aback. "You'd have a strong case if you wanted to file a complaint. There are officers who'd be willing to support you in that if you wish. And I will give you my backing as well." His voice was grim and rough. "You deserve better, Elenie. Persecution does not sit well with me and I won't stand by knowingly and let it happen."

He sounded a little bit pompous, a little bit stilted, as if the words weren't flowing too easily for him either. As if he'd maybe practiced them in advance but found it harder in person. It helped somehow. Some of the tension dissipated like dandelion seeds and Elenie considered how to reply. They both sat in silence. She flicked at the pages of the book in her hand. Sometimes, there was nothing to offer but the truth.

"Chief Roberts had no reason to be a fan of my family." Achingly uncomfortable, she couldn't look at him. "They've run rings around him for years. My stepfather's just smart enough, just enough of a loose cannon, to make his job extremely difficult. Scarier men than Chief Roberts handle him with care. I guess it was easier for the chief to take his frustration out on me. I'm fair game."

Martinez frowned. "No, you're not. The law is supposed to be impartial and objective. It sounds like Chief Roberts abused his position. You have options if you want to take this further."

She wondered if he really meant that. "My family is an unholy mess. I'm not after sympathy or revenge. I just want to be left alone." Elenie glanced sideways, caught his gaze, and immediately slid her eyes away again. "Thank you, though. It means a lot that you would take the time to say what you've said."

"We all make our own choices, Elenie. For some people, that takes a hell of a lot more courage and determination than it does for others.

"*Quem não tem cão caça com gato.*"

He blinked. "And that means?"

"'He who doesn't have a dog, hunts with a cat.'" Elenie eyed him steadily. "It basically means you do what you need to do with the resources you have. It's Portuguese."

Slowly, very slowly, the corners of his mouth curved into a cautious smile. It was hesitant, like something little used that had been dusted off and brought out for a special occasion. In the space of seconds, Roman Martinez went from distracting to devastating.

"If we remain on the same side, I will give you any support you need."

"Great. That's just—great." Elenie tore her eyes away from him, with a mental kick to reboot her brain and remove her heart from her throat. *Safe topic. For God's sake, find a safe topic and find it quickly.* But she didn't have the confidence to know where to start.

Chief Martinez climbed smoothly to his feet. "I have a call to make at the fire station, so I'd better get on. I'm glad I caught you."

Hook, line, and sinker.

Elenie murmured a goodbye. Her gaze followed his broad back until her view was blocked by a row of shelves. She fought the sensation of being reeled in like a lake trout, but it was a losing battle.

* * *

Over the next week, while she walked to work, took food orders, served drinks, and chatted to diners, she replayed the police chief's words and killer smile on repeat. She had thought nothing changed in a small town like Pine Springs, but here he was—the unexpected—and suddenly her world held just a little more hope and a little more promise than it had done for as long as she could remember.

Elenie found herself hyperaware every time the door to the diner swung open. She absolutely wasn't waiting for Roman Martinez to walk in and take those long, unhurried strides to the counter to order himself a hot tea. He wasn't occupying her mind any more than should be expected—any more than any other customer.

Much.

Out of necessity, Elenie kept herself to herself. She'd learned it was better that way. Nursing a magnetic attraction toward the new police chief, of all people, was as sensible as offering to floss the teeth of a tiger. At best, she should be hoping for a genuine ceasefire in hostilities, but already she felt lighter. Energized. And it wasn't all down to the relief of escaping from the oppressively sizable shadow of Chief Roberts.

Elenie knew little about Martinez other than the few snippets she'd overheard here and there, but she had begun to collect information about him. He'd grown up in Pine Springs, was a five-tool player on any baseball field that would have him (Nathan Reyes was still telling anyone who would listen) and seemed to send the temperature of almost every female within the town boundaries soaring—other than possibly Delia, whose veins Elenie suspected were filled with formaldehyde. The rest of his family were local. She'd served all of them in the diner, though not regularly, and his closest friend was an accountant with a small firm just off Main Street. Like she did most people in town, Elenie knew Milo Walker by sight, but had never said more to him than "Here's your Americano." Martinez had left Pine Springs in the same year the Daxes had arrived. He'd progressed through the ranks of the

Detroit PD, was on track to make lieutenant at a young age, and now he'd returned, unexpectedly. There were few further details that could be gleaned by eavesdropping. Unless you listened to the more bizarre gossip, that is—and there was always bizarre gossip in Pine Springs. Most of it sounded so wildly improbable it couldn't be true. As a seasoned victim of inaccurate chatter herself, Elenie felt a tentative kinship with Roman Martinez, which strengthened with every unlikely tale that reached her ears.

"Morning, Otto." She smiled at her favorite customer as she passed him with a tray of bagels and coffee. "How are you today?"

"Definitely the better for seeing you." The silver-haired charmer twinkled over his cinnamon Danish. As always, warm bubbles of pleasure burst under Elenie's skin at the way his face lit up when he saw her.

"I could join you for a go at the crossword in a minute. I'm due a break soon."

"Praise be! I'm getting nowhere with it today. I think my brain cells are dying off quicker than I can stimulate them with sugar. Hurry, girl—hurry!"

Elenie was laughing as she grabbed the next tray. Facts were her thing. You knew where you were with a crossword. People, not so much, but letters in boxes—yup, she could do that. Carrying a couple of hot drinks and some fresh brownies over to a table by the door, she fumbled her grip as she recognized Dougie Taggart's girlfriend, Summer Daley.

"Two coffees and two brownies." Elenie laid the plates on the table. "Good choice. The brownies are freshly made. They have walnuts in them."

Three cheers for Most Vacuous Statement of the Day.

Opposite Summer, fanning herself with a laminated menu, was Caitlyn Walker, wife of the police chief's best friend. Fiery red curls spilled over her shoulders, her pale, rounded cheeks dotted with enough freckles to make cute war with sexy. Caitlyn gave her a measured look but didn't smile.

The girls met several times a week at Diner 43. Summer's open, friendly face had never been open or friendly toward Elenie, even if neither woman was outwardly rude. They were polite but reticent, and that was it. If sometimes Elenie's chest ached from hearing them laugh, seeing their closeness as they swapped news and chatter, well, that was something she'd learned to deal with. Being on the outside wasn't a new experience for her.

Summer cleared her throat, a flush high on her cheekbones. "Hey. I want to thank you for looking after Dougie when he had his accident. He said you were so calm and helpful." Her fingers fidgeted around the handle of a teaspoon.

"I hope he's doing OK?" Elenie ignored the thanks, unsure of the right response.

"Better by the day—and a little embarrassed, I think, which is nuts. He says there's nothing cool about being shot with a BB gun by kids."

"Would have been worse if they shot him in the ass." Caitlyn's dry aside made Elenie's mouth twitch.

"Sorry." Summer gestured to her friend. "This is Caitlyn. We were at school together."

Elenie's eyes flicked to the redhead, then involuntarily down to her stomach and back up again.

"Yup, due in the fall," Caitlyn confirmed with an eye roll and a lazy drawl. "I'm praying for a baby so good it teaches me all the shit I need to know."

Elenie relaxed a fraction, enjoying her easy humor. "I hear parenting's a piece of cake. I mean, how hard can it be to take one hundred percent responsibility for a small human?"

Caitlyn gave a guarded smile and took a huge bite of brownie.

"I guess Officer Taggart's still off work?" Elenie asked, for want of something else to say.

"Roman's told him he can go in for desk duty next week," Summer said. "Dougie's not good at resting. He's bitching about not getting the dressing wet yet and pacing around our apartment, threatening home improvements." She winced. "Last time he tried to change a washer on our kitchen faucet, we had to clean the dishes in the bathroom for a week."

"More than three hundred people each year are killed falling off a ladder," Elenie remembered. "Tell him he should quit while he's ahead."

Summer and Caitlyn blinked in unison. "Weird fact," stated Summer.

Delia yelled Elenie's name across the diner. "Hey! I've got orders stacking up here!"

"I'm so sorry. I'd better—"

"No, I'm sorry." Summer gave a grimace of understanding. "We didn't mean to keep you."

"It was nice to meet you properly anyway." Elenie shared a small smile with the two girls.

"Maybe, if you were free sometime, would you like to come out for a drink with Cait and me? One evening—perhaps Friday next week?" Summer looked like she even meant it. Caitlyn's expression didn't change.

Walking back toward Delia's impatient glare, Elenie raised one hand in an awkward wave as a swirl of warmth spread through her chest. "I'd like that, thanks."

Would it happen? She doubted it. But an unfamiliar bounce stayed in her step for the rest of the day.

* * *

She heard the bite of strong words the moment she opened the front door and her jaw clenched. For a second, Elenie considered going somewhere else, anywhere else, but she was tired, and gray clouds, heavy in the sky outside, threatened an evening rainstorm.

An object hit the floor of the living room with a bang.

"I'm not asking, I'm fuckin' telling you. If I don't have it in forty-eight hours, I'll be paying you a visit. And I won't be bringing apple fuckin' cobbler." Frank's ominous monologue rolled through the small house, thick and dangerous. She couldn't hear anyone else; he must be on the phone.

Gripping her hoodie close to her chest, Elenie moved soundlessly down the hall and darted up the stairs to her room, closing the door behind her. Dean's bedroom door was also shut, but the lack of music told her he wasn't inside. With any luck, they'd think she was out too. No one paid much attention to her coming or going. Being forgotten or ignored was usually the best-case scenario. And she still had one last new book from the library so the evening wouldn't drag.

Getting anything from the kitchen was unwise in the short term. When Frank was kicking off, staying out of his way was essential. Fortunately, in the pocket of her hoodie, she'd tucked a napkin-wrapped pecan pastry from the diner.

Who needs a balanced diet anyway.

The irony never escaped Elenie that, despite smelling of fried food almost all the time—the combined scent of cooking fats and caffeine clinging to her hair and her clothes, stuck in her nostrils 24/7—her stomach was rarely full. And neither were the cupboards in the kitchen. They'd never been a "wholesome meal around the table" kind of family.

One day, she swore to herself, she'd have a place of her own. An oasis of calm, cleanliness, and fresh groceries. She'd get so far away from this house that it would only be a bad memory in a sea of contentment and exciting experiences. In the meantime, she'd plan, manifest, dream, and scheme her way toward financial independence and emotional emancipation. Things would change. She'd make them change.

Roman Martinez had not been wrong when he'd said she deserved better.

Elenie lay back on her thin mattress, staring up at the ceiling, and tried to think of two men who were more opposite ends of the spectrum than Chief Martinez and Frank Dax.

Shameless, cunning, and unpredictably vicious, her stepfather was always on the lookout for the next way to screw someone over, right a perceived snub, or bend a law in his favor. He took pride in breaking as many as possible when bending didn't work. A barging ram of muscle, force, and noise. No subtlety, no nuances. He was a man of self-serving actions, almost all of them unethical.

Roman Martinez seemed to wear his scruples like armor. There was something innately dependable about him, as if he would show up whenever he was needed, deal with any problem thrown at him, and tie off all the loose ends. Hard to read on the surface, maybe. From their limited number of meetings, Elenie suspected he had more going on than he cared to reveal. He was clearly happier to listen than talk. But she thought he might be someone you could rely on. Sincere, honest, and utterly decent.

And hot, she added to herself. My god, the man was hot. A breathtaking mountain of sexiness, impossible to ignore. His body was ridiculously toned. Chief Roberts may have ruined her appreciation for a uniform until now, but only a dead person could fail to notice how Roman Martinez wore his like a made-to-measure suit. And Elenie was far from dead.

She was also a realist. Most likely, there was an equally attractive and intimidatingly successful girlfriend waiting at home for the police chief. Respectable and confident. Someone with qualifications, a career path, savings. Someone whose mother wouldn't blot her lipstick on a lacy thong pulled from her jeans pocket.

Grabbing a pillow to prop herself up on the bed, Elenie reached for the E.V. Huxley book she'd just begun. A distraction was necessary; no good could come of pipe dreams. Once he'd been back in Pine Springs for more than a few weeks, she'd be lucky if Roman Martinez ever spoke to her again. Outside of a police cell, that was.

Footsteps sounded on the landing and Elenie's eyes flew to the door handle as it turned. Athena didn't bother to knock; she never did. Her mother sauntered in, a chipped mug in her hand.

"That for me?" A smile lifted Elenie's lips. She could kill for a coffee.

"I wasn't sure you were home." Athena took a long sip and leaned against the closet at the foot of Elenie's bed. It wobbled alarmingly. Ash from the cigarette in her other hand dropped onto the carpet. She rubbed the toe of her boot over it, blowing a stream of smoke through Cranberry Kiss–colored lips. Elenie sighed and studied her, wearily.

"Got any cash?" Athena asked. "I'm going food shopping."

By food, she meant drink. And by drink, she meant vodka.

"I'm all out. Frank's already had my wages for rent." She'd be damned if she'd give up the few tips she had in the pocket of her hoodie.

Athena eyed her suspiciously and pulled open one door of the closet. There wasn't much inside but she jiggled the front of Elenie's denim jacket in the hope of hearing coins, huffing when it made no sound at all. Elenie raised an eyebrow but didn't comment.

"They never tell you raising kids will be so expensive," her mother groused around the cigarette. "This family keeps me poor."

Sober Athena without access to a drink could be as self-absorbed as Drunk Athena.

"I don't ask you for money, Mom. And I buy my own food." The emptiness in Elenie's stomach swelled to fill her chest. Her mother's comment wasn't an original one. Nor was her own response.

"I just want some vodka. It's not too much to ask for," Athena mumbled without heat. She stubbed her cigarette out on the side of the closet and dropped the butt onto the floor.

Elenie was tired, hungry, and done with this conversation. "Nor is a carpet without burn holes and the chance to bring home a nice boyfriend, but I'm not doing so well there either."

Her mother gave her a hard look. She muttered something dismissive about the male population of Pine Springs and drifted back out of the door.

Elenie closed her eyes, her book falling into her lap. She wondered what it would feel like to be part of a normal family.

Chapter 8
Roman

Since his shift pattern allowed it, Roman had accepted an invitation to Sunday lunch at his sister's house. Typically, the whole family heard about it via the Martinez jungle drums and pitched up en masse to join the party.

"It's so good to have you back home!" Thea squeezed his face between her hands, pinching his cheeks for good measure. "I've missed you, little brother."

Roman rolled his eyes. "Eleven minutes, T. You're only eleven minutes older. And I'm the fucking police chief. Have some respect."

When he first moved away, he'd missed Thea like he'd miss an arm. She knew it, too. It wasn't easy keeping secrets from a twin. Heaven knows, he had even more to keep from her now.

Thea laughed and looked over his shoulder. "Did you bring Dougie? I told you he was welcome."

"I asked but he and Summer have movie plans this afternoon." Roman pulled a bottle of chilled beer from the fridge and a flying body hit him from behind like a boxer's punchbag. "Ooof!" His younger sister, Florence, clung to his back, her arms wrapped around his neck. "Jesus, Flo—you're too old for this shit! And if you're not, I am."

He twisted at the waist, shaking her off onto the tatty old couch pushed against one wall of the sprawling kitchen. Florence bounced once and jumped back up.

"Why do I never see you?" she complained. "There's no point in having you home if you're always working. I had to hear from Thea you were coming today!"

"I'm not always working. I'm just avoiding you, muppet." Roman brushed her off with a smirk he dragged up from beneath a sudden wave of adrenalin. Florence stuck her tongue out and he forced a laugh, relieved she hadn't heard the truth in his words. "What are you—twelve?"

He let out a jagged breath as she turned away, deliberately unclenching tight fists. Eyes on the back of her head, her mass of rich curls, he forced down the image of a butchered Florence, dead-eyed and broken, on a filthy bed in a Detroit suburb. *Not* actually Florence. She hadn't been his sister. But, God, they'd looked so similar. Even now, Roman felt the shock of it. Staring down into the face of someone so like his sister, he'd thought for just one minute—

His heart had stopped for a beat. Two beats. And it had taken him months to be sure it was working properly again.

Roman ran a hand over the stubble on his jaw and took a swig from the beer bottle. It hit him in his knees every time he had one of these sudden flashbacks; his legs felt shaky beneath him. Unreliable and numb. He'd seen dozens of dead bodies through his homicide years. He'd seen even more brutal injuries. But none had floored him like the impact of the poor, battered girl with Florence's face.

He swallowed down a surge of sickness and pulled himself back into the moment. Thea's kitchen. Familiar and comfortable. All was well and his family was fine.

Out on the deck, his mother and father sat at a table made by Thea's husband, Luke. His brother-in-law, quiet and laid-back, was a talented carpenter. He'd become a very good friend. When Roman needed a more measured opinion than Milo's, or some easy company, he could always turn to Luke. He was a stand-up guy.

"My son!" His mother stood up to give him a hug as Roman finally stepped out through the door. He rested his chin on the top of her head. "You look tired, mijo! Elias, doesn't he look tired?"

"Thanks, Ma." His voice sounded rough but steady. "Just what everyone wants to hear." Roman squeezed his dad warmly on the shoulder, pulling out a chair to sit down. Luke, leaning against the rail, raised his beer in welcome.

His mother waved away the comment. "You know what I mean. Are they working you too hard already?"

He smiled at her. "I don't know who *they* are but I'll be putting in some long shifts until I'm completely familiar with the new role and my team." It didn't faze him. Every shift had been a long one as a city cop.

"Milo and Cait are joining us," Thea shouted from the kitchen. "They'll be here soon and they're bringing pie!"

It was chaos when they all got together. Everyone talked over each other, mostly forgot to listen, and told stories that grew gradually more raucous as the afternoon continued. There was teasing and laughter and affectionate gestures by the bucketload; it'd always been the same in his family. He'd missed too many of these lunches during his time in Detroit. He might be the serious one, the most buttoned-up, the one who found it hardest to relax and let his guard down, but here, it didn't matter and no one judged.

It was great to be home. Although he had no idea how to break it to them that it wasn't for good.

"How's your week been?" His dad was always interested and finally Roman felt able to share. Now his days weren't filled with brutalized bodies, misery and degradation—confidential horrors he wouldn't have dreamed of revealing in the middle of a family Sunday lunch—he could talk about work like a normal person.

"Still trying to identify where the Westlake girl got hold of the drugs she took. Other than that, we were called to a burnt-out lodge down Beggar's Track a couple of days ago, which might be an insurance job. And Peggy Winterburn reported her neighbor for cutting down a tree that she said was hers. It's been a steady week." He took a swig of his beer.

His dad chuckled. "That woman could have an argument on her own in a locked room."

"I saw Arianne Westlake in the hardware store yesterday." His mother stroked his arm. "She looks wrecked."

"I often see Millie go past the salon, usually with her basketball friends." Florence worked as a hairstylist on Main Street. "They all seem so confident."

"On the surface maybe. Underneath, they're just immature kids with insecurities, who make stupid decisions without thinking of the consequences." Roman said it without heat. "Just like we did and just like others will in the future."

"But, as a parent, you always pray your children will escape the worst fallout from those decisions." His mother gave a sad smile. "And not all of us are lucky."

"She's fortunate she survived at least." Roman laid a hand over hers. "Now we need to do what we can to shut down the supply." He cast around for a subject change. The one he found was a close link. "I also met the Daxes recently. I called at their house with Dougie to ask Frank Dax some questions. Could be coincidence, but I had two flat tires on the patrol car when I left work that afternoon."

His father's eyebrows drew together.

"Fuckers." Luke muttered into his beer and gave his mother-in-law a guilty glance. "Sorry, Ava."

"Tyson Dax is a dick and Dean's not much better," Flo chipped in. "Sorry, Ma!"

"Was this about Ray Parker's truck?" Luke asked.

"Can't say, I'm afraid." Roman pulled an apologetic face.

"Poor Ray. He's such a sweetie. Mrs. Elliott lives on the corner of his road. Ray and his partner clean her gutters every year." His mother frowned. "I've only seen Mr. and Mrs. Dax a handful of times in person, and never together. We don't really mix in the same circles but I've heard all the gossip. Seems amazing we can live in such a small town and rarely cross paths."

Roman could see that Athena Dax wasn't the type to join his mother's book club. "Not a bad thing, Ma. Elenie—the daughter—seems OK but I wouldn't ask any of the rest of them to water your plants if you go away."

"Frank Dax sure does love a lighter." Luke set his empty bottle on the edge of the table. "He'll pull one out of a pocket and flick it on and off with that dead-eyed smile of his. It's his way of saying, 'Don't mess with me or I'll burn down something you love.'"

Ava shuddered and his father reached over to smooth a hand over her hair. Roman would have smiled at the casual touch if he hadn't been focused on Luke's words.

"When have you come across Frank Dax?" he asked.

"I put a new roof on the garage at the back of his house a long time ago now. The business was in its early days, wasn't it, T?" Luke directed the question to his wife; Thea answered with a nod. She ran the books and dealt with the orders for Luke's construction company.

"Yes, sometime in the first couple of years," she confirmed.

"That was enough to tell me I didn't want to work for him again. I got the job done quickly, he paid me, and I got out. I overpriced next time he came back and I didn't hear from him after that. There's no way any business he does is legitimate. Everything about him smells off. But he always seems to go under the radar."

Roman filed the information away with a nod and steered the conversation onward by asking Luke and Thea about their current workload. He'd done more than enough talking for one lunchtime.

When Milo and Caitlyn arrived, the volume dialed up another notch as his mother went into pregnancy interrogation overdrive. Milo gave him a chin lift from the other side of the deck but was stopped on his way over by an embrace from Roman's dad. His friend had been around so long he was practically a surrogate son, and Elias Martinez had enough warmth and love for a whole host of children. Strong, quiet, loyal, and with a laugh no one could resist, his father had been Roman's hero from the time he could crawl. He couldn't imagine being without his unshakable support.

Roman wondered who he would be if he had grown up with a father figure like Frank Dax instead.

He sat back and lost himself in thoughts of work again. However much he might warn his parents off, it seemed there was not a chance in hell that he'd get to keep his distance from the Daxes while he was police chief of Pine Springs. He might only be here on secondment, but Roman wanted calm in the town. A safe space for the families he'd grown up alongside and for the future he hoped to build for his friends. It would take more than a couple of slashed tires to scare him off.

Chapter 9
Elenie

Sliding into one of the booths at the Rusty Barrel, the bench seat cool beneath her thighs, Elenie shot a nervous smile toward the girls and slid off her jacket.

Summer pushed a tall glass filled with a colorful cocktail across the table. The white t-shirt she wore featured the name of a band Elenie hadn't heard of, with tour dates from two years ago. A miniature silver daisy hung from a thin chain around her neck.

"It's Purple Rain—vodka, lemonade, blue curaçao, grenadine, and lime—and it's on Dougie. His treat as a small token of appreciation for your nursing assistance." Summer's blond, choppy bob danced as she gave a happy shimmy. Elenie allowed herself a relieved puff of breath that she might escape the evening without being financially embarrassed. There was just enough tip money in her pocket for another round of drinks if needed. "I said he should buy you some new underwear too, but he muttered about us doing a girls' shopping trip for that, so yay!"

Elenie flushed and caught Caitlyn's eye.

"I'm on the orange juice and not jealous at all," said the redhead. Her reserve was still firmly in place, despite Summer's instant friendliness. It suggested Elenie was being given a chance, but the outcome, on Caitlyn's part at least, was currently in the balance.

Despite low expectations, it had been a pleasant surprise when Summer actually followed through on her original invitation, catching Elenie on the way home one afternoon and making her promise she would join them at the Barrel. Tonight, the bar was humming but not packed; it smelled of spilled beer and wood polish. She tried not to check around for unfriendly stares or outward hostility. It'd been a long time since her last night out, and this slim chance of friendship meant the world. She wouldn't mess it up.

"Is he feeling better?" she asked. Elenie avoided using his name—both "Officer Taggart" and "Dougie" seemed out of place. "How's the leg?"

"Yeah, loads better, thanks. He's still got a bit of a sexy limp but he's back at work and far happier for it."

"Good." The conversation lagged for a moment and Elenie felt the stirrings of panic. Why had every iota of small talk she'd ever known disappeared from her head?

"So, this is interesting, isn't it?" Caitlyn contributed, in what seemed to be her usual dry style. "Here we are—getting to know each other after only, what, ten years or so of living in the same town? Who'd have thought."

"I've been here twelve years." Elenie made her tone equally dry. So, they weren't going to dance around the elephant in the room. It was a relief in many ways.

"Wait." Summer frowned. "Were we at school together? I don't remember you being there."

"How old are you?" Caitlyn asked.

"Twenty-seven."

"We must have been in the grade above then."

"You probably wouldn't have noticed me anyway." Elenie shrugged. "I mainly kept my head down."

"Because your stepfather is a psycho?" Caitlyn was bold.

"Mostly." She gave a tight smile. "Don't forget Tyson and Dean are my stepbrothers and they've pissed off everyone Frank's missed." Elenie lifted her chin, her fingers white against her glass.

Summer grimaced. "They are pretty gross."

"I didn't get to choose or I'd have picked differently." Eyeing her jacket, Elenie wondered if she should start putting it on.

"It's fortunate there's more alcohol where those came from," said Caitlyn, waving a finger between the glasses on the table. "You've got more reason than most for drowning your sorrows."

Elenie blinked as Summer chuckled. And then she sat back as the two took control of the conversation, steering it with the chaotic speed of a runaway bobsled through a dizzying array of topics. None of them involved her family and all were light, fun, and frivolous. They were letting her off the hook for now.

Summer had the unguarded openness of a child; she was irresistibly appealing. Talking twice as much as Caitlyn, she explained she'd been dating Dougie for almost three years. Caitlyn, more measured, sarcastic and brutally blunt, continued to study her—reticent but not unfriendly. She and Milo had been married for eighteen months.

"Roman and my husband kicked up hell, side by side, as teenagers. Now they've turned into a couple of the most responsible, upstanding men the town has ever seen. I tell Milo I've been short-changed. I fell for a bad boy, not a pillar of the community. What the hell?"

"Nice is always underestimated." Elenie sipped her drink. "And kind and honorable is absolutely everything." She pictured the strong, trustworthy face of the police chief and felt a pull in her chest.

Caitlyn leaned forward, elbows on the table, and wiggled her eyebrows suggestively. "Roman Martinez is also fucking hot."

Elenie came close to snorting Purple Rain from her nose. A flush roasted the back of her neck.

"More drinks?" Summer gave her glass a forlorn tilt.

"I'll go—it's my turn." Elenie stood and gathered the empties.

"Another orange juice for me, please," sighed Caitlyn.

Wiggling into a gap at the bar, Elenie waited her turn, humming the chorus to a Taylor Swift number. She felt carefree and young, her shoulders relaxed for once in her goddamn life. It made it all the more shocking when a sweaty pair of palms skimmed the sides of her thighs and pushed upward under her skirt.

"Dammit, Craig—keep your hands to yourself!" Elenie careered into the person behind her.

"Ah, but that's no fun, Ellie." Leering and swaying in equally alarming measures, Craig Perry reached for her again, eyes on her chest despite her simple t-shirt being far from revealing. "It's about time we had that date you've been promising me." He leaned in, pushing her back against the bar. His breath smelled of cigarettes and peanuts. "You know you want to."

Loud and brash, Perry was in property development, hung around occasionally with Tyson, and had "business dealings" with Frank. Elenie didn't trust him as far as she could throw him. Proud of his English roots—"Essex boys have heard it all, seen it all, done it all," he'd told her more than once—Craig made her skin crawl. She smacked his hand away.

"But I don't want to." Elenie retreated as far as she could. "Girls don't like it when you grope them without asking. And cocky guys who won't take no for an answer are a bit of a turn-off."

He let out a low, sarcastic whistle. "Wow, full of yourself much? Remember who you are, love. You're a Dax. A waitress. You're nothing special. And, if I ever do decide to get my hands dirty and take you out, you'll count your lucky stars."

He crowded her closer, his aftershave burning the inside of her nose, eyes alight with the thrill of a chase.

"I don't think so." Caitlyn's voice was deadly. A glance over Elenie's shoulder found the two girls flanking her, slight but fierce. Caitlyn, no less scary for her baby bump, looked ready to take on the entire British Army, not just one underwhelming expat. "I'm pretty sure our friend said 'no,' dickface."

Elenie swung back to Craig and cocked an eyebrow.

He swore under his breath, raising both hands in mock surrender. "Christ, this is why people talk about you, Elenie. You're such a fucking loser." Grabbing his beer from the bar, he pushed past her and headed back to his friends.

Summer signaled the bartender; Caitlyn bumped against her in unspoken sympathy. Elenie blew out an embarrassed huff of breath.

"*Skitstövel,*[1]" she muttered. "Sorry, girls. Way to ruin the mood."

"You're kidding, aren't you?" Caitlyn smirked. "That's the most fun I've had in months. There's nothing like taking down a sexist scumbag to bring girls together."

"Let that be a lesson to sleazeballs everywhere!" sang Summer, drumming on the bar with her delicate hands. "More drinks for the Dream Team over here—as quick as you like!"

---

1   Skitstövel (shitboot / asshole)—Swedish

Chapter 10
Roman

Roman watched her leaning on the wooden fence and took a moment to raise an imaginary hat to small-town living and familiar faces. The possibility of seeing Elenie Dax had been a consideration when he'd accepted the request to judge the fancy dress riding class at the town fair.

She was his way into the inner circle of the Dax family. If he stood any chance of getting the lowdown on Frank, it would have to be through her.

Face relaxed, she ran her eyes over the gaggle of children in costumes as they ran to their ponies, boosting themselves into the saddles and drifting out to ride in a wonky, egg-shaped circle. He hadn't seen her out of her waitress's uniform before and she looked like a summer's day. Her cropped jeans were the palest blue, soft and worn like old favorites. She'd paired them with a simple tank top, striped in white and pale green. Elenie closed her eyes and lifted her face to the sun. He hesitated to disturb her.

"So, which one is your pick?"

His question startled her but she recovered quickly. Her arms, resting on the rail next to his own, remained slack but he didn't miss the careful glance she shot over his shoulder. Roman tilted his head toward the children.

"It would be Jasper for me, I think." She pointed to a small boy dressed as a scarecrow. A row of cardboard carrots hung from each half of his reins. "He's adorable. Looks like he made his own costume, too. He lives with his grandparents—they're nice people."

Roman nodded thoughtfully, taking in the line of colorful competitors. One child was dressed as an astronaut and another couple were superheroes in capes and tights. In addition, there was a host of obligatory fairies, princesses, knights, and cowboys, all equipped with glitter, streamers, swords, or hats.

"Excuse me a moment." He ducked between the fence rails and strode across the grass.

Meeting Mrs. Magellan, the mayor's wife, all smiles and primary colors, in the center of the circle, he took a large red rosette from her hands. She thanked him for coming with a squeeze of his elbow and a slightly alarming flick of her hair. Roman backed away to award the first prize to a delighted scarecrow. He rubbed his hand up and down the neck of Jasper's pony and took a moment to ask the small boy a few questions.

Jasper had one of his own, pretty standard among kids of his age. "How many people have you shot?"

"No one today," Roman replied seriously, and gave the boy a wink.

As he handed out the rest of the prizes, he was aware of Elenie, in the periphery of his vision, clapping among the gathered spectators. When he excused himself from the group and walked back to the fence, she didn't even try to shut down the grin that broke over her face. It wasn't huge and it was a little shy, but Roman almost missed his step when he saw it. It hit him like a bolt from an electric fence square in the chest, and maybe a little lower too.

The pull he felt toward her was unexpected, inconvenient, definitely unwise. The impulse to keep that light on her face was concerning. "Ice cream or cotton candy? Or both? My treat," he asked.

Elenie hesitated. Another glance, over her own shoulder this time.

"Please." He took a step away, hoping she'd follow if he gave her more space, and waited.

It took almost half a minute.

"I've always wanted to try cotton candy."

"It's so sweet it makes your teeth hurt. But a town fair's not a town fair without it." A warm sliver of satisfaction slid between his ribs when she let go of the fence to walk by his side.

They wandered slowly through the milling crowd. Roman took in the surroundings and marveled at the contrast between a homicide shift and this casual afternoon on duty at the Pine Springs fair. The setting made Detroit seem like a distant chapter in his life. It was surreal.

But, even with the mingled scent of hot dogs and horseshit in his nose, he still had a job to do. And he needed to get Elenie Dax talking.

Digging deep into unfamiliar reservoirs of chatter, Roman told Elenie of other town fairs he remembered from the past, including when Milo had once eaten nine corn dogs and thrown up on his shoes. "And not even that long ago either."

She smiled and listened. He thought for a moment that she wasn't going respond.

"Last year, Lilian Dankworth mistook dried garlic for coconut flakes," Elenie said eventually, "and baked a cherry cake that stank out the food tent."

A smartly dressed older man passed them, wearing a navy bucket hat and licking at a scoop of mint ice cream. He raised his cone in greeting, a warm smile on his lips. "Good afternoon, my dear. How lovely to see you outside of the diner."

"It's closed this afternoon for the fair." Elenie flicked Roman a glance. "Otto, have you met the new police chief?"

He stepped forward, hand outstretched. "Roman Martinez."

"A pleasure to meet you." The old man's eyes were shrewd, his face friendly and his grip firm. "Perhaps I could buy you a coffee the next time our paths cross in Elenie's place of work?" He leaned in. "I can tell you where she's buried the bodies . . ."

Roman chuckled. "I'd very much like that. You'd save a lot of legwork."

Elenie gave the old man a gentle shove with her elbow and he walked on, tipping his hat to them as he went. Roman thought how different her face looked when it was less guarded. Younger, happier. It tightened again when they skirted the beer stand and she turned her head away from a small group of preppy-looking guys standing under the awning. Her shoulders hunched a little. She put more distance between them. He ran his eyes over the men, fixing their faces in his mind.

Roman bought two huge sticks of cotton candy bigger than his head from a chirpy teenager with a cart, and passed one to Elenie with a flourish. Her smoky eyes flared as she popped a large pinch into her mouth. "That is—so sweet! And kind of disgusting. But also, amazing!"

He couldn't help the grin. "An accurate assessment, eloquently put."

A short, rounded woman with a tight crop of graying curls and bustling elbows turned from a stand selling local preserves to give them a hard look over her shoulder. Elenie and Roman were clearly the topic of conversation between her and Josephine Alberty, the Pine Springs librarian.

"That's Elfrida Alberty and her daughter," murmured Elenie beside him. She took another pinch of her cotton candy.

He could see the resemblance now she'd pointed it out. Roman tilted his head and considered the options.

"Mrs. Alberty." He approached the women with an easy stride, offering the hand free of cotton candy to the older of the two. "Roman Martinez—I'm the new police chief."

Mrs. Alberty nodded grandly. "Hello, Chief Martinez. This is my daughter, Josephine."

"Yes, we've already met." Still holding Mrs. Alberty's hand, Roman's eyes dropped to her wrist and the familiar bracelet draped around it. "What a coincidence that we should bump into each other when I was just talking to Elenie." He turned to beckon her forward. "This is the kind lady from the diner who handed in your bracelet. I don't know if you were aware of that?" Elfrida's cheeks hollowed as if she were sucking a lemon. Josephine's eyes darted from her mother to Roman and back again. "She came straight from Diner 43 to the station," he continued with a hard smile, "and gave me a list of everyone she could remember seeing. I can only imagine how grateful you must feel to have your jewelry back, safe and sound. All because of Elenie here." He held her eye and waited, folding his arms across his chest.

There was a long pause as various expressions warred with one another on Elfrida's face. None of them were gratitude.

"Yes, indeed," she said finally. "That was most kind. Thank you."

The stupid woman still regarded Elenie with the same look she would give a maggot in her meatloaf, but she inclined her head stiffly and Roman decided to let it go.

"You're very welcome." Elenie's voice sounded strangled.

"Enjoy the fair!" Roman called after the Albertys as they bustled away.

"Wow." A small smile quirked the corner of Elenie's lips. "You played her like a two-bit fiddle, Chief Martinez. Great job."

* * *

The cotton candy was long gone, replaced by paper-wrapped soft pretzels, salty and still warm to the touch. Legs extended, they leaned up against a tree. Shadows were just beginning to stretch across the park, but the area around them was flooded with more people rather than less. It shocked Roman that the last hour had passed so quickly.

"Pennsylvania produces the most pretzels in the US. They eat the most, too. And there's even a National Pretzel Day each year on 26 April." Elenie licked a salt flake from the corner of her mouth.

"And you know that how?" He dragged his gaze away from her lips.

She shrugged. "I read a lot, I look stuff up and I have a good memory. One day I'll use it for more than food orders and takeout requests."

Roman frowned, studying her long enough that Elenie colored and tore off another piece of pretzel. She was an unusual combination of interesting and different, but he could not afford to like someone with Elenie Dax's background. That was so far past messy, it ventured into potential chaos. He was trying to get his life back on track, not derail it altogether. He pulled his professional reserve around him like a cloak and heard its echo in his voice.

"That kind of recall could be helpful if there was anything you wanted to tell me about your stepdad's business. Or even about Millie Westlake."

Elenie went as still as a wood frog in winter. Her fingers tightened around the remains of the pretzel, her hand poised on one bent knee.

"You give me the impression that you want more for yourself than a life of petty crime." Roman pushed a little harder. "Can't be easy living with a man like Frank Dax. Why do you do it, Elenie? Why don't you leave?"

He watched her throat bob around a ragged swallow. She wiped her hand across her mouth. Carousel and folk music blended with the sounds of tractors and trucks. Happy screams came from the direction of the Ferris wheel, and the scent of dozens of different foods melded in the air. And Elenie Dax gradually withdrew from him until all the gentle animation had left her face.

Roman felt its loss with a sharp edge he didn't like to examine.

"They still give a prize for the town's largest pig," she told him eventually. "I think I'll go check it out." She screwed up the pretzel paper in her hand and climbed to her feet, looking around for the nearest trash can. "Thanks for a nice afternoon, Chief Martinez."

He sat on the ground for a full ten minutes after Elenie cut through the throng of people standing in line for bumper cars and disappeared out of sight. Somehow, she took all the pleasure of the fair with her.

Chapter 11
Elenie

Elenie made herself a cup of coffee in the tiny, grubby kitchen, rinsing the mug before she used it because she shared the house with animals.

The day stretched out before her. Maybe she should grab her library book and take the long walk down to Weller's Lake. She could escape and read and chill for the afternoon. And keep her mind right away from dark eyes or corded forearms.

It'd been so easy to forget who she was at the fair. Dazzled by the attention of Roman Martinez, his support of her to Mrs. Alberty, the easy conversation, the sexy damn heat of his closeness, she'd let herself get swept away. As if he actually wanted to spend time with her. As if he hadn't tracked her down because of who she was. She knew better, dammit. It was embarrassing how much his change of tack had blindsided her. Elenie still felt the mortification through to her bones.

The volume of her unruly thoughts drowned out Frank's footsteps in the hall. His sudden appearance in the kitchen doorway startled her, and Elenie's coffee slopped until she steadied her hand.

"Clumsy!" she murmured, giving him a half-smile and reaching for a cloth.

The force of the backhand across her face split Elenie's lip, coming from nowhere as it did. Her head whipped to the side; white-hot pain bloomed from her cheekbone. Scalding coffee spilled over her hand and her wrist, the mug shattering against the kitchen counter. Her forehead smacked the edge of the fridge as her legs gave out beneath her. Stupid with incomprehension, she lay in a crumbled heap, half leaning against one of the cupboard doors at Frank's feet, brain scrambled.

His boot caught her in the side and her ribs screamed. Elenie curled into a ball to protect her poor, battered body. Blood from her mouth dripped onto the floor.

"Think it's funny to make a joke out of me?" Frank's face was as cold as concrete.

"I didn't—" she began, not even knowing what she was saying.

"Did you think no one would see you chatting with a fuckin' cop like you're best fuckin' buddies?" He pulled her off the floor—one hairy hand clamped around her wrist and the other gripping the sleeve of her t-shirt. Elenie heard it rip, felt it give. A pained cry forced its way through throbbing lips. "You're a part of this family whether you like it or not. And we don't like cops, we don't talk to cops, we don't fuckin' *think* about cops!" She flinched when the spittle from his mouth landed on her face. "Get your goddamn act together and choose where your loyalties lie."

Frank let go and she collapsed onto the floor, colliding with one of the kitchen chairs, which rocked on its legs then crashed over on its side. He stormed out of the kitchen and into the entryway. The screen door rattled when he slammed it behind him.

Shaking with shock in a pool of cooling liquid, Elenie gasped through swelling lips, too dazed to move, broken pieces of the mug scattered around her. There was dirt under the fridge and the corner of one sticky floor tile near her hand had lifted because the adhesive was old. A trip hazard, she thought randomly.

Dizzy and sick, she couldn't even push herself up to a sitting position. The side of her face, where Frank's knuckles had caught her mouth and cheekbone, felt hot, numb, strange for a moment or two. And then pain began to kick in like an absolute bitch, stealing her breath and pounding under her skin. Air wheezed in and out of her chest.

Breathe, she told herself. *Just breathe.* Moving could come later. Elenie closed her eyes and even that hurt. Helpless tears trickled into her hair. It was hard to tell how much time went by.

This was an awful, sickening first; Frank had never hit her before. Despite his bluster and threats, she'd never thought he would. She'd been an idiot to imagine the danger only radiated outward, away from the house.

Light footsteps paused in the doorway. Her mother's feet were bare, toenails painted a delicate shade of coral. Elenie looked at them but couldn't speak. Slowly, very slowly, she lifted her chin. Athena's narrow face was a flicker book of expressions—confusion, shock, pity, denial, and, finally, weariness.

"Oh, Elenie," she said eventually. And there was judgment in her tone. Not toward Frank. Never toward Frank.

Picking her way through smashed china and coffee, Athena stepped around the fallen chair, over Elenie's ankles, and lifted a pack of cigarettes from the window ledge. She headed for the door, then paused. Elenie drew in a juddering breath as her mother turned back. But Athena just closed her fingers around the neck of a vodka bottle on the countertop and left the kitchen without saying another word.

Chapter 12
Roman

Roman needed food and he needed it fast. There was just time to drop in to Diner 43 for a quick takeout at the end of the Monday lunchtime rush.

Near the doorway, he sidestepped to let a woman pass him on the sidewalk. It was Josephine Alberty. Roman paused to speak to the librarian and they exchanged pleasantries for a few minutes.

"Will we see you back on the baseball field soon? I've heard impressive things but I'd like to see the proof." She was a good deal more approachable out of the presence of her mother.

"That depends on the workload. I've hit the ground running, but once things quieten down I might get the chance."

"At least you found time to take in the fair!" Josephine laughed.

"Wouldn't have missed it." He immediately thought of Elenie and her quicksilver mind and something occurred to him. "How are you doing for staff in the library?" he asked.

"Oh, we're always short-staffed." Josephine's reply was rueful. "I'd like a day off here and there, if only the budget allowed."

"Well, if you're ever looking to hire, Elenie Dax would be a good candidate to consider. She's smart and hard-working."

The smile disappeared from Josephine's face. "I'm not sure she'd be the right fit."

"No? And why's that?"

Josephine glanced away, up the street. She swapped her purse to the other shoulder. "The Daxes aren't popular in town."

"I get that. But we're more than the sum of our parents, aren't we?"

Listen to him, the hypocrite. As if he wasn't keeping Elenie at arm's length, just like everyone else. Roman rubbed at the scruff on his jaw.

"No, no, you're quite right." Josephine Alberty backed up a few steps. "But, as I said, our budgets are tight. We're not hiring right now. And I'd better head off and open up again for the afternoon!"

She scurried away from him, practically jogging along Main Street toward the library.

Roman tugged at the door of the diner. His eyes scanned the tables as he crossed to the serving hatch, pulling his wallet from his pocket. "One fiesta wrap to go, please, Delia."

The dumpy diner owner grunted an acknowledgment and turned from the hotplate.

There was a flash of burgundy by the far booths and Roman caught sight of Elenie from behind as she leaned over a table, offloading drinks from a large tray. Delia packaged the wrap and pushed his lunch across the counter.

"Thank you." Dropping the money into her hand, he scooped up the takeout bag.

Elenie turned with the emptied tray and froze the moment she saw him. Her damaged face hit Roman with the force of a sledgehammer.

"What the—"

In an instant, she went into reverse. She spun away, dumping the tray on the counter. Jerky steps took her through the doors leading to the restrooms and staff area. He caught up with her in the corridor beyond and grabbed her elbow.

"Elenie. Talk to me."

She looked everywhere but at his face and fury whipped through his stomach like a fire devil. The embarrassment in her eyes made him want to smash something. A livid bruise darkened her cheekbone and the socket of her left eye. It highlighted the exhaustion that pumped off her in waves. Her lip was raw and blood-crusted. Elenie vibrated in his grip and Roman, his nostrils flaring, held her gently upright.

"Take off your apron," he ground out. "You're done here for the day."

She pulled her arm away from him, still without meeting his eyes. "No, I'm not. I've got one more hour and then I'm finished."

Roman swore violently and Elenie flinched. When she finally looked at him, his heart twisted at the defeat in her eyes.

"People like me don't get second chances. I need this job."

He looked at his watch. "You finish at three?" Elenie nodded. "I'll be back then," he promised.

It took every ounce of will he possessed to turn and walk away from her.

* * *

There was a bite in the air as he waited outside the diner an hour later. Clouds split the sky, blue to one side, black and threatening to the other. A downpour would be on them before the afternoon was out. The sidewalk was quiet.

When Elenie finally emerged, slowly, carefully, holding her ribs, she looked like someone at the very end of their tether. Roman had no idea how she'd thought she would get home.

He stepped forward, steering her carefully toward his truck, just a couple of yards away, pulled up on the verge. He'd gone home to swap the police Interceptor for his own F-150, aiming for a lower profile.

"This way." Roman opened the passenger door and stepped aside, waiting for her to climb up.

Elenie shook her head. "No. This is a bad idea. I—"

Her face took on a clammy sheen; she swayed on her feet. Swearing harsh and low under his breath, he gripped her gently around the waist and slid his other hand to the back of her thighs. Elenie's protest ended in a small groan of pain as he lifted her into the truck.

"I'm so sorry," he said gruffly.

Roman stretched across her to fasten the seatbelt. Elenie turned her head as if it was too heavy for her neck and closed her eyes. Before he'd reached the top of Main Street, she'd tumbled headfirst into sleep. It seemed her body had reached its capacity for powering through and she was out for the count when Roman pulled up outside his sister's house.

She stirred when he lifted her out of the truck, resettling against his shoulder with a whimper as he kicked the front door instead of knocking. Thea was frowning when she pulled it open.

"I need your spare room." He brushed past her into the foyer.

"What the hell, Ro!" Thea whispered as she followed him up the stairs.

His muscles bunched solid with suppressed rage, he carried Elenie into the bedroom and laid her on the sheets. He felt the jagged sigh she expelled, her eyebrows notching in pain, like a punch in the stomach. With gentle hands, he eased off her shoes and socks, hissing out a breath at the bloom of bruises revealed between the hem of her top and the waistband of her skirt.

Thea gripped his shoulder. "That's Elenie Dax."

Roman nodded. He lifted Elenie's polo shirt just a fraction to check out her ribs. Red, black, blue—the angry discoloration spread over her left side. Fuck, that had to hurt. He straightened the material with tender hands and drew the sheets up to her shoulders. Elenie's teeth chattered.

"I'll fill a hot water bottle," Thea offered softly.

When she left the room, Roman slumped heavily into an upholstered chair facing the bed. Propping his elbows on his knees, he scrubbed at his face and deliberated calling a doctor. He guessed nothing was broken or Elenie would have struggled to put in a full shift at the diner. She might have strong feelings one way or the other but he didn't plan to wake her up and ask. Getting medical help could wait for now.

His mind churned. He'd already known her life was more challenging than many, but seeing it spelled out this way in violence on her skin was like a kick in the balls. And he realized he knew next to nothing about her at all. He hadn't even begun to scratch the surface of what made Elenie tick.

With her measured smiles and watchful eyes, she was so different from Thea and Flo and their casual confidence—from anyone else Roman knew. Frank and Athena Dax didn't give out nurturing vibes. He wondered what it was like to go home to that house at the edge of the town. And suspected he might now know the answer.

Hours passed and Roman didn't move. He sat by the side of the bed while Elenie slept, flooded with a wash of emotions that rampaged like a bull leaving a bucking chute.

As the afternoon faded to evening, Thea called him downstairs, dishing up a huge plate of pasta, topped with chicken and red peppers. She brought another helping to the table for herself.

"That smells amazing. Thanks." He added a couple of twists of black pepper and dug in.

When she picked up her fork, Thea's eyes were stormy. "What happened, Ro?"

He shook his head, mouth full. "I don't know, but I'll find out. D'you know her?"

Thea shook her head. "I've spoken to her a couple of times in the diner but nothing personal. She's Frank Dax's daughter?"

"Stepdaughter," said Roman, in between forkfuls.

"She must keep a really low profile—I've never seen her out. Although the Dax boys are always in the Rusty Barrel and they're pretty hard to miss. Usually right in the middle of it if anything kicks off." She poked at a piece of chicken but didn't start to eat. "Did she tell you anything?"

"Nothing at all." Roman blew out a breath of frustration. He itched to get back upstairs to check on Elenie. "I saw her at the town fair and she was fine. When I went into Diner 43 today, she was working—God knows how—and she looked like that." He gestured toward the stairs. "She wasn't up to saying anything and I couldn't take her to my house. Sorry to bring this here, T."

"Not a problem. You did the right thing. She doesn't deserve that. Even if the Daxes are a nightmare."

"Elenie's not a nightmare," he grunted. His sister flashed him a surprised glance. "From what I can make out, she stays out of trouble and works hard. She's smart, too. And she helped Dougie when he got shot in the leg." He ate the last piece of pasta. "Haven't you talked to Caitlyn recently? She was out with Summer in the Barrel last Friday. They asked Elenie to join them as a kind of thank you. Seems they got on well."

Thea shook her head. "I've been snowed under with work. Luke and I were planning to catch up with her and Milo this week." Without asking, Thea dished out a second helping of food for him. "I'll make some soup. She might be hungry when she wakes up."

He spent a restless night dozing in a chair and jerking awake each time Elenie whimpered. Fury was a vicious, winged creature, clawing at his chest, and it kept him company during the long hours of darkness.

His heart ached when silent, pained tears leaked through her hair and onto the pillow.

* * *

Roman dropped the lid of the sugar canister on the countertop and swore at the noise. He grabbed for it, fumbled and dropped it again, glancing toward the stairs with a wince.

Elenie stood in the doorway, still dressed in her uniform, her face worse than yesterday, the bruising darker and the swelling more pronounced.

"I'm awake," she said, unnecessarily.

Roman assessed her and knew he'd have no luck in talking her out of working. "How are you feeling?"

She gave him an empty half-smile. "It's amazing what fourteen hours of sleep can do for a person."

He smiled back. "And yet you still feel like shit, don't you?"

Elenie shrugged, avoiding the question. She wrapped her arms around her body and he realized suddenly that she'd woken to find herself in a house she didn't know. "This is my sister Thea's place—we're twins. She lives with her husband, Luke. He's away overnight visiting his dad and she isn't up yet. She's not an early morning person." Keeping his tone light, Roman reached for two mugs. "Coffee and toast before work? Or would you prefer tea?"

"Coffee would be lovely, thank you. And a piece of toast. If that's OK."

Moving smoothly around the kitchen, aware of her eyes on him, Roman forced himself not to badger her with questions.

"I worked alongside a Brit in Detroit. He was a great guy, older than me by quite a bit. Moved over here in his twenties but still mainlined tea like a junkie. Since the coffee at the station was almost always disgusting, I picked up the habit and it's stayed with me." He laid a plate on the table in front of her, added a slice of hot toast, and passed her a knife. Elenie slid carefully onto a chair. "Peanut butter, if you want it," he pointed.

They ate in silence for a couple of minutes. Roman's nostrils flared as Elenie tore off tiny pieces of bread to pop into the less damaged side of her mouth.

"I want you to take my number," he said.

"I don't have a phone anymore. It . . . went missing. I haven't gotten around to buying another one."

He nodded. It wasn't a surprise. "We will be talking about this." Roman made a small, sweeping gesture which took in her face and body. Elenie flushed and looked away. "I'll give you a ride to work on my way to the station."

His fingers settled near hers on the tabletop and she withdrew her hand, letting it fall onto her lap.

"Could you drop me a little way out, please?" Elenie fixed him with unreadable eyes. "It's best we aren't seen together."

His gaze sharpened. "Why?"

Elenie shrugged and, though he opened his mouth to pursue it, Roman decided to let her eat in peace and added that to the list of things to discuss later.

When he entered the diner mid-morning, he'd already achieved a lot. There was a satisfying dent in the large pile of paperwork that littered his desk and he'd had time to run a few errands, too. Roman scanned the room, eyes settling on Otto, who was bent over his newspaper, coffee cup in hand. Elenie was behind the counter, dividing a carrot cake into equal slices. She didn't see him as he slid into a seat opposite the old man.

"Good morning, Chief." Otto's greeting was subdued. He flicked a glance in Elenie's direction. "Have you seen our lovely friend yet today?"

Roman's mouth tightened as he nodded. "I have, Otto. I have. I'm on it, don't worry."

Otto shook his head and wiped a hand over his mouth. His clever eyes were sad. "I don't know, Chief. It's just not right."

Roman pushed a padded envelope across the table toward him. "This is for Elenie," he said. "Would you mind passing it on to her? I'd appreciate your help. And I haven't forgotten that coffee we said we'd have, but could we make it another time? I've got a lot on today."

Otto closed his hand over the package with a nod. "Whenever you like, Chief. I'm often here."

Roman watched Elenie for a few more seconds, then made himself look away, said goodbye to the old man and left.

Chapter 13
Elenie

Weak and queasy, Elenie lowered herself gingerly onto a rickety chair in the staff area. Everything hurt. Resting her head against the wall, she tried to relax her jaw. Her breaktime and the chance to sit down for ten minutes had been all that kept her going through the morning.

She studied the package in her hands and turned it over a couple of times. Otto had given it to her when she'd refilled his coffee. Finally pushing a finger under the flap, she tugged it open. A piece of paper and a box containing a cell phone slid onto her lap. Elenie unfolded the note.

I want you to be able to reach me if you need to. I've put my number into the contacts on this phone under Thea's name.

I've added Summer's number as well. She can pass a message to Dougie if you can't get hold of me.

If anything happens to this phone, I will replace it.

Roman

Elenie read the words multiple times, mainly because she kept getting distracted by the angular sweep of Roman's writing and the knowledge that he'd held the paper, touched the package. It was so unexpectedly generous. Why would he do this?

She was used to people backing away. No one wanted to get involved with anything to do with the Daxes. Although it sucked, she didn't really blame them when they judged, belittled, and attacked, depending on their previous exposure to Frank or the boys. It had been tempting to think things were looking up with the hint of a couple of new friends and one afternoon in the company of a man so far out of her league it wasn't funny. But none of them would stick. No one ever did. Martinez just wanted his intel. That was the bottom line. The last few days had hammered home the folly of fanciful hopes.

But Elenie would remember last night as if it were a rip in the space-time continuum.

Though her face had throbbed and wrenching cramps sawed at her ribs, she'd never felt so safe. The layers of sleep, so deep she couldn't quite fight her way to the top, adding to the feeling of an alternate reality. She'd drifted in the relief of half-consciousness, with no idea where she was or how she'd got there, knowing Roman was close by because his scent surrounded her. The cotton sheets the smoothest, cleanest bedding she'd ever slept in. Everything still and peaceful.

Halfway through the night, she'd woken, her body too sore, limbs too heavy, to move. The room lay in shadows, a pale wash of moonlight cast over the floor. Roman was asleep in an armchair by the window, long legs stretched out in front of him, his strong, dark features just visible in the half-light. He looked uncomfortable, yet utterly relaxed. A sexy sentinel. A rumpled god of the night. She'd watched him without moving for as long as she could stay awake.

Elenie gave a tiny groan and held the note against her face, the paper cool on her cheek. What a mess. She had nothing to offer the police chief. She was a liability to the calm and order of other people's lives and any contact with him was a huge risk for her own. Elenie would be wise to steer well clear of Roman Martinez. And he would be even wiser to stay away from her.

She filed the shameful memory of rubbing her cheek against his arm when he'd pulled the soft covers up to her shoulders. And tried her hardest not to dwell on the fact that it had stilled next to her skin for just a moment.

The door was thrown open. "Ten minutes, Elenie, not twenty!" Delia yelled.

It had been nine.

"I'm coming." She dragged herself to her feet.

"This is not a good look for the diner." Delia grumbled as Elenie passed her in the corridor. "There's a reason I didn't give the uniform to Terence Crawford, you know."

Elenie lifted her chin. "Short-sighted of you. He'd look good in burgundy."

Delia stormed back to the kitchen, muttering something about Elenie being no better than her "goddamn useless, waste-of-space brother"—an insult far worse than most others. Delia had hated Tyson with a passion ever since he'd thrown a manhole cover through one of the largest diner windows when he was high as a kite. He'd laughed in her face at the suggestion he pay for the damage and it looked likely she'd take the grudge to her grave.

"*A holló vájja ki a szemed.*[2]" Weary to her bones, there was no bite in Elenie's insult and no one to hear it anyway. But her pride insisted on a comeback, if only for her own satisfaction.

---

2   A holló vájja ki a szemed (May the raven gouge out your eye / fuck you)—Hungarian

Otto had his nose in a book and looked like he was making himself comfortable for a long stay. He ordered lunch and an iced tea. His smile, as warm as vanilla sauce over apple pie, soothed her tattered senses. "I've got nowhere else to be today so I plan to relax here with my friend, Stephen King."

"Is it good?" She gestured to the book.

"Terrifying."

"Terrifyingly good?"

"That too." Otto's chuckle was throaty.

"I finished the E.V. Huxley I was reading. I think you'd like it. Great twist at the end."

Elenie's foot slid, a piece of paper beneath her sneaker stealing the traction. The pain in her ribs flared and dots swam in front of her vision. One of the flyers for the business guild's gala dinner lay the floor. She held her side as she picked it up, wincing at the discomfort as well as the font and color combination while she scanned the familiar details.

"Will you be going to the Local Event of the Year?" Elenie asked Otto, placing suitable emphasis on the grand description.

"Unlikely, I'd imagine. I like to be in bed by ten thirty. You?"

"Still waiting for my invitation from Prince Charming." She attempted a flippant grin, which tugged at the healing scab on her lip. Gala dinners weren't a big feature in her life. Nor were fun evenings out, nice clothes, or dates with dashing men.

Moving stiffly along to a new table of customers, pad at the ready, Elenie tried to ignore the hopelessness that weighed on her shoulders.

Come see me, Fairy Godmother. I'm here and I'm ready for you to makeover my life.

* * *

Elenie's legs were shaking when she opened the front door after work. Her heart thumped, throat tight. Coming home was never fun, but this utter dread was new. Everything had gone to shit so fast she still felt dizzy. A line crossed that could never be uncrossed.

Her mother and Dean were in the kitchen. There was no sign of Frank. Both turned when Elenie walked in and both slid their eyes away almost immediately.

"Hey."

"Hey," Athena echoed.

Dean poured a mound of Cheerios into a bowl, holding out the box to Elenie. "Want some?"

It was easily the nicest thing he'd said to her in months. The ever-present beanie plastered his straggly hair to his forehead; blue eyes peered through the strands.

"I'm good, thanks." She had no appetite at all. Maybe later her stomach would settle.

Athena added sugar to her coffee and stirred, discarding the teaspoon next to her mug. She spun it with one finger, leaving a dirty circle of liquid on the wooden kitchen table. "I had a word with Frank." She waved a hand at Elenie's face, unease setting her mouth into harsh lines. "He went too far. It won't happen again."

Dean sloped out of the room. Elenie nodded, lost for a reply.

That's OK, Mom.

No problem.

Thanks for asking your husband not to backhand your daughter.

She rubbed her eyes, tired beyond belief. Her mother was kidding herself if she thought she had Frank on any kind of leash. "I'll get something to eat later."

Elenie couldn't stand to be in the house so she grabbed a book and slowly climbed the small hill behind the garage to sit in the calm stillness of the dusky evening. As she drew her knees up under her chin, she soaked in the quiet and tried to empty her head. A half hour went by with only the *chip, chip, chip* of a song sparrow disturbing the peace but her mind refused to rest. She couldn't even read.

She thought of Millie Westlake again, as she'd done every day since the overdose, and wondered how her recovery was going. Had the pills come from Frank? There'd always been drugs in their house. Elenie knew they passed through Frank's hands. Now and then, he'd even gotten on her case about pushing some at school. It had been pretty bad for a while when she was younger, but she'd always refused to get involved and had never caved. Ty and Dean were willing enough anyway. Frank hadn't needed her in the end.

She thought of Ray Parker and his truck—just another victim of Frank's heavy-handed intimidation tactics. Elenie didn't even know the background to that one. She considered all the times Frank had stolen property stored in the garage or disappeared for days on undiscussed delivery runs. It wasn't guesswork. Tyson often moaned about unloading the huge quantities of boxes that came and then went again.

She thought about her mother and her lack of reaction to Frank's attack. When had Elenie stopped expecting more? Maybe it was finally time to accept things as they were, rather than bartering her soul for a fantasy that would never solidify into real life.

She rubbed a finger over the screen of the new phone in her pocket. It was the first gift she could remember receiving. The invisible link to Roman Martinez felt like a lifeline.

Despite all that had come afterward, Elenie couldn't regret the time she'd spent with him at the town fair. Walking and chatting, sharing food—the most wonderful kind of ordinary. Roman's company was undemanding. Irrespective of his lofty job title, his ego seemed non-existent. She thought he looked healthier than he had that first day in the diner. Less angular, some of the tightness gone from his face. He'd been dangerous then, with the hint of darkness behind his eyes. Now, he was lethal.

She wanted to message him but Elenie recoiled at the thought of getting it wrong. Yes, he was being kind. He might want her to be safe—his job was to keep people safe. It didn't mean he'd welcome more involvement than that. She already knew he was a decent guy. Reading too much into his attention would be stupid and she'd already been stupid enough.

Shifting her position on the grass, Elenie pressed a fist to her side. Her bruises were blooming into a violent rainbow of colors, the pain turning slowly from a fiery stab to a strong and steady ache throbbing through her bones. It was exhausting. She was exhausted.

She did not want this life. She'd had enough. What she could do about it, though, was another matter.

Chapter 14
Roman

"Any chance Craig Perry had anything to do with it?" Dougie's face was grim as they discussed Elenie's injuries in Roman's office.

"What makes you say that?" Since Elenie had told him nothing, Roman was none the wiser about who had hurt her. The lack of knowledge rubbed raw on his simmering temper.

Dougie relayed what Summer had told him about the run-in with Perry at the Rusty Barrel, plus the little he knew about the Englishman. Roman had an inkling Milo would be able to tell him more. Leaving the station on time for once, he placed a call and they arranged to meet up for an early drink. He'd pick Milo's brains about Perry at the bar.

As he turned his key in the ignition, Roman's cell pinged in his pocket. Elenie's name, next to the text, was unexpected.

Elenie:

Thank you so much for the phone. I will guard it with my life. Please don't pity me.

What could he say to that?

He did feel sorry for her—sorrier than he could express. Not pity exactly. But compassion, definitely.

And he was angry, too. Furious at whoever had lashed out and hurt her. Was it Perry? Or was it Frank Dax? Exerting power and control through brute strength was repellent. Somehow, Roman would find out what was going on. Police work was regularly more of a marathon than a sprint, and he had grim persistence in spades. No one knew better that swift justice and easy arrests were the exception rather than the rule. Pushing his phone back into his pocket, Roman headed for the Barrel.

Luke, just back from his dad's house, caught a ride to the bar with Milo. They beat Roman there and had beers already lined up when he joined them.

"Craig Perry's a dick," Milo said when he asked about the Brit.

"Say what you mean, buddy." Luke snorted. "How do you not upset more of your clients?"

Roman raised an eyebrow. "A dick in what way?"

"Every way. I don't like the guy. He's just too much of everything—too loud, too confident, too smiley, too slick. If he came with instructions, they would just say, 'Don't trust me. I'm a dick.'" Milo took another swallow from his bottle. "He's ruffled a few feathers at the business guild, although a lot of people think there's some merit in his plans for a new business center."

"Ruffled them how?"

"Initially, he put feelers out for local investors. When they didn't jump in as fast as he wanted, Perry piled on some pressure, playing people off against each other. It didn't go down well."

"And?"

"Seems now he's looking outside of the town for the money. There's been talk he won't get the planning application he needs anyway, so who knows if the project will even get off the ground."

"If it does, it shouldn't. It's a crappy site for a business center," Luke interrupted. "It used to be the old fuel station owned by the

Deerings. I've seen an overview of his construction budget and it's a joke. He's made no allowance for removing the underground fuel storage tanks. The valves and pipe vents are still there. You can see them from the access road. To get that site ready for construction will cost a hell of a lot more than he's allowed, whether he gets the planning application through or not."

"Why're you interested in Perry?" Milo asked.

"This got anything to do with Elenie Dax?" Luke leaned back in the booth.

While they finished their beers and started on another three, Roman gave them the rundown. Though his expression never changed, underneath he seethed, quietly and coldly. If Perry was the cause of Elenie's bruises, he would find out.

Bone-weary from a night of broken sleep, he ate a late dinner when he got home. Not in the mood for silence, Roman flicked on the TV and slumped on the couch, stretching out across the cushions.

He watched a soccer game, commentary droning in the background, with one eye on his phone. The temptation to answer Elenie's earlier message tugged at him, but he couldn't think of a suitable reply. Professional boundaries were a minefield in his line of work. Although he could and would argue his right of free association with anyone who wasn't a known felon or a drug user, Roman hadn't ventured onto shaky ground before this. It took him aback to feel so conflicted now.

When his cell pinged with an incoming message, he knocked it straight off the arm of the couch; it skittered across the floor. He hit his elbow on the coffee table. "Crap, damn, and double fuck!"

Zena:

We need to talk.

Great. The phrase every man, everywhere, most wanted to hear.

Roman couldn't think of a single reason for Zena to get in touch and had no interest in knowing. She'd made her feelings clear the last time they'd seen each other, and he was fine with that. Just six weeks into being home, his life in the city with Zena was already beginning to feel like it had happened to someone else.

No, we really don't

It was remarkable how fast his ex-fiancée had faded from his mind—how wrong she seemed for him now. He hadn't opened up to her when he was crumbling in Detroit, when every day was a pit of horror and he woke each morning soaked in sweat. They should have been able to talk about it, but he could never get the words out. And somehow she hadn't noticed the difference in him, even when he saw the dread written clearly on his face in the mirror.

Zena had reacted to his secondment like he'd chosen to do this just to mess with her, when the choice hadn't been Roman's at all. Her lack of empathy and understanding was the death knell in their relationship. He'd been desperate for someone to catch him, but she'd stepped back and let him fall. His head too full of ghosts to spare room for her disdain, he'd felt nothing but a numbed relief when they parted ways.

Throwing his phone down onto the coffee table, Roman headed upstairs to grab a shower. He was on another early shift tomorrow, so turning in soon would be a good idea. Zena was out of his mind before he hit the top step.

* * *

A chance meeting with Otto the next morning gave him enough distance and an unexpected reason to send a simple text to Elenie.

How are you today?

There was no answer until mid-morning, when his cell pinged just as Roman was mulling over timesheets and staffing rosters. He opened her message and a slow smile lifted his lips.

Elenie:

Feeling a little better, thank you. I might still make the Unicycle Championship qualifiers next month. Fingers crossed.

Why use two wheels when you can use one?

He beat a tattoo on his thigh with his pen and waited. She must have been on a break because his phone pinged almost immediately.

Elenie:

My thoughts exactly.

Milo had a unicycle. Neither of us could stay on the damn thing. What's your secret?

Elenie:

A good breakfast, the right shoes and a little magic.

Roman rested his forearms on his desk, enjoying her quirky humor.

We went with balance and determination.

Elenie:

Naive

With a chuckle, he decided to grab the moment he'd been leading up to, even as he remained torn over the wisdom of the suggestion he was about to make.

> I saw Otto in town this morning. You up for pizza on his deck tomorrow night?

This time more than a couple of minutes went by before Elenie began typing. The message bubble appeared and disappeared several times, while Roman fidgeted like a child at a church wedding. He told himself he needed to question her about the assault. He had an official duty of care to explore the matter further. That's why he'd fixed this up with Otto. The old man was concerned about her. Roman was concerned about her.

He expected an excuse but yet again she surprised him.

Elenie:

Sounds good. What time?

Duty aside, it was disconcerting how much her acceptance eased the tightness in his chest.

Chapter 15
Elenie

They swapped slices of pizza, laden with multiple toppings, until the night began to draw in and Otto flipped on the outside lights.

Elenie's eyes were drawn again and again to Roman as he sat on the deck, leaning up against the handrail. She didn't even know when he'd found the time to bond with her old friend to the point that they were all here, sharing food. But it felt so good to find this bolt hole for the evening, she refused to question it. She'd let it ride and pretend that these relaxed moments, eating pizza with a police chief, were ordinary rather than exceptional.

Always gorgeous in his uniform, Roman was even more appealing in casual clothes. His well-worn jeans and navy t-shirt made her mouth dry. His tousled hair lay a touch messy, brushing his collar, as if he hadn't thought to smooth it after tugging his top over his head. It added to his charm rather than detracting from it. Her eyes snagged too often on his legs, his chest, his smile, and she had to keep dragging them away.

Otto waved yet another piece of pizza in her direction. "Just two left and I am done. Don't leave me any leftovers—I'm too old to find cold pizza appealing in the morning!"

Elenie laughed and took the slice from his hand. She hadn't eaten so well in a long time; the pizza was spicy and satisfying. As long as she took small bites and left the crusts, it didn't hurt her mouth too much. Roman leaned over to pluck the last piece from the box on the deck. He cupped a hand underneath to catch any falling debris.

"So good," he mumbled around a mouthful, his head resting against the wooden post at his back. Inky eyes twinkled in the dusk. "No one makes a chicken Florentine pizza like Jerry's. It tastes of home."

Elenie curled up on the comfy, padded cushions of an outside wicker chair, Otto nearby on the right-hand side of a small bench, one leg crossed neatly over the other. Low music drifted out through the open back door from a radio inside the house. The men had drained a beer each while Elenie chose to pop the top of a can of Coke.

Otto's house was small and charming. It was the perfect place to meet, tucked away at the end of a small no-through road in a quiet part of town. No danger of anyone passing by. She'd taken pains to evaluate the safety of this get-together; she had a feeling Roman had done the same.

"I don't know about you two, but a coffee would hit the spot." Otto stopped Elenie from jumping up with his hand. "You stay there. I could do with a leg stretch. I've sat still long enough." He moved stiffly to the doorway. "Coffee for three? Or can I get you anything else?"

"I'd love a coffee, please."

"Could I have a hot tea instead, if you have it?" Roman lifted an eyebrow. "With milk and sugar. I'm not much of a coffee drinker."

"Not a problem, son." Dropping a blanket in Elenie's lap as he passed, Otto disappeared inside. They could hear his slow and steady movements in the kitchen as he opened cupboards and ran water to put on the stove.

Elenie pulled the woolen softness around her legs and snuggled in. The silence felt different when it was just Roman and her in the soft light. She knew he wanted some answers and the time to avoid them was running out. Her nerves began to vibrate.

"I can hear you thinking from over here." Roman's voice was low.

A tiny huff of amusement left her lips of its own accord. "Not me. I'm a blank." She turned her head to find him watching her. "You must be tuning in to someone else who isn't in a pizza coma."

"When are you seeing Caitlyn and Summer next?" The innocuous question was a relief.

"We said we might meet up for coffee soon." Elenie was still struck with the novelty of having dates in her social diary.

"They're nice girls."

"Yes. Very." There was a brief pause. "So, you're a twin, huh?"

"I am." She heard the smile in his voice.

"In Nigeria, they think twins are special children from God."

Roman chuckled. "My mom might beg to differ. We were little nightmares."

Otto brought two mugs out to the deck and asked if they minded him drinking his inside, in front of a favorite quiz show. He urged them to stay put and relax on the deck. "My bones begin to ache if I get too chilled. My couch and the television are calling me now, but please stop a while if you're happy to."

The night was clear and still. Only the occasional distant engine interrupted the rhythmical clicking of cicadas in the shrubbery. Elenie wanted just a little more time before he knew all her dirty secrets.

"What was it like to be a city cop?"

Roman's out-breath was barely audible, but she caught the way his jaw flexed.

"It was intense," he replied eventually. "Antisocial hours, tough cases, hard work. I made detective, did a four-year stint in fraud and then crossed over to homicide."

"Did you like it?"

He didn't answer for a while. "I enjoyed it for a long time. The work in fraud, especially. Pitting myself against a challenge and coming out on top was a buzz. But homicide is brutal. There's always another case to replace each one you close." He wiped a hand across his mouth and shot her a sideways look. "In Pine Springs, the toughest part of my day is getting a cup of tea before someone else swipes the last of the milk."

Elenie recognized the deflection away from his work in the city and let it go. "So, you're happy to be back?"

"I'm not back for good. I'm on a temporary transfer." Roman frowned, as if he'd surprised himself with the words. "That's classified, actually. I haven't told many people. Anyone."

Elenie made a small gesture with her mug, even as her chest cracked open like a walnut. "Who would I tell?"

I don't want you to leave.

The words were so loud in her head, she was amazed he couldn't hear them. She counted the brightest stars in the sky and tried to squash down a sense of loss for something she'd never had.

"Who hurt you, Elenie?"

The blunt question hung in the air. She'd expected it before, but now it caught her unprepared.

Elenie exhaled and shifted. Standing up and bringing her coffee and the blanket with her, she lowered herself onto the deck next to Roman. She perched on the wooden top step, which led down to the backyard. Blanket around her shoulders, she drew her knees up beneath it, wrapping her hands around the welcome heat of her coffee cup.

"Craig Perry saw us at the fair—we passed him by the beer stand—and he told Frank. My stepdad's not a fan of the cops," she clarified, unnecessarily.

Roman's grip was tight on the handle of his mug. When Elenie focused on his knuckles rather than his face, he seemed to make a conscious effort to relax his fingers and took a swift gulp of tea.

"Talk to me," he invited.

There was another period of silence.

"I don't really know where to start," she admitted.

"Anywhere will do."

Elenie stared out into the dark. "I've never met my dad. My mother wasn't sure who he was. Falling pregnant with me was a disaster for her. It ruined so many plans, apparently. Maybe if she hadn't been drunk or high so often, she'd have noticed sooner and I would never have existed. But she missed the signs and ended up with a baby she didn't really want. As mothers go, I guess I wouldn't have chosen her either." Elenie took a sip of coffee. "We stumbled along together when I was small. Every now and then I had a spell in foster care, but the child benefit was appealing and sometimes there was nothing else to buy cigarettes with."

She could feel the weight of Roman's whole attention. He had a way of studying her as if he could read every thought in her head, every expression on her face or movement of her body.

"We moved around a lot. Mainly because Mom struggled to hold down a job, so the rent didn't get paid regularly enough to keep landlords happy for long. The partying and the drinking were endless. She loved a good time. When she met Frank, they just clicked and got married inside of a month. It was a match made in heaven."

"What's Frank's story?"

"His first wife left him with the boys and disappeared." Elenie flicked a glance his way. "I don't blame her a bit. They were little shits then and they're worse now. My mother loves the perks that come with a husband who pays the bills, stepkids who don't want mothering, and a lifestyle on the wrong side of legal. He has a network of shady contacts, breaks some faces, delivers stuff for people, and torches a truck—" *Damn!* She almost slapped herself. "—or something else, here and there. She drinks too much, spends his money, and genuinely loves him. I think he loves her, too." Elenie shuddered. "In any case, it seems to work well for them. They all fit together perfectly, like a crappy jigsaw puzzle of lowlife bliss."

Roman's voice was husky when he spoke. "And how do you fit in?"

"I don't. I never have." Elenie tried to assess his reaction to her words. "I always knew I wanted the exact opposite of the life my mother dragged me through. That hasn't changed. Honestly, I think she's baffled by me. My thoughts and feelings don't make sense to her. I'm not sure she has a moral compass." She traced her fingers along the wooden grooves of the deck which ran beside her leg. "I worked hard at school. I loved learning. It was a welcome escape. And I've refused to get involved in any of Frank's criminal shit over the years. It's caused more fights than I can even remember. My plan was always to leave. I dreamed of walking away and putting down roots somewhere else. I still do."

Roman stared at the empty mug in his hand, twisting it around and around, and she wished she could tell what he was thinking. The grubby details of her life lay dirty and shameful between them.

"Why don't you?"

She closed her eyes. "You must think I'm pathetic."

"I don't."

Elenie doubted that. "There are two reasons. Athena might not win any Mom of the Year awards but she's all I have. It's pretty scary to make that final break. I keep thinking our relationship will improve somehow and it will be worth sticking around for."

The grunt in Roman's throat was acknowledgment, if not agreement. "And the other reason?"

"I don't have any money."

He shot her a quizzical look.

Elenie curled over her knees, wincing a little when her sore ribs twinged. "Frank takes most of my wages for rent. I buy food with the rest, so saving the money I'd need is almost impossible."

A muscle bunched in Roman's cheek. "Why do you work in the diner when you could choose to work anywhere in town?"

Elenie gave a tiny smile which lacked humor. He had no idea. "It's not as simple as that. I didn't really choose Diner 43. I planned to work somewhere else. There was a wonderful, pokey bookstore on the corner of Stewart Street when we first moved here and I thought it'd be the coolest thing I could imagine to surround myself with books, all day, every day. Books are so much easier than people."

"You're not wrong there," Roman agreed. "I remember the bookstore."

"The French use the phrase 'ink drinker' instead of bookworm. Don't you just love that?" He gave her that dangerous, lopsided tilt of his lips which set fire alarms screaming in her ears. "Mr. Reagan was a nice guy. Reserved but fair. He gave me a job after I left school, but Frank got involved. When Mr. Reagan wouldn't pay my wages straight to him, Frank smashed a window in the storeroom and started a fire." She tugged the blanket tighter. "That's the sort of thing he does. All those beautiful books and a man's livelihood— gone. I don't think the insurance ever paid out and Chief Roberts certainly didn't bust a gut to find out who was behind the attack. The store stayed closed, and Mr. Reagan moved out of town. I will never stop feeling guilty about that." Elenie wiped her hands over her face. "I tried everywhere else to get a job, but being Frank Dax's stepdaughter isn't the reference you need to open doors in Pine

Springs. I work at the diner because no one else will hire me and Delia's so awful she can't get any other staff. Frank leaves the diner alone because far more people would kick up a fuss if anything happened to keep them from their breakfast than they would over a little used bookstore." She summoned a touch of flippancy. "It's not all bad, though. Sometimes there's spare pie."

It didn't feel cleansing to spill out her pathetic life story. The facts hung in the air like a layer of pollution, threatening the chances of another night like this one or more time in the company of the magnetic man beside her. Elenie's skin felt raw, too thin, too sensitive, and not just from the bruises. It prickled with the shame of not being able to lead an ordinary life when everyone else seemed to manage it.

Roman placed his mug down on the deck, slowly and deliberately. "Would you consider pressing charges against Frank?" Solemn eyes searched her face. "It's not OK to live like this."

She gave an involuntary shudder and looked out across Otto's backyard. "Things are changing," she said finally. "I've been doing a lot of thinking recently and I'm trying to decide where to go from here."

"And Craig Perry?"

She hadn't expected that question. "Craig? Why do you ask?"

Roman's voice was gruff. "Summer told me he gave you some grief in the Barrel. How do you know him?"

"I don't know him well. He's been to the house, talking business with Frank, and he's a bit of a creep. Very cocky."

A small breeze ruffled her hair, blowing a feather-soft curl across her eyes. Roman lifted his hand. She flinched and he froze.

Stupid.

"Sorry, your hair was—"

"No, I know . . . I, uh . . ." Elenie's face burned with embarrassment.

113

The long moment of silence was leaden with unspoken words before Roman broke it. His eyes had darkened almost to black.

"You're not on your own anymore. You have friends now. And you have choices."

His words sounded like a promise, but Elenie wasn't sure it was true. Her choices felt as limited as always. And Roman Martinez was not staying in Pine Springs.

She searched his face intently—what for, she didn't know— and tucked the blanket tighter around her legs. They sat without speaking for ages, the narrow space between them as uncrossable as the Darién Gap. The hum of Otto's television drifted out through the open doorway.

It was almost eleven when Roman said he'd better make a move.

Elenie, stiff and sore though she was, the top step imprinted on her butt, would have stayed there until morning given the choice. Soaking up the quiet comfort of Roman's company, his heat warming her bones even without any contact.

"Can I give you a ride home?" He reached out a hand to pull her up, his huge palm callused against her skin. The touch seared like a static current right through to her core.

Elenie shrugged off the blanket, folding it neatly to give herself something to do. "Otto offered me his couch for the night." She glanced at the open back door. "It'll take me ten minutes to walk to work in the morning so it seemed a good idea. I brought some things with me."

"Will anyone wonder where you are?"

Elenie lifted the less-damaged corner of her lips. "We don't really keep tabs on each other in my house."

"Have you ever considered asking Otto if he'd put you up on a full-time basis?"

She shook her head before he'd even finished the sentence. "There's no way I'd bring him to Frank's attention like that. Otto's been the closest I've had to a friend in years. I won't risk his safety."

They walked into the house together.

"I'm heading home," Roman told Otto. "Please don't get up."

The older man reached for the remote control and turned down the volume. "I was just thinking about turning in myself."

"Thank you for a lovely evening. Your deck is the perfect place to unwind. It was kind of you to invite us." Roman bent down from his great height, his strong hands gentle around the gnarly bones of Otto's fingers.

"You're welcome any time. And if you make a habit of bringing food too, I'll get you a key cut." Otto chuckled and waved them away. "Elenie, will you lock up after our police chief, please?"

They moved into the foyer and stopped by the front door. Roman jiggled his car keys in his pocket. "I hope you sleep well. That looks like a comfy couch."

"Thanks for the pizza. It was delicious."

"Thanks for the company," Roman replied. He was shrouded in shadows, as if the night was his to command. Elenie thought he might say something else. She stepped a little closer so she could read his expression, her skin still sparking with that same electricity that threatened to arc and jump the short distance between them. His hand on her shoulder speared a plume of heat through her cotton shirt as he gave it a light squeeze.

A simple gesture. One that made it impossible to keep her eyes on his face.

He's a decent man. You're not used to them, but they do exist. Don't overthink it.

Roman's voice rasped. "Sleep well. Don't forget to flip the latch after I've gone."

He pulled the door closed behind him before Elenie could speak, and she stood in the silence, listening to his truck start up, a starburst of conflicting emotions blooming in her chest.

Chapter 16
Roman

The next week passed in a steady procession of minor incidents, including a fistfight at last call outside the Rusty Barrel, a small fire on farming land, and a traffic accident that took out the main stoplights in town.

Roman sat through an interminable meeting of the town council mostly hijacked by Peggy Winterburn and her cronies for a lively discussion on speed bumps. He took Dougie with him to the high school, where they conducted an open, no-nonsense talk about the facts, laws, risks and consequences of alcohol and drug use. Millie Westlake, recently back at school and warned in advance, chose to sit it out, but the interaction from other students was rewarding.

Maggie celebrated a birthday and Roman bought in pastries for everyone to share. When Dougie gave her flowers with a flourish and Forsberg and Morgan sang a loud and out-of-tune rendition of Stevie Wonder's "Happy Birthday," he felt an unfamiliar glow of contentment, grateful to be a part of the small team and its vibrant new energy.

And all the while, in amongst the ordinary, Roman thought of Elenie and what she'd revealed about her life. The simple words, calmly delivered with little self-pity, had turned him inside out. She might not relish being viewed as a victim, but what she was dealing with would have broken someone weaker.

Fuck. He'd been trying to pump her for information at the town fair, and just talking to him had put her in danger. He felt like a monster.

There was a disconcerting jostle against the sides of the cardboard box he'd stuffed his feelings into over the past couple of years. The firmly folded flaps buckled and bowed. The broken body of the girl who'd looked like Florence was giving over her almost-constant presence in his mind to someone very much alive. A waitress with suspicious eyes, a clever mind, and a tentative smile, who would put herself at risk to protect an elderly friend.

Something about Elenie reeled Roman in. He swore to himself he'd provide the backup she needed from now on—for as long as he could. And he wondered if the impact he'd been wanting to make so desperately when he'd chased his career toward the crazy, tough, and violent was waiting for him back home after all.

Halfway through a run of late shifts, Roman was called to a drunk and disorderly at the liquor store. He arrived to find the door pulled shut, blinds open. Nathan Reyes was hovering and rushed to let him in with a grateful smile and an audible huff of relief.

Athena Dax wandered the floor, idly swinging a bottle in each hand and humming softly to herself. Her eyes lit up when she saw him. "Officer Big and Beautiful! So good to see you again."

She wore a beige cropped tank with no bra, and pale jeans so tight it looked as if she'd been sewn into them. A silky, knitted cardigan draped off one skinny shoulder and pooled around her elbow. Roman had never seen a woman sashay before, but sashay she did until she stood in front of him, just a little closer than was comfortable. The smell of drink on her breath was overpowering. He exchanged a sideways glance with Nathan, who mouthed the word "Wasted!" at him just out of Athena's eyeline.

"I was heading home," she purred, reaching up to stroke his chest but hitting him with one of the bottles instead. "Unless you want to take me for a drink somewhere quiet?"

"You're not leaving with the vodka unless you pay for it." Nathan's voice was firm.

Athena pouted up at Roman. Everything Elenie had told him ran through his mind and he was hit by a strong wave of repulsion for every way in which her mother had let her down. "I've come out without my purse and I've asked him very kindly to put it on my tab. I'll settle up another time. No big deal."

"You don't have a tab." Nathan sounded frustrated.

Roman crossed his arms. "You heard the man," he said. "No money, no booze. Pay for it or put it back."

Athena tried to outstare him for a minute, hampered by her eyes crossing behind a lank, cherry-red lock of hair that flopped over her face. She wrinkled her nose. "You are no fun at all." Twirling away, she tripped over her own feet and Roman grabbed her elbow to stop her falling. She wrenched it out of his grasp, shooting an icy glare over her shoulder. "We could have been very good friends but I don't think you're my type after all."

Nathan snorted.

"We all have our crosses to bear," Roman said evenly. "I'll have to try to live with it."

Athena shoved one of the bottles under her arm—both men feared for its safety—and squeezed the tips of her fingers into her front pocket. When she pulled out a crumpled pile of bills, Roman wasn't the least bit surprised.

"Here." She slapped them down on the counter. "Happy now?"

Nathan rang them into the register without comment.

Roman opened the door of the store. "Come on," he said to Athena. "I'll take you home."

In the confines of the police car, the smell of alcohol was even stronger. Athena raked thoughtful eyes over him as he drove. It was a quiet night in town. They passed minimal traffic as they left Main Street and headed uphill toward the Daxes' house.

"So what do you see in my daughter?" Athena's voice was harder now. The vodka lay in her lap and she picked at the seam of her jeans.

Roman heard warning bells louder than downtown Detroit. "I hardly know your daughter."

"Oh, really?" Athena mocked him with an arch look. Then she laughed and there was no humor in the sound. "Take a tip from me and stay well clear. You might have a stick up your ass but you can seriously do better." Roman's hands clenched around the steering wheel, knuckles white. Athena ran a hand through her hair. "When I was her age, I had so many men chasing me, I could choose a different one every day of the week. There wasn't a party that took place without me and not a single one where I went on my own." Her expression soured. "Being an adult is so dull, don't you think? Less parties, less fun." She squinted at Roman, eyes unfocused, face bitter. "You don't look like you have much fun, Chief Straight and Narrow. When was the last time you let your hair down?"

"You sound like my ex," Roman murmured as they pulled up a little way from the house.

"So you do date!" Athena's mercurial mood shifted again. An alcohol-fueled loose cannon in action, she unclipped her seatbelt and leaned toward him, providing a view straight down the front of her tank top. Elenie's mother ran her hand up his arm. Her touch was cool, her nails painted and bitten short.

"Good evening, Mrs. Dax. Be careful getting out of the car." Roman's voice was as neutral as he could make it.

For a moment, neither of them moved, then Elenie's mother sat back. Her eyes clouded.

"Stay well clear," she repeated, each word slurring into the next.

Roman held her gaze until she pulled at the handle on her door and spilled out onto the pathway. He expelled a long breath as Athena wobbled away toward the house.

Chapter 17
Elenie

Coming down the stairs, Elenie bumped into her mother in the hall. "I didn't see you in the dark," she said uneasily. "Has the bulb blown again?"

Athena gave her a look she couldn't read. "No idea. I didn't try it."

Her mother weaved into the kitchen and placed two bottles of vodka noisily on the table. Coordination taxed by the removal of her cardigan, she saved herself from overbalancing by grabbing the back of a chair.

Christ. One of those nights.

"Want some toast?"

Athena waved her away, reaching for a glass instead.

Elenie pulled a loaf of bread out of the cupboard, checked it for mold, and dropped two slices into the toaster. Her hope of grabbing some food and retreating upstairs faltered as the front door opened and slammed.

Frank was on the phone. "I'll take a Navigator or an Escalade. Whatever you can get me by next Friday. I can change the plates myself. Let me know when and where for the pickup."

She heard Ty hack up a cough and someone else's voice in the hall, drowned out by Frank's conversation. Elenie made a conscious effort to look relaxed as she watched the doorway.

The third person was Craig Perry.

"Hello, ladies!" His greeting was smooth. The smarmy douchebag crossed the crowded kitchen to take Athena's hand for a kiss. Elenie gave an internal eye roll, shoving both of her own hands behind her back and shifting up against the counter.

"Hey, babe." Athena dropped onto a chair, her body listing toward Frank.

He grabbed a four-pack from the fridge, popped the top of one and dumped the rest on the table. Laying broad hands on her mother's bony shoulders, he gave them a surprisingly gentle squeeze, pressing his mouth to the top of Athena's head. Elenie looked away, a pain throbbing in her damaged jaw from the clenching of her teeth.

"Elenie." Craig nodded in her direction. He gave no reaction to the bruises on her face, even though his snitching had put them there.

Her toast popped up. Tyson, standing nearest, swiped a slice and took a bite. *You are a cretinous asshole*, she told him with her eyes. Ty grinned, a diamond stud glistening in each ear. Elenie grabbed the other piece of toast, reaching for a plate from the cupboard and a knife from the drainer.

"I've got a business dinner next Saturday, Ellie. Wanna keep me company?" asked Craig.

She didn't bother to look up as she buttered her toast. "No, thanks." Her knockback in the Rusty Barrel hadn't made a lasting impression then.

"Have a think about it and let me know tomorrow," Craig pushed.

"Don't need to," she told him around a mouthful. "I can't make it."

Frank stepped between Elenie and the doorway as she tried to leave the kitchen. The scent of strong bar soap scoured her nostrils. Her pulse raced. "Don't tell me you have a better offer." His eyes flicked over the marks on her face.

"It's not that," she said, taking courage from the number of people around her, friendly or not. The handle of the knife bit into her palm. "I'm just choosing to focus on myself right now."

"Be careful, darlin'. Be very careful." Frank spoke the words quietly against her cheek. His breath brushed her ear.

Elenie's stomach rolled like a washing machine on a slow cycle. Pushing past him, she headed for the stairs, blocking out the sound of Craig and Tyson laughing as she hit the first step.

* * *

It was a bolt from the blue when Roman sent a text the following afternoon, asking if she'd like to have Sunday lunch with his family.

After a shift that had crawled by, she was waiting in Mocha Magic—a cute little café in sorbet colors—for Summer and Caitlyn to arrive. Seven hours of carrying trays had made her bruised ribs ache and her feet hurt. It was good to sit down.

She stared at her cell, debating so long over how to reply that a second message pinged through.

Thea (Roman):

I can hear you thinking from here

An echo of the words he'd said to her on Otto's porch. Elenie gave a silent laugh and another text followed.

123

Thea (Roman):

Just say yes

Oh, God. She wanted to.

That's not a good idea.

Thea (Roman):

It's just lunch. I can get you there safely

She closed her eyes.

Sunday lunch was not an occasion in the Dax household. No one ate together. In fact, Elenie couldn't remember the last time the oven had been used. The stovetop maybe. Fried foods and pasta with jars of sauce were how Frank and the boys stayed alive. Elenie, too. Her mother existed mainly on booze.

The idea that Roman Martinez even wanted to ask her for lunch, after everything she'd told him, spread like hot buttered rum beneath her skin.

Was it so bad to want to see what normal might feel like?

Just once.

Thea (Roman):

Please

Your family will hate me.

Damn. Why had she sent that?

It was her biggest fear. Even bigger than inciting Frank's wrath. Roman answered immediately.

Thea (Roman):

Unlikely

"He's right." Summer's quiet voice behind her made Elenie start. "Sorry for reading over your shoulder but I totally think you should."

She sat down, dropping a cute corduroy tote bag onto the floor.

"Should what?" Caitlyn—louder, bolder—pulled one of the remaining chairs out far enough to leave room for her stomach and sank into it with a huff. "What have I missed?"

"An invitation from the chief to join the Martinez family for Sunday lunch," Summer told her.

"You should go. It's a thing they do. Roman's probably been given an open invitation to bring whoever he likes. Milo and I will be there." Caitlyn sounded so matter-of-fact it took Elenie aback.

"But they don't know me."

"Strangers are just people the Martinez family haven't met yet. They're pathologically friendly." Caitlyn shed her cardigan and looked around. "I wonder if they'd boost the air conditioning in here if I asked?"

"I can see why you might be worried." Summer brought the conversation back to Elenie. "But they're really nice people. Dougie and I went a couple of weeks ago. It's usually 'the more, the merrier' in the Martinez house."

"I just . . . don't know. I can't see why they would want me there."

Caitlyn fixed her with a steady look. "How will people see you differently if you don't give them the chance?"

Elenie glanced away. "I don't remember anyone giving me much of a chance."

"That's a fair point. But maybe this would be a good place to start." Caitlyn leaned back in her chair, her hands on her bump. "It isn't really you that people object to, anyway. Not the real you. Just the connection to your family. At least, it was for me. Summer, too. You've just ended up as collateral."

Summer nodded, chewing her lip. "I assumed you were like them."

"It's OK. I get it. I've always got it. But I'm hardly the poster girl for someone you want to introduce to your parents. Especially right now." Elenie circled a self-conscious finger around her face. The girls exchanged sober glances and Elenie's cheeks heated.

"Was it Craig?" Caitlyn asked.

"No." Elenie kept her eyes on her empty mug. "I pissed off my stepfather by talking to Roman at the fair. Another reason to bail on the lunch invite."

Summer laid her hand on Elenie's arm. "I'm so sorry."

"None of us were gossiping, I swear to you, but Milo told me you were hurt," Caitlyn admitted. "Roman was on the warpath about it and it's not often Ro shows his emotions. He wanted info on Craig Perry because of what happened in the Barrel."

"How are you feeling?" Summer asked.

"I'm fine, thanks," Elenie lied.

"You know Roman's folks live at the back end of town? Milo and I could pick you up and either stop for Ro on the way or see him there. It would just look like you were going out with us," Caitlyn offered.

"It's madness. Seriously, the guy could take his pick from anyone else in Pine Springs. I don't understand why he's asking me." She tried to explain her doubts. The fear of Frank finding out was a whole other matter. It curdled in her stomach like spoiled milk.

"Well, he doesn't seem to want to pick someone else." The redhead gave a shrug. "Roman's super private. He only brought the snotty lawyer he was seeing in Detroit back home once—and they were engaged."

Elenie blinked rapidly, a chill spreading through her bones.

Summer's mouth fell open. "He has a fiancée?"

"Had. They broke it off before he came back."

"I need coffee. And I need details." Summer scooted out of her chair. "Don't start without me!"

Elenie brushed at some dust on the screen of her cell. If the chief was getting over a breakup, this was a pity invite. Nothing more. Nothing less.

Caitlyn kicked her under the table. "Say yes. What's the worst that could happen?"

I could fall for him. Elenie shoved that thought way down where she didn't have to acknowledge it.

"Um, they might not let me in. Or they might let me in and then be rude to my face. Or they might be icily polite but take Roman to one side where they know I can still hear them and ask him what the hell he's thinking. And then kick me out."

Caitlyn just stared at her. "But apart from all of that, it could be fun. Just say yes."

Elenie stared at her phone for so long the screen went blank. Eventually, she swiped back to her messages. Nerves cramped her stomach as she began to type.

> OK. I'd like to meet your family.

Roman's answer was immediate.

Thea (Roman):

> Fantastic. Let me know where I can pick you up and I'll see you at midday on Sunday

"What have I missed?" Summer dumped a tray holding two coffees and a hot chocolate onto the table.

"She said yes."

"Good." Summer smiled, dimples flashing. "Now, dish the dirt on the chief's ex, Cait. We need to know what you know."

"You'll be disappointed, I'm afraid. I could tell you more than I ever wanted to know about Zena's job. She didn't shut up about that when we met her. But she wasn't exactly open about anything else." Caitlyn dumped extra sugar into her hot chocolate. "I'm not even sure they had a life outside of their work while they were together."

"Describe her," Summer demanded.

"Tall. Long blond hair. Pointy features. Beautiful clothes. Very elegant. Legs up to her ears." Caitlyn gestured vaguely with her hand.

"She sounds stunning," said Elenie, battling the sensation of barbed wire around her lungs.

"They weren't very touchy-feely. No public displays of affection that I saw. Roman mainly caught up with Milo. He looked tired. A bit remote."

Elenie knew the look she meant. She'd seen the shadows in his eyes. Reserved, professional, contained, Roman was still undeniably, underwear-meltingly handsome. But when his face relaxed and his eyes warmed with humor, he was a whole other level of delicious. Something in him called to every part of her. She could still feel his hand on her shoulder in Otto's foyer. He'd literally just touched her shirt and every ounce of her focus had centered on his fingers. Elenie, lost in the memory, almost choked on absolutely nothing.

"They met through mutual friends. Zena's a corporate lawyer with a big firm. I think she advises on mergers and buyouts. And she's very ambitious." Caitlyn was still talking. Elenie felt like a small and pathetic underachiever; it was an embarrassing nudge from reality. "I don't know if they ever set a date, but I can't imagine having a family would feature any time soon in her plans."

"What went wrong?" Summer asked.

"Milo said things went sour before Roman came back home. Zena wasn't on board with his decision to leave the city, I know that."

"Dougie says Roman doesn't talk about his old job." Summer fiddled with her mug. "He doesn't really talk that much at all."

"For someone who looks like they have everything under control, I don't think Roman is as together as he seems." Caitlyn propped her chin in her hands. "It's hard to tell what he's thinking. He used to tell Thea everything but she says he's more closed off now. He's always been the quietest one in his family. The rest of them are lovely but full-on."

"As you'll find out on Sunday." Summer nudged Elenie, who gave a nervous swallow and sipped her coffee.

"Let's talk about something else."

They chatted all things work and babies for the next hour, sharing stories and finding out more about each other. Elenie, more grateful for the company and burgeoning friendship than Summer and Caitlyn would ever know, deliberately pushed Roman's invitation and his previous relationship from her mind.

There would be time to worry about that again later.

Chapter 18
Roman

He retched as he jerked awake, his stomach rebelling against the rolling horror in his dreams. Through the rough rasp in his throat, Roman struggled to drag enough breath into his chest. Elbows on his knees, head in his hands, he braced himself and tried to clamp down on the sickness by focusing on his surroundings.

The air felt clammy. He'd need to change the sheets again. They were soaked.

The sweat was cooling on his back by the time he was steady enough to stand. Quads trembling, he took slow, deliberate paces toward the glazed balcony doors and watched his reflection run shaky fingers through tousled hair. The sky was clear above the treetops and as black as pitch. Stars, like backlit pinpricks through a sheet of cardboard, shone stark and comforting. A reminder of all that was beautiful in the natural world. Not like the ungodly mess regularly created by humans.

His heart rate steadied as the branches of the pine trees dipped and swayed.

His dreams had meshed an array of realities together. The young girl with his sister's face was still dead, still draped unseeing on the single mattress in that grim, abandoned house on a decaying Detroit street. But alongside the wounds Roman had seen, catalogued and studied, and the track marks in her arm, her broken body was mutilated with a kaleidoscope of injuries from other victims and other cases—his unconscious mind drawing on atrocities from across the years. So much blood, so much suffering. Bones snapped, skin flayed, puncture wounds bubbling, body parts missing. Everywhere, the scent of death, rot, and fluids that he sometimes doubted would ever leave his nose.

Roman shuddered, turning from the window. He needed a shower, middle of the night or not. He needed something to drive the dream from his head. Stripping off his shorts and leaving them on the bathroom floor, he stepped under the showerhead and turned the heat up as high as he could stand. As the room filled with steam, he braced a hand on the tiles and hung his head.

The trigger tonight was a meeting with Millie Westlake and her parents. All three had been hollow-eyed and exhausted, the overdose infecting the whole family in a myriad of different ways. Millie looked thinner, almost ghostly. As if her experience had sucked the life and confidence right out of her bones. Her mother and father, gray and strained, flanked her with an intensity that broadcast their terror of what might have been.

He'd explained that Michigan's Good Samaritan law meant no possession charges would be brought against Millie. Her use of what she'd thought was MDMA would result in a misdemeanor charge but, as a first-time offender, it was likely she'd avoid a prison sentence and the fine would be low. Without further information from Millie, there was nothing more Roman could do about tracing the source of the drugs.

The relief on her parents' faces was palpable. Millie remained dazed and uncommunicative. He'd left the house sick and frustrated, a pervasive feeling of failure on his shoulders. There would be no winners in this case. Another one tucked, for now, into the devastatingly bulky folder marked "Unresolved" in his head.

At least Millie Westlake had escaped with her life. She'd get over this, even if she never forgot it. She had a future to look forward to. She would make new memories and fresh mistakes. But Roman had gone to bed with other failures lurking like specters in the corners of his bedroom, waiting until he slept to pounce.

He shut off the water with a curse and stepped out of the shower, pulling clean shorts and a t-shirt from his dresser. Padding down to the kitchen with bare feet, he flicked on a solitary table lamp and made a cup of tea. His eyes gritty, his body clumsy, he stared at the digital clock on the front of the stove. The idea of Sunday lunch with his family, introducing Elenie to everyone amidst the usual noise and mayhem, was suddenly overwhelming.

Standing in the dark, with a head full of heaviness, the draw he'd felt toward her at Otto's house was intangible, out of his grasp.

Why had he talked her into it? What the hell was he thinking?

He had enough on his plate without this as well. Elenie Dax was not a safe or sensible person for him to spend time with. He must be out of his mind.

And he was a mess. So screwed-up, he couldn't talk to his family. Under pressure to fix himself in a timeframe chosen by other people.

What a catch.

Roman groaned and stared up at the ceiling, his mug burning his fingers. The minutes ticked by, the house silent around him. Beneath his feet, the rug was rough and textured. Concentrating on the sensation kept his mind from spiraling free. He doubted he'd get any more rest before morning.

* * *

Elenie wore a simple cotton shirt dress, the color of fall leaves. Face bare of makeup, her expression was a smooth mask but he could read her well enough now to see the nerves. Her tongue flicked toward the healing cut on her lip. Tension burned in his shoulders and Roman felt a flash of regret at putting them both through this.

"We can leave any time you want," he said. Elenie's eyes were on his face when Florence pulled the door open with a shriek. "Welcome to chaos." His words were both gruff and apologetic.

Roman handed a bright bunch of sunflowers to his mother, bending to kiss her cheek, edgy and awkward.

"My son looks concerned for your safety. Or maybe your sanity?" His mother's usually blinding smile danced on her lips at reduced wattage. She held out a hand, blatantly assessing Elenie with a shrewd once-over that missed nothing. "I'm Ava. It's nice to meet you properly."

"Thank you for letting me join you." Elenie's polite response was stilted and defensive. There was a pause which made Roman's head thump. He rolled his shoulders and tried to relax.

"Any chance we can come in? I really need to take some of the weight off my feet." Caitlyn's voice came from behind them. She winked at Roman.

"My darling! Of course, of course. Come on, everyone. Move out of the hall. Our lovely pregnant mama needs to sit down!" Ava led Caitlyn tenderly into the kitchen.

"Nicely played, wife of mine," chuckled Milo, following on behind. "By the way, anything he's said about me is probably exaggerated, unless it's intellectual." He winked at Elenie, blue eyes twinkling, punching Roman's arm as he passed.

In the kitchen, Thea was checking on something in the oven. Lunch smelled wonderful; his stomach growled. Both his parents loved their food.

Elenie took a long, slow look around the large, sunny space and Roman wondered what she was thinking.

"Can I get you a drink?" Luke had one hand on the open fridge door.

"Thank you. I'll have any soda there is, please." Elenie gave him the glimmer of a smile.

Roman did a quick round of introductions, silently beating himself up as he waved a hand toward Florence but avoided catching her eye. Last night's dream lurked too close for comfort. Overtired and oversensitive, he was struggling to shake free of its grasp. As everyone grabbed drinks and exchanged news, his dad crossed the room to say hello.

"I'm Elias." He clasped one of Elenie's hands in both of his. "I can see why my son is a fan. Welcome to our home."

She blinked, the smallest tilt tugging at her lips. "It's lovely to be here. Thank you for inviting me."

Roman's mother called across the kitchen, wanting advice from Milo on buying a paper shredder which Roman knew she'd never use. On the couch, Florence talked to Caitlyn's stomach, sharing fashion tips and ridiculous life hacks with the baby. When Thea slid her arm around Roman's waist, he saw Elenie tense.

"Your home is very beautiful," Elenie said to his sister, embarrassment giving an edge to her words. "I hope Roman passed on my thanks for letting me stay."

Thea reached out to give Elenie a hug. She squeezed her gently, her lips close to Elenie's ear. "Whoever did that to you is an asshole. Come and stay anytime you like." His sister drew back and Roman flicked her a grateful wink.

"OK, people—grab a dish and take it to the table with you!" his dad called out.

"Florence, get the enchiladas out of the oven. Milo, can you take the sweetcorn?" Ava started handing out food. The gold hoops in his mother's ears caught the sun as they swung. She passed Elenie two small bowls of spicy salsa and guacamole, before giving Roman a huge dish filled with a colorful salad, topped with beans and crumbled feta, which looked as if it would feed twenty people.

When they sat down around the large rectangular table that had hosted every family gathering for as long as he could remember, he reached beneath it to touch Elenie's hand. She jolted and gave him a sideways glance. Her fingers had warmed up and Roman ran his thumb once over her soft skin, startled by the flicker of heat it lit in his stomach. He drew back again.

"You OK?" he mouthed.

"I'm fine." She looked a little shell-shocked, though not uncomfortable.

The table buzzed with noise. Plates of food were handed back and forth, serving spoons passed and sauces exchanged in a dance of hands, laughter and *excuse me*'s.

"So, you work in the diner on Main Street, Elenie?"

"Yes, I do."

"I've seen you in there. That Delia can sure work a griddle but she doesn't break a smile as often as she should." His mother's understated observation was spot on.

"I think there's a lot of things in life that disappoint Delia," Elenie said, just as carefully. "It's a challenge each day to work out what is top of that list and, when I can, I try to avoid adding to it."

"One of the reasons I like working for myself," chipped in Caitlyn, waving her fork. "The only moods I have to deal with are my own."

"And that's what the chocolate in the top drawer of your desk is for," added Milo.

Caitlyn grinned. "He knows me well."

"What do you like about working in the diner?" his mother asked. Roman remembered the conversation on Otto's deck and wondered how Elenie would answer.

She took a moment to swallow a spicy mouthful. "It's busy, so there's no time to be bored. A lot of people are in a hurry or they're socializing with friends, so they don't want much of a personal approach. Just a few come in because they want some company or a change of scenery." She was clearly talking about Otto. "It matters to them to have a connection with the person who's bringing them their order. Those customers, I give more time, when I can. I like that best. It means a lot to them. And to me."

His mother nodded without comment and Roman swiftly asked Luke about a refit he'd just completed at a shop unit in town. Elenie looked more than happy for the conversation to move on. All the different threads of chatter began to merge and spool around them—crossing, linking, and weaving. His dad, retired from the fire service for more than fifteen years, told Elenie about the red-tailed hawk he'd seen by the roadside during the week. Milo and Caitlyn, keen hikers, discussed their plans for including a baby in their future adventures. His mother had just started to dabble in watercolor painting, using one of the upstairs bedrooms as a makeshift studio. "And she claims the twins were messy when they were teenagers," Luke told Elenie in a muttered aside, getting two matching clips around the ear from Thea on his right and Ava on his left.

Roman usually loved listening to everyone as they talked over and around each other. It was just what his family did. Today, the weariness of a broken night pressed down on him and he felt over-sensitized to the noise. He struggled to relax his face, unclench his teeth. He drummed restless fingers on his leg, counting the beat of each as they tapped in turn against his thigh. When he glanced up, Elenie was watching him with cool, guarded eyes.

Before long, it looked as if the table had been attacked by possums and everyone headed outside onto the deck for dessert and freshly brewed coffee. The afternoon was balmy. They lounged on a medley of outdoor chairs; none of the furniture in his parents' home was new. Everything well-worn and well-loved, kept for comfort and happy memories.

"You won't eat a better pecan pie than Ava's," Caitlyn told Elenie around the biggest spoonful she could get in her mouth.

"There are over a thousand varieties of pecan nuts." Elenie studied her plate. "Lots of them are named after Native American tribes."

"I didn't know that." His dad smiled.

Elenie ducked her head and grimaced, then shot Roman a sideways glance and mouthed, "Sorry."

"What for?" He leaned toward her, his voice a low rumble to keep it between the two of them.

"For coming out with such a boring-ass fact," she muttered.

His lips twitched and he was grateful for the moment of levity. "You are many things, but boring isn't one of them."

Elenie's smile was golden. It caught him like a gentle brush of fingers around the tight muscles in his chest and soothed. The waning sun seemed warmer, the colors of his parents' backyard more vibrant. What did it matter that his head was a little scattered, the atmosphere a little forced, and his mother's attitude toward Elenie reserved, though not wholly unfriendly.

He was just beginning to think the afternoon could still be saved when, in an instant, it all went to shit.

Chapter 19
Elenie

Roman had rolled up the sleeves of his casual shirt and those sun-kissed forearms, all dark hair and sexy muscles, were exposed for Elenie to drool over.

He didn't seem like himself today. He'd been distracted from the moment he'd climbed into Caitlyn and Milo's car outside the most stunning A-frame cabin Elenie had ever seen. Torn between out-and-out begging to go in and look around and noting the subtle signs of strain on his angular face, she'd opted to stay quiet, wondering how much he regretted asking her to join them. The worry burned at her skin like poison ivy.

Full to bursting but determined to finish her pie, Elenie found it harder and harder to keep her eyes off him. Every now and then, he looked her way, lifting an eyebrow to check she was OK. Each time he did, her heart gave a thump. She felt like she'd been picked up and dropped into a parallel reality. There had never been an afternoon like this one in her whole life. Although she'd dated a little, no one had ever taken her home to meet their family. And Elenie had never had a close friend who'd asked her either.

She tried to think of anything that linked Ava to her mother or Elias to Frank, but came up short. They were as different as apples and bicycles.

No one laughed in the Dax household unless it was at someone else's expense. Conversation never went both ways because no one wanted to listen. The affection that Roman's family shared hung in the air, as obvious as the food on the table or the sun in the sky.

It wasn't about money, because the Martinez house was far from grand. And Frank and Athena didn't struggle for money themselves. Yes, it was a bit all or nothing. Cash either spilled out of Frank's pockets, or he lost himself in a funk for a couple of weeks when things got tight. There was certainly enough that their house didn't have to be so dirty, scuffed, and soulless. There could be food in the fridge or nice meals on the table. Things didn't need to be broken or neglected. It was just that no one gave a shit.

Never had Athena teased her the way Ava teased her children. Never had she tugged her close with a careless, loving arm and pressed a kiss to her cheek. Pet names and casual touches flew between each person around the table and it was intoxicating. The desire to have a different life hit Elenie again like a sucker punch. If there could be a home and a family like this in her future, she wanted it with an intensity that made her heart hurt.

Looking up, she found Roman's eyes on her face. He was tapping again, muted stress in the rhythmical movement of his fingers. It brought her out of her reverie. She was just about to ask him if he was OK when Elias flung out his hand in an expressive gesture, upending Florence's glass of sangria down her front. Red wine spread from her neck over the pale cream of her lacy top. Florence shrieked and leaped to her feet; Elias too, apologies abundant. Thea grabbed a paper napkin while Ava ran for a cloth, scolding her husband over her shoulder as she disappeared indoors.

Roman's eyes were fixed on Florence's neck and the brilliant stain of red. He swallowed roughly, the movement of his throat jerky and pained. His breath lodged in his chest. Skin waxy, he had the look of a man drowning on dry land.

"Roman?" He gave no sign of having heard her. "Roman?" Elenie gripped his arm and found it solid and chilled, like an iron bar beneath her fingers. She dropped to her knees in front of him, placing herself directly in his eyeline and blocking Florence out behind her. Her hands on his face, she forced him to look at her. The grate of his stubble rasped against her palms. "Roman, you need to breathe." Those inscrutable eyes of his, tortured and burning, finally met and held hers. He took a long, wheezing gasp of air and then another. "That's good," she said. "Really good. It's alright. You're alright."

Everyone else faded into the background. Elenie forced him to watch her, breathing loud and slow so he could hear and copy her. She could see the shudder of Roman's heart as it thumped beneath the cotton of his shirt, and hers pounded in tandem. He buried his head in shaky hands, struggling for control. She glanced around. Florence, his parents, and Thea were all busy in the kitchen.

Milo stepped up to Roman's shoulder. "You alright, bro?" He sounded at a loss, quiet concern in each unfussy word.

Elenie made a swift decision. "Let's go for a walk." She took Roman's hands from his face and pulled gently. "Stand up," she told him. He rose to his feet without a word. "Come on—I'd like to see the backyard."

Luke handed her a bottle of water and Elenie shot him a silent smile of thanks. She threaded her fingers through Roman's, the action so alien and yet so right as they descended the steps onto the grass. Their shadows led the way—his tall and rangy, and hers pressed close to his side. She gripped his hand without speaking and kept their strides slow.

Ava and Elias's yard was wide and long. They walked over mown grass through well-tended borders and into an area left more natural. The end boundary seemed to lie beyond an assortment of greenery, dwarfed by an old, gnarled chestnut, out of sight of the house. The tree had thrown out one long bough, parallel to the ground, at the perfect height to sit on.

"Want to keep going?" Elenie searched Roman's face, relieved to see his color had returned.

"No, let's sit." He slumped onto the chestnut's limb with a ragged exhale of breath. Elenie perched next to him, her shorter legs swinging. The bark was barnacle-rough against her thighs, even with the material of her dress in between. Roman gripped the back of his neck with both hands, staring up at the sky—and, damn, if his beautiful biceps weren't extremely distracting even as she examined his face with concern.

Five minutes passed. The breeze through the leaves was a soothing whisper in the air. Eventually, he met her gaze, weary-eyed but present again. She handed him the bottle of water without speaking.

Roman unscrewed the lid and took several long swallows. He studied the label. "Have you spent much time in Detroit?" he asked eventually.

"None at all. I only know what people say about it."

"Most of it's true, although some areas are getting the attention they deserve. There's a lot of regeneration but there's a long way to go. It still has one of the highest violent crime rates in the country. Almost everyone carries a gun." His breath remained unsteady. "I spent most of my time in the worst parts, where it's a chaotic mess of gang wars, drug use, and debt. Streets that look like they've been hit by a natural disaster. Block after block of abandoned houses. A few families living in amongst the mayhem." He picked at a piece of bark. "There were so many bodies. People who were just in the wrong place at the wrong time. Who died because of it. And every time I crouched beside another one, every time I broke the news to another family, the cases we solved, the cases we didn't—they all built up on top of each other, higher and higher. Until it reached a point where I just couldn't do it anymore." Roman's eyes met hers. They were flat and honest and open.

"Did you talk to anyone about it?"

The corner of his mouth twitched. "I'm not much of a talker. I should have spoken to someone sooner, but for a long time I just accepted it. I chose to work homicide. I wanted to be a detective. I thought the violence came with the job. I didn't feel I had the right to complain or feel overwhelmed when everyone else was in the same boat, and they were all coping." Roman rubbed at his chest. "And the thing with the crime scenes, the victims—it's bad enough when you can't get rid of the memories yourself. You don't want to put those kinds of images inside the heads of the people you love. I couldn't do that to them."

Elenie's heart felt bruised. She reached out her hand until it bumped his, linking her little finger through Roman's much larger one. "Years ago, before we moved to Pine Springs, someone Frank knew had his throat slit when he skimmed off a couple of jobs. Photos got sent out to everyone the dead guy worked with as a warning. Frank left them on the kitchen counter for a week before he threw them away. I was about fourteen." Roman shot her a look of fury and disgust and she shrugged. "I've seen all sorts. You can talk to me."

And so, over the next hour, he did. Slowly and painfully at first, then with calm, quiet relief. He told her how he'd been stressed but functioning, overworked, overtired but managing. Until he wasn't. Until the call came in that took him to the trap house on the East Side and the young female victim who'd been stabbed in the neck.

He told her how she'd been lying face down, how he'd kneeled beside the mattress on the floor and gently turned the body over.

Mouth tight, voice rough, Roman described how like Florence she'd looked—similar brown eyes, the same olive skin, his sister's dark, long, wavy hair and full lips, her curvy build. "So much blood," he told Elenie. "It covered her. It covered the sheets. It was drying and crusty. More like fake blood than real." He wiped a hand over his face. "I got this buzzing in my ears and it wouldn't go away. It started to drown out everything else. We had so little to go on. Never even found out who she was, let alone who killed her. I couldn't move past it. Drawing a line under the case meant accepting she just didn't matter. Or that's how it seemed. And it ruined me. I tried to carry on as usual but I couldn't focus. I felt completely detached. I couldn't sleep. And the less I slept, the harder it was to keep a grip during the day." He stared at Elenie, although she wasn't sure he really saw her, and she could see the hell he'd been through in his eyes. "My heart would pound so hard at night I thought I was having a heart attack. I saw a doctor and she told me I needed to look at my life and make some serious changes." Roman smiled, a faint and empty version of the one that usually did her own heart so much damage. "I finally spoke to my superiors at work. There were meetings and discussions. We agreed to a twelve-month secondment so I could step away and get my head sorted. And that's why I'm here. Back in Pine Springs, trying to get my shit together, instead of pushing forward on the fast-track to make lieutenant."

He looked down at where their fingers were still linked on the bark of the chestnut limb. Much of the tension had drained from his body and he flanked her like a solid wall of heat in the cooling afternoon air. He was so strong and dependable and reserved, offering that unshakable support of his to anyone who needed it. But who did he allow to take care of him?

Elenie wanted to bring up his fiancée. His ex-fiancée. But she couldn't find the courage. "Have you talked to your parents at all?"

He shook his head. "I haven't even had the guts to tell them I'm not back for good. They'd want to know why I took the transfer and I don't know where to start."

"They love you." Of that, Elenie had zero doubt. "You're kidding yourself if you think your parents haven't noticed something's up. They don't seem like easy people to fool."

Roman grunted an agreement.

"Just talk to them. You'll feel better for it. And they'll support you. I think you're underestimating their strength."

He stared down at her, his brows knotting and his beautiful mouth softly vulnerable. "Thank you for not thinking worse of me. It's not what you expected, I guess. Not what anyone expects of the high school baseball star and the new police chief in town."

Elenie bumped his shoulder gently, aching for him and the broken pieces he'd been hiding. "I'll be honest, you're still an improvement on the last one."

Roman chuckled, rusty and low, but he sobered as he continued to search her face. The air crackled. Elenie's spine grew taut.

"If things were different . . ." he began. There was enough heat in his eyes to melt tungsten. No one had ever looked at her that way before.

"I know."

He swallowed. His voice was pained. "If I wasn't leaving again . . ."

"Yes. And if I wasn't who I am," she whispered.

Roman shook his head. "I would never want you to be someone else."

The feelings in her chest banged on her ribs to be let out. She ducked her head so he wouldn't see the ridiculous desire written all over her face.

Looping a strong arm around her back, Roman pulled her closer, his fingers closing tightly on her hip bone as if he wanted to keep her there. Elenie's shoulder bumped his shoulder and it felt like the most daring thing in the world not to move away. They sat in silence, breathing synchronized, in the calm embrace of the chestnut tree.

* * *

The atmosphere had evidently shifted when they returned to the house. Roman's meltdown and her handling of it had obviously been discussed in their absence and the family didn't hold back. Elenie, overwhelmed by the subsequent outpouring of warmth that flowed from everyone, reeled from the non-stop chatter.

His parents made her promise to visit again soon.

"Let's see that movie together next month," Florence, in a borrowed t-shirt, gave her a kiss on the cheek when they stood up to leave.

"I'd like that."

Thea squeezed her arm, rubbed it, then squeezed again. Her eyes glittered with heartfelt gratitude and Elenie fell a little in love with Roman's twin.

Roman's mother opened her arms and swallowed Elenie up in a hug which caught her completely by surprise. Her hands fluttered, not knowing where to rest, until they tentatively settled on either side of Ava's waist.

"Thank you, little one." The whispered words encompassed so much more than just her presence over lunch, and Elenie's cheeks heated with pleasure.

Ava and Elias waved them off from the doorstep as Milo put the car into gear and pulled out of the drive. In the back seat,

Roman gave her that barely there smile. Everything about him seemed calmer than earlier. His face was softer, his mouth curved, brown eyes tired but warm.

"Are your ears ringing?"

Elenie laughed. "Your family are just—wow."

"Yeah." Roman looked pleased. "They are."

A comfortable silence settled between them all as they drove along the quiet roads that linked his parents' house to the back of the town.

"What's the age gap between you and Florence?" Elenie asked.

"Thea and I are six years older. We're thirty-two and Florence is twenty-six. I think it took my parents that long to catch up on their sleep." Roman's phone rang; he tugged it from his jeans pocket and she saw Zena's name lit up on the screen. His eyebrows pulled together into a frown. "I don't need to get that."

He swiped to disconnect the call. Elenie's fingernails bit into the palm of her hand. She slowly spread her fingers out against the material of her shirt dress, feeling like a bucket of cold water had been tipped over her head.

"You on an early tomorrow, Ro?" Milo asked over his shoulder. They discussed meeting up for a beer later on in the week until, way too soon, the car pulled up in front of Roman's cabin. Elenie wished the drive had been longer.

Greedy for a final moment of privacy with him, she climbed out of the car once Cait and Milo had said their goodbyes.

"Will you be alright?" she asked.

"I'll be fine." He looked like he meant it. Their eyes locked and held. She could have sworn he swayed toward her, but his hands stayed in his pockets.

"Thank you so much for the invitation. *Lo pasé bomba.*[3]"

---

3 Lo pasé bomba (I had a blast)—Spanish

"*Yo también, hermosa.*[4]" He shot her a slow, wide smile, which lit his face and cracked the shields around her heart. "You won't get away without a repeat visit, you know. My sisters are limpets when they like someone. And embarrassing me is what they love to do best."

His endearment stole her breath. "I'll look forward to it."

"See you soon, Elenie."

"Bye, Roman."

He watched them drive away, his tall, shadowed outline unbowed and stable again for now.

Something about Roman's struggle reached out to the parts of Elenie that doubted and feared. She was as stuck in her own nightmare as he was in his. There had to be a way out for them both.

The expansive love of Roman's family, reflected in the food, the jokes, the casual touches, had shone a spotlight on the irreparable flaws in her own. She'd pushed him to turn to his parents and his sisters for support. Maybe she should use them for motivation.

It was time to stop hanging on for something she'd never find within the walls of the Dax family home.

It was time to let it go.

---

4   Yo también, hermosa (Me too, beautiful)—Spanish

Chapter 20
Roman

Dumping his keys and phone on the table, Roman leaned against the kitchen counter and took a long, deep breath. He felt contented but keyed up. Wrung out and fucking horny.

Sweetness blanketed the stench of death and squalor that had filled his nostrils for months. He didn't know if it was shampoo or bodywash, but Elenie's scent cleansed his brain like waves moving through a rockpool. Just being close to her sent pins and needles through the parts of him that were numb.

No matter how many times he reminded himself that his attraction to Elenie had nowhere to go, his body wasn't listening.

He'd have given everything for a Pause button during their time on the chestnut tree.

Roman's eyes narrowed on his cell. Damn Zena for her untimely interruption when he'd wanted to enjoy those last few minutes with Elenie—especially after the shitshow he'd made of the first half of it. What the hell could she want?

With a sigh, he dialed her number.

"I'm glad you rethought your decision to decline my call." Zena's voice held the sharp edge he was well used to.

"I was busy. What do you want?" Roman pulled a mug out of one of the cupboards. There was a brief moment of silence during which he could almost hear her switching gear.

"I miss you," she said finally. "I've been thinking we should give our relationship another try."

He laughed without humor. "You miss me? Do you really, Zena? Have you forgotten how uptight and unemotional I am?"

She had no idea.

"I never said that."

"They were your exact words." Roman's tone was dry. He felt absolutely nothing—not wounded, angry, upset, nor regretful.

"Well, maybe I made a mistake." Zena sounded annoyed rather than sorry. "You needed time to get your head together. I assume you're managing to do that now. Let's put it behind us and have a go at a long-distance relationship. I'm happy to give it a try if you are."

He placed the kettle on the stovetop, craving his bed and a solid night's sleep. "Here's the thing. I think we made the right decision. I'm here, you're there, and I don't miss us as a couple. That tells me it's time to move on." She drew in a breath, trying to regroup. "I think that's all I have to say, Zena. Take care of yourself." Roman ended the call and dumped a teabag into his mug, reaching for the kettle.

He hoped he'd been blunt enough without being hurtful. He didn't feel the need to sling mud but he had no interest in reviving a relationship that had been dying a death for a long time.

Elenie had made him realize how much it'd been lacking.

Her company made his blood hum and his nerve endings sizzle. She was pleasure and pain in feminine form, comfort and temptation. Roman ached to get closer even as he warned himself off. He'd never felt the same heated need for Zena, not even at the beginning when he was flattered by her interest and turned on by her ambition. He'd asked her to marry him with ambivalence he'd hidden from everyone. It had felt like a business deal. A sensible next step to build the life of his dreams—lieutenant, captain, commander, loving wife, big house, comfortable life.

Now, Zena was barely a passing consideration. Someone he once thought he knew.

Spilling his feelings to Elenie had been painless once he'd started, a little of the pressure inside his chest easing with every sentence. She was slight, but goddamn was she strong. He hadn't worried about her being able to handle it, didn't wonder for a minute if she'd judge him for his weakness.

His mom and dad worked like a team. Being in a relationship should be like that—two people pulling on the oars of a boat in time with each other. Up until now, Roman had either felt like he was rowing on his own or whoever he was with was rowing in the opposite direction. Even with everything against them, he wished he could try rowing with Elenie.

He dragged in a deep breath. Reaching for his phone, he dropped onto the couch and dialed the most recent number from his contacts.

"Hey, Ro. We just walked in the door." Thea answered almost immediately. He heard the muted clatter of her shoes as she kicked them off in her foyer.

Roman took a deep breath. "You got time to talk, T? I need to tell you something."

* * *

When Elenie appeared unexpectedly in the doorway of his office mid-afternoon the following Saturday, the frown slid off Roman's face. The tight coil in his middle loosened and warmed.

"Dougie said I could come on back." Her smile was tentative, a little edgy.

His deputy was fully fit, but riding the reception desk as it was Maggie's weekend off. Forsberg and Morgan were out dealing with a truck that had shed its load near Quarry Pass.

"Of course. Come in." Roman narrowed his eyes. "What's up?"

He waved her toward one of the chairs on the other side of his desk and leaned back, fiddling with a ballpoint pen. The desk sat between them like a Victorian chaperone. Elenie wore her uniform; he guessed she'd come straight from her shift. The bright sun, sneaking between the slats of the blinds, lightened her eyes to pale gray. It was good to see the bruises on her face were fading.

"I've been thinking a lot. About Millie Westlake and the drugs. About my family. About your family."

Roman frowned. "And?"

"And I need to find a way to make some serious changes in my life. Like you have." Elenie blew out a breath. He searched her face while he waited for her to link the two statements. "What you need is information, and someone who doesn't have anything to lose."

A chill raised the hairs on the back of his neck. In a moment of horrible realization, he had a suspicion he knew where this was going.

"I was wondering if police informers are an actual thing?" Elenie asked. "Because I want to be one."

Roman's reaction was instant and instinctive. "No." He didn't give it any thought. This idea was one that needed shutting down as soon as possible. "You're not involved in the criminal side of Frank's business, so you're not party to any information that would be useful."

"But I could be." Elenie leaned forward. "Imagine if I could turn things around and find out something you could use against him." The desperation in her eyes floored him. "I need to do this. I can't carry on living in that house, and I don't have the money to escape them. I'm just going through the motions of living my life—I don't think I can stand to do it much longer. I have to find some way to move on."

Roman gripped the pen he was holding, staring intently at his hand, the desk, anywhere but her face. A pain in his jaw told him he was gritting his teeth.

"Help me do this, please?"

Silence stretched between them.

"Stay there." To give himself time to think, Roman grabbed a bunch of keys from his top drawer and stalked out of his office. Reaching the reception area, he pulled the front door shut and turned one of the keys in its lock. "My office, please," he growled at Dougie on the way back.

His deputy followed him, shooting a quizzical glance at Elenie before taking a seat in the empty chair next to her. Roman leaned against the filing cabinet, too restless to sit.

"What's up?" Dougie asked. Elenie flashed him a nervy smile.

"We need to talk something over. It's far from decided and I want your input." Roman's gaze bounced between them. He gave Elenie a brief nod. "Go on."

"Um . . ." She cleared her throat and twisted one of the buttons at the neck of her shirt. "I'm offering to be a police informer. Against my family. I think I can find out details you might be able to use to put Frank away."

Dougie looked between Elenie and Roman, his normally sunny face serious. "OK. Shit. That was not what I was expecting."

"I've thought about this a lot. Not just in the last week. It's the right thing to do. To have a hope of getting anything on Frank, you need information. And you need it from someone who can't be bought or intimidated. Someone close to Frank."

"But will he trust you with that information?" Dougie frowned. "Why would he tell you anything now? Especially since he reacted so well to you getting to know the boss."

"It would take some work," Elenie admitted. "But I've considered that, too." She looked at Roman with determination. "Frank would need to think I've hit rock bottom. That something has happened—on top of what he's already done—to knock the fight out of me. Nothing would make him happier than knowing I'd been broken enough to crumble."

His chest hurt with the urge to punch something.

"If he genuinely believed I'd given up all hope, he'd love to get me back under his thumb and into the family business," Elenie said. "I know how his mind works. He'd figure the dirtier he made my hands, the more hold he'd have over me."

"And how would you go about convincing him you've hit rock bottom?" Roman's voice was rough.

Elenie twisted the toe of her sneakers against the floor. "I think you'll have to date me and dump me." Her eyes didn't waver from his face. "You need to walk all over my heart."

Chapter 21
Elenie

If she hadn't been so tense, Elenie might have laughed at the way Roman blinked.

Dougie coughed. "Sorry," he said. "Swallowed the wrong way."

"No."

They both turned as Roman pushed away from the filing cabinet, his eyes stormy and explosive. He ran a hassled hand through his hair, which left a tuft sticking out on one side, just above his ear. Elenie's fingers twitched with the desire to flatten it.

"That won't work."

She felt an arrow-sharp stab in the heart. "I know it might not sound that believable but—"

"That's not what I meant." Roman cut across her. "You got hurt the last time Frank heard we spent time together. I'm not putting you in that position again." He began to pace behind his desk.

"But if the timing was right," Dougie tugged at one ear, "Elenie's idea is a good one."

"It is," she insisted. "Hear me out. If we could stage a public breakup and humiliation, everyone who mattered would hear about it. And Frank would take advantage." Elenie sat firm under Roman's glare. "I could make him believe it. I know I could."

"I don't like it."

"It's about controlling the narrative," Dougie chipped in. A flicker of approval crossed Roman's face, before it was chased away by more thunderclouds as he continued his pacing. "How about a relationship reveal and breakup on the same night? In public. Somewhere you know you'll be seen and heard. That way, by the time it reaches Frank, it'll already be over—if you get what I mean. He'll be more focused on the split than the date. There'll be no point in him kicking off."

"Yes! He'll be so busy gloating, we'll skip right over the beating-me-to-a-pulp stage." *Hopefully.* Elenie's mind raced, turning over the idea, examining it for holes.

Roman winced, his eyebrows knotted. One hand gripped the back of his neck and the other was stuffed deep into the pocket of his pants. He looked pained, riled, and oh so sexy. "It's too risky. Frank Dax is a loose cannon. And he's not stupid."

"No, but he is slippery," Elenie pressed. "Nothing ever sticks to him despite the whole town knowing he's shady. If anything goes down that's the wrong side of legal, he's mixed up in it every time. We had two drug raids on our house before we came to live here and no one's managed to pin anything on him so far. You need my help. And I need yours." She leaned forward. "I've lived with Frank for nearly twenty years. Mostly, I know how to stay safe around him. Yes, there are risks, but I'm willing to take them. I've thought it over—this isn't a spur-of-the-moment plan. He likes to watch things burn. Who better to set his house on fire than someone on the inside?"

In the end, they called for takeout pizza and ate it sitting in the office. Dougie rang Summer to say he'd be late home.

"It's more complicated than you're imagining." Roman glared, unseeing, at the pizza box. "We can't just organize and run this operation on our own. You'll need to be registered as a confidential informant and your suitability tested. You'll have to sign a code of conduct and confidentiality agreement and be given an official handler. The circle of trust would be us, you, either one or two handlers—and no one else."

"Can't you be my handler?" Elenie hadn't expected that. She trusted Roman but placing her trust in someone else was unnerving.

"No, I can't." His eyes pinned her with an unreadable intensity. "I have a personal relationship with you already. That makes it unethical for me to be your handler." A spark of molten flame flickered in his pupils, flashing pinpricks of heat all over her body like the searing sting of fire ants. Then he blinked and it was gone. "We wouldn't want any risk of the information you gather being compromised—for whatever reason. Or the whole thing would be for nothing."

Elenie gave a slow nod and pushed her pizza to one side, appetite dead. She didn't like it but she understood.

"It'll take a little time to set up. And, however careful we are in the meantime, you're at risk until Frank knows there's nothing happening between us." Roman watched her. She had the impression he could read her every thought.

"But this could work, Chief. Distancing yourself from Elenie in public would serve two purposes." Dougie ticked them off on his fingers. "One, it would make her position safer. And two, if it convinced Frank that she's got no chance of running to you, she would be in a better position to gather information from the inside." Dougie spread his hands. "The guy's like Teflon—nothing ever sticks to him. Frank's our top suspect for any and every burglary, arson, or assault. We know he's involved but we can't prove it. The Daxes have been a one-family crime wave in Pine Springs since they arrived. Our possession charges alone have gone up twenty percent in the last ten years. Sorry, Elenie." He shot her an apologetic glance.

Roman seemed to look at Dougie without properly seeing him for several minutes. Dozens of different scenarios were clearly running through his mind. The office was silent.

"OK," he said finally. "Let's make a plan."

* * *

The following Friday night, when Elenie walked into the Rusty Barrel, her heart was beating so loudly she could hear it in her ears.

The tables, floor area and bar seating were all busy; she'd never seen it so packed. For a second, Elenie panicked that she wouldn't find him. A nonsensical thought. He was the very first person she focused on, as if her eyes would always track him down in every crowd like some kind of homing device.

He saw her, too, from his position at the bar, raising his glass to catch her eye.

Her feet felt clumsy and she didn't know what to do with her hands. She was on a date—well, a kind of date—with Roman Martinez, the local police chief. If that wasn't the craziest thing to ever happen to her, Elenie didn't know what was.

They'd decided to move on this part of the plan while Roman got in touch with his contact at the County Sheriff's Office. He'd warned her he wouldn't be able to set everything up at the drop of a hat but was adamant her safety was paramount. And so here they were. Ready to put Elenie back on the Pine Springs PD blacklist.

"Hi." It was the only word she could manage to get out.

Roman gave her a slow smile which lifted one corner of his beautiful mouth and spread until his angular face eased. She couldn't take her eyes off his lips.

"Hey, Elenie." He stood up from the bar stool, towering above her, and leaned down to press a kiss against her temple.

What. The. Fuck.

She almost whimpered.

He smelled of washing powder and aftershave. So damn clean. It was all she could do not to rub her face against his chest like a cat and breathe him in.

"What can I get you to drink?"

"Huh?" Elenie looked up at him and blinked.

"Drink?" Roman asked again, pointing to the bar. "What can I get you?"

"Oh, uh, I'll have a gin and tonic, please. If that's OK."

He stepped away from his bar stool and pushed it toward her. "Take a seat."

Elenie shrugged off her denim jacket, laying it across her lap. Her flowery cotton dress was old and worn, just like her ankle boots, but it was pretty. She fiddled with the material under her fingers and straightened the hem on her thighs, wishing her stomach would settle.

Roman, rumpled and casual, was dangerously handsome in black jeans and a soft, khaki Henley. He pushed his sleeves up as he waited at the bar and she swooned a little more. His hair was slightly damp at the ends. Elenie wondered how recently he'd been in the shower. Her cheeks warmed and she forced herself to stop staring.

She wasn't the only person checking out the police chief. Looking around the bar, she counted at least four girls plus a guy in a flannel shirt who were studying him with hungry eyes. It was hardly surprising. He was drop-dead throw-your-panties-over-your-shoulder-and-have-a-defibrillator-on-standby gorgeous. That he seemed so unaware made him all the more compelling.

This is not a real date. This is make-believe. Perhaps if she kept telling herself that, it would save her from making a fool of herself.

Roman slid a drink in front of her. "One gin and tonic."

158

"Thank you so much." Elenie, desperate for something to do with her hands, picked it straight up and took a gulp. She shivered as the tart iciness slid over her tongue.

"There'll be quite a crowd in tonight. There's a band playing soon," he said. "Should work in our favor."

Elenie let herself be reassured by his steady confidence. She gave a jerky nod. "Yes, it'll be fine."

But she wasn't sure she believed it.

Chapter 22
Roman

If only subtlety was a language Frank Dax understood, they wouldn't be going through with this farce.

Every time he thought about putting Elenie in danger, Roman's stomach plunged and rolled, cement-mixer style. His objectivity was shot. The only thing stopping him from shutting down this whole plan—forcefully, instantly, permanently—was the hope he'd seen on her face.

It absolutely killed him.

How could he know how it felt to go home every night to that house? To a mother who had treated the care system like a crèche and chosen Dax over her daughter. To a man who mocked her, ignored her, or hurt her.

Thea kept sweet popcorn in her cupboard for him when she and Luke only liked salty. Florence left him a voice message every Halloween, singing a ridiculous song about witches they'd found funny when they were kids. His parents had sent regular care packages of food and books to the city, as if he hadn't had access to any shops himself. It was something he'd taken for granted. Even laughed about.

Elenie had no one. He'd seen the hunger in her eyes at his parents' house.

If Frank was at all suspicious that Elenie still had the ear of the local PD, there was no way she'd be able to gather the intel they needed. His default setting was mistrust; he was never going to simply take her word for it if she promised to keep her distance from Roman. There needed to be witnesses to an implosion that left no doubt.

Men like Dax dealt solely in things that went *boom*. Fingers crossed, this performance should solve that.

They needed a brutal, public face-off to shatter any question of an ongoing link. But to do that, they had to confirm the connection first. It was this part that had the potential to blow up in Elenie's face if they didn't play it right.

Roman hooked a second bar stool and pulled it closer to Elenie's, settling in behind her and drawing her back to sit between his thighs. His stomach muscles rippled. Her hair smelled heavenly, like sugar and ice cream. He fought the urge to wind the soft waves between his fingers and press another kiss to her temple. God, how he wanted to.

She was temptation with a ramrod-straight backbone.

This whole charade was fucking dangerous. And half of that danger had nothing to do with Frank Dax.

"Is this OK?" Roman murmured next to Elenie's ear.

Her nod was a firm jerk of her head. "Yes. It's good. People are looking."

The band members appeared to raucous applause. They cut through the patrons and took up their instruments, jumping straight into a fast-paced country song that got the audience clapping and stamping. The reverberations thrummed through the floorboards. Gathering his professional control around him as tightly as he could, Roman rested his hands on Elenie's waist, trying his best to make it look intimate but feel unthreatening. He ran a deceptively casual eye around the bar.

He'd had a couple of evenings in the Barrel with Milo and Luke since his return, knocking back any flirty encounters with closed body language and a reserved smile. It wasn't usually as busy as this but he'd chosen a good position. Their location at the bar left them wide open to the attention of others. He tried to assess how much interest they were getting. A group of women nearby threw glances their way, before turning back to gossip among themselves. Roman was pretty sure they were the subject of it.

"See anyone you know?" he asked Elenie, his mouth close to her ear. She gave a tiny shiver; his fingers flexed on her waist.

"Uh, Craig Perry's sitting in a booth near the corner. He's with a couple of friends."

"Describe him."

She screwed up her nose. "Navy tweed jacket, mustard-colored t-shirt and jeans. Medium height, sandy hair. Stupid, punchable face." Roman flicked a glance in the direction she mentioned and identified him in seconds. "He's in our house too often for comfort these days and he likes to brush past me in doorways so he can touch my breasts."

Roman struggled to keep his face impassive. "D'you know the guys he's with?"

"Yeah. The meathead with curly hair is Vince Detler. He hangs around with Tyson, too. I wouldn't trust him to babysit a dog."

He grunted and shot them another look.

"Some of Ty's other friends are in the booth next to them," she continued. "I can't see him or Dean."

She tapped nervy fingers against her glass and Roman covered them with his own. His thumb drew calming circles on the back of her hand. "That's no bad thing. Better they hear about it, rather than see us and kick off in person."

Now he knew who Craig was, he was aware of the Brit looking over in their direction every now and then. When he next caught him doing it out of the corner of his eye, Roman made a point of brushing one of Elenie's curls out of her face. She drew in a sharp breath but threw him a flirty smile over her shoulder.

He closed his eyes as his groin tightened and bloomed with heat. *Not the place, dammit.*

Roman shifted his position and rested a casual hand on Elenie's thigh, the butter-soft cotton of her dress catching on his rough fingers. If only they were anywhere else but here, somewhere else alone. But those wishes were not his to make. Elenie wasn't his to claim.

He focused hard on the performance of the band's lead guitarist. This secondment was an opportunity to get himself steady again. If he did his job right in the meantime, he might leave Pine Springs in a little better shape than before. Those were his goals. And he couldn't let a gray-eyed woman from a family of criminals disrupt them.

The next hour passed slowly.

They did their best to chat and act like a normal couple on a normal date. An enamored couple on a normal date. They ordered more drinks and listened to the music. Roman tried to make Elenie laugh; he was delighted when he succeeded. She leaned tentatively against his chest. He held her loosely, the seam of his jeans skimming either side of her thighs. The tension gradually eased from her body and she relaxed in his grip.

Zena wasn't a fan of public displays of affection but she'd also complained he was too uptight when they attended social gatherings or work events. He'd never been quite sure what she wanted from him. And he'd always thought himself too private to ever want to make out in public.

If this was a proper date, Roman realized he wouldn't much care who was watching.

When Elenie laid a cautious hand on his leg, the heat in his body climbed a few degrees. He rubbed the stubble on his jaw against her hair. She drew in a breath and held it.

"You make it difficult to remember why we're here," he growled in her ear. The words forced their way out, even as he tried to hold them back. She immediately lifted her hand from his thigh. Roman caught it, mid-air, and placed it slowly back where it had been. "Leave it there."

Electricity sparked between them. He could feel it crackle in the humid air, like a summer storm waiting to break. Elenie's fingers curled against his jeans.

Behind him, someone pushed someone else who collided with Roman's back. He jostled Elenie, automatically tightening his grip around her so she didn't tip off her stool.

"Easy, buddy."

A gangly young man, wearing far too much aftershave, wilted under his ferocious stare. "Sorry, dude—my bad." He held up both hands in apology.

Roman let him off with a nod and put a little distance between himself and Elenie. She didn't return her hand to his leg.

Tyson's friends played drinking games. Rowdy jeers and back-slapping accompanied each round of shots. Someone knocked over a beer. The band moved into their final song of the evening. Last call rang out and people flooded the bar to refill empty glasses.

"Let's move out of the way," Roman suggested.

He led Elenie away from the band, toward the opposite end of the bar, where they leaned against a wall just behind Craig's booth. Roman looped a casual arm around her shoulders, fingers tapping a deceptively relaxed beat against her collarbone. As the last chords of music died away, the noise level began to drop.

They gave it another quarter of an hour or so, each pointing out people they knew by sight, relating stories they'd heard about them or experiences they'd had dealing with them. Roman found her observant and funny, as always. It reminded him of the afternoon at the fair. Talking to Elenie was easy.

Finally, their conversation tailed off. There was no delaying the next step.

He turned her to face him and gave both of her shoulders a squeeze, wanting to pull her closer and whisk her out of the bar. Instead, he smiled and the moment belonged to just the two of them.

"Best fake date I've ever had," he said.

Elenie tilted her head. "Been on many?" she asked.

"None."

She huffed out a laugh. Her smile flashed bright, then faded.

"Ready?" Roman's hand closed over her own, removing her denim jacket from her fingers. Elenie's mouth twisted. She nodded. "OK, then. It's showtime."

Chapter 23
Elenie

Roman held out her jacket and Elenie slipped her arms into the sleeves. He pulled her back against his body, wrapping his arms around her from behind and stuffing his hands into her front pockets. The heat of his chest burned like a brand of fire, a tattoo on her skin she'd wear forever. She summoned a laugh and pressed backward, the butterflies in her stomach no longer from desire.

When Roman's body went still behind her, Elenie's heart stuttered, struggling to beat within the icy crust forming around it. He removed his hands slowly from her pockets.

"Are you kidding me?" He held a small plastic bag in his fingers. Inside were two tiny, colorful pills. His face had transformed to a grim mask of disdain and the change was devastating.

She held her breath.

"For Christ's sake, Elenie. What part of 'I'm a fucking police officer' don't you get?" Roman's voice, carefully moderated to reach and penetrate the conversations of nearby drinkers, was dangerous.

"I didn't—"

"Save it." His disgust pierced her chest, even though she'd steeled herself to expect it. Roman pinched the bridge of his nose, then wiped a hand across his face. "Everyone told me not to trust a Dax. I should have listened."

He towered before her like a rockface. A statue of untouchable masculinity, so far above her that she'd never felt so small.

"Roman, it's not mine. I didn't know it was there. Please!"

All chatter had died in their section of the bar as everyone listened avidly to Elenie's unconvincing denial. She reached for his arm, dropping her hand again when he stepped back. The distance felt like a chasm.

"Forget it. You're not worth the risk to my career." His eyes could cut glass. The cruel twist of his mouth was alien. "You're barely worth an evening of my time."

She flinched as his words hooked themselves right into her soul. Undeniably true and achingly painful. They hurt even knowing why he said them.

Roman shoved his hands into his pockets—bag, drugs, and all—and walked away from her. Weaving between the late-night drinkers, he pushed through the doors of the bar and strode out into the dark.

It felt symbolic to be left behind. It felt like foreshadowing. While Elenie's head knew the plan and exactly what to expect, her heart didn't seem to get it.

Tyson's buddies had noisily shushed each other to eavesdrop but now they let out a whooping round of applause. Several of them reached for their phones. All had big mouths and a love of trouble; it wouldn't take long for the gossip to spread.

Craig Perry pushed himself up from the table. "That was bloody priceless, babe! Let me know in advance next time and I'll sell tickets."

Elenie took the half dozen steps needed to stand in front of him. Lifting a full shot glass from the tabletop, she downed it in one, wiping her mouth with the cuff of her jacket. "He's an arrogant fucker."

Her voice broke on the last word. She let her lips tremble, made sure Craig noticed. Swiping at her eyes with heels of her hands, she turned away and left the bar.

Roman was nowhere in sight.

The night air wasn't cold but her teeth chattered. Shuddering inside her thin jacket, she squinted across the parking lot, indecision freezing her feet. Where to go and what to do? Her brain felt like cotton candy. And cotton candy made her think of Roman.

A breathy sob escaped Elenie's lips before she clamped them together. She would be OK. She could get through this. All was going as expected. The pills she'd lifted from the pocket of Dean's ripped jeans, dumped on the floor of his room, had served their purpose. Although he'd kicked off when he found them missing, Elenie was right at the bottom of his list of suspects and she'd flown under the radar of his temper tantrum.

She lifted her chin. Going home tonight wasn't an option, so she just had to think of somewhere else to hole up for a while. It wasn't something they'd discussed. She didn't like to disturb Otto this late but his house was only a fifteen-minute walk away and the moon was more than three-quarters full.

"Hey!"

She turned toward the soft call. Caitlyn stood by the open passenger door of an SUV. Milo, his face mostly in shadow, leaned against the fender.

"Here!" Caitlyn called again. "Jump in."

Elenie ran over. Flicking a grateful smile at Milo, she ducked behind Caitlyn to pull open the rear door. "Thank you so much!"

She didn't realize she'd let out a wobbly sigh until she met Milo's eyes in the rearview mirror. There was quiet sympathy in his smile. He started the car and drove smoothly out of the lot.

Five minutes later, they pulled up in front of a pretty little house, painted in soft green, near the center of town. Caitlyn ushered Elenie inside.

"Alcohol, coffee, or a cold drink?" she offered, heading for the kitchen.

Elenie was studying their wedding portrait on the wall of the living room with a raw heart when the hammering started on the door. Wired but exhausted, edgy and unsettled, her nerves jangled. There was no going back now; the plan was in motion.

"Did you find her? Is she here?" The front door slammed, footsteps sounded in the entryway, and Roman surged into the room. He checked his stride for a second when he saw her. His eyes flashed with relief as he crossed the floor to stand in front of her, laying careful hands on her shoulders. "You OK?"

"I'm fine." Only an iron will stopped her from swaying toward him.

He searched her face. She knew he knew she wasn't fine. "You were great."

"You didn't need to send them to find me." The concern in his eyes nearly melted her. What she wouldn't give to slip back into a fantasy land where he might look at her like that because he really cared. But in the real world this man could never be hers.

Roman grunted. "You're not on your own in this, Elenie. You've got people looking out for you now. And you've got me. They only know we've done this to keep Frank off your back. Nothing more."

He might have continued but Caitlyn barreled into the room, leading with her stomach first.

"You didn't get a chance to answer so I've made us all hot chocolate. Since I can't drink, I don't see why you can't all keep me company." She plonked four mugs down on the coffee table, kicking off her sneakers with a sigh of relief. "I've even given you marshmallows. Don't tell me I'm not the best hostess ever."

169

Roman pulled Elenie down next to him, leaning forward to snag them each a mug of chocolate. Milo perched on the arm of Caitlyn's chair and stroked a hand over his wife's fiery curls. Elenie blew across the top of the hot chocolate to cool it, a wave of exhaustion rolling over her. Roman's arm pressed against hers and the closeness made her unruly heart scurry.

"I've always wanted to be a getaway driver," Caitlyn said around a mouthful of marshmallow.

"Strictly speaking, you were the getaway passenger." Milo gave his wife's ear a tug. "But you kicked ass whichever side of the stick you were on."

Chapter 24
Roman

"Any chance Elenie can use your spare room?" Roman asked. They'd been talking for more than an hour and it was late.

"Sure, bro." With a yawn, Milo began to gather the empty mugs.

"I'll grab you one of Milo's tees, Elenie." Caitlyn levered herself up from the armchair.

Five minutes later, Roman stood in the bedroom doorway feeling like a vampire who hadn't been asked inside. He hooked his hands into his pockets for want of something better to do with them and kept his eyes deliberately away from the queen-size bed. Mental snapshots of their "fake date" taunted him; a sliver of heat licked at the base of his spine.

"Didn't think to bring my own sleepwear," Elenie said weakly, holding up the cotton shirt she'd been given.

"You need to get some rest. It'll be morning before you know it." He smiled to ease the tension. "If you need anything, I'll be on the sofa right downstairs."

"OK." She fiddled with the curtain ties on the other side of the room.

Roman forced himself to turn. "Goodnight, Elenie."

"Night." Her reply was so quiet he barely heard her.

His tread was silent on the stairs. Behind Caitlyn and Milo's door, he heard the rumble of low conversation, and unexpected splinters of envy jabbed at his ribs. In the kitchen, Roman closed his eyes and braced his arms on the counter. The clock on the wall ticked loudly and steadily; he waited until his breath matched its pace before raising his head. Pouring a tumbler of water, he drained it in five long gulps and refilled it.

A movement in the doorway caught the corner of his eye. When Roman turned he found Elenie watching him.

She'd changed into Milo's t-shirt and her feet were bare. As still as the center of a hurricane, only her fingers fidgeted. Face scrubbed clean and ready for bed, she was the perfect picture of casual familiarity, and an aching sense of the forbidden danced with the swirl of heat that smoldered in his gut.

"You OK?" He was grateful his voice emerged measured and steady.

Elenie cleared her throat. "I think the world record is fifty-four people on a single bed."

Roman tipped his chin. "I see." He didn't see.

"The one upstairs is a queen."

His brain couldn't form any kind of answer to that.

She pushed her hair back from her face with an agitated hand. Her eyes clung to his and stole the breath from his lungs. "Would you sleep upstairs with me tonight? I don't want to be alone."

The strangled request came out in a rush, as if asking anyone for a favor was an alien experience for her. Roman's heart turned over yet again and he wondered when Elenie would stop sneaking beneath his defenses. How could he say no?

The silence seemed to expand and she huffed an embarrassed laugh. "Unless you don't want to. It's fine if you don't."

Roman couldn't bear to listen to her backtrack. He nodded. "Sure. Of course. No problem."

He could do this. It was his job to protect and that's what Elenie was asking for—protection, support. He could give that to her.

She smiled the ghost of a smile and turned. Roman gave her a few minutes to pad silently back up the stairs. He filled a second tumbler of water and then followed in the footsteps of the woman who threatened his equilibrium more than anyone he'd ever met.

Elenie was already under the covers when he entered the bedroom. She'd left a small lamp glowing by the bedside. In the dim light, he couldn't see her eyes. Roman tugged his Henley over his head and tossed it onto a chair in the corner, leaving his undershirt and jeans on. Crossing to the other side of the bed, he lay down on top of the covers. He would rather be uncomfortable himself than make Elenie feel awkward.

She reached over and turned out the light. The bedroom was silent but the hush that fell between them held a dozen unspoken thoughts.

"It's been a weird night." Elenie murmured into the dark.

He smiled at the understatement, staring up at the ceiling above him, muscles tense. "You did so well. Everything went exactly how we planned."

She gave a hum of agreement. "I bet either Craig or Vince called Ty before they left the bar."

Roman frowned and shifted position, raising an arm to cradle his head. The urge to look at her whispered through his sinews but he resisted. Long moments ticked by and the air grew thicker. His mind refused to settle, leapfrogging restlessly from one subject to another.

"I told Thea I've been struggling. I told her everything. We talked for ages. I should have done it before."

He heard Elenie turn her head and her eyes warmed the side of his face. The fruity scent of her shampoo did strange things to his chest. "Did it help?"

"It felt good. I've never kept secrets from Thea."

"Will you tell your parents?"

"Already have. I went round to theirs the next day. Told them about the transfer, too. They were disappointed I'm not planning to stay, but they were more upset I hadn't told them how bad things had gotten."

"They love you." Her voice was soft.

"Yeah." The hand lying on top of the covers bunched into a fist. Tension snaked through the darkness. "Just Florence to go now."

There was a rustle of cotton and Elenie reached out. He opened his grip at her touch; she threaded her fingers through his own. Offering comfort to him, even now when she needed it more. She was so slight in build, so resilient in person. He admired every feisty inch of her.

The night threw a blanket around the bed, insulating them from reality, and Roman turned to look at her then; he couldn't help himself. Her slate-gray eyes held whole worlds he was desperate to visit, and he swallowed. Elenie's gaze shifted to his throat. His groin tightened, his breath caught. Neither of them moved. Then, her eyelids flickered shut, eyelashes forming perfect half-circles against her pale skin, and Roman sagged into the mattress.

Torn in two with wanting what he couldn't have, Roman let himself imagine what life could be like if things were different. He wished he'd met her in simpler times—when he had his life together and she had found her freedom.

As the quiet minutes passed, their breathing slowed, steadied, and blended. He held her hand gently like a wild thing; Elenie's chilled skin warmed beneath his touch. Ever so slowly, her fingers slackened in his and, although he could no longer see her, he guessed that she was sleeping.

It was a long time before Roman followed suit but, when he did, he crashed deeply. And Elenie kept the nightmares and shadows away with just the rise and fall of her breath.

Chapter 25
Elenie

She changed into the spare uniform she kept at work and got stuck into the familiar routine that kickstarted every shift at Diner 43. As Elenie unloaded the dishwashers and sanitized the surfaces on autopilot, the craziness of the last twelve hours ran on repeat in her brain.

She'd woken early enough to watch the sun rise across the stunning face of Roman Martinez just inches from her nose. They weren't touching, though she was pretty sure she'd drifted off with her hand in his. Barely breathing, Elenie watched him like a stalker for as long as she could, greedy eyes taking in the relaxed lines of his face.

As she pulled on her clothes from the night before, Roman rolled onto his side in his sleep, his arm denting the pillow beneath his head. The silver scar along his jawline called to her fingers. At some point in the night he'd pulled the comforter over one leg, his undershirt bunching just enough to show an inch of tanned skin above the waistband of his jeans. His body was insane. It had physically hurt to drag herself away.

Caitlyn's little house was silent, the hum of town life outside different to the sounds at home. No one stirred as Elenie stealthily opened the front door and headed to work.

The first ninety-five percent of their fake date in the Barrel might well have ruined her for every real date to come in the future. Roman Martinez was an impossible act to follow. Elenie shivered at the memory of his midnight-dark irises focused on her face, spearing her with heat. She would sell her soul for someone to look at her like that when they weren't pretending.

"I swear to God, if you don't pull your finger out and start moving, Elenie Dax, you won't make it to the end of your shift!" Delia's threat brought her straight down to earth.

An apology fell from Elenie's lips. Daydreaming was for other people. Not her. She would still be here long after Roman had headed back to his life in the city.

Otto's smile was kind. He patted her wrist when she poured his coffee. "Ignore her, Elenie. She wouldn't know how to manage without you, and that's the truth. That woman is so jealous of you, she doesn't know how to control it."

"Jealous? Of me?" The idea was comical.

"Of you." Otto nodded. "You're clever, you're young, and you're beautiful. Your whole life is lying ahead of you, filled with endless possibilities. It makes perfect sense that she'd be jealous."

New customers filled another booth and he waved her away with good humor, spreading his newspaper out on the table. She stared hard at Delia when she collected the next order, trying to process and evaluate Otto's words. He must be wrong. People loathed or mistrusted the Daxes. They were wary, often angry, sometimes fearful. Never jealous.

Elenie skipped her break, choosing to ignore how exhausted she felt from a stressful evening and too few hours in bed. The morning flew by and the flow of diners was steady.

A familiar, dark-haired woman called in for pastries. As she laid a book on the countertop to dig in her purse for the right money, Elenie realized she recognized her from the library.

"I've read that one," Elenie said, unable to resist. "I love E.V. Huxley. I recommended it to a friend, too." She pointed at Otto.

The customer gave her a blinding smile and tugged her glasses free of a tangled curl. "That's amazing! I work with the author. This is one of her early titles. I reread them constantly."

"E.V. Huxley's a woman?" Elenie grinned. "I wouldn't have guessed."

"Her name's Esther. I'm Leah."

"Nice to meet you. You have a cool job."

"It's the best." Leah's smile flashed again, freckles dotting her pale cheekbones like cinnamon on steamed milk. She handed over the payment for the pastries, said a cheery goodbye, and headed for the door. It burst open as she reached it. Leah made a quick and fluent side-step, eyeing Dean warily as he barreled past her.

Shit.

Elenie approached him quickly before he could make a scene. Face flushed, mouth twisted, he grabbed her arm. "You stole my fucking drugs!" he hissed in her ear.

With no other option open to her, Elenie stuck with outright denial and thanked God Dean wasn't very smart. "No, I didn't."

"Bullshit! I know what I had in my pocket. Then abra-fucking-cadabra, I'm told it was in yours last night." He pushed his face toward hers. It wasn't his best angle. "I'm glad he dumped your sorry ass for it! I'm glad you looked like a skank in front of a whole bar full of people!" Dean twisted her wrist. "You're no better than the rest of us, Elenie."

"Actually, she's worse."

Like two choreographed dancers, they both spun around. Elenie's mouth opened in a surprised "O."

Caitlyn stood in the doorway, hands on hips and side by side with Summer. "We heard all about it, too." Pushing Dean out of the way without sparing him a second glance, she jabbed her finger into Elenie's chest. "In case you hadn't noticed, I'm about to have a baby and drugs are a hard no for me. Look what they did to Millie Westlake! Does that mean nothing to you?"

Elenie had a moment to secretly admire the way Caitlyn pitched her voice just low enough to keep the conversation between the four of them, before Summer stepped forward and took the Oscar for Best Supporting Actress. A perfect tear shimmered on her lower eyelashes.

"Oh, Elenie." Her bottom lip quivered. "I'm so disappointed in you."

Elenie let out a forced laugh. Dean took it all in, slack-jawed. "Join the line, babe. I've been letting people down since I was born." She took a quick glance over her shoulder to check Delia wasn't listening. "Can I get any of you a table or would you like to fuck off now?"

Surprisingly, none of them stayed.

Either Delia's bat ears hadn't picked up on the ruckus or she pretended not to hear in order to keep the diner operational. Either way, Elenie finished her shift with a job to return to and a ridiculous amount of adrenalin coursing through her body at the thought of going home after last night's drama.

Her fingers tingled with it, her heart pounded. There was a genuine possibility she might be sick. Suddenly, it all seemed very real.

A text from Roman came silently through on her cell phone as she reached the top of the hill.

Thea (Roman):

Hey. You there?

She knew he wouldn't text more unless she answered.

I'm nearly home.

Thea (Roman):

Caitlyn told me what happened in the diner. If you don't feel safe at any point, please get out of there and call me. I will meet you anywhere. Get in touch when you can.

Elenie rested the screen of her phone against her forehead, committing his message to her memory before deleting it. Shoving her precious cell to the bottom of her bag, she walked toward the house.

Craig Perry's six-year-old Jag was parked next to Frank's truck and Elenie sagged with relief. Usually, she would go to any length to avoid the slimeball but, today, he might just be the key to saving her skin.

Closing the front door behind her, Elenie wrapped herself in the cloak of the character she'd been working on all the way home.

Despairing and pathetic, she recited to herself. *Defeated, beaten, and humiliated.*

Athena appeared in the doorway of the living room. They looked at each other silently. Elenie bit her lip. "Mom." Her voice sounded shaky and needy in the dim entryway. Not all of it was an act.

"One of these days, you're gonna push it too fucking far." Sympathy flickered on her mother's face, driven out by a tired resignation which was far more familiar. When Athena drifted back into the living room, Elenie forced herself to follow.

Frank lounged in an armchair, glass in one hand, open bottle of whiskey within reach. Craig sat at one end of the couch. Her mother slumped onto the cushions to curl up against the opposite arm. On the television, an action movie she'd seen before rolled toward a climax. Her hands shoved into the front pocket of her hoodie, Elenie watched a fireball engulf two tanks on the screen. There was chaos, screaming, multiple admirable death throes from multiple different actors.

"Craig's been telling me about last night." Frank's tone was dangerous. Elenie tried to estimate how much he'd had to drink. She effected a listless shrug.

"It was a fucking car crash." Craig grinned. "You should've been there." His phone was in his hand, thumb idly scrolling as he spoke.

Elenie's skin prickled as Frank examined her face. She kept her eyes on the television and imagined one of the exploded tank drivers was the love of her life, his fiery death, slow and painful. Her soulmate lost to the cinematic battlefield. She scrubbed the back of her hand over exhausted eyes which were satisfyingly hot and moist. The silence lingered way past comfortable. Athena picked her nails, casually alert. Frank watched Elenie.

Craig, seeming oblivious to the undercurrents, tucked his cell into his jacket pocket. "Tell you what, babe. I'll give you a do-over. To help you out. The business guild gala dinner is on the twenty-fourth and I need to go. Come with me and I'll even sort you out with something pretty to wear." He ran his eyes over her body in a way that both creeped her out and had her fuming at the same time.

Fuck.

She hadn't expected to be put on the spot like this. Frank knew she'd rather die than date Craig; she'd told him often enough. If Elenie wanted him to believe she was crushed, this was a good place to start. She tried to imagine what Roman would say. Craig, Frank, and Athena were all waiting for her to answer.

"Whatever." Elenie shrugged again. "Might as well."

"Good choice, Ellie."

Don't wink at me, you dick. I swear to God if you wink at me . . .

Craig winked at her.

"I'm hungry—I need a sandwich." She waved a hand in the direction of the kitchen.

"I think I'll come too." Elenie's steps faltered as Frank clambered to his feet. She shot a look at her mother.

Athena caught hold of Frank's wrist as he passed the couch. "Play nice, now."

"Nice is my middle name." He bared his teeth in a crocodile smile and followed Elenie to the kitchen.

The silence held the weight of a boulder as she moved between the fridge and the cupboards. Frank looked relaxed but his body language was deceptive. Faded tattoos moving over the muscles of his arms, he pulled a lighter from his jeans pocket. Elenie's tongue darted out to wet her lips; there was no saliva in her mouth.

"Seems I didn't make myself clear enough." His tone was conversational. "Either that or you're a fuckin' idiot." Her stomach rolled; her armpits were damp. Frank flicked the lid of his lighter open and shut. A smirk hovered on his lips. "Are you an idiot, El?"

Elenie kept her gaze fixed on her sandwich, layering a cheese slice between the bread with total concentration. Would he gloat or lash out? She couldn't tell yet. Her throat was tight, her heart galloped so fast her head spun.

"I bet you feel dumb now. You look as dumb as fuck from where I'm standing." She flinched when Frank shifted, propping himself up against the counter, so close that her elbow brushed his solid stomach. He grinned, feeding off her fear, a master of intimidation. "Craig's more than you deserve so don't screw that up." Frank lifted a hand, crisscrossed with fine scars, to grip her chin. Elenie held herself rigid, nostrils flaring, letting him feel the shudder that tremored under her skin. "Do us all a favor—keep your mouth shut and open your legs when you need to." He pushed her face away from him, eyes hard and cold. "Craig's a damn sight more use to us in the family than a fuckin' cop. Don't make me have to remind you of that."

They stared at each other for a moment.

"You hearing me this time, Ellie?"

Controlled menace rolled off Frank like drugstore aftershave.

"Yes." Her reply was a whisper. Elenie dropped her eyes, shoulders hunched.

He pushed away with a satisfied grunt and she leaned sweaty palms against the countertop as he strode out of the kitchen.

* * *

You girls make fierce enemies. And WTF Summer? Real tears!

Summer:

Looked like a distraction was needed. U impressed?

Caitlyn:

I nearly high-fived her performance but I was too OUTRAGED!!!

Yh I got that.

Summer:

U home?

Caitlyn:

Give us an update.

It went some way toward settling her stomach to have friends who cared that she was OK.

Craig was here when I arrived. Probably made things calmer than they could have been.
BUT he asked me to go to the business guild dinner with him. Right in front of Frank.

Caitlyn:

Fuck.

Summer:

What did you say?

It didn't feel like I had a choice. What do you think?

Caitlyn:

. . .

Summer:

. . .

Girls? I need help!

Caitlyn:

I hate to say it but I think you're right. Shit. Roman will flip.

Summer:

He's not going to like it.

You've forgotten he dumped my sorry ass in the Barrel.

Caitlyn:

Yh true. Thats OK then. See you at the gala dinner ☺

You're going??!!

Caitlyn:

Milo, me, Luke, Thea, and Roman. Couldn't keep us away. Last year's main raffle prize was a voucher for 2 new tires at Jeffersons Motors.

Kill me now.

Summer:

My mom's staying that weekend so Dougie and I can't make it ☺

That's good! The less people I know, the better. Now I just have to make Craig understand I'd rather put a campfire out with my face than sleep with him.

Summary:

Summer:

Caitlyn:

Chapter 26
Roman

Roman was in a foul mood.

He was tense to the point of snapping at the thought of Elenie becoming a confidential informant. When she'd messaged to say things had gone as smoothly at home as could be expected, he'd relaxed just a fraction. And then she'd hit him with the news about dating the fucking Brit.

He wished he had the right to tell her not to do it, even though he understood the reasoning. He'd discussed it with Dougie, who'd heard about Perry from Summer. They chewed it over together, neither of them happy with the development. But Elenie insisted it made sense and he could see what she meant. If it helped her cover with Frank, he'd let it go for now. But Perry was in his sights, alongside Dax, and every single move he made would be under Roman's scrutiny.

His initial contact with the County Sheriff's Office had led to a preliminary meeting with Chief Deputy Shawn Booth. Unfortunately, Booth, subjected to a barrage of anti-Dax rantings from Chief Roberts over the years, proved a hard sell on Elenie's suitability as a CI. They'd butted heads with icy politeness— goddam bureaucratic paper-pushers—until Booth reluctantly agreed to pass the details through to the Drug Enforcement Agency. Roman suspected the current fentanyl crisis was the tipping point; there was pressure from higher up to show steps were being taken to deal with the sharp increase in fentanyl-related deaths.

Subject to a successful background dive and a positive first meet-up, which Roman wouldn't be allowed to attend, it looked like Elenie might be in.

He hadn't seen her for more than a week while he worked behind the scenes on setting everything in motion. The niggling need to be somewhere near her rubbed awkwardly in his rib cage.

Pushing open the door of the diner, he scanned the busy hub inside with a casual glance. Otto raised his coffee cup in greeting, a welcoming smile on his lips. Roman strode over and slid onto the opposite bench seat.

"Good to see you, sir," Otto twinkled. "It's been a little while."

"It has. I'm sorry. Things keep cropping up." He could swear he smelled her before he saw her.

"What can I get you, Chief?" Elenie's voice was polite and low. He heard the hesitance behind her reserve.

"Just a hot tea, please."

Roman tried not to look at her but his eyes were traitors who flipped him off and sought her face regardless. However flat he kept his gaze, however impersonal he made his words, just a glance at her eased the tightness inside his chest and he soaked her up.

"Coming right up. And Otto—can I get you a refill?" She mastered the perfect blend of awkward and stilted, so far removed from the more relaxed Elenie of pizza night on Otto's deck.

"No, I'm fine, thank you." Otto smiled but he was too sharp to miss their tense exchange. The older man sent him a searching look.

They chatted about the weather, the proposed plans for the new business center, local politics, and neighbors. Elenie delivered

Roman's tea, setting it gently on the table without saying a word. He didn't thank her. When she walked away, he watched her go.

Otto laid surprisingly strong fingers on his forearm and squeezed. "Roman. I'm asking as a friend. Please don't let that girl down. I think she needs you."

"Sometimes people let themselves down." He took a long swig of tea and raised his eyes to Otto's. "I'll tell you what I told Elenie. As long as she stays on the right side of the law, she'll have my support." The old man examined his face. Roman wasn't sure what he saw, but Otto nodded and the frown lines that had wrinkled his brow smoothed out. It was too tempting to hold back the question. "How long have you known her?"

With a smile in his eyes, Otto leaned forward. He ran a gnarled finger over an old mark on the table. "It's been about three years now, I guess. I was getting lonely at home and decided to make more of an effort to get out of the house, so I started coming in regularly for breakfast. I lost my wife, Bea, two years before that. Bea was the best friend a man could want in a wife. We used to talk all the time. Not about anything important—just ordinary stuff. I missed the sound of her voice in our home so much." Roman gave him a sympathetic chin lift. "I'm lucky to have shared my life with her and the memories are happy ones. But it was the right decision to get out more. The exercise is good for me and the company is even better. It's become a part of my routine. Elenie wasn't chatty to start with but we always exchanged a few words. The first time I earned one of her smiles was a golden day for me."

Roman knew exactly what Otto meant. He glanced her way automatically, his eyes following her easy strides across the room.

The old man chuckled. "Don't tell her I said this, but Elenie reminds me of a stray cat—all wary and distrustful, poised to scratch or hiss. Yet it only takes the smallest iota of kindness to unlock all the sweetness she has to offer."

Roman was hit by an image of himself gently stroking Elenie's skin like a cat. Heat bloomed in his chest and he shifted in his chair.

"Probably not the most flattering compliment to pay a lovely young lady and I'll deny it if you tell her." Otto's smile was mischievous. "She's clever too. I've read a lot in my time but she gobbles up books like cinnamon buns. Her capacity to remember facts is amazing—the more obscure the better. I find her so interesting to talk to. Did you know she can speak four languages fluently? And insult you in about fifty!"

Roman grunted. There was too much about Elenie he didn't know, and he didn't like it.

Otto's eyes turned distant. "Bea and I never had children. We worked, we travelled, we were too selfish to share each other or make any compromises. I have no regrets." He lifted his coffee and drained it. "But if I had a daughter, I'd have been very proud to have one like Elenie."

* * *

Of all the people he might have expected to see on the afternoon of the gala dinner, his ex-fiancée wasn't one of them. She followed Maggie into Roman's office just after lunchtime.

"Visitor for you, Chief."

Glancing up from a case report, he blinked and blinked again. Maggie harnessed her curiosity and left them alone.

"Hello, Roman." Zena folded herself elegantly into one of the chairs.

"Uh. Hey." He shook his head to clear it. What the hell was she doing here? "You got business in Pine Springs?"

"Hardly." She gave a polite little laugh. "We didn't get anywhere when I called, so I finished up a contract I was working on and decided to pay you a visit." She flashed him a confident smile. "I'm here for the weekend. You can show me around."

Zena ran her eyes over his office with interest and he didn't doubt for a minute she was registering its small size, minimal technology, and lack of bustle. She was immaculately dressed as always—cropped black pants and a black satin strappy top, pale green tailored blazer and flat shoes, just the right amount of makeup and tiny, tasteful jewelry. Most likely a lot of time and money had gone into the outfit, but Roman only noticed the lack of warmth on her face.

"Did you listen to anything I said on the phone?" He tried to keep his voice mild but heard the edge of irritation when it crept in.

"Yes, I did. I just don't think you've thought it through properly. Maybe we could go out for dinner, chat things over, and you might feel different when we've spent a little time together again." Zena lowered her voice to a persuasive purr. "I've given you space, Roman. I've given you time. I was hoping you might have laid some ghosts to rest by now."

He flinched at the phrase. Then cursed himself for the reaction.

"I'm out tonight. There's a business dinner I have to attend." Roman opened the top drawer of his desk and rummaged for a pen.

"The one at the Elite Lodge?"

"How the hell do you—" Roman stifled a groan. "That's where you're staying, isn't it?"

"It is. There wasn't a wide choice." Zena smiled. "I could be your date."

He leaned back in his chair and actually considered it. Florence had laughed in his face when he'd asked her to go with him. There wasn't anyone else he felt comfortable using just to provide him with the cover he needed for one night, now that Elenie would be there with Craig Perry. Zena was a different matter. And she was offering. It would help to cement the impression with Perry that he had other irons in the fire. That Elenie wasn't of any importance to him. Some extra camouflage would be a good thing. And yet his skin prickled at the idea of taking Zena anywhere as his date.

"Well?"

Roman didn't miss the annoyance in her voice when he took his time answering. "OK," he said finally. "If warm white wine floats your boat, you're welcome to join us." Zena smirked. "But it's a one-off thing, for old times' sake. Nothing more." It seemed best to spell it out again. "I meant what I said on the phone."

She stood up to leave. "Seven o'clock in the lobby?" Roman gave her a brief nod. "Wonderful. I look forward to it."

It took the rest of the afternoon and two open windows for Zena's sultry perfume to disappear.

* * *

"That's the dress you brought with you in case we went out for dinner?" Roman raised one eyebrow.

"Well, I know this town lacks classy restaurants but I thought we might find somewhere less backward. I like to be prepared." Zena's silver evening gown swept to mid-calf with a tasteful slit at the side. A diamanté clasp held it securely on one milky white collarbone. Her sleek blond hair lay ruler-straight. She'd already made several wearisome comments about the facilities at the Elite Lodge, the cleanliness of her room, and the smell inside the elevator on her way downstairs.

The evening stretched ahead, a polar trek to be navigated in sliders.

Roman broke it to Thea and Luke that Zena was his date when he picked them up on his way to the hotel. They were far from impressed. Milo whispered a "Seriously, Ro?" in his ear when Zena's head was turned, and he wasn't looking forward to Caitlyn cornering him on his own. Safe to say his ex was far from a hit with his friends or his family. He felt foolish for not fully realizing it before. But then his head hadn't exactly been in the game for a while there.

The lobby, tired and in need of a revamp like the rest of the hotel, led through to the bar area and spacious conference room where the dinner was taking place. Old-fashioned swags and tails dressed the windows, with some of the braiding hanging loose. The carpet, once a rich shade of blue, was now faded and patchy, suspicious stains drowned out in the main by a gaudy pattern. There hadn't been money spent here for some time.

"Charlie, Charlie, Charlie—persons of interest have entered the building." Caitlyn's hiss came from somewhere behind him. Roman turned, calmly, casually, with a studied lack of interest.

Inside the main door, Elenie paused, her path blocked by a gaggle of newcomers. Perry ushered her onward with an impatient gesture. She shrugged a thin black jacket from her shoulders and Roman's conscious thought process short-circuited and died. His ears buzzed. His mouth opened and moved but didn't produce any words.

Unveiled, Elenie was a riot of sparkles. She wore a scarlet body-hugging, off-the-shoulder mini dress, so wantonly erotic the heat surged to his groin. He almost groaned. Edged with a wide band of lace, it dipped low across her chest, the swell of her breasts curving suggestively over the top of the neckline. The glittering material hugged her bottom, ending obscenely high on her thighs. Black high heels drew his eyes down her slim, bare legs. In all, it was just the wrong side of tasteful but Elenie carried it off.

Her hair was loose, curling gently above her shoulders, with one side pulled back and held above her ear with a jeweled clip. Roman swallowed as he soaked her in.

"Who's the hooker?" Zena's voice held amusement as she followed his gaze.

He couldn't answer.

"Well, I think we can guess who chose the dress," Milo murmured.

"Someone get the girl a cardigan." Thea was part-horrified, part-awestruck.

Roman dragged his eyes away and ignored the contemplative look Zena shot in his direction.

"Do we know this couple?" she pressed again.

"She works in town," said Caitlyn. "And her boyfriend's a bit of a creep."

Roman's mouth clamped into a tight line. He caught the sympathetic glance Luke threw his way as his brother-in-law steered Zena toward their table.

Goddammit, this is going to be a long night.

"How are we playing this?" Thea asked quietly in Roman's ear. "I'm scared I'm going to mess up."

"Just keep it as natural as possible. He knows she's been out with Caitlyn, but it's best if he doesn't realize she's met you and Luke as well."

"He's an egotistical douchebag with the sensitivity of a slug so I doubt he'll pick up on any subtle undercurrents." Caitlyn's head bobbed between them. She pulled a sour face before sailing onward like a pint-size torpedo.

"Jesus, this is painful." He pinched the bridge of his nose.

"I'll get the drinks in," said Milo. "It might help."

"I'll give you a hand," Roman growled.

"If I see you looking like you're gonna kill him—or even her," Thea watched Zena pass her shrug to Luke as if he was there to serve her, "maybe I could get Cait to go into fake labor or something."

"Probably still wouldn't stop me," Roman muttered grimly, as he stalked toward the bar.

Chapter 27
Elenie

Elenie resisted the urge to tug at the hem of her dress. She felt ridiculous, out of place, her pulse skipping wildly in her throat. Craig pushed a glass of wine she didn't want into her hand and the conference room gradually filled up with people. His head whipped from side to side as he tried to spot anyone worthy of conversation. She wasn't even a footnote on the list.

"Well, well, well." Amused and gleeful in equal measures, Craig chuckled and Elenie's heart dropped like a stone.

She turned slowly to find Roman a few paces away, Milo by his side. Both had their hands full with a selection of drinks from the bar. Both wore careful expressions of indifference. Despite willing her game face to hold fast, all the feeling went from Elenie's fingers and she fumbled her wineglass. It dropped to the carpet, snapping at the stem and showering lukewarm liquid over her feet.

Idiot.

She crouched to scoop up the pieces, only remembering as she did so that her dress could not be relied upon to stay in place. Elenie dropped the broken glass, her hand flying to the lace neckline to make sure she hadn't just flashed the entire bar. Her cheeks blazed.

"For fuck's sake, Elenie, leave it for someone else." Craig dragged her upright. "Great to finally meet you properly, Chief Martinez. I've heard so much about you from Ellie. I'm Craig Perry."

The Englishman offered his hand to Roman, who looked pointedly at the drinks he was holding and shrugged a dismissive shoulder. His face was cold. Such a different Roman to the one who teased his sisters and held her hand in the dark.

"Excuse my girlfriend—she's extremely clumsy. Easy on the eye though, aren't you, babe?" Craig's shit-eating smile was calculated to cause maximum offence as he smirked at Roman. Elenie burned with mortification. She opened her mouth to say something, anything, and Craig's fingers clamped painfully on her hip. "A powerful man needs a way to let off steam at home. Am I right, Chief?"

Made brave by the throng of people surrounding them, he was baiting Roman and humiliating Elenie at the same time. It was Craig at his obnoxious worst; she could tell he was loving it.

"In my experience, the most powerful men usually downplay the self-promotion." Roman's voice dripped with boredom, his eyes shuttered. "If you'll excuse us." He made to move around them, giving a clipped nod to Nathan Reyes from the liquor store who was on his way to the bar.

"I know your date went sour the other night. I was there. It was quite the spectacle." Craig wasn't done. "Hopefully no hard feelings, though? Easier for me to have lower standards than you, I guess. People might expect you to keep better company but I prefer something sparkly and simple. Makes me look smarter." Typically, Craig seemed to have mistaken his own misogynistic shit for cocky banter. Elenie wanted to be sick.

Roman's eyes were chilled with disgust. "I'm happy for you both, Perry. But now I'd like to get back to my date."

She recoiled but refused to show her shock on her face. *Oh God, he's brought someone with him!*

Craig just grinned and grabbed Elenie's wrist, fingers closing tightly enough to bruise her bones. Roman's nostrils flared imperceptibly at her wince.

"I believe we're sharing a table tonight, so we'll come too and you can introduce us." Craig looked delighted to deliver the news. "I don't know about you, but I'm starving. Let's find our places and get the booze flowing!"

Tugging her along behind him, he strode away, pausing to slap a couple of men on the back and greet others with a gleaming smile as he crossed the room. Elenie concentrated on walking steadily in her heels. She could feel Roman's eyes burning a hole between her shoulder blades and it was all she could do not to turn.

His group had yet to take their seats. Every face was familiar to her, bar one. Elenie flicked a polite smile at Thea and Luke, avoiding eye contact with Caitlyn until she was sure she could keep her face blank. Her friend glowed with health, rounded stomach encased comfortably inside a stunning satin wrap dress in olive green.

Craig waved a general greeting but zeroed in on the woman who stepped forward to link her arm through Roman's.

"You must be here with the chief," he said, extending his hand. "He was just telling us about his date but he forgot to say how beautiful you are. I'm Craig. This is Elenie."

"Fiancée." The blonde extended her hand and the engagement ring on her finger burned Elenie's retinas like a thousand suns. "I'm Zena and I'm Roman's fiancée, not just his date."

Craig's reply was lost to Elenie as she gave thanks for a lifetime of disguising her feelings. That Zena was there with Roman hurt her heart in ways she didn't have time to examine. Hearing the woman introduce herself as his fiancée was a spear straight to the abdomen.

It was little comfort that Caitlyn, Thea, Milo, and Luke appeared just as blindsided.

Side by side, Zena and Roman made the perfect couple, her pale hair and skin a glorious contrast to his tanned darkness. She matched his easy grace in spades, her poise and self-confidence as instinctive as his air of authority. Just being near her made Elenie feel so much less in so many ways.

Her eyes locked on Roman's. His lips were clamped. A muscle jumped in his cheek. Did she imagine that tiny shake of his head because she wanted so much to see it?

Elenie turned away.

The group drifted over in ones and twos to take their seats. And the evening began in earnest.

Picking at the unimaginative melon and prosciutto appetizer, she wrapped the remains of her dignity around her like a shawl and ran her eyes around the table of ten. It was possibly the most awkward scenario Elenie could have pictured.

Howard, a baby-faced but belligerent colleague of Craig's, sat on Elenie's left with his wife, Ruby, on his other side. Ruby was both shrill and dull; Howard possessed a habitual sniff which started to grate within the first five minutes. She hadn't met either of them before and was in no hurry to ever see them again. The conversation was forced and sticky around the table.

What a farcical situation. Torn between despair and hysteria, Elenie had no idea which, if either, would win out. And all the time, her skin bristled with awareness of the tall man with a face like stone who sat three seats away on her right-hand side. She could swear she felt the rumble of his low voice in her breastbone every time Roman spoke. So damn gorgeous in the navy suit that fitted his lean, muscular frame to perfection, he'd already shed his jacket, too warm in the overfilled room. He wore no tie, his midnight blue shirt unbuttoned at the neck.

She wanted to stare and stare; she was so thirsty for the sight of him. Even the presence of his fiancée couldn't keep her thoughts in line. Elenie's eyes flicked to the bare skin under his collar once, then twice. She imagined running her tongue along the groove at the base of his neck and had to stifle a moan. His skin would be warm against her mouth. Their fake date in the Barrel had taught her how hot Roman's body temperature ran. She could almost feel the burn on her lips.

Thank God that Zena was mainly blocked from her sight, sitting as she was on the other side of Craig. Her flawless appearance wasn't something Elenie needed in her eyeline. The glossy hair, immaculate makeup and elegant dress screamed high-class. Elenie knew what her own look screamed and it had nothing to do with good breeding. Used to being judged and found wanting, she was well aware that Zena had taken one look and found nothing to concern her at all.

Craig's bark of laughter rang in her ears and Elenie pulled herself together enough to smile. At what, she didn't know. The background noise made it hard to hear conversations around the table. She could only focus on the nearest ones. The ones she was least interested in. Being lonely in a crowd was so much worse than being lonely on her own. She wished for just one person to talk to. Or failing that, a book.

"There's no point in remodeling and renovating crappy buildings like this one. It's throwing good money after bad. My plans for the new business center will blow this kind of venue out of the water." Luke looked less than thrilled to be at the end of Craig's cocky boasts or his jabbing finger. "Small outfits like yours are better off sticking with home renos and decking. Leave the bigger jobs to those with a larger workforce and the experience to project-manage a proper commercial site. It's all about the contacts, mate. You might have a copper in the family but when I choose to mingle, I make a point of rubbing shoulders with the guys who dish out the money that matters. Businessmen, local councilors who have the casting votes, and people with influence, like the mayor."

"And yet still we find ourselves blessed with your company tonight." Caitlyn's words were sweetly delivered as she refilled her glass with water and offered the bottle to the rest of the table.

Trust Cait to provide the light relief. Elenie wiped away a smile that fought to surface against her will. Finding no ready answer to the putdown, Craig leaned back in his chair and began a loud conversation over his shoulder with someone on another table as they waited for their entrées.

Zena delicately buttered a wholewheat roll. "What do you do for a living, Melanie?"

"Elenie," said Caitlyn and Roman together.

"I'm a waitress."

"Interesting," Zena said in a voice that could not have been less interested. "Are you looking for a real job?"

Elenie's fingers tightened around the stem of her glass.

"Zena." Roman's use of his fiancée's name was glacial.

"I'm so sorry. I didn't mean to be rude. I'm happy for you if you like what you do." She wrinkled her perfect nose the perfect, adorable amount. "But I couldn't work in that kind of sweaty, steamy atmosphere day after day. I can feel my pores weeping in sympathy just thinking about it."

Across the table, Thea rolled her eyes.

Elenie took a sip of wine. "Did you know your skin loses its elasticity as you get older? That causes it to sag, making your pores seem larger. If you can feel them doing anything, they're probably drooping rather than weeping." She flashed Zena a careful smile. "Not that you're old. Just older than me."

Roman's fiancée gave a tight laugh. "It's so interesting to have you and your boyfriend here. Your attendance fills a much-needed gap in the guest list." She laid her napkin with deliberate care on the table and rose to her feet. "Excuse me for a moment. I need to use the bathroom."

"Wow," Caitlyn murmured sarcastically to Milo. "Roman's *fiancée* is kind of an ass. Who knew."

Thea glared at Roman. "No wonder you only brought her home once."

Elenie hoped the tips of her ears weren't as hot as they felt. "Sorry," she mouthed at Roman. The air crackled between them as their eyes caught and held. For a searing, molten moment in time, nothing else existed. Roman's pupils flared.

Craig chose that minute to swing back to the table, slamming Elenie's shoulder as he did. She jolted forward, catching her glass with her hand and sending white wine spilling across the tablecloth. "Bloody hell, babe," he groused. "It's a good job the wine's included in the ticket. You threw the last one I bought you on the fucking floor!"

A waitress appeared at her shoulder with a plate of food and Elenie had to fight to find her voice. A sideways flick of her eyes caught unguarded fury on Roman's face for just a second. He looked one small step away from a table-flipping rampage. Was it so wrong to hope he was fighting an overwhelming urge to grab Craig by the collar and smash his head into the table? Just the thought of Roman breaking Craig's nose into a plate of mediocre beef tenderloin and gravy gave her a sense of grim satisfaction.

Zena slid back into her seat.

Howard speared a carrot and eyed Elenie. "You're related to Frank Dax?"

"He's married to my mother."

He gave a sniff, his eyes flat like pebbles behind round glasses, and turned his shoulder to her. She was doing well with the small talk this evening.

Elenie focused on her meal; the food smelled better than it looked. It was warm and tasty but she could barely eat a thing. The lemon and blueberry cheesecake dessert, both sharp and sweet on her tongue, should have been delicious. Instead, it stuck to the roof of her mouth and she struggled to swallow it.

Zena held court while coffee was poured, recounting legal battles she'd fought and won. She was enviably self-possessed. Over the rim of her cup, Caitlyn caught Elenie's eye, rolling her own in an arc so huge she nearly sprained them.

Eventually, Craig pushed back his chair. "We're going to love you and leave you. It's been a pleasure but I need to socialize." He winked at Zena and circled an impatient hand in Elenie's direction. "Come on, Ellie. Chop, chop!"

Then he whistled at her. Like a dog.

Caitlyn's eyes went wide and then narrowed. Milo let out a strangled cough which sounded suspiciously like "what a dick." Elenie appreciated their support even as a flush of embarrassment climbed her neck.

"Excuse me," she murmured quietly, tucking her chair under the table. "It appears I have to chop. Twice."

Thea snorted. Caitlyn grinned. Elenie gave Roman a sideways glance and then she followed Craig across the room.

The evening dragged painfully on.

Craig drank more and laughed louder. He either ignored her or grabbed her ass, depending on whether he was talking shop or trying to impress his buddies. Less and less networking was conducted as his alcohol consumption increased. Two of Craig's friends hit on Elenie with him standing right beside them. He roared with laughter and took it as a direct compliment to his manliness, rather than the insult to his date their lewd comments implied.

She forced herself not to seek Roman out. For the most part she couldn't even see him and assumed he was still sitting at the table, chatting with the others. Craig dragged her onto the dance floor, where Elenie propped him up as best she could while he danced with drunken enthusiasm.

"Did you know the police chief was hiding a fiancée?" His voice was loud above the music. "Can't say I blame him for dumping you when he had her on speed dial. She's proper classy." Elenie refused to let him provoke her. "Maybe he just wanted a quick fuck while she was out of town." Jerking her closer, Craig clamped her tightly against his groin. "Did he discover you're just a tease who doesn't put out?" He started to laugh. "Jesus, given the choice, I'd give the hot lawyer one, too!"

Elenie leaned away when he tried to stick his tongue in her ear. "Martinez was a mistake. I should have known better."

She suspected Craig was too hammered to pay any attention but it was worth making the defense. There was no doubt in her mind he would report anything she said straight back to Frank. If he remembered it.

As the song came to an end, Elenie fought her way out of his grasp. "I need to go to the restroom."

"Be my guest!" With a mocking incline of his head, Craig slapped her on the ass and headed back to the bar.

Elenie pushed through the double doors leading out from the conference room, desperate for a little air, craving some space. The lobby was deserted. She considered heading outside but it was late, the night was a cool one, and her dress was ridiculously tiny.

"This way." Roman's voice, as tight and deep as a bass chord, raised instant goosebumps on her skin. He took her elbow and swept her swiftly through another door. In front of them, a flight of stairs stretched upward but he ignored them and turned right into a short corridor. After checking inside, he guided her into a tiny, darkened room and closed the door behind them. It looked as if they'd found themselves in a small office space. Maybe one also used for storage, she wasn't sure.

All of Elenie's focus was on the man in front of her anyway.

Neither of them spoke.

Roman pushed at the shirtsleeves cuffed at his wrists and closed the gap between them. Her breath hitched at the firestorm blazing in his eyes. He was so close she could have run a finger along that narrow scar beneath his jaw. He smelled delicious. Oak and pepper combined with the scent of his skin to send her senses tumbling like dominoes.

"Zena is not my fiancée." Each word was a stone dropped into the puddle of tension.

Elenie wet her lips with her tongue. "She seems to think differently."

Roman dragged a long, ragged breath in and pushed frustrated fingers through his hair. "I didn't plan to bring her. She turned up in my office this afternoon and it seemed like a good idea at the time. I made it clear we're not back together. She just chose not to listen."

Elenie examined his face for a lie. She wanted so much to believe him. "She's everything I'm not."

"Yes, she is."

Wow, that hurt. Elenie closed her eyes for the briefest of moments. When she tried to turn away, Roman reached out to grip her wrist.

"She's judgmental and ruthlessly ambitious. She's not very kind, has zero sense of humor, and she doesn't make my heart beat out of my fucking chest."

He pulled her a step closer with the lightest of pressure. Elenie's knees turned liquid in relief. A gasp caught in her throat at the need etched on his serious face.

"Can I kiss you?" he asked. A battle raged in his eyes.

He was leaving. This was dangerous. It couldn't work. And she didn't care.

All the logical, sensible reasons why he shouldn't disappeared like wisps of smoke on a strong breeze. In this moment, none of them mattered.

Unable to summon proper words, Elenie nodded.

The air quivered around them and a lifetime passed before Roman finally lowered his head, so very slowly, watching her with fierce intensity until the second his mouth met hers. He pressed a gentle kiss to the center of her lips, a low rumble rising from his chest. His touch was warm, the contact feather-light. His fingers trembled. Elenie gave a shuddering sigh, every nerve pathway flooded with a rip current so strong she couldn't fight it. As her mouth parted, his tongue dipped between her teeth. It tangled, smooth and insistent, with her own, and she curled her fingers around his forearms, tighter and tighter. Hands pushing into her hair, he kissed her again and again.

"Finally." Roman growled against her lips. "Fucking finally."

A wave broke over them both and they surged together.

His body slammed into hers, backing her against the door, and she moaned. Sandwiched between the unforgiving wooden surface and Roman's solid muscles, Elenie grabbed a handful of his shirt to keep her afloat. He tasted of lemon and Malbec, the hot sweep of his tongue driving her insane. He was a rigid wall of unstoppable need, trapping her like a car crusher. And Elenie felt herself falling apart. Pieces here, pieces there, breaking off and spinning into the air.

Roman's hands moved from her hair to her neck, sparking lightning shivers over the surface of her skin as they brushed her bare shoulders. His rough fingers skimmed lower, tracing the curves of her body, his mouth an addictive obsession. Reaching her hips, he pulled her even closer, his hardness grinding against her stomach, a groan wrenched from his throat, tendons tight beneath his jawline.

Warmth flooded through her; her skin was on fire. Her fingers gripped the soft strands of hair at the back of his neck and she arched into him, demanding with her hands, offering with her mouth. Roman grasped her thighs, lifting her against him in a fluid, powerful motion, muscles bunching. Elenie fought against the stupid dress. Its body-hugging shape restricted her movements, sequins catching on his clothing. Shoving the hem up and out of the way with a raw curse, Roman wrapped her legs around him.

There was nothing gentle about this kiss. It seized and blazed and feasted and looted. Their need was desperate. The desire explosive.

Elenie had never felt so wanted. The ridge of his cock, pressing against her panties, flooded her with heat. The ache at her center was unbearable. She pulled him even closer with her legs and a growl rumbled deep in his chest. His huge hands, like brands on her bare thighs, lifted her roughly, rubbing her up and down against his erection. He caught her gasp on his lips.

"Oh God—" Roman pulled his mouth away, his chest heaving against her breasts. His face so close to hers that Elenie felt each rasping breath on her lips. Her eyes were unfocused. He held her, still trapped between his heavenly body and the door, and searched her face, his hair wild and tousled by her hands. "I have wanted to do that for so long." The confession was a whisper in her ear. "I've been going quietly out of my mind all night."

Chapter 28
Roman

"I think it might be the stripper dress." Elenie's laugh was wobbly.

He kissed her again because he couldn't help himself. Dipping his head and tasting her soft, open lips, so deliciously warm and wet. Watching her eyelids flutter and close.

"It wouldn't make any difference if you were wearing your uniform. It's not the clothes. It's you."

Roman gentled his touch, worrying he'd already been too rough and knowing he was still dangerously near to tipping over the edge. It made no difference. The passion ignited again, raging in his blood, and his cock throbbed with the need to lay her down and drive into her beautiful, sexy body.

Leaning his forehead against hers, he bit off a curse. "I couldn't watch him mauling you for one more minute. And now, I'm doing the same."

He slowly lowered Elenie to her feet, catching his breath as she slid down his body, rubbing against the parts of him that throbbed. She caught her lip between her teeth, gray eyes fixed on his face as she tugged her dress back into place. The heat in his groin was intense, his hardness flexing against the fly of his pants.

"The difference is that I have been wanting you to touch me. I never dreamed you would feel the same."

Roman's laugh was hollow. "How could I not? You're everything I see when you're near me. You're all I can look at. You've no idea how hard it's been to hold back."

The cautious smile that lit Elenie's face dazzled him. Roman couldn't tear his eyes away. Her body felt like perfection against him, his hands belonged in her hair. He couldn't think of another time when he'd felt this connected to someone else. Even as he pulsed with wanting her, he could have held her like this forever.

Unable to resist, Roman dipped his head to take her lips again. Softly, he nibbled, tasted, and teased. Their tongues danced and flicked, touching and retreating. It was gentle, tender, and nowhere near enough.

"I need to go back." Elenie's voice was unsteady.

Her words were a rock in his chest even though he knew she was right.

Stepping away was torture. Elenie ran her hands over her body, smoothing down her dress, and he wished it was his hands pulling it back up again. Her eyes were luminous and her lips—made for the shadow-light brush of his mouth—velvet-soft and swollen. Roman's muscles bunched beneath his clothes as he fought the urge to grab her and run.

She felt like his. He didn't want to let her go.

With a chokehold on his restraint, he tucked a stray curl behind one of her ears. "You go first. I'll give it some time before I follow." He would need those minutes to get his body back under control. She nodded and turned to open the door. Roman stopped her with a hand on her elbow. "We'll get through this. It'll be OK."

With a tiny quirk of her lips, Elenie slipped through the doorway.

Roman blew out a shaky breath, clenching his fists and his jaw at the thought of her returning to Perry's side. He shouldn't have kissed her. He knew he shouldn't. His professional reserve lay in tatters and Roman couldn't bring himself to give a fuck.

With the need still pulsing through him from the feel of Elenie's body on his, he was prepared to walk through fire for the chance to hold her again. Gathering the shreds of his composure together in a steely grip, he strode back into the conference room, aching, unsettled, and more than a little pissed.

He re-joined his friends, fighting to keep his face neutral, and tried his best to focus on the conversation. And, all the while, Roman cursed his formal outfit, the incessant chatter of his ex-fiancée, and the scruffy hotel.

This wasn't where he wanted to be when he realized how far gone he was over the bewitching woman in the stripper dress.

"We're ready to head out," Milo announced, at last, as the evening began to wind down. "Anyone else?" It turned out to be a popular suggestion.

They had to pass Craig and Elenie to reach the exit. Zena curled her hand around his elbow in an unwanted, possessive move. Roman wished he could remove it with his finger and thumb without looking like an ass. Perched on a stool at the bar, Elenie eyed them as they approached. He could still taste her on his lips.

Perry threw an arm around her shoulders. He gave Caitlyn a cocky smirk as she drew level. "Turns out your mate had no defense against my charm and persistence. Or maybe my money and my body. Who knows!"

He planted a bruising kiss on Elenie's mouth and rage seared the lining of Roman's lungs.

"I've met some pricks in my time but that guy's a fucking cactus," Milo muttered beside him, swooping in to wrap an arm around his wife's waist. "Craig. Elenie." Nodding goodnight, Milo led Caitlyn away before she could form a response.

Thea and Luke followed, Roman and Zena bringing up the rear.

Craig swayed in front of them. "Night, Chief. Take care getting home now."

Roman gave him a tight smile. Zena offered her cheek to the Brit, who kissed it with a flourish like the jerk he was.

"Nice to meet you, Zena. Goodbye, Chief Martinez." Elenie directed the words to the second button down on his shirt. Her smoky gray eyes smoldered as she took in the faint creases she'd left there when she'd crumpled it in her fist.

Roman's pulse thumped in reaction, his throat tightening. A wordless chin lift was all he could manage but it looked suitably dismissive.

They were stopped multiple times on their way to the door. Local residents, all of whom he now knew and recognized, wished him goodnight. Their interest in the woman on his arm grated and he stubbornly refused to introduce her. From beneath heavy brows, he eyed the sagging promotional banner that hung across the foyer. Roman's mouth twitched. The Pine Springs "Local Event of the Year" had been more memorable than he'd expected.

Desperate to be on his own, he managed to brush Zena off with a quick goodnight by the elevator in the lobby. The price he paid was agreeing to meet for a coffee in the morning before she headed back out of town.

Thea gave him grief on the way home. He answered her mainly in grunts, relieved beyond measure to drop her and Luke off at their house.

He hated leaving Elenie with Perry at the hotel; even the peace of his cabin couldn't soothe the raw jealousy in his chest. It was impossible to close a lid on the memory of their kiss. He tried to rebuild the smashed and shattered boundaries but failed completely.

Roman stripped off his suit and crawled into bed, the touch and taste of her torturing his thoughts, scorching his airway. His skin burned like a furnace.

Aching to have her next to him, under him, surrounding him, Roman slid his hand into his shorts. Muscles clenched, sheets rumpled beneath him, he got himself off to the memory of Elenie's scent and the feel of her body against his. He came hard in his hand, on his stomach, chest heaving, and couldn't remember the last time he'd felt so out of control.

* * *

Showered, composed, but irritable, Roman slumped at a table in Mocha Magic. So far, his precious day off was a bomb. He'd done nothing from the moment his eyes opened but rerun the events of the gala dinner.

"Sorry to keep you. Checking out took forever. Apparently preparing a bill for one solitary hotel guest is a challenging concept." Zena draped her jacket over a chair and parked a neat travel bag beside the table leg.

"Coffee?" Roman asked.

"Please. My usual."

There was no line and he returned with her espresso and a mug of tea for himself within minutes.

"So, last night was interesting." Zena gave him a sideways look.

"Right from when you introduced yourself as my fiancée," Roman agreed.

She smiled and shrugged. "I miss wearing the ring. It looked good with my dress."

"The ring is yours. Do what you want with it, but don't tell people we're engaged when we're not."

"You're not even tempted to give us another go?" She seemed curious, rather than upset.

"I don't want to go back to how things were. I'm trying to move forward." He stirred some sugar into his tea.

"Yes, I can tell that."

Roman wasn't biting. His eyes swept the almost empty café. "I don't have long this morning. I've got things to do."

Zena sighed and her demeanor changed. "OK, cards-on-the-table time." She set her cup down. "I'm in a spot of bother at work."

Roman raised an eyebrow. This was unexpected.

"Remember Ben Barrett? I've been seeing him for a while and his wife has heard rumors. Not ideal, as I'm sure you can imagine."

He found himself completely lost for words.

Zena plowed on. "I've told her that you and I are still an item, totally committed, even though you've taken this post for a year. I said we're fine with the whole long-distance thing as it has an end date." Her cool eyes searched his face for a reaction. "I need you to come back for a few work functions to convince her."

"You've got to be fucking kidding me," Roman said eventually.

"I'm not," she assured him.

"So, the whole 'Let's give it another go' thing is a crock of shit?"

"I was just testing the ground. It might have been worth calling time on it with Ben if you—"

He cut across her, his eyes flashing with danger. "How long have you been seeing him?"

Zena gave a sigh, straightening the watch on one narrow wrist. "Does that really matter?"

"Yes, it really does."

She met his eyes with a level stare. "About six months or so."

Roman hissed out a breath between clenched teeth. She was unbelievable.

"Let me get this straight. You were cheating on me before we split with one of the partners at your law firm. One of the married partners at your law firm, who is married to one of the other partners at your law firm?" Zena toyed with the handle of her coffee cup. "And you want me to either forget about this and take you back, or go along with it and pretend we're still dating, so you can convince your married lover's wife—one of the people who sign your fucking paycheck—that you're not sleeping with her husband."

"I've worked hard to get where I am and I don't want to lose my job." She remained completely unruffled.

Roman was reminded of Athena Dax and Elenie's comment that her mother had no moral compass. On the surface, the two women couldn't be more different but, studying Zena with incredulity, he found himself repulsed by the same trait in her.

"Goodbye, Zena." Roman pushed back his chair and stood up.

"Wait—where are you going?"

He fixed her with a disbelieving stare.

"I knew you'd be like this!" She made a sound of frustrated annoyance. "Yes, there was a bit of an overlap in relationships. But it wasn't working for us and we both knew it. Now I need your help, and you'll want to give it to me." Her look was challenging, no hint of an apology in her voice. "Sit down, Roman."

He stood for a moment longer, gathering the fragments of his temper. Though the urge to walk out was strong, he sat back down. Two more minutes. He'd give her two more minutes.

"I'm a smart woman and it was blindingly obvious there were . . . undercurrents . . . last night." Beneath the table, Roman's fist clenched against his thigh. "You disappeared for a while toward the end of the evening. And I couldn't help but notice the sparkly waitress was nowhere to be seen at that point either." Zena's tone dared him to take issue with her avoiding Elenie's name. Roman's face remained blank. "Want to tell me where you were?" He stayed silent while she studied him closely. "Well, you might have nothing to say but I'm sure Craig Perry would be keen to talk it over. I can find out if he's the type to share."

"Like your boss?" Roman bit out.

Zena's eyes glittered. "There's no need, is there? All I want from you is a little help with a tricky situation, in exchange for keeping my nose out of whatever you've got going on in this cultural backwater. And frankly, I'm not that bothered about finding out. But I will if I have to."

"Even if it puts Elenie at risk?"

She raised her eyebrows. "Is it me putting her at risk, Roman? Or is it you? There's a fine line between an ethical relationship and an improper one when you're chief of police."

Roman seethed, weighing up his options. "What do you want, Zena?"

"I told you. I have some work events coming up and I need you to accompany me to them."

"How many events?"

"Let's say three."

Roman tapped his fingers on the side of his empty mug. "I'll go to one with you."

"Two and we have a deal."

"Send me the details."

Roman pushed to his feet. Stalking out of the café, he cursed himself for the signs he'd missed while they were dating.

Chapter 29
Elenie

It had been a long twenty-four hours since the gala dinner, and Elenie craved Roman's dark eyes and serious face with a force that staggered her. She rubbed a palm over her heart as she walked. Sunlight dappled through the trees, spilling onto the track beneath her feet, and the back of her neck grew damp from the heat.

Even as her lips still buzzed from the scrape of his stubble and the pressure of his mouth, she'd read herself the riot act.

Don't be an idiot.

Don't get ridiculous ideas.

Don't think that your life can ever be some kind of crazy-assed fairy tale with a happy ever after.

Yes, he'd kissed her. Yes, they appeared to have a physical connection. A thrilling, stomach-flipping, physical connection. But Roman was in a different league. Even if he wanted her now, she would never be enough to keep him.

Not with Zena hovering in the background.

Elenie didn't believe he'd treat her badly on purpose. Every inch of him seemed honest and genuine. He might consider himself remote, but she found him easy to read. His integrity shone like a beacon. The things he'd seen, the horrors of his work, added faceted layers of gravity that only added to his appeal. He was complicated, wounded, and careful. Not perfect. Just nearly perfect.

It was an unavoidable fact of life that men like Roman dated women like Zena. Not girls who collected facts rather than cosmetics and smelled of waffle batter. Even if he *had* kissed Elenie like he would never get enough. And sent texts that mangled the breath in her chest.

Thea (Roman):

Hey. You there?

> I'm here.

Thea (Roman):

Thinking of how you taste every other second. It's making it hard to get much done.

Maybe that was the fascination of something different. Takeout after fine dining. Or tinkering under the hood of a rusty Jeep with a sleek Corvette in the garage. She'd reread his message a dozen times before she could bring herself to delete it.

The next text he'd sent had brought her here, walking the quiet back road out of town just as Sunday afternoon was turning to early evening. No one had asked where she was going. No one cared. Her stomach rolling nervously, Elenie sauntered, just as she'd been told to.

Lost in her thoughts, the unmarked electric car nearly scared the crap out of her when it pulled up alongside, silent and ominous. The rear window whirred down; a hand inside flicked open and held up an ID wallet.

"Please get in." It was a pleasant voice. Female, melodic.

The appearance of the car, although it had made her jump, was expected. The request, too. Elenie swallowed and took a steadying breath. Fingers and toes tingling, she pulled open the door and slid in.

"I'm DEA Special Agent Faith Dorsey." The agent handed over her ID so Elenie could read it properly. There was a second one with it; she read that too. "Thank you for meeting us."

The driver eyed her shrewdly in the rearview mirror. "Chief Deputy Shawn Booth," he said as the big car pulled away again. "I'm with the County Sheriff's Office."

"There's a turnoff a little further along here. We'll be able to park up and run through a few things." Dorsey turned to face the front and Elenie took a moment to study her.

She guessed the agent's age to be somewhere around mid-to-late forties. Tall and muscular, with a fierce pixie cut so current it made Elenie feel like a scruffy child, she looked firm but approachable.

Booth turned the car onto an unmarked track, drove another couple of hundred yards into an area surrounded by Northern red oaks, and killed the engine. He undid his safety belt and twisted to face them.

Dorsey broke the silence again. "The DEA are pleased to have you on board as a confidential informant. I will be your handler. Although we thought a two-officer approach was best for this initial introduction, in-person meetings will be limited after this to avoid breaking your cover. OK?"

Elenie nodded, her eyes shifting from Dorsey to Booth and back again. She wished Roman was there.

"We need to be convinced of your suitability before it's full steam ahead." Booth's brows were heavy.

Dorsey tapped short fuchsia nails against the paper file on her lap, the pink standing out boldly on sepia fingers. "We will complete a suitability report today and then you'll be issued with a code name and CI number to protect your identity. You'll be given a cell phone with my number and we will speak every third day. If I leave you a message, I expect you to get back to me within twenty-four hours." Dorsey waited for another nod. "Your role will encompass passive observation and active evidence-gathering, so you need to be sure you feel comfortable with that."

"And we need to feel comfortable that you can come up with the goods. In a realistic timeline." Booth again. There was an antagonistic edge to his words. Elenie's eyes flashed to him, then returned to the special agent. Her fingers clenched on her lap.

"Let's get started." Dorsey opened the file.

The registration process took nearly two hours. Multiple times, Elenie wondered what the hell she was doing. There were questions about her personal history, her current knowledge of Frank's criminal activities, colleagues, movements, and as much detail as she could give on past offenses. Dorsey asked about her social life (pretty non-existent) and her connection to Roman Martinez (complicated). Elenie tried to answer as simply and honestly as she could.

As the agent laid out the DEA's expectations and discussed what was needed, Booth pinned her with a stare that reeked of his resistance to her involvement. Elenie's head ached. The nerves she'd been trying to ignore began shredding her intestines. Especially when Dorsey started talking about recording devices and mobile forensic tools, two-party consent and the eavesdropping statute.

This was her life now. She was Elenie Dax, diner waitress and nemesis to the criminal fraternity. She served pancakes and ice cream sundaes, had wrapped her legs around the waist of the local police chief, and was signing up to feed information to the DEA.

What. The. Actual. Hell.

"This wouldn't be happening if Chief Roberts was still in office."

Elenie's hand stilled on the CI Agreement in her lap, pen poised above the signature strip. She looked at Booth. "I'm very glad he isn't, sir."

"Not a fan of yours, is he?" Mistrust coated the statement like buffalo sauce.

She tipped her chin. "That goes both ways."

"I worked with him for years and I had no reason to doubt his views. He served Pine Springs long enough to know his town."

"Sometimes a fresh view gives a clearer picture." Elenie pressed her knees together so neither Booth nor Dorsey would see the tremble.

"Chief Martinez is not involved with this operation. You will not be keeping him in the loop or running to him for backup. Understood? He can pass on information as a last resort and that's it. You say you're friends. He says you're friends. We've taken that under advisement only because this is a small damn town and everyone knows everyone. But you use any personal connection to him in the wrong way and you're out." Booth unwrapped a stick of gum and folded it into his mouth.

Dorsey's calm voice broke in. "Moving forward, we need to trust and depend on each other. It's the only way to ensure your safety. And that is the ultimate goal, above and beyond gathering information."

Booth grunted. "But you're no good to us if you can't nail Frank Dax and his associates. We want results."

"I wouldn't have said I can do it if I didn't think I had a chance." Elenie kept her eyes on Dorsey.

The agent nodded. "I believe you can," she said.

Elenie scrawled her signature across the agreement and handed the papers over. Dorsey held out a cell phone. Honestly, now she was making a collection of them!

Booth met Elenie's eyes in the rearview mirror again and started the car. "In my experience, criminal informants think they're VIPs when really they're just a royal pain in the ass."

* * *

Double life or not, Elenie was back in the diner as usual for her shift the next day. She stacked a tray with the empty glasses, cups, and plates from a recently vacated table, her head all over the place, focus shot to pieces. Fortunately, Diner 43 was all but empty, bar Peggy Winterburn and old Mrs. Elliott who sat chatting together in the far corner.

Placing the tray on the counter, Elenie turned back to the table with a cloth and found Craig leaning against the wall.

"Hey, Ellie." He flashed her a smile of white teeth and empty promises.

"Hi, Craig." As she did every time she'd seen him recently, Elenie compared him to Roman and noted the million ways in which he came up short.

"Looking hot in your uniform, babe. Polo shirts bring me out in a sweat. They remind me of sports and gym skirts at school."

She met his mocking eyes with careful gray ones that hid how many fucks she gave. "I've got stuff to do, Craig. I'll have to chat later."

He caught her arm as she tried to walk past. "I have a couple of business dinners. One on Thursday and one on Saturday. I need you to come with me."

"Oh?"

"They're networking meetings and I could use a date." He grinned. "Fortunately for you, I've chosen to support the underprivileged and blown out everyone else in my little black book."

She looked down at the cloth in her hand so he wouldn't see the roll of her eyes. "Great. Give me the details and let me know the dress code."

Craig pulled her closer and ran a finger along her lower lip. Elenie was tempted to bite it. "It'll be smart during the evening, but you can take off as much as you want afterwards, babe." When she tried to step away from him, his hand gripped tightly enough to leave a mark. "Maybe we should renegotiate our business terms. I'm not sure I'm getting all the benefits I could be."

He walked her backward until she was pressed up against the wall. Trying to avoid his breath in her ear, Elenie smacked the side of her head on a wooden shelf. He was crowding her so closely she could count the hairs in his nostrils. She wished for the luxury to knee him in the balls.

"Dammit, Craig. Were you bullied in those gym classes or something?" Elenie blew the frustrated question through tight lips. "Why do you always have to be such a dick?"

An unexpected shadow flitted across his eyes. It was the first time she'd seen anything approaching vulnerability on his face and it surprised her. Maybe she wasn't so far off the mark.

"I would steer well clear if I were you." Caitlyn's drawl shattered the moment. The redhead had hitched herself up onto one of the stools by the counter. She watched them with her chin on both hands. "It was only recently she was asking me if I thought she should see the doctor with a particularly personal complaint. If you get my drift."

A look of alarm and distaste flashed across Craig's face.

Elenie stifled a snort. "Mind your own business, Caitlyn. The rash is a lot better now. It hardly itches at all."

Craig stepped back, shoving his hands into his pockets. "I have to go. Be ready on Thursday. I'll pick you up at half six." He pushed through the door of the diner like it had personally offended him.

Elenie leaned a tired shoulder against Caitlyn's. "Hot chocolate on the house for my savior?" she offered.

"It's the least you can do," Caitlyn answered, with a twinkle in her eye.

Chapter 30
Roman

"Good timing." The corner of Roman's mouth hitched as they pulled up behind Frank Dax's truck at the stop sign.

He flipped the roof light on and caught Frank's glance in his rearview mirror as it flashed. Both vehicles cleared the intersection and pulled over at the side of the road. He took his time exiting the police car, strolling leisurely to the driver's door of the Dodge. Officer Forsberg followed.

"Mr. Dax."

"Chief Martinez." Dax nodded. "Anything I can help you with?"

"May I see your license?"

Frank Dax dug into the pocket of his jeans, took out a dog-eared wallet and flipped it open, handing over his license without another word. Roman passed it to Officer Forsberg, who walked back to the Interceptor to make the checks.

Leaning toward the window, Roman ran his eyes over the interior of the truck. A tangle of jumper cables lay on the passenger seat, next to a bottle of water and a pack of cigarettes. A thick pair of gloves had been tossed on the floor. The rear of the cab was clear, but one end of a baseball bat stuck out from underneath a discarded sweatshirt in the footwell.

Roman raised an eyebrow.

"I like a knockabout with my boys here and there." Frank followed his gaze. His burly shoulders were relaxed, hands propped casually on the bottom of the steering wheel. "By all accounts, you were quite a player, back in the day. Maybe we'll end up on the same team sometime."

"Stranger things have happened." Roman kept his tone genial, while the non-professional core of his being ached to pull the older man out of the truck through the window. He lifted his eyes from Frank's tattooed knuckles, tore his mind away from the thought of them connecting with Elenie's face. Flames of rage licked low in his stomach. He'd never stop coming after Dax for that alone.

He let the silence draw out before he spoke again. "I had a call from law enforcement in Battle Creek. They pulled over a Grand Cherokee early hours of this morning. Brand-new plates." Roman paused as Officer Forsberg stepped back up to his elbow. He waited for a huge semitruck to rumble by so his words wouldn't get drowned out. "Brand new, but false. The car turned out to be stolen. They took a couple of young guys into custody and your name was mentioned." Frank's expression didn't change. "Any idea why that might be?"

This was nothing more than a fishing expedition. All his colleagues had been able to say was that one of the little shits, not blessed with the sharpest of brains, had let slip Frank's first name before zipping up and refusing to give anything further. The other hadn't said a word. It was nothing to go on, far from conclusive. No hard proof Dax was involved at all. And only the local knowledge of the Battle Creek police had tied the possibility of this particular "Frank's" involvement to the case. The car had likely been stolen to order. Roman suspected it could well be another dirty Dax sideline exposed to the half-light.

"My name?" Frank Dax gave a slow blink.

"Yes."

"I have no idea why that might be, Chief."

"If we look into it, will we find any connection between you and these guys?"

Dax lifted one beefy shoulder. "I know a lot of people."

"Any false plates lying around in your garage?"

"Not last time I looked."

"Maybe I should be the one looking." Roman took Frank's license from Officer Forsberg and tapped it against the palm of his hand.

"I tell you what." Frank's eyes shifted between Roman and Officer Forsberg as the corner of his lips twisted. "You get a warrant and I'll give you a guided tour."

Stalemate. There was no hope of a warrant without more proof. "Seems to fit your remit though. Stolen cars have featured heavily on your rap sheet in the past. You can see why I wanted to have this chat."

"I can, Chief. I'm only sorry I can't help you. Especially since Chief Roberts and I found a way to rub along together just fine."

"Roberts and I have very different priorities." There was a clear warning in Roman's tone.

Frank brushed at a speck of dust on the dash. "Is that all? Only, I have places to be."

Roman nodded, considering his options. They were few. "I won't keep you any longer then, Mr. Dax." He handed Frank back his license and stepped away from the Dodge. "You have a good day now."

Forsberg let out a low growl as Dax pulled away. She tightened her ponytail with jerky fingers. "That guy pisses me off. He seems to come out on top every single time. Pulling him over achieved nothing."

Roman allowed himself a small smile. "Not exactly." They strolled back to the car. "He had to have heard his boys got taken in, but now he knows we don't have any hard evidence he's involved. The more he thinks we're floundering around in the dark, the more invincible he'll feel. And then he'll make mistakes."

"He's not wrong though. We are floundering and he does seem invincible."

"For now, maybe. But his time is coming. I'll look in on Millie Westlake again on Monday. A little space might have given her a different perspective on things."

"Think you can get her to talk?"

"I'll do my damnedest."

He'd be a friendly face, a safe haven, a supportive and nonjudgmental ear. However many regular visits it took to the teenager and her parents, Roman would let the Westlakes know they could trust him. He was convinced Millie held at least one of the cards they needed to scupper Frank Dax's winning streak.

"The guys have been talking, boss." Forsberg angled herself toward him. "Your idea of a no-blame, anonymous Drug and Alcohol Helpline is one we all want to get behind."

"Good." He'd never doubted it but the support of his team was gratifying.

"Everyone wants to sign on for a shift. Maggie, too. We're all happy to be on a rotational standby but I'd like to take the lead on it, if you'll let me."

"It's yours if you want it, Kristina."

"Thanks, boss." Her previous frustration discarded, Forsberg straightened her shoulders. "Maybe we can provide a safety net for the next teenager before they take the leap, rather than afterward."

"That's the idea."

For the ten minutes it took them to return to the station, they discussed how to get the helpline up and running.

Back behind his desk, Roman logged his notes and caught up with the rest of his paperwork. Dougie and Officer Morgan arrived for the late shift, chatting with Maggie on their way through. For a few hours, the open office buzzed with shared jokes, good humor, and teasing. When school finished, the Renner kids appeared. Dougie set one up with a pile of shredding and had the other cleaning windows, slipping them both a cookie from the stash in his desk.

Roman glanced at his watch. After an early start, he was more than ready for a shower and some food, but going home to an empty house wasn't appealing. On impulse, he picked up his phone.

You there?

Elenie:

I'm here.

Any chance you can get away? I'm picking up takeout. I can get enough for two and meet you anywhere you like.

He hadn't seen or talked to Elenie since the gala dinner last weekend. They'd exchanged a couple of brief texts but he needed more details about her meeting with the DEA.

Grabbing his jacket and his keys, he closed his office door, checked with Dougie that there were no last-minute issues, and headed out of the station. As he crossed the parking lot, his phone lit up with a reply from Elenie.

Elenie:

Give me half an hour and I can meet you up at the point off Archer's Road?

Roman's lips lifted. He knew the spot from his teenage years; it was a good place to meet. The track had been a deathtrap for vehicles way back then. He'd ripped a cable out of the transmission case housing on an old Mustang at seventeen. He guessed it could only be worse now and almost definitely secluded.

He made it there in twenty-five minutes, his battered F-150 handling the terrain far better than the patrol car would have. Roman parked halfway up the narrowing track and walked the last part, food tucked under one arm.

Elenie was already waiting, and a small smile lifted her lips as he turned the corner. Her jeans and t-shirt combo bore no resemblance to the glitz of the red dress, but his chest hitched regardless. Damn, she was potent.

An unexpected rightness spread through him. Attraction layered over respect layered over destiny, as if he was walking toward everything that mattered. Elenie, the transmitter, sending an energy pulse that resonated through his every cell, calling him onward.

"Hey."

"Hey."

"No problem getting away?" He raised an eyebrow.

Elenie shook her head. "No sign of the boys. And Frank and my mom were getting ready to go out. They're seeing a movie later. I cut through the woods without touching the road."

Roman nodded. He searched for a response, digging for smooth, reaching for charming, chatty—anything—and came up empty. A thousand unspoken words whirled in the air between them, like a flock of birds, twisting and diving in soundless motion. The gala dinner, their kiss, the touchpaper that smoldered between them, impossible to extinguish, threatening to blaze. He wanted to reach for her but stopped himself. Wanted to tell her how much she'd been on his mind but didn't know how to begin.

Instead, he smiled again. She smiled again. And it was enough.

The food smelled good when Roman unwrapped it. He was starving. They tucked into the tacos with greedy delight. The pork belly was juicy; the salsa and slaw made for messy eating but it was delicious. Any awkwardness disappeared. Elenie shot Roman a sideways glance and grinned.

He made sure he didn't have sauce on his chin. "I don't know what you're laughing at. Most of your filling is in the bottom of the carton. At least I'm getting mine in my mouth."

Her eyes flicked to his lips and the tiny movement was incendiary. Roman's dick twitched in his pants. He shifted slightly, smothering a curse under his breath. She was pure temptation. And the pull between them seemed to grow stronger every time he saw her.

It was impossible to chat while they ate but Roman asked about Elenie's meeting with the DEA once they'd finished up.

"Don't give me any details, but did you feel comfortable? Did they explain everything you needed to know?" He'd had his own dealings with CIs before now and knew the fine balance of the relationship well.

Elenie shuffled her feet. "The DEA agent was fine."

Roman frowned as he wiped his hands. "Who else was there?"

"Chief Deputy Shawn Booth. From the Sheriff's Office."

"Damn. Yeah, he seems a bit of a hardass. Did he give you a tough time?"

"No, he just made it clear he wasn't one hundred percent on board with the whole thing." Elenie picked at the grass. "It'll be fine. Special Agent Dorsey was nice."

It was so damn frustrating being outside of the loop. He wanted to quiz her further, make her tell him everything from start to finish—especially whatever it was that weighted her words with reserve—and yet he knew he couldn't. "If you're having second thoughts—"

"I'm not. It was just a lot to take in. And it feels kind of unreal now I need to actually get started. But I'm committed. I'm ready. I just need to work on the way Frank views me and I'll have more chance to wiggle back into the trusted circle."

"I've got a plan to help you there."

He talked her through it. She was nodding before he finished.

"Yes. That's just what I need. I can carry that off." There was wicked determination in the smile that inched across her lips.

Pride bloomed beneath his skin. She was so fucking impressive. Roman had to look away before she saw something on his face neither of them was ready for. His hand had a mind of its own, though. It covered Elenie's, long fingers closing around hers. Her skin, so much paler than his own, was soft and warm. A breeze sent the leaves above them rustling. He felt her eyes on his face even without turning.

"How are you feeling?" she asked. "Have you been sleeping any better?"

"I have." He squinted sideways at her. "Getting it off my chest helped a lot. And I've had other things to think about when I go to bed."

Elenie colored, studying her Converse with concentration. "I'm glad." Her voice was husky. "About the sleeping."

"Not the thinking?"

"That too." Her flush deepened, but she was smiling. "Dean told me you stopped Frank this morning."

Roman let her change the subject. "We did. I won't lighten up on him from my side, Elenie." If anything, he'd be doubling down on his efforts, doing anything and everything he could think of to bring an end to the vulnerable position she was in as a CI. "This isn't all on you. I'll keep digging, keep nudging, keep asking questions. And I don't give a fuck if he thinks he's untouchable. No one is."

Elenie chewed on her thumbnail, shadows in her eyes. "He might not be untouchable but he is vicious when he's crossed. You should be careful."

"I've come up against worse." Roman's smile was dangerous. "Maybe he's the one who should be careful."

Chapter 31
Elenie

The house was in darkness when she got home, the driveway clear of cars. Her heart rate quickened as she walked up the path and turned her key in the lock. She'd known before meeting Roman that a potentially empty house was too good an opportunity to waste.

"Hey?" Elenie flicked on the light. "Ty? Dean?"

There was no answer. Still, she went room to room through every part of the house to make sure everyone was out. She even traipsed out back to the garage, just to check, finding all the lights off and the heavy chain locked through the door handles.

Back inside, mouth dry and palms sweaty, Elenie ran through the possibilities open to her. Frank's phone was a non-starter. It'd be in his pocket right now; he never left it at home. And the key to the padlock on the garage doors would be on Frank's keyring, also in his pocket. That left a search of the house for money, drugs, or his laptop.

A quick glance around the living room told her his laptop wasn't there. Elenie headed swiftly upstairs to the main bedroom, careful as always to avoid the most worn treads where the gaps in the carpet liked to snag unwary toes. Neither her mother nor Frank had made the bed. The air smelled faintly of cigarettes and dirty laundry, with a touch of her mom's perfume thrown in, the partly open window helping to disperse anything more pungent. Elenie let the bulb on the landing illuminate the room, so no one pulling up in the driveway would see a light on in the bedroom.

Again, there was no laptop. In Frank's nightstand, all she found were cigarettes, empty gum packets, a handful of loose change, three disposable lighters, and a strip of condoms which made her gag a little. Elenie slid a clumsy hand beneath the drawer, thinking of hidden compartments or taped paperwork, but there was nothing. Of course. Because her life wasn't actually a TV show, even if it felt like one.

She flinched at the sharp snap when she closed the drawer harder than she'd meant to.

Inside the closet, she went through the pockets of Frank's jackets and pants. Balled-up receipts for gas, more loose change. His clothes were surprisingly tidy. Her mother's, not so much. Elenie bent down to look under the bed and grimaced at the layers of dust covering the carpet. One sock, discarded and forgotten, lay like a dead mouse a couple of feet in. She crooked her neck to scan the underside of the wired bedframe and mattress. No bundles of drugs, no wrapped wedges of cash. Frank wouldn't be making this easy for her.

"Dammit."

She tapped her way carefully around the bedroom floor, checking for loose boards, and dug her fingers gingerly into the edges of the carpet to see if it came away easily at any point along the walls or in the corners.

Elenie checked Athena's nightstand, her dresser, and even inside the pendant lightshade in the center of the room. And all the while, her chest grew tighter and her palms damper; the silence screamed in her ears. She was drawing a blank.

Where else could she look?

A set of headlights dipped and bobbed their way up the drive, casting moving shadows on the bedroom wall. Elenie ducked instinctively, bending at the waist, and slid across the carpet on silent feet.

By the time Tyson and Dean crashed in through the front door, she had made it to the safety of her own room, beads of sweat drying on the back of her neck. As her pulse slowly settled, she pulled open her closet. When Dean passed her door five minutes later, he found Elenie studying her limited outfit choices for her date with Craig the following night.

* * *

At least this time most of the company was pleasant and the food was excellent.

Elenie smiled across the table at June Reed Sanders—a smart woman in her late thirties who managed to be funny, glamorous, clearly ambitious, and yet friendly at the same time. Her husband, Owen, reminded Elenie in many ways of Roman, with a calm and dependable air that was enormously appealing. She loved the affectionate touches they shared without embarrassment as the evening wore on.

"I'm time-poor at the moment while I get my current project onto a more secure footing," June told them.

"Doesn't stop her looking for anything that will pay more cents on the dollar than tucking money away in the bank." Owen's words were dry but full of humor, as he squeezed his wife's hand on top of the tablecloth.

Craig continued the smooth spiel Elenie was familiar with by now, intent on encouraging June's investment into an overseas project currently at the drawing-board stage. Or so he said.

Elenie knew for a fact there was little chance of the scheme ever getting off the ground. Craig had told her so himself. He laughed at what he called the "easy targets," looking to boost their property portfolios, who would fall over themselves to invest once he rolled out some slick marketing ploys and inflated profit projections. Expecting him to be a miserable but necessary distraction while she gathered dirt on Frank, Elenie had been side-swiped by the extent of Craig's brazen scams. Now it looked like she might end up with a catalogue of damning information against the property developer as well.

Despite Craig's arm stretched across the back of her chair, they didn't give off the convincing vibe of a loving couple. Anytime he got close to touching her, Elenie couldn't stop herself from moving away, the quiet force of one magnet being repelled by another. And she felt the irritation coming off Craig in waves whenever she did.

He wanted her to back him up. Not have any opinions— oh, Lord no. But she was supposed to chirp in with positive reinforcements to echo what he was saying, give brief anecdotes to support his trustworthiness, build him up to June and Owen, just like he'd told her to build him up at the previous dinner he'd dragged her along to. The problem tonight was that she really liked this couple and she had no intention of selling them down the river for Craig's benefit. She just needed an opportunity to give them a heads-up.

Elenie studied June and Owen across the table and tried to read their thoughts. June's eyes met hers for a second. There was calculated interest in the look they shared.

"If you could live a different life, Elenie, what would you choose?" Owen's question drew her attention back to the table. Craig let out a stifled laugh but wiped it from his face when he saw the other couple were genuinely interested.

Wow. She hadn't seen that one coming.

A kaleidoscope of images and sensations assaulted her, none of which Elenie could share. Even if she wanted to.

Roman. The serious version, the tortured version, the sexy, smiling, stunning version. Every different Roman there was. The press of his body, the band of his arms. The desperation in his kisses. The laughter in his parents' home. His mother's hug. Thea's kindness. Summer and Caitlyn's friendship and all the fun it brought with it.

Elenie's heart squeezed so hard she almost doubled over.

Love. She'd choose love every time. And Roman Martinez.

"Good question." She took a sip of her drink because her throat felt raw. It bought her a little time to think. "Cowgirl or trapeze artist, maybe. It's hard to choose between them."

Owen chuckled.

"Did you know you can scoop up water in a Stetson hat?" Elenie reached for a random fact. "They're designed to keep out the weather, but with the side benefit of being able to water your horse as well."

The conversation confused Craig. "I didn't know you could ride."

"Well, no. I can't exactly. I've never had a chance to try."

"So maybe the trapeze artist might be a better fit?" June suggested.

"Possibly. It might not make me rich, but what a buzz."

"Money isn't as important as following your dreams." June was laughing. "You wouldn't get me on a trapeze, but I'll come and watch the show if you make it to the big time."

Craig couldn't hide his impatience. "Luckily, money does make me happy. And it makes me even happier when I'm making it for other people, too." He waved a waiter over with a commanding gesture. "More wine, June? Owen?"

"Actually, if you'll excuse me a moment, I need to go to the restroom and then I think it might be time for us to call it a night." June gave Owen one of those looks true couples had perfected. And Elenie missed Roman even more.

"I'll come too." She pushed away from the table.

"Women, huh?" Craig rolled his eyes at Owen. "Terrified of a little alone time, even when they need to pee." When he laughed, he laughed on his own.

Fortunately, they turned out to be the only two people in the restroom.

"So, how long have you known Craig?" June's question was polite but her eyes were shrewd.

Acutely aware there was only limited time, Elenie rinsed her hands in one of the washbasins and chose to leap straight in. "Look, Craig's a dick. I know it and I think you know it. Please don't give him any of your money and please, please don't tell him I asked you not to." She drew in a deep breath.

The mirror reflected June's surprise. "Well, I did not expect that."

"I think you did, maybe just a little?"

"You seem an unlikely couple."

Elenie made a face. "We're not really a couple. Not a proper one like you and Owen." She smiled tentatively at June. "I really like you both. And I'd hate it if you got caught up in something I had the knowledge to save you from."

June tipped her head to one side. "And you? Are you caught up in this, too?"

"Right now I am. Unfortunately. But I have people looking out for me, like I want to look out for you. This business deal Craig's offering isn't genuine. Please save your money and don't get involved with him."

"OK, I believe you." June didn't take long to think about it. "I wasn't getting a good feeling from Mr. Perry. I would have looked into his project in a lot more depth before deciding but he isn't someone I'd be keen to invest with. I'd be surprised if Owen doesn't think the same."

"I'm so glad to hear that."

"I take it you can't give me more details?"

"I don't think I should right now. And we'd better not be too much longer. Although I'd rather chat with you than go back to the table."

June studied her face. She seemed to be weighing up everything Elenie had said, plus everything she hadn't.

"Would it help," June suggested, "if I led Craig to believe I was interested in taking this further? Maybe I could ask him for more information, which might be useful to you in the long run."

"Oh, God, yes! That would be great, if you could. I know someone you could forward it to. He's one hundred percent dependable but I can get him to contact you to give you any reassurance you need. He's in law enforcement."

"And your face lights up when you talk about him. How interesting!" June smiled and Elenie fidgeted. "Right, here's my card. Text me or call me so I have your number and let me know how to contact this man of yours. If I can help you, I will." Elenie took June's business card and was surprised to be pulled in for a tight hug. "Thanks for the warning. I think it was a brave thing for you to do." June reached for the door handle. "I don't like the way he talks to you, Elenie. I hope whatever you're mixed up in comes to an end soon. Craig Perry is not a good man for you to be around."

The faintest of frowns tugging at one of Owen's immaculate eyebrows told Elenie he'd had enough of Craig's hard sell while they'd been gone. June was smooth and unruffled when she declared that she had a lot to consider but would be in touch shortly. They stood to say their goodbyes.

Imagining a done deal, Craig missed June's outstretched hand and turned instead to clap Owen on the back, oblivious to the other man's wince. "Let's leave the ladies to their shopping or spa dates next time and hit the golf course, shall we? My treat."

Owen didn't give him an answer, just a tight smile as he reached for his wife's hand. "Elenie, it's been lovely to meet you." He bent to kiss her on the cheek.

"Likewise," she told him. "I hope I see you again."

"I think you will," June murmured into her ear as they embraced. The couple left the restaurant hand in hand.

"Suckers." Craig slipped on his jacket and called for the check. He drained the last drops of wine in his glass, shooting Elenie a smug look. "That was a good move. Two couples having dinner together is the perfect cover for a soft sell. Puts a woman more at ease than negotiating in a boardroom."

Sure. She suppressed a smile as he paid with his card and they got up to leave. She'd bet good money it would take more than a conference table to intimidate June. The fact that Craig couldn't see it only emphasized his density.

"Elenie?" The crystal-clear call brought her to a halt just shy of the main doors to the restaurant.

Ava and Elias Martinez sat at one end of a buzzing table of six. Gold and black "happy birthday" balloons danced above their heads, an air of celebration surrounding the group they dined with. A delighted smile lighting her face, Ava stood to wrap Elenie's stiff body in a hug. Elias waved his glass in her direction to excuse not being able to reach her.

"What a surprise to see you out of town! Isn't this a fabulous place? Our lovely friend at the end of the table has reached a grand old age that shall remain a secret and we are helping him forget." Ava's joyous chuckle was echoed by the rest of the group.

"Damn cheek!" A bearded giant of a man shook his head in mock rebuke.

Roman's mother wore a silky turquoise dress with large diamond teardrops in her ears. She shimmered like a kingfisher, luminous in the muted light of the restaurant.

"What are you doing here?" Ava's eyes travelled between Elenie and Craig and back again.

Elenie cleared her throat nervously. Beside her, Craig gave an impatient huff as he pulled his phone out of his pocket to check the time. "Um, we had a business meeting. That is, Craig had a business meeting. He's a friend—"

"Good to meet you, but we were just heading out." Craig slid an arm around her waist and tugged. He barely looked at Roman's mother. "Come on, Ellie. Let's go."

Afraid Ava would mention Roman's name, Elenie willed her with her eyes and a tiny shake of her head not to say anything more, her heart racing like a train. A restrained expression drifted across Ava's face. It made Elenie want to cry.

"Well, it was nice to see you, anyway." Her voice was noticeably cooler, carrying shades of their first meeting.

"Enjoy your evening." Elenie forced a smile and allowed herself to be swept onward by Craig, Ava's eyes following them all the way to the door.

As they stepped out onto the sidewalk, she braced herself for an inquisition.

"Fucking hell, it's raining," Craig griped. He shoved his hands into his jacket pockets and hunched his shoulders. "Hurry up, babe, or the car seats will be soaked."

He set off without waiting to see if she followed.

Elenie breathed easier, realizing the moment with Roman's parents had barely been a blip on his radar. But, picturing the disappointed look on Ava's face, she felt sick all the way home.

Chapter 32
Roman

A knock on his front door before eight o'clock on a Sunday morning was a rare thing.

Roman pulled a t-shirt from one of his drawers and tugged it over his head as he jogged down the stairs. Flipping the latch on the inside of the door, he gave it a hard pull, making yet another mental note to sort out the swollen frame when he next got some free time. He did a double take when he found Elenie standing on the front porch.

She gave an awkward wave, lips lifting briefly. "Hi."

"Elenie." Fireworks burst in his chest; a smile tugged at his mouth. "This is unexpected." He cursed himself when she took a step back, hands plucking at the pockets of her jeans, gray eyes huge, uncomfortable, and defensive again.

"I'm really sorry."

"No, no—come in!" He stood back, opening the door wide. When she hesitated, he took a gamble and walked away from her, heading for the kitchen. "Give the door a hard shove," he called over his shoulder. "It sticks a bit."

He didn't hear the sound of the door closing until after he'd filled the kettle and placed it on the stovetop. Roman allowed himself another small smile.

"How d'you get here?" he asked when Elenie finally appeared in the doorway.

The taste of her skin was as clear on his lips as it had been every day since the gala dinner, the urge to kiss her again almost overwhelming. Roman's muscles tightened, need burning low in his stomach. Smothering it all, he turned to open a cupboard.

"Tea or coffee?" He held up a mug, his voice a little rough.

"Coffee, please." She took a step into the kitchen and stopped again. "I, uh, walked. Here, I mean. This morning."

Elenie looked around. Her face softened as her eyes darted from place to place. Roman followed her gaze. The open-plan kitchen and living area was fairly tidy. He allowed himself a moment of relief that he'd done the dishes last night and hadn't left any clothes tossed over the couch. He'd picked up some more furniture recently. Seeing the place through her eyes made him realize how much he had settled in.

She only walked the rest of the way into the kitchen when he placed a steaming mug of coffee on the counter and pushed it toward her. Rather than pick it up immediately, she fiddled with the handle.

"Must have taken you a while to get here."

"I hope you don't mind?" Her eyes flicked to his face.

"I'll be honest, it's the best start to my day I can remember having." She took a few sips of coffee and Roman saw her shoulders relax slightly; he felt like he'd won a prize. He'd never been someone to wear his heart on his sleeve but he was willing to say whatever was needed to put Elenie at ease. "Why did you come?"

She cringed. "I went to a business dinner with Craig last night."

Jealousy kicked him swiftly in the balls. "Oh?"

"We met another couple at a restaurant in Kalamazoo. Your parents were there."

Roman lowered his mug to the counter. "Ah."

Elenie paced across to the huge window that almost filled one wall of the sitting area. She looked out at the tall trees for a moment, then turned back to face him, leaning against the glass. "I didn't see them until we left. Your mother spotted me as we walked out and I couldn't avoid speaking to her. Craig had his hand on my waist—it was so obvious we were there together." Mortification colored her cheekbones. "I'm used to people thinking badly of me, I really am. It's something I try to ignore."

She crossed the floor to straighten his radio on the countertop and then moved again to the coffee table, bending down to look at the back of the thriller he was halfway through. Roman followed, taking a seat on the couch, his elbows on his knees. Elenie ran her hand back and forth along the velvety back of the armchair.

"But your mother looked like I'd disappointed her and I can't bear it. As if anyone would ever choose that *dummkopf*5 instead of you."

Roman's heart turned over with a thump. "It's OK."

"It's not OK!" She pushed away from the chair. "They were so kind to me when I was there for lunch and now they'll be thinking I'm this shitty person who is out with a different guy every day of the week."

"Hey, stop." Roman stood up and reached for her elbows, wanting to reassure her, wanting to touch her. It was impossible not to compare her obvious distress with Zena's calculating deception.

Elenie frowned, eyebrows knitting. She chewed on her lip. His eyes dropped to her mouth and he was lost.

Slowly, gently, he kissed her. Her breath shuddered on his tongue and his body clenched with need. She let out a soft moan, heating his blood with the sound. He pulled her closer, hands sliding around the small of her back. She was so slight, so delicate. When she raised herself on her tiptoes, pressing her palms against

---

5   Dummkopf (moron)—German

his chest, he caught his breath. The feel of her sliding against his groin set him on fire.

"Oh, sweetheart." He whispered the words against her mouth.

Elenie's fingers skated tentatively upward to twist in his hair as they tasted each other. His tongue dipped between her lips, the warmth welcoming him, enticing him further. Soft and delicious. She tasted of coffee. The scent of fresh air and grapefruit in her curls filled his nose. Hunger burned and spread under his skin. Roman had never wanted anyone so much.

His hands found her bare waist under the hem of her t-shirt and he breathed a groan into her mouth. His fingers inched higher, stroking her skin, brushing the fabric of her bra. Her breasts teased him, inviting his hands to cover them and his mouth to explore them. A tremor rippled his stomach muscles as he forced himself to hold back.

"You taste so good," Roman rasped against the curve of her neck. She shivered and the sensation set off an answering pulse in his cock. An electrical current travelled up his spine. "Fuck, you drive me wild."

Somewhere in the back of his mind, he knew he was due at work. Talking would be more sensible, with the few opportunities they had. But he couldn't move away from her to save his life. Couldn't focus on anything other than the feel of her skin and the heat in his blood. He'd thought nothing would be able to top the first time they had touched, in the back room at the Elite Lodge Hotel.

This embrace, this kiss, blew his mind.

With an iron will that made his hands shake, Roman kept his touch gentle and lost himself in her lips.

Chapter 33
Elenie

Roman's body was unreal. His tall frame, the firm muscles, his arms—dear God, his arms. She wanted to grip them, stroke them, lick them. They were ripped and defined. Elenie loved them. She was officially an arm freak. Arm-obsessed.

Why had she never realized how sexy arms could be?

Maybe because she'd never closed her fingers around the taut, tanned biceps of Roman Martinez before.

And as for his chest—

Elenie's mind had become a fickle thing. Every part of him she touched, every sculpted ridge she stroked was her new favorite place. She was torn between pressing into him and needing enough space to run her hands everywhere. Never had she felt this desire to explore someone's body so thoroughly. She wanted to map him out and memorize him. Hours could pass and she would never tire of kissing Roman.

Elenie pushed her hips into his hardness and he uttered a broken curse into her mouth, his hands clenching in her hair. She could feel every inch of him straining against the zipper of his pants. A pool of need centered between her legs and she ground into him again.

Roman tore his mouth from her lips. "God, Elenie, we have to stop this." His voice was hoarse. She raised glazed eyes to his beautiful face. Roman's eyes were almost black, his hair ruffled by her fingers. "I want to take you to bed so badly." Her stomach flipped and leaped with desire, lips parted and swollen. "And you looking at me like that doesn't help." Roman's words were wry, his mouth lifted at one corner in the way she adored the most, his chest heaving as if he'd just completed an assault course. He gave another pained groan as he took a small step away from her. "I'm on shift today. I need to head to the station."

"Yes, of course." Elenie straightened her t-shirt. "I'm sorry."

"Are you? I'm not." Roman fingered a strand of her hair. The look on his face stole her breath again. "I've thought about kissing you more times than I can count in the last couple of weeks. And I don't think that'll stop anytime soon." All of Elenie's words, in every language, deserted her. He bent to collect their mugs from the coffee table. "The only thing I'm sorry about is that I have to go now."

Roman smiled at her and she almost melted like cheese on a griddle. He ran a hand through his hair to smooth it but only rumpled it more. Watching him as he rinsed the mugs, Elenie wanted to throw herself at his back and cling onto him like a koala.

"Let me grab my shirt and I'll drop you wherever you want on my way to work."

She heard him taking the stairs two by two and leaned against an armchair, inhaling her first full breath in what felt like a lifetime. He was back in less than a minute, buttoning his uniform as he strode into the room. She hadn't moved a muscle. His presence was magnetic, drawing her eyes and making it impossible to look away.

"What are you doing today? Got any plans?" Roman's voice still sounded husky.

Elenie shook her head, dumbly.

He paused as he tucked in his shirt. "Stay here." It was part command, part invitation. "Please. I'll only be at the station until two. I can come straight back afterward. And we could go and see my parents after that." He reached her side in three strides. "If you haven't anywhere else to be, I'd love you to make yourself at home here." Roman gently cupped her chin in his hand. His fingers trembled just a little. "I've wanted you in my house so many times." He dipped his head and pressed a kiss on the corner of her mouth.

Elenie clenched her fists to stop herself from grabbing a handful of his neatly ironed shirt. "I can stay."

She nodded. Roman nodded. For a while, they both forgot to stop.

"What I wouldn't give not to be rushing out and leaving you alone." He spoke the words against her hair. Rubbed his cheek on her temple, sighed, and stepped away. "I'll be back as soon as I can." He opened one of the kitchen drawers and placed a key on the countertop. "That's a spare," he told her. "Keep it and lock up if you need to go for any reason. Otherwise, I'll see you soon. Don't worry about my parents—we'll fix it."

Elenie heard him lift his own keys from a table in the entryway. Roman gave the sticky door a hard pull, slammed it behind him, and was gone. His truck fired up and, minutes later, the engine faded away, leaving nothing but silence behind. She sank down onto the couch and blew out a shaky breath. Her thoughts were scattered, her body tingling. Minutes passed and she looked around.

Roman's cabin was filled with light. It flooded into the living room and kitchen through enormous windows and bounced off the warm timber walls. The leaves on the tall pine trees outside filtered the watery sunshine into broken dapples which lay on the wooden floor like pebbles at the bottom of a stream. There was no sound at all. It was like being wrapped up in a blanket of peace.

Her house was never like this. Even when no one was home, the atmosphere felt strained and unwelcoming. On her guard the minute she opened the front door, she never knew what she was walking into.

Elenie wandered a circuit of the living room. She trailed her fingers along a bookshelf that ran either side of the fireplace. Nonfiction and true crime took up most of the space, sitting alongside thrillers, some autobiographies, and the odd tattered classic. It looked as if he'd brought all his books with him even if this was just a temporary move.

Roman had no ornaments—or "dust-catchers" as Otto called them—but the few pieces of furniture in the room were well chosen, colorful, and solid. A big blue lamp stood on a wooden sideboard and a rust-red rug covered most of the floor beneath the couch. It was a very comfortable space.

Elenie couldn't get over the fact that he trusted her enough to let her stay. He'd left her a key, as if she was someone special, from a regular family. He hadn't thought twice about it. Every single other person in town would assume she'd rob them blind. He saw her, he knew her. And it made her want to cry.

Tempted to curl up with one of Roman's books, another idea hit her instead. Elenie rummaged through a couple of cupboards in the kitchen and took a peek inside the surprisingly well-stocked fridge. With a quick evaluation of her finds, she narrowed down the options, giving a triumphant cry when she found three fresh lemons in the fruit bowl.

Half an hour later, Elenie placed a lemon pound cake into the oven to cook in a loaf pan she'd unearthed from the back of one of Roman's cupboards. If it came out looking halfway decent, she would at least have a peace offering to take to Ava and Elias later. She cleaned up, wiped down the countertops, and made herself another cup of coffee. When Elenie realized she was smiling, she gave a little laugh and shimmied across the kitchen to grab the milk from the fridge. This was the best Sunday she could remember in forever.

With the cake baking in the oven, Elenie picked up the book Roman had left open on the coffee table, broken spine and all—the horror. Curling up at one end of the couch, she read quietly for the next hour until the kitchen was filled with a wonderful smell and the lemon cake sat cooling on the counter.

Worried about overstepping but needing to find a bathroom, Elenie headed for the stairs. At the top of the landing, she found two doors opposite one another; both were ajar. Pushing open the one to her left, she discovered a compact bathroom that was almost entirely taken up with the most jaw-dropping shower she'd ever seen. The faint scent of Roman's shampoo or shower gel lingered in the air. An involuntary moan escaped her at the thought of standing under the huge showerhead with a steady stream of hot water raining down on her body.

Lucky, lucky Roman. And lucky, lucky shower to get to wash Roman's muscular frame clean.

Elenie used the toilet quickly, washed her hands, and stepped back out onto the landing. Giving in to curiosity, she gently pushed open the second door.

Roman's bedroom was simple. A large bed made up with moss green linen sat against one wall, covers pulled roughly into place. Next to it was a small mahogany nightstand with a lamp on top. There was a dresser, a tall, old wardrobe, a long mirror, and that was it.

Two glazed doors made up most of the wall at the far end of the room. They opened onto a small balcony, with the woods stretching out beyond. Transfixed, she crossed the room, pressed her hands against the glass, and gave a sigh. Sleeping in here would feel like being in a treehouse. The view was heavenly. She hoped the woodland setting had been a comfort during those nights when Roman's sleep was broken.

Turning to leave, Elenie paused by the bed. With a hesitant glance toward the door, she sat down gently on the edge of the mattress, her hand drifting over one of the pillows. She leaned down and inhaled. The linen smelled of Roman; Elenie would recognize his scent anywhere. Picking up the pillow, she buried her face in it. Her blood fizzed in her veins.

I've officially lost it.

I'm a freaky, odor-obsessed lunatic who should be locked up.

He needs protecting from me.

Hit with a wave of exhaustion and unwilling to let go of the pillow, Elenie curled up on the very edge of the bed, hugging the feathery softness against her chest.

She would lie there for just a few minutes and Roman would never know.

Chapter 34
Roman

"Just like Goldilocks," Roman murmured to himself from the doorway.

Unable to concentrate on paperwork and with nothing else needing his attention—not even a littering offense to write up—he had closed the station soon after midday. People could call him if they needed to. Driving home, he found himself praying Elenie would still be there. He was jittery, buzzing; anticipation tingled in his bloodstream.

The smell of baking greeted him the moment he opened the door, and the cake sitting on the side in his kitchen brought a smile to his face. A big, wide grin he'd used so rarely in the past few years that it felt rusty. The house was quiet. An empty mug on the coffee table, her sneakers on the rug, and his book on the arm of the couch had the muscles at the back of his neck easing.

And now, here she was.

Her hair lay in a cloud around her head, her skin pale against the rumpled sheets, face as relaxed as he'd ever seen it. Her lips were slightly parted, her arms wrapped around one of his pillows. Roman moved closer. He couldn't help himself. He could hear his own heartbeat as he sat down on the edge of the bed.

Elenie stirred and turned toward him. A curl fell across one eye, catching on her dark lashes. It must have tickled her nose because she twitched; a frown creased her brow. He caught hold of the stray strand and lifted it away from her face. It slid through his fingers.

Barely breathing, heart full, Roman placed his palm against Elenie's cheekbone. She gave a small sigh and turned her head into his hand. Her drowsy gray eyes opened slowly. Roman felt the punch of them in his groin.

"I fell asleep."

"It would appear so." His own words emerged as a husky rumble.

A flush broke over her face. "Oh, God, it can't be after two o'clock already! I'm so sorry—I honestly wasn't snooping. I came up to find the bathroom."

"Don't worry. It's not even one yet. The station was dead and for some reason I was keen to get home."

Elenie's eyes slid away from him. "I just—I didn't sleep well last night and your house is so peaceful. You said to make myself at home . . ." She trailed off.

"So really it's my fault that you couldn't resist my bed."

She gave a tiny snort and scrubbed her face. "One hundred percent. You lured me here with your upstairs bathroom and your woodland silence and then I could swear your soft, soft quilt cried out, 'Lie here, just for a minute, you weird snooper!'" She flashed him an awkward grin.

Roman shrugged and held out his hands. "Honestly, what's a girl to do, huh?"

"I was powerless." Elenie slid past him and stood up. Pacing over to the double doors, she looked out at the trees. "This view is unreal. I could look at it forever." She clasped both hands above her head and gave a feline stretch.

In an instant, he lost all power of thought as the blood raced south to his cock.

"Unreal," he echoed, his eyes fixed on the sliver of bare skin between the waistband of her jeans and the hem of her t-shirt. He knew how it would feel under his fingers, how silken she would be against his rough hands.

The thump of Roman's heart beat a pulse in his throat and he wasn't even sure if Elenie had spoken again. How did she do this to him? How could she take all the strength from his legs without being aware of the effect she had on him?

To prove to himself that he could move, he pushed up from the bed and walked to the window. Pausing behind her, Roman caught Elenie's eyes in the faint reflection in the glass. His own burned with an intensity that would have surprised him if he hadn't already been aware of the fire blazing through his body. She was still, shoulders slightly tense. And though his stomach trembled with the effort it took him to hold back, Roman lifted gentle hands to trace down the outsides of her arms.

"I think I could look at you forever," he said to her reflection, voice low and gruff. "But maybe we should head downstairs and put a little distance between us and my soft, soft bed." He forced a wry smile onto his lips, hoping to God there would be another time when she might want to visit his room.

She turned slowly from the window. Her eyes searched his face. He didn't know if she found what she was looking for. Each breath dragged from Roman's chest. Elenie took a step nearer.

"Do you know what I think?" she asked.

Her hands fluttered slightly as if to reach for him, and his muscles clenched in anticipation of her touch. It was all he could do not to lean into her.

Roman shook his head. "What do you think?"

"I think that maybe we're wearing too many clothes."

Chapter 35
Elenie

She wasn't sure where she found the words that hung in the air between them. Couldn't believe she'd let them escape. But her need for him was so huge and his care for her feelings so breathtaking, they'd fallen naturally from her mouth. Her doubts dissolved. Her common sense evaporated. She knew he wanted her. And her body was burning up from his heat.

She wanted this. Even if it was just once. Even if there was nowhere for it to go.

Roman drew in an audible breath and closed his eyes. "Elenie, you don't—"

She interrupted him, stepping closer, wrapping her arms around his waist and leaning her cheek against his chest. "I do. I want to. I want you." Roman's erection pulsed against her navel and her body tightened in reflex, straining toward him. She couldn't get close enough. His arms went around her like a vise. For a moment, there was no sound other than their labored breathing. "I want this so much."

"You have no idea," his voice rumbled against her ear, "how desperately I have wanted to hear you say that."

Elenie lifted her chin and pressed a kiss at the base of his neck, where he'd undone the top button of his uniform. Roman swallowed; his pulse juddered beneath her lips. Remembering how she'd looked at his throat from across the table at the gala dinner, she marveled at this opportunity to fulfil what she'd thought of as a hopeless fantasy and dotted more soft kisses on every part of his neck she could reach. He stood frozen beneath her hands and her mouth.

"Elenie—" Roman's voice was hoarse.

"You smell so good," she murmured. "It's why I ended up on your bed earlier. You smell amazing and your sheets smell of you. I think I'm addicted."

The sound he made was half-laugh, half-moan. His hands moved from her waist to her hair. "No, it's you who smells amazing. You only have to be near me and your scent makes me so fucking hot." He took a handful of her hair and pressed it to his nose. She felt his cock flex against her stomach. "See?"

Elenie's whole body was as tight as a bow. "Roman. Please." She didn't know what she was asking for.

He lifted her chin and their lips touched. Elenie's mouth opened beneath his. His tongue dipped inside to meet hers, tasting and stroking. Their breath mingled. She made a strangled noise which sounded ridiculous to her ears, but seemed to inflame Roman, who swore and pulled her closer.

Taking hold of each side of her t-shirt, he lifted it swiftly over her head. The cool air caressed her skin and she wished with all her heart that she owned sexier underwear.

"I only had two bras," Elenie whispered through numbed lips, "and you cut one of them in half."

Roman lifted a finger to trace each cotton strap and the swell of her breasts. Fire blazed in his eyes as he followed the path of his hands. Elenie couldn't breathe. "I'll buy you more. I'll buy you all the bras you want."

Her eyelids fluttered closed as his hands slid around her back and undid the clasp. It wasn't a smooth maneuver. The fact that his fingers fumbled slightly made her smile. Gave her the courage to open her eyes again as he swept the straps gently off her shoulders and dropped her bra to the floor.

"Christ, Elenie. Maybe I won't buy you any bras at all." He brushed one large thumb over the nipple of her left breast; she arched into his touch.

"Roman." His name was a plea on her tongue as he stroked her again.

"So fucking lovely," he murmured.

His hands were heated as they moved over her skin. The fine hairs on her arms stood on end, his fingertips dragging ripples of sensation through her body. Her nipples tightened into small pebbles which he caught between his finger and thumb, triggering an immediate ache at the junction of her thighs, partway between bliss and torment.

"Too many clothes." She gave a dazed shake of her head. "You're still wearing too many clothes."

Her fingers went to the buttons on his shirt and Roman sucked in a sharp breath. Elenie watched her own hands, transfixed, as she undid each one, his shirt gaping wider the further she went. When it hung loose on his shoulders, he shrugged it onto the floor. She grabbed a fistful of the soft t-shirt that lay underneath, pulling herself up on her tiptoes to catch his lower lip between her teeth. Roman groaned and dragged her closer, his hands on her ass and his rock-hard length pushing into the dip above her hip bone. His mouth was hungry, hot, and heavy on hers. He smelled like the woods and tasted of strength and temptation.

"I want to feel your tits on my chest," he grated. "But I might just explode if I do."

She gave a breathless laugh. "I might just explode if you don't."

Tugging on his t-shirt, Elenie drew it up his sides, uncovering tanned skin beneath. Impatiently, Roman whipped it out of her grasp and dragged it the rest of the way over his head. Hair ruffled, eyes glazed, he stood in front of her and she couldn't breathe.

"Oh, my God. You are—" She lifted her face to him and he smiled his enticing, uneven smile. "Gorgeous," she finished on a whisper. "Roman, you are gorgeous."

"No. You are."

When he reached for her and pulled her into his chest, they both moaned. The smattering of hair that covered his firm muscles teased her nipples, sending shivers of sensation over her skin. She shuddered and Roman's body tightened in response. His breath was coming in gasps. His fingers went to the button of her jeans, moving more urgently. The moment they were undone, he pushed them off her waist, over the curve of her rear and down onto her thighs. Elenie stepped away to wriggle out of them, dragging her socks off at the same time.

Without taking his eyes from her face, Roman undid his pants and slid them past the bulge in his shorts to the floor. His own socks soon joined the scattered pile of clothes. When she reached for the sides of her panties, he shook his head and held out a hand.

"Come with me."

Catching her fingers, he tugged her gently toward the bed. Elenie stumbled and followed him.

Roman sat on the edge of the mattress. When he opened his legs, she stepped between his knees. He gripped her hips to pull her closer, pressing his lips against her stomach. Her skin rippled in response; she curled her fingers into his hair. Licking and kissing in random patterns that made no sense to anyone but him, Roman

255

muttered broken sentences, telling her how beautiful she was, how much she turned him on. His fingers slid over cotton. Elenie's inhale was tortured. He didn't press any further, just stroked the soft skin of her thighs until her legs shook.

"You feel like heaven," he told her. "And you taste like heaven. And your smell drives me completely insane. My cock is so hard right now and it's all because of you."

She flexed under his touch. "You make me feel so sexy," she breathed.

"Christ, Elenie. If you were any sexier, I'd lose the ability to speak at all. I'd only be able to grunt like a caveman." Roman turned his face to rub his jaw against her stomach. The rough scrape of his stubble on her sensitive skin made her eyes roll. "Lie down with me."

His words were so soft, she barely heard him. But Elenie answered his tug on her hips immediately, climbing onto the bed and stretching out with a sigh.

Roman kneeled over her, midnight eyes raking her body from head to toe. He placed a hand at the base of her throat and trailed it gently between her breasts, over her stomach, and farther down to rest on her panties. His chest rose and fell as if he'd just finished a workout.

"Please—" Her hands closed on the quilt. She rolled her hips and his gaze shot to her face. He looked wild and rumpled, on the edge of losing control. The thrill of having such power over him lit her up inside like a sparkler.

The mattress dipped as he leaned over her to pull open the drawer of his nightstand. Roman rummaged inside and dropped a foil packet onto the bed. With hands that shook, he gently peeled away her underwear, then impatiently pushed down his own. His length sprang free and Elenie reached for him, eyes cloudy with need. She was desperate to feel him.

"Not yet." He closed his fingers on her wrist, voice like sandpaper. "I want to explore you first."

Roman lay slowly down on top of her, a sensual weighted blanket covering every inch of her body. Muscles bunched in his upper arms. She wanted to close her teeth on his taut skin. Dipping his head to take her mouth again, he slid one leg between hers, nudging her knees apart and moving against her. He closed his fingers gently on her neck, slid them to her collarbone, the curve of her shoulder, the smooth expanse of her chest.

He brushed his palm over one nipple and traced it with his fingers. The sensation was exquisite. Elenie's head twisted from side to side. She was losing her mind to the feel of Roman's touch on her skin, the pressure of his hardness against her thighs.

He stroked her stomach, the back of his hand teasing the underside of her breasts with every sweep. And all the while, his mouth painted hers with kisses so tender and warm that a knot of emotion lodged at the base of her throat.

Roman's hand slid lower. His eyes burned into hers as he paused above her center.

"Yes," she murmured. "Touch me. Please." They both drew matching jagged breaths when he obeyed.

"Elenie." His voice sounded pained. "Fuck, I didn't think I could get any harder." His fingers dipped into the silky wetness between her legs, gliding back and forth in a gentle sweep that sent her hips rolling against him. "You feel like velvet," he whispered into her mouth.

She clenched when his thumb brushed her clit, a million nerve endings tingling all over her body. Her muscles tightened and cried out for release from the delicate touch, the too-sensitive vibrations. When he pushed a finger deep inside, she moaned against his neck. Another joined the first and the delicious stretch sent tremors through her shaking thighs. He stroked her with his thumb, circling, teasing, exploring. A starburst of colors flickered beneath her eyelids. She bit her lip, poised on the edge of a cliff dive of sensations. Wanting more. Needing more. So ready to fall.

"Let me taste you." He grunted the words into her hair, raising himself onto braced arms and prowling down her body. "I want you to come on my tongue."

Elenie tensed.

"I don't . . . I've never—Roman, let me—" When she pressed her legs together and reached for him instead, he lifted his head. His eyes were intense, his pupils huge and drug-dazed.

"I want to make this good for you, sweetheart. Your pleasure comes first. You come first. Let me do this for you."

And, oh God—that feeling! Of being seen. Of being wanted. Of being worshipped. It spread through her like sunlight between November clouds and he almost tipped her over the peak with his words alone.

A small sob escaped Elenie's lips as she submitted completely. Her thighs parted. Knees spreading, she opened herself up for him. Roman groaned, pressing his mouth to the hollow of her hip. She could feel his breath against her center. And then his tongue swept over her, staggeringly intimate, achingly tender.

Her breath came in gasps, her hands fisting in the bedsheets. She was a writhing mass of need and want. With iron control, he tasted her and teased her. Every upstroke was silken. Every downstroke, ragged. The light stubble on his jaw left trails of fire on Elenie's inner thighs. His hands bit into her hips, taut with focus and possession. Each time she nearly fell, he paused and drew back.

"I'm not finished." His voice was rough and unsteady. He traced her folds with his tongue, over and over, until finally she begged him. Then Roman's fingers pressed back inside her, his mouth hot and insistent. The stretch was too intense. "Come for me, sweetheart," he said finally. "Come for me now."

With a cry, Elenie shattered and broke under his touch, her climax fueled by the vibrations of satisfaction that hummed on his tongue. He lapped at her until her body stopped shaking and her vision cleared. She tugged on his hair to lift his head.

Roman's body was rigid as he shifted to kneel above her, a light sheen of sweat covering his skin. "I need to be inside you," he told her hoarsely.

She nodded, hips lifting in invitation. "Yes."

He reached for the condom, tore open the foil, and rolled it swiftly onto himself with purposeful hands. A whimper broke from Elenie's throat at the sight; she'd never seen anything so erotic. Roman centered his weight over her until they were chest to chest, his cock hot and heavy between her thighs. When he pressed into her, inch by unhurried inch, she gasped. He sank deeper, his lips bumping her temple. Unintelligible words fell from his mouth. Stretched around him, gloriously full, Elenie's breath panted from her lips.

"So good. You feel so good," he murmured into her hair.

Roman began to move and she could swear her eyes rolled. His biceps under her fingers felt like rock. The friction, both friend and foe, spiraled them higher and higher, almost painful, wonderfully tender, the center of everything. Slow strokes, juddering breaths. He was the heat of the sun, burning her up from the inside out. Consuming her, one thrust at a time.

One hand slid to her ass, fingers gripping her cheek, as he buried himself further with each roll of his hips. She lifted her legs to wrap them around his thighs and pulled him even closer. Her ankles crossed, encasing him in a prison of eager limbs, and the change in position was the undoing of them both.

"Fuck! Jesus Christ, Elenie." Roman ground the words out, nostrils flaring. "I can't hold on."

"Don't." It sounded like a sob. "Don't hold on!"

He came with a hoarse cry and a series of shuddering pulses which shook his body and sent her free-falling into her own blissful climax. She tightened around him as they clung together, riding crashing waves which stole their breath and all their words.

Roman rested his forehead on hers, his chest heaving, body still trembling with aftershocks. He pressed hot, slow kisses to her mouth. "That was incredible. You turn me inside out."

When he tried to lift some of his weight, Elenie gripped her wobbly legs around him and pulled him back down.

"No, no, no," she sighed. "You need to stay here forever."

Chapter 36
Roman

He rasped out a laugh and compromised by rolling onto his side, catching his breath at the slide of skin on sensitive skin as she moved with him.

"You won't say that when I've squashed you like strawberry jelly." His voice sounded shaky to his own ears. Roman felt her laugh against his skin and a wide smile spread across his own mouth. "Damn, Elenie. I wanted that to take twice as long, but you blew my mind. I was hoping to impress you with my incredible stamina and lothario moves."

Elenie tipped her chin to look up at him. Her gray eyes shone in the afternoon sun and Roman's heart turned over. "Count me impressed," she told him. "Lotharios are not to be trusted. I'd rather put my faith in the new chief of police."

Her grin was infectious. He would happily lie here for hours and just look at her face. With the echoes of his climax still tingling in his muscles, he already wanted her again. He was officially sunk.

"I'd better head for the bathroom." Sliding unwillingly out from under her, Roman stood up from the bed. He didn't mind a bit when Elenie's eyes followed him. "Back in a moment."

He dealt with the condom in seconds and paused in the doorway of the bedroom. She lay stretched out on top of the quilt, the look on her face shy but unselfconscious. He ran his gaze over her body.

"I may have mentioned it before, but you are absolutely stunning." Roman crossed to sit on the edge of the bed. "I'll probably keep telling you and your head will get huge and you'll be all cocky and unbearable and everyone will get fed up with you. But I don't think I'll be able to help myself."

She sat up and pulled her knees into her chest, wrapping her arms around them. Her beautiful breasts disappeared from sight and he frowned automatically.

Elenie laughed. Her face shone. "You're just saying that because you got lucky."

He knew without a shadow of a doubt she'd never been told how lovely she was. It broke his heart more than a little. Roman swore to himself that he would tell her at every opportunity until she was forced to believe him.

"I certainly did." Unable to resist, he leaned in to taste her lips again. "I consider myself to be the luckiest bastard in Pine Springs right now." Elenie quivered under his touch and he made himself pull away, even as he felt the familiar tug in his groin which he was powerless to control. "I would love nothing better than to curl up with you all afternoon. But maybe, if we're planning to visit my parents, we should go sooner rather than later. What do you think?" He hated to see the cloud that drifted across her face. "Honestly, I don't want you to worry. This will be fine—you'll see." Standing up, he held out a hand to pull her up from the bed. "Would you like a quick shower?" His length twitched at the words, drawing Elenie's eyes. Roman stifled a moan. Grabbing his shorts from the floor, he held them in front of himself like a shield. "Ignore that," he instructed her, fiercely. "My cock isn't running this show and, just

262

because I'm picturing you in my shower, doesn't mean I'm going to jump on you again like a hot and horny teenager."

Elenie giggled. She paused in the doorway of the bathroom and looked over her shoulder. Roman's eyes devoured her gentle curves. "How disappointing. I was kind of hoping you would."

He felt the smile on his lips grow until it spread across his face. With a growl, he threw his shorts to one side and followed her into the bathroom.

* * *

They took the back roads to his parents' house, and it was late afternoon by the time they pulled up on the roadside. Elenie paled at the two extra cars parked on the driveway.

"It's just Florence, Thea, and Luke. And Thea and Luke know the score already." He jumped down from his truck, walking around to the passenger side when she didn't move. "Come on, tiger."

She lifted her chin, squared her shoulders, and still managed to look as if she was heading for the gallows. Her fingers had a death-grip on the cake in her hands. His mother answered the ring on the doorbell. Her face lit up when she saw it was him and fell when she noticed Elenie behind him. They were back to square one again.

"Roman. Elenie."

"Hey, Ma." He leaned down to give her a kiss. "You plan to let us in?"

Ava stepped back and held the door open. "Of course."

They followed her into the kitchen, where Florence was making coffee. Everyone else sat around the table.

"I thought you were working today!" Florence's smile disappeared like the lights snapping off in a power outage. "OK, so this is awkward—"

"No, it's not. There are a few things we need to tell you." Roman pushed Elenie gently in front of him toward the table.

"I brought you a lemon pound cake," she said and set it down on a counter.

"My favorite. I'll grab a knife!" Warm and friendly, his dad sounded just like he always did. Ava, on the other hand, was assessing them carefully and Florence's face was stormy. Luke pulled out the chair next to him in invitation. Elenie shot him a grateful look and slid into it without saying anything more. Thea gave her a sympathetic smile.

Roman took hold of Elenie's hand, deliberately placing it on top of the table, despite her tug of resistance. The gesture wasn't missed by anyone. "I know you saw Elenie in Kalamazoo last night. She told me first thing this morning."

"Craig Perry? What are you even thinking!" Florence thumped two cups of coffee down in front of them. Elenie's fingers flinched in his grip.

"You know him?" Roman's voice was sharp.

"Not really, but he comes into the salon to get his hair cut. Jordan usually does it." Florence wrinkled her nose.

"You don't like him?"

His sister gave him a look. "Hairdressers tend to prefer it if you don't grope them when they bend down to plug in the blow dryer. Sexy English accent or not. Pretty sure he chooses the salon over the barbershop because we all have breasts."

His mother looked furious, his father horrified. Elenie shrank a little further into her seat.

"None of this is how it looks," Roman said firmly. "It's complicated and, when I've explained, I want you to keep what I tell you to yourselves."

He explained Frank's reaction to them being seen at the town fair, the public breakup to convince him their relationship was over, and how Elenie was fake-dating Perry to secure her safety. He left out any mention of her CI role. Beside him, Elenie's shoulders curved inward when he described the violence she'd met with at home. He hated that she was embarrassed by something she had no control over. She kept her eyes pinned on his face, muted stress pulsing from the pores of her skin.

"Milo and Cait are in on this. So are Dougie and Summer. Thea and Luke knew already because they came to the gala dinner. And now you three know as well. But that is it and we need it to stay that way." He looked from his mother to his father to Florence. "Elenie's position is vulnerable and we're working on a longer-term solution. But it needs to be handled sensitively at the moment. OK?"

"Fuck." Florence blinked.

"Yes." Roman gave a tight smile. "Fuck."

There was a brief silence.

"My dear." His dad stood up from the table. "I'm so sorry you're dealing with all of that." Unruffled and accepting, he squeezed Elenie's shoulder with a large hand and picked up her mug. "Let me heat up your coffee."

"I could not get my head around you dating that prick. I'm so glad to hear you're not delusional, because I really like you." Florence's smile was tentative. "Plus, now we don't hate you, we can eat your cake." She jumped up to gather some plates from one of the cupboards. Luke gave a dry chuckle.

"I was dying to say something after the gala dinner, but it was so hard to pick out what I could and couldn't mention that I thought I'd best keep quiet about the whole thing!" Thea put her hands to her temples and shook her head. "Caitlyn nearly exploded from the pressure of keeping her mouth shut that night."

Elenie gave a weak smile.

While the cake was being sliced and handed around, Roman looked across the table at his mother. Ava's open face was deeply concerned.

"I don't like this at all." She gave a tiny shake of her head.

He felt every muscle in Elenie's body go rigid next to him. "I'm so sorry," she said stiffly. "I hate to involve you all in this. It's bad enough that Roman's been roped in, but my options are limited. My family is messed-up."

Ava pushed back her chair. "That's why I don't like the sound of this, mija." She bustled around the table to sweep Elenie up in her arms. "It breaks my heart to hear what you've been dealing with." Roman swallowed a lump in his throat as his mother rocked Elenie back and forth in a lavish hug. "We're here for you in any way you need. All of us. Don't you worry about that." When she finally let go, Ava's eyes were damp and Elenie's shimmered in a shell-shocked face. "Let's have some cake. You can tell us more if you want to and we'll talk about something else if you don't."

Elenie's smile trembled at the edges. "What I'd really like to know is how the watercolor painting is going."

And with that, his mother was off and running. Ava talked about a class she might join and a new technique that was currently defeating her, leapfrogging effortlessly from art to fitness to relatives he barely remembered to childhood memories in the way only his family could. Roman leaned back and let the conversation roll over him.

A lightness settled on Elenie's face, banishing the blankness he hated with a passion, as Florence explained how she was responsible for the scar below his jawline.

"I was ten. He was an ass! What can I say? I had no idea the buckle on my schoolbag would turn it into such a deadly weapon." His sister shrugged, any repentance she might have once had long gone. "I like to think I've given his face the character it lacked."

266

"You're blowing my cover." Roman hushed her without heat. "I've been telling people I got that scar in a sword fight."

Elenie snorted, and he would have taken ten more schoolbags in the face to hear it again. "I heard you saved Mrs. Alberty from a coyote attack. You mean that's not true?"

He aimed a lazy grin her way. "I'd have left her to it. Those coyotes would rue the day they had the nerve."

He stretched his arm along the back of her chair and stroked his thumb gently up and down her spine. The memory of her bare skin under his touch flared in his mind. Roman wrenched his thoughts back to the present before he was forced to adjust himself under the table. Luke caught his eye and gave him an imperceptible wink. It seemed he was not as unreadable as he'd been led to believe.

Chapter 37
Elenie

"Guess whose truck is still smokin' out at Pedlar's End!" Ty bounced on the balls of his feet in the doorway, scrubbing stubby nails over his buzz cut.

Frank looked up from the television. Elenie closed her book around a finger, grateful beyond measure for the interruption. She'd forced herself to join him in the living room, but twenty minutes of sharing the same space had her climbing out of her skin.

"I'll give you a clue. It's a black F-150. And it's fuckin' gutted."

"Martinez?"

Tyson's grin showed all his teeth. "Got it in one."

"Devastated to hear that." The corners of Frank's eyes crinkled. He stretched out his legs, ankles crossed, and folded his arms behind his head, satisfaction in the ripple of his biceps. "Good job, Ty."

"Wasn't me." Tyson slumped onto the couch.

"Dean?" Frank cocked an eyebrow.

"Nope. He was with me."

Elenie uncurled her legs and headed for the door. "I thought it'd be harder to get it started but the seats went up really quickly."

Their faces were comical.

Ty snapped his slack jaw shut. "You're shittin' us. *You* torched it?"

"He had it coming." She pulled the lighter from her jeans pocket and rolled her thumb over the spark wheel a few times. Frank's eyes followed the movement.

"Fucking A, Elephant!" Tyson held up his palm and Elenie high-fived him as she passed the couch. It was a strange moment.

Roman had nailed it.

And soon, she had the first indication that his plan was having the desired effect when Frank caught her in the entryway on Tuesday evening.

"I need you to do a job with Dean."

"Tonight?" Elenie frowned. She'd been thinking of heading to bed early.

"Yes, tonight! Got something better on?" Frank crossed to the bottom of the stairs and bellowed Dean's name.

Answering rhetorical questions would definitely not be in her best interests. "What is it?"

"There's a package to pick up in Saginaw. I don't want Dean to go on his own."

"You're kidding." That was nearly a two-hour drive away; it would be well after midnight before they'd get back. But it was a great opportunity to gather information.

Frank ignored her. Rummaging through the messy drawers of an old cabinet, he pulled out a padlock with a key in it and stuffed it into one of his pockets.

Dean's footsteps thumped down the stairs.

"You ready?" Frank asked.

"Just need something to eat," Dean grunted, heading for the kitchen.

"Why can't Ty go with him? Or Athena?" Elenie hesitated to poke the bear but knew Frank would expect some kind of protest. "I have work tomorrow."

Her stepdad took two slow strides toward her. With a wall behind her, Elenie had no option but to hold her ground. Lifting his hand to bunch the hair at the nape of her neck, Frank tugged her head back to stare down into her face.

"Either you're in or you're out, Ellie." His hot breath fell on her cheek; her heart jumped in her chest. "Are you fuckin' in? Or are you fuckin' out?"

Elenie nodded as best she could. "I'm in." Her voice cracked.

Dean loped out of the kitchen, a folded piece of bread held in one hand, nothing inside it. His mouth was full of something else and he chewed messily, noisily, wiping crumbs from his lips on the arm of his sleeve.

"I'll just grab a hoodie." She ran up the stairs without waiting for a reply.

Five minutes later, they were pulling off the drive in Frank's truck. Elenie's small backpack was by her feet, Roman's phone tucked into an inside zipped pocket. She didn't dare carry the DEA cell, too. That was hidden, with the other gadgets Dorsey had given her, inside a box of tampons on a shelf in her closet.

"Let's go, Road Trip Ho!" Dean snickered at his own wit.

It was going to be a long night.

"Where's Ty?" she asked.

"Him and Dad have gotten another job."

"And Athena?"

"Pissed." Dean leaned forward to fiddle with the radio.

"Why aren't we taking your car?"

"Gearbox is fucked." He found a station that suited him, cranked up the volume, and drummed along to the music with a rhythmless tattoo on the steering wheel.

Frank's Dodge was pretty luxurious, with plush seats and multi-speaker surround sound. Elenie propped her feet on the dash and leaned her head against the window. Dean fidgeted, smoked, chewed gum, and grumbled, but his eyes looked focused and he stuck somewhere around the speed limit.

"What are we picking up?" she asked. The air conditioning raised the hairs on her arms and legs. She turned it down. Dean turned it back up.

"Couple of packages."

"What's in them?"

"Don't know." He shot her a quizzical glance.

"What?"

"How'd you get the chief's truck to Pedlar's End?"

"I lifted his keys in the diner."

Dean's head bobbed. His mouth twisted in an impressed smirk.

It wasn't true. Roman and Dougie had handled the arson themselves and his truck currently idled unharmed in Milo's locked garage. The torched ringer, a write-off with duplicate plates to Roman's F-150, had come from a junkyard.

They lapsed into silence and, for the next ninety minutes or so, Elenie let the long, straight roads with their tree-lined woodland edges lull her into a soporific daze. She passed the time lost in dirty thoughts of one very sexy lawman.

The GPS took them to the outskirts of Saginaw. It was late when they pulled up curbside in front of an ordinary-looking house with a host of cars on the drive. Dean killed the engine. Memorizing the address, Elenie watched her stepbrother type out a message on his phone.

"Now what?"

He ignored her.

A couple of minutes went by and the front door opened. Dean's fingers drummed on his leg. Two muscular thugs strolled toward the truck and he lowered his window. One had pulled the fabric hood of his sweatshirt up, the other wore a baseball cap over a mainly shaven head.

Thug One peered in through the window. He eyed them both. "Got something for me?" His voice was surprisingly high. Elenie suppressed a nervous giggle and bit her lip. This was beginning to feel like a scene from a bad movie.

Dean leaned over to pull a fat envelope from the glovebox. He passed it through the window. Thug One broke the seal, glanced inside, and gave a brief nod. Thug Two slouched behind him, staring at the screen of his phone.

"Give us a minute." They walked back up the path. Dean blew out a breath and gave her a cocky wink. Elenie watched the front door. Five minutes went by before the men re-emerged. This time, Thug One passed Dean something bulky, wrapped neatly inside a plastic bag.

"Tell Frank I'll be in touch." He leaned on the car window sill and squinted at Elenie. "Who's the Fuck Bunny?"

Dean snorted. "This is my sister. She's more of a Fucking Pain In My Side."

Elenie dredged up a fake grin and a finger wiggle. Dealing with Frank had taught her it was all about the attitude.

His eyes lost interest. With a jerk of his chin, he tapped on the side of the truck. The two men melted back into the night.

Dean dropped the package in her lap; it was heavy and very solid. "Shove that under your seat."

"What is it?" *Worth another try.*

He started the truck and didn't answer. Elenie bent down to push the bag between her feet, wedging it under the passenger seat just behind her ankles.

Twenty minutes later, Dean pulled onto the forecourt of a gas station. "Dad wants the truck back full," he grunted and climbed out.

Elenie watched him through the window, her heart beginning to jump. He reached for one of the pumps and she heard the thrum of the gas when it started to flow. It seemed to take an age to fill the tank, but finally Dean pushed the filler cap closed and sloped off toward the kiosk to pay.

As soon as his back was turned, she grabbed the package from under her seat and dragged it out into the footwell. Her hands weren't quite steady as she unwrapped it and reached inside. Three items slid onto the mat. Two clear plastic bags held a multitude of tightly packed pills—some white, some blue. There were thousands of them. Elenie began to sweat.

The third item was wrapped inside a folded piece of old cloth. She swallowed compulsively when she picked it up. Its shape and weight were unmistakable. A quick glance at the kiosk, where Dean stood in line to pay, revealed just one person in front of him. Scrambling through her backpack, Elenie pulled her phone out with one hand and unwrapped the cloth with the other.

The handgun lay between her feet—black, menacing, and dangerous. A breathy whimper escaped her lips. Her trembling fingers flicked the camera to selfie mode by accident. Righting it swiftly, she snapped four quick photographs of all three items, plus a close-up of the gun.

Glancing through the windshield, she saw Dean push away from the counter. Her stomach rolled. With the speed of a professional gift wrapper, Elenie closed the cloth around the handgun. She stacked it on top of the drugs and pushed all three items back inside the plastic bag, praying to God the gun had its safety on. With seconds to spare, she shoved them under her seat, texting the photographs she'd taken to Roman as Dean sauntered across the forecourt. When he pulled open the door of the truck, she'd just dumped her phone into the backpack on her lap.

"I could have sworn I had some cookies in here somewhere," Elenie muttered, keeping her hair across her face in a curtain while she tried to stop her lips from trembling. She put her bag back down by her ankles and shrugged. "Must have eaten them, I guess."

Dean grunted and smirked. He pulled a chocolate bar from his pocket, tore open one end, and bit into it.

"Asshole." She smiled sweetly at him. "Any chance we can go home now?"

"One more stop first."

Half an hour later, Dean signaled and took a turn down a long, sandy track that led to a rustic campground in the woods. He pulled over in a deserted passing place and asked Elenie to hand him the package from under her seat. She tensed. Would he notice it was wrapped differently than before? But Dean barely glanced at it before casually pulling out the drugs and handing her back the plastic bag with the gun inside.

He gestured through the windshield. "If you follow that path for a bit, you'll get to the lake. Chuck this as far out as you can."

Elenie blinked at him. "I'm sorry?"

He wiped his nose on his sleeve. "Throw this," he pointed at the bag, "into the lake."

"Why?"

"Because it needs getting rid of."

"But it's dark."

"I don't give a shit."

"I'm no good at throwing."

"Just lob it good and hard."

"What if it doesn't sink?"

He looked exasperated. Even under these circumstances, it was entertaining to see how far she could push Dean. Thinking on his feet wasn't one of his greatest talents.

"Of course it'll fucking sink! It's made of metal."

"You said you didn't know what's inside. Why don't you do it?"

"Because I've done the goddamn driving and so far you've done zip."

She took a gamble. "And if I tell Frank you didn't do it yourself?"

Dean's mouth twisted into a sloppy grin. "I don't think you will. And I'm not gonna. Dad doesn't need to know everything."

Elenie considered that and shrugged. "I might be a while."

He put his feet up on the dashboard, tipping back his head. "You've got fifteen minutes."

She grabbed her backpack as she climbed out of the truck. Oh God, she hoped she'd done the right thing in sending the photos to Roman. Without the second cell phone, she had no idea of the contact details for Special Agent Dorsey. What to do now was the question.

Five minutes along the trail, out of sight of the truck, Elenie tugged off her hoodie with just enough light from the waxing moon to see what she was doing. Clouds loomed ominously above, threatening to take even that away if she didn't hurry. She wrapped the bulky material around the package containing the gun and pushed the whole bundle into the bottom of her bag, burying it beneath two library books. The cool air tugged at her shirtsleeves but adrenalin had her blood pumping like a diesel engine. She fumbled with her cell, saw that Roman had received and viewed the photos, prayed he'd saved or forwarded them immediately, and pressed Delete. Then she erased them from her camera roll and from the trash folder too. He'd also sent her a message asking if she was OK. With the allotted time ticking by too fast, Elenie deleted that without answering.

When she returned to the truck, she was out of breath, her sneakers were muddy, and her phone was stashed safely back in her bag. Dean was asleep.

She slammed the door with a little extra force. "All done."

He pushed himself upright, and started the engine. She felt as if the backpack was glowing red as she tucked it between the door and her legs.

When they reached home, the lights were still on in the living room, the flickering of the television visible from the driveway. A wave of sickness churned in Elenie's midriff. Dean crossed the hallway, lounged against the doorframe and gave his dad a chin lift.

"All OK?" Frank paused with a glass of whiskey halfway to his mouth. Her mother was asleep—passed out?—on the couch, one hand trailing on the carpet.

Dean gave a huge yawn, showing all his teeth. "Fine."

He threw the two packages across the room, one after the other. Frank caught them neatly, turning each bundle over in his hands with a grunt.

"And the other?"

Elenie stood silently beside Dean, her limbs heavy, head pounding.

"Gone. Like you said." Her stepbrother sniffed and shifted his feet.

Frank pulled himself upright. As he crossed the room, Elenie dropped her eyes and prayed her legs weren't shaking enough to be obvious. Instinctively, she tucked her backpack behind her body. The movement drew Frank's eyes and she realized she'd made a dangerous mistake.

"What are you hiding, Ellie?" Frank's voice was deceptively soft. Her stomach threatened to heave its way out of her throat.

"Nothing. It's just my bag."

Dean, sensing trouble, ducked out of the way and headed for the stairs. Frank prowled relentlessly closer, like an oncoming natural disaster. Elenie's throat bobbled. She could swear her lip throbbed where he'd backhanded her weeks before. He reached out, made a beckoning gesture with meaty fingers.

She turned hot and then instantly cold.

Shit.

Fuck.

The gun.

She was a dead woman.

Mouth, hands, gut, all encased in ice, Elenie passed him her backpack. Frank undid the clasp and flipped open the top. He peered inside, then stuck a careless hand into the depths. She closed her eyes and forced a ragged swallow to take away the saliva pooling in her mouth.

"What do we have here then?"

Despair and resignation clouded the fear. Elenie opened her mouth with no idea of what to say, no voice to say it with. Her eyelids, each weighted heavy from the backwash of adrenalin, lifted slowly and she focused on the object in Frank's hand.

It wasn't the gun. It was her phone.

"Been holding out on me, Ellie? I didn't know you had a cell." He pressed a few buttons, the lock screen lighting up his double chin. Elenie's tongue felt too big for her mouth. "Open it."

Frank pushed the phone toward her, dropping her backpack next to his feet. She took it with trembling fingers, typed the passcode in wrong the first time, right the second, and handed it back. He scrolled for a couple of minutes, opening her messages and the photo gallery, both of which had minimal content. Innocent pictures, innocuous chats. Reading through the short list of names in her contacts, he pressed on one number and connected the call, his eyes boring into her own as it rang. Elenie's stomach swooped again.

Please don't let it be Thea's. Don't let Roman answer.

"Hey, Elenie—it's a bit late for you. Everything OK?" Frank was close enough that Summer's voice, light and sleepy, was crystal clear. Without saying a word, he ended the call. A snarky smile lifting his lips, Frank pushed her phone into the back pocket of his jeans. He sauntered to his armchair, reaching for his whiskey, and took a long, leisurely swallow. On the couch, Athena sighed in her sleep. Frank dug around for the TV remote and changed the channel.

Elenie was dismissed.

Scooping her bag up off the floor, precious cargo still inside against all the odds, she headed for the stairs on jelly legs, praying that Summer or Roman wouldn't leave a message. One cell phone down but internal organs in place for now.

She had to get rid of this gun.

Chapter 38
Roman

Roman and Milo had a couple of beers each throughout the evening—"Look at us being responsible adults!"—before brewing a pot of coffee like a couple of old men. Remnants of the chili Caitlyn had cooked sat in a large pot in the middle of the dining table, but they'd carried all the plates out to the kitchen and made a civilized stab at cleaning up.

Roman had been struggling to keep the grin off his face since he'd arrived; it hadn't escaped the attention of his friends.

"Happy suits you, Ro," Milo told him. "You're less of a miserable bastard now Elenie's on the scene. When you're as good-looking as we are, it's only fair to share it around. Sometimes I look at Cait and think, damn, she's a lucky woman."

"You're full of shit, Milo Walker." Caitlyn's voice drifted down the stairs.

Happy or not, Roman had no intention of sharing any details. Every time he thought of Elenie, his chest flared and his body temperature cranked through the roof. He wanted her again with an obsession that floored him. To keep Milo from prying further (and he knew he would), he told him about his parents seeing Elenie out with Perry.

"I hate this whole situation. I want it to be over already." And that was without even getting started on the CI nightmare. Roman stared up at the ceiling.

"How d'you think Elenie must feel." Milo's words were uncharacteristically grim. Neither of them spoke for a while.

"Well, I suppose I should make a move. I'm on an early shift in the morning." Roman's phone pinged multiple times, in quick succession. He dug it out of his pocket, an automatic smile pulling at his lips when he saw Elenie's name. Opening the first photograph, it took him a moment to work out what he was looking at. He jolted upright. "What the fuck."

Milo did the same. "What is it?"

Roman scrolled through the other pictures, surroundings forgotten. His eyes raked over each shot, examining them for details and an explanation. He went through them again and again, an icy tangle of concern roping his limbs.

"Ro?" Milo's second query came from behind him. It was too late to hide the images as the phone was plucked from his grasp. Roman wiped a hand over his face, his mind racing. "What am I looking at? Spell it out for me."

"Drugs and a gun. In a car footwell, I think. And Elenie's feet." He would recognize her scuffed Converse anywhere.

"Shit." Milo's mouth dropped open. "Can you call her?"

He shook his head. "Her phone will be on silent and I never call her because I can't tell who she's with. They don't know she has a cell." He pushed to his feet, unable to sit still. "Dammit, why no message? No details, just the pictures." Roman was muttering to himself. He took his phone from Milo's hands and typed out a text.

Are you OK?

Elenie didn't open the message and there was no reply. The two men looked at each other silently. Automatically, Roman emailed the photos to himself and took a screenshot of each one for backup. He knew she wouldn't chance leaving them on her camera roll for long.

"I guess you'll have to hold on and trust her." Milo's voice sounded far from certain. "There's nothing you can do. You don't know where she is or whose car that is."

Roman heard Caitlyn coming down the stairs. "This is confidential. You have to keep what you've seen to yourself. Promise?" There was no one he trusted more than Milo but it needed saying.

"Of course."

"I thought you boys were aiming for an early night?" Caitlyn smiled as she walked into the living room.

"I was just heading off," Roman said, his voice strained.

"What's up?" Caitlyn looked instantly suspicious. She glanced between them.

"Nothing, babe. It's all good. And definitely time for bed, I think." Milo pulled his wife in for a brief hug and shot Roman a conspiratorial grimace over her head.

Grabbing his keys from the arm of the couch, Roman shoved his phone into his pocket. "I swear this baby grew while you were upstairs." He laid a gentle hand on Caitlyn's stomach as he kissed her goodbye. "Take care of yourself. I'll see you soon."

Milo followed him to the front door. "Keep in touch. Let me know what happens."

Roman nodded. His mind was already miles away and he wanted to be gone.

By the time he'd reached home, he'd already driven himself mad with a hundred different possible scenarios. A cloud of vapor hung in the cold evening air when he huffed out a breath. He looked up at the stars, his nerves as taut as a power line. Banks of clouds were gathering in the sky, dense and heavy. A few fat drops of rain hit his shirt. Another bounced off the toe of his shoe. Roman ignored them.

Where was she and what the hell was she doing? How could the evening have deteriorated so fast?

It wasn't until he lay in bed well after midnight, unable to sleep and surrounded by the smell of her on his sheets, that he finally got a reply from Elenie. This time it came through from her DEA cell phone.

Elenie:

I'm home now but can't talk. Frank's got the cell you gave me so don't use the number anymore. Please tell Summer and Cait too.

Roman propped himself up on his pillows and typed back.

I need to know you're OK

Elenie:

I'm fine. Did you save the photos I sent you?

Yes

Elenie:

I've deleted my copies. Can you email them to Dorsey and I'll text her an explanation?

He held off from answering when he could see she was typing again. Her next message came from left field.

Elenie:

Also, any chance you could phone through an order for donuts in the morning and come into the diner to pick them up? It's kind of urgent.

Roman frowned.

Of course. Do I need to specify the fillings?

Elenie:

Let me surprise you.

Sweetheart, you keep surprising me and I don't know if I can take it

Elenie:

Good night.

You too

He flicked off the lamp, his heart just a little lighter in his chest, wondering how the hell donuts linked with drugs and guns. When he slept, fully expecting a disturbed night and bloody dreams, his thoughts were only of the way Elenie had felt around him and the bliss of being buried deep within her body.

And in the dark, he burned for her.

Chapter 39
Elenie

Roman strode into Diner 43 just before ten the next morning, and an aeronautical display of butterflies let loose in her stomach.

His face was set and fierce, his long strides eating up the floor as he crossed to the counter. Anyone watching them would have taken the way his gaze raked over her as possibly aggressive, definitely unfriendly. Elenie saw the concern in his intensity as clearly as if he'd shouted it, and knew from his rigid posture how hard he fought not to reach for her. Desperate to fling herself at him, she recognized the conflict. Why was life this complicated?

Lifting the tray she'd just loaded up, Elenie shot him a quick glance. "I'll be with you in a moment."

Business had been steady all morning and she knew she didn't have much time to spare. Delivering a selection of cooked breakfasts and drinks to a family of four, she emptied the tray and headed around the back of the counter.

Roman slid a takeout bag and an empty disposable drinks cup toward her. "Get rid of this for me, would you?" He stood like a watchful statue, brooding and serious. His eyes never left her face, fingers tap-tapping on his thigh.

"Sure." Elenie chucked the featherlight cup into the trash can and paused with her hand on the screwed-up paper bag. It wasn't empty. Reaching down to one of the lower shelves beneath the counter, she stuffed it to the very back, behind a tall stack of crockery. Then she retrieved the takeout box she'd filled earlier from its position nearby, right in the corner where no one else would see it. Not that there was anyone else but her who might. You still didn't mess around with a special order like this one, though.

Placing the box on the counter, Elenie pushed it toward him. "Your donuts, Chief Martinez."

He closed his large hands on either side of the cardboard and picked it up. One eyebrow flickered when he registered the weight.

She held his eyes for a moment. "I hope you enjoy them."

Roman gave her a brief nod. Elenie could smell his aftershave, his cleanness, in the air around him. A yearning twisted in her stomach. He looked like he wanted to say something and the silence stretched heavily between them. Then Delia clattered another pair of plates through the serving hatch and the opportunity passed.

Thanks to Dean and his laziness—plus a huge slice of knee-tremblingly good luck—inside the box, beneath a wedge of paper napkins and some artfully displayed donuts, lay the handgun. In used condition with who knew how many careful owners. She suspected Roman had guessed what was inside. Whether the gun would link back to any crimes was a gamble but Elenie knew for sure that not every family made late-night collections like this. And the instruction to toss it into the lake? Well, that wasn't your average way to pass on an unwanted firearm.

She'd had to get it out of her house, couldn't wait for a meetup with Dorsey. It was far too dangerous to hang onto the gun any longer—she had nowhere safe to stash it. Instead, she'd messaged the special agent a full explanation last night, along with the address in Saginaw where they'd made the collection and a description of the two guys they'd dealt with. Dorsey could arrange a handover of the evidence with Roman, and Elenie had not a single care if Chief Deputy Shawn Booth didn't like it.

He wasn't the one who had to live with Frank.

New arrivals through the door of the diner made them both turn around. Roman bit off a curse as his mother and father called out their surprise to see him, his fingers reflexively tightening their grip on the box in his hands.

"What wonderful timing—we didn't expect this!" Ava reached up to cup his face, planting a kiss on his cheek. His dad gave him a slap on the back. Elenie shot them a careful, guarded smile and moved quickly away, grabbing the next order from the hatch.

"If you'd like to find a table, I'll be right with you," she said politely over her shoulder.

Serving two groups and taking an order from another, Elenie took a few calming breaths and found that Roman had introduced his mom and dad to Otto. The four of them were now sitting together at his table in the corner, chatting like old friends. Well, three of them were. Roman still had one hand on the takeout box and an exasperated expression on his face. She shared his concern. Of all the days, why had his mother and father chosen this one to come into the diner? She was so unsure about how to play this.

"Hello, everyone. Do you know what you'd like yet or shall I give you more time?" Reserved but friendly, she maintained a little distance between herself and the table.

Roman's eyes held an apology. He gave her the smallest of shrugs in a "what the hell?" kind of way. Ava and Elias did their best to rein in their natural urge to shower her with attention. They placed their orders in stilted voices, flicking glances at Roman for his approval as they chose from the menu.

Otto watched them all with the genial half-smile he wore most of the time. He raised his eyebrows at Elenie, blue eyes sparkling. "It must be my lucky day to share the morning with such special company."

When she returned to the table with their food, a tea to go for Roman, and a refill of coffee for Otto, Ava was asking about the box. Elenie's heart stuttered in her chest. Her eyes flicked first to Ava, then to the innocuous cube of white cardboard and finally to Roman's face. He pushed the box casually away from his mother, tucking it against the wall at the far end of the table.

"Donuts for the team." His calm and steady tone gave nothing away. "A bit of bribery now and then keeps the wheels turning smoothly." He tipped his takeout cup. "That's why I can't stay long this morning. It's dangerous to keep the guys from their sugar fix."

Everyone chuckled and the crisis passed. Elenie clenched her hands on the empty tray so no one would notice the tremble in her fingers. Stress and sleep deprivation were taking their toll on her nerves. She needed to get a grip. "Would anyone like any sauces or more napkins?"

Behind her the door of the diner opened again. A subtle charge seemed to run through Roman's body. Achingly aware of him with every nerve ending she possessed, Elenie turned her head and looked slowly over her shoulder.

It was quickly becoming another day measured in WTFs per hour.

Chapter 40
Roman

Could the morning turn into any more of a shitshow?

As if it wasn't enough that he was sitting in the diner with what he suspected was a fucking handgun in a takeout box, his parents had decided to show their support for Elenie, despite knowing they couldn't let on they knew her. Roman silently cursed the huge heart of his headstrong mother. The cardboard box sat openly on the tabletop; he was desperate to get it back to the station.

Only now, Frank and Athena Dax were wandering casually up to the counter and pulling out a couple of bar stools. They sat down just a few feet away and Roman knew he wouldn't be going anywhere for a little while yet.

Elenie excused herself, her beautiful face the blank mask he most hated seeing. He clenched one hand into a fist beneath the table. Otto shot him a quick, concerned glance and he nodded.

"Get us a couple of coffees and two breakfast specials," Frank growled at Elenie.

She gave him a cool look. "Money first."

"Don't be such a little shit." He leaned toward her but she stood her ground. Without betraying the slightest hint of awareness that others might be watching or listening, she regarded him steadily, eyes completely flat. It was the first time Roman had seen Elenie with any of her family.

"You're tedious and I'm thirsty. I need coffee!" Athena's voice was a breathy whine.

Elenie raised one eyebrow and walked away to take another order.

"Is that—?" Roman's mother bumped his shoulder, nodding toward the counter.

"Frank and Athena Dax. Elenie's mother and stepfather."

Ava's eyes narrowed.

Athena was jittery. She ran slim hands through her hair and fiddled with the clasp on a small green shoulder bag. Frank, leaning sideways, rested one bulky arm on the counter. He ran a casual gaze around the diner, following Elenie's path as she piled a tray with empties and returned to unload it. With heavy brows, he pushed a couple of bills toward her. She took the money without a word, rang it up at the till and wrote up their order for the kitchen. Within minutes, she'd handed them each a steaming cup of coffee. Athena took a pack of cigarettes and a lighter out of her bag.

"You can't smoke in here," Elenie told her.

"Fuck off, Cinderella." Her mother didn't even glance in her direction. Beside him, Ava caught her breath. Roman felt cold fury surge in his throat. Her cheeks flushed, Elenie whipped the lit cigarette from Athena's fingers and threw it into the sink beneath the counter. She stepped back out of her mother's reach. "You little bitch!" Athena's rage went from zero to one hundred in seconds. Frank didn't move.

"You can't—they're not my rules. It's the law. If Delia doesn't enforce it, the police chief will." Elenie jerked her head in his direction. Roman locked eyes with Frank Dax for a long minute. Then the older man raised his coffee cup in a mocking salute, sending a tight smile their way with a dip of his chin.

"Sergeant Starchy!" Cigarette immediately forgotten, Athena crossed over to their table. She leaned toward him, treating his mother and father to an inappropriate view of her unfettered breasts. "Well, if this isn't the greatest of pleasures."

Roman resisted the urge to place his hand on the box next to him. "Mrs. Dax."

Frank watched them, amusement twitching his lips. Athena sent a bright and birdlike glance around the table. "Won't you introduce me? I thought we were friends."

Elenie appeared at her shoulder, embarrassment darkening her smoky eyes. "Mom, your breakfast will be ready in a moment."

Athena acted as if she hadn't spoken. She held out a hand toward his father. "And you are?"

Genetically unable to be rude, Elias shook her hand and smiled. "Elias Martinez. And this is my wife, Ava."

Athena straightened. "Martinez? So you must be—" She flicked a finger from his dad to Roman and back again.

Elenie tried again. "Mom—"

"Shut up." Athena held a hand up to her without even turning.

"My mother and father." Roman supplied the information in a flat tone.

Elenie's mother turned icy blue eyes to his parents. "How wonderful for you. You must be so proud. A law enforcement officer in the family, and such a handsome one, too." His mother held back from answering. Athena leaned toward her. "I can only imagine that the benefits of birthing someone who can make a parking fine disappear must make the hideous experience of having children worthwhile. Am I right?" She laughed at her own joke. "Elenie won't even give me my breakfast on the house."

Roman heard Frank's low chuckle as Delia pushed their order out through the serving hatch. Athena flicked them all an on/off smile, instantly bored, and drifted away from their table.

As Elenie passed next to him, Frank caught hold of her elbow, fingers closing tightly enough to make her wince. Roman ground his teeth. Frank pulled her closer, his mouth moving against her ear. Elenie nodded stiffly once and then again. More words were spoken. She flinched just a little and Roman ached to drag Dax to the floor and sink his fist into the older man's face. Elenie answered him in a low voice, pale lips barely moving. Then she tried to step away from him. Frank's grip tightened and twisted. She drew in a pained breath. An unpleasant smile hovered at the corners of his mouth.

"I say when we're done, baby. Not you. It's never you." He released his fingers and gave her a push.

When Roman's mother laid a gentle hand on his leg, he realized it was vibrating under the table. Delia snarked something crabby through the hatch. Elenie squared her shoulders, blew out a tense breath, and got on with her work. She looked unruffled but her hands were shaking.

Roman wouldn't have put money on his own being completely steady.

By the time Dax pushed his empty plate away, Athena had only picked at her breakfast. She played with the cigarette lighter between fidgety fingers, a nicotine addict jonesing for a smoke. They left soon afterward without another word to anyone.

Roman headed out too. He didn't say goodbye to Elenie but at least he'd managed to slip her a new cell phone inside the used takeout bag. There were tears in his mother's eyes when he kissed her on the cheek. His dad was frowning.

"I'm handling it, Ma," he promised her. "She'll be OK."

And handle it he would, even if it killed him.

* * *

Back at the station, after safely removing the incriminating evidence, Roman delivered the donuts to an enthusiastic reception and beckoned Dougie to his office.

Taking a huge bite out of a glazed donut, Dougie studied the evidence bag containing the gun. "What now?" he asked.

"I have to pass this up the chain of command for examination and tracing." Roman pinched the bridge of his nose. "It looks like Dax is up to his ears in some serious shit." He'd shown Dougie the photos of the drugs and the gun, even though it was strictly DEA business now.

"So Dax and sons are running drugs—probably dealing, too—and one of their goon-for-hire services involves disposing of firearms." Dougie licked his fingers and spoke his thoughts aloud. "I wonder if finding out what Elenie knows will give the DEA enough information to apply for a search warrant for the Dax place?"

Roman grunted, his movements contained and focused. He could feel the familiar buzz of the chase rippling through him. They were close on Frank's heels. It only needed one trip-up from him, one twist on the path that worked in their favor, and they would have enough to pin down the fucker.

His phone buzzed on the pile of paperwork where he'd dumped it earlier. He swore at the name on the screen.

"I'll leave you to it, Chief," Dougie told him cheerfully, around a last mouthful of donut, and pulled the door closed behind him.

Roman swiped to answer the call. "Yes?" he grated.

"Charming." Zena's voice was teasing in his ear. "Anyone would think you weren't missing me at all."

He frowned and shook his head. What the hell was she talking about? "Did you mean to call me? This is Roman."

She gave a flirty little laugh. "I'm at work, so I've only got a few minutes. I'm calling about next weekend."

And just like that, he understood. Roman wondered who was listening to Zena's end of the call. He felt his irritation building and fought the urge to hang up on her.

"Right. Your work event. When and where is it?" His voice held all the warmth of a slushie.

"It's at the Monarch Club, at the top of the Metropolitan Building. Saturday from seven p.m. Evening dress. I can't wait to see you, darling."

"I'll check my schedule and see what I can do."

"I'm sure you'll be able to work something out. It's so important for us both to find the time to get together."

He didn't miss the warning in her words. "I'll be in touch."

Hanging up in the middle of her goodbye, Roman chucked his cell onto the desk. The exchange left him feeling grubby, complicit in something he wanted no part of. Damn Zena for adding another layer of complication where it wasn't needed.

* * *

A night out with friends toward the end of the week was a welcome change. The Rusty Barrel was busy for a Thursday, but Milo, Cait, and Summer, arriving first, had managed to snag one of the booths. Luke finally fought his way to the bar, ordering and handing back bottles and glasses to Thea, who ferried them to the table.

By the time Roman and Dougie had closed down a busy shift, both were in desperate need of a drink. Running his hand through hair still damp from the quick shower he'd had at the station, Roman rotated stiff shoulders and hoped a beer would take the edge off.

Dougie pulled Summer in for a firm kiss. "Needed that!" he drawled. She curled into his side and Roman pushed down on the swirl of envy in his chest.

"Tough day?" Thea took a seat at the end of the booth.

"Just busy." He shrugged. "Trying to pull a lot together at the moment. On top of the usual." He was in the mood for company but not for talking. Hopefully, he wouldn't need to offer much. There were enough people around the table who enjoyed chatting a lot more than he did.

Proving him right, Milo, Cait, and Dougie kicked off a discussion about living off-grid, fueled by a recent documentary. Dougie listed all the things he'd be unable to live without. Cable TV and takeout, mainly. A man of simple tastes.

Roman let his attention wander and took a long swallow of beer.

A chilly blast of evening air hit the back of his neck as the door of the Barrel swung open again and a small group entered the bar. It was as if he'd conjured Elenie up in person from plain wishful thinking. Craig Perry laughed with Tyson Dax, who had his arm slung around a curvy blonde. Another couple he didn't recognize led the way and, following along behind, stopping to close the door, was Elenie, casually dressed in jeans and a thin shirt. Roman forced his face into impassivity and watched her out of the corner of his eye.

The group drifted toward the bar. Dax and Perry pushed their way to the front; Elenie hung back and looked around. She tucked a stray piece of hair behind one ear, a habit of hers he loved. He remembered how it had felt between his fingers when he held her face in his hands, the scent of her shampoo in his nose. Roman shifted in his seat. Her wary gaze zeroed in on him—and swept straight past. He allowed himself the tiniest lift of his lips. This gorgeous girl who held his heart in the palms of her hands was one tough customer.

Perry pushed away from the bar, holding a bottle of beer and nothing for Elenie. He headed for the pool table. Cheapskate. In a smooth, fluid movement, Roman unfolded himself from the booth and strolled unhurriedly to the bar. Seconds later, he knew without turning that Elenie stood next to his elbow. The desire to study every inch of her face was overwhelming. It actually hurt to ignore the pull. He kept his stance relaxed, forearms on the bar, his eyes on the bustling bar staff as they served each customer. A fractional movement to the left and his leg bumped Elenie's hip. He kept it there, lightly pressing against her. That tiniest of touches silencing the need that burned inside him.

He caught the eye of one of the bartenders—Kai Mason, cohost of the party which had proved so memorable for Millie Westlake for all the wrong reasons. Roman didn't hold it against him, no matter how much Kai flushed every time their paths crossed. House parties were a rite of passage. For most people it didn't end up being one of the worst nights of their lives. He gave Kai his order and tacked on a gin and tonic for Elenie. When it appeared on the bar in front of him, he pushed it gently her way. "It kills me not being able to talk to you or hold you when I see you." Roman ducked his head to murmur the words in her ear, still not looking at her as he spoke.

Elenie gave an involuntary shiver. She dipped her chin. "Same."

He gathered up a handful of drinks and strode back to the booth. When he returned for the rest, she was already on the other side of the bar, watching Perry and Dax playing pool.

The evening passed pleasantly enough. Florence joined them just after ten, walking in with a guy he hadn't seen before. She was happy and lit up; her date was quiet but attentive. Roman listened and assessed and decided his little sister didn't need his input. But if she did, he'd be there for her. Right now, it was enough that he could look her in the eye without losing himself to dark memories of a squalid trap house.

And all the time, even as he enjoyed the company of his closest friends, he maintained a razor-sharp awareness of everything happening on the other side of the bar.

Tyson Dax was drinking heavily. More friends had joined them and the group was getting rowdy. Perry's overloud belly laugh rang out repeatedly. Round after round of shots were necked, although Elenie still seemed to be sipping the drink he'd bought her. She sat quietly on a bar stool tucked into a corner until Perry decided to drag her off it to play pool. One day, Roman swore he would make the Brit pay for all the times he'd laid his hands on her so roughly. Elenie's reluctance was obvious, but she eventually shrugged, taking the pool cue from Perry like it was a foreign object, while he pushed her toward the table.

"Every time I think that guy can't be more of a dick, he manages it." Thea mirrored his gaze. Roman grunted.

Elenie missed almost every ball she aimed for. When she bent over anywhere near Perry, he either slapped her ass or grabbed her thighs.

"Fuck off, Craig."

Roman read the words clearly on her lips and it made him smile. A second later, a sixth sense for trouble wiped the grin from his face.

Tyson Dax was squaring up to a guy built like a barn. Anyone else might have considered backing down but Dax, fueled by alcohol, was hampered by a hair-trigger temper and no sense at all. Whatever the cause of the argument, it was never going to end well.

Roman moved the second Elenie chose to step between the two of them. She was apologizing on Tyson's behalf, her hands on his chest, when her stepbrother threw the first punch over her head. The Man-Barn lunged forward, barreling into Dax and Elenie, and the trio disappeared into a writhing heap on the floor. Glasses and beer bottles smashed. Tyson's date screamed. Perry put his hands to his mouth and whooped, careful to keep the pool table between him and any flying fists.

Taking a double handful of sweatshirt, Roman heaved at the top body on the pile. Dougie, close behind him, grabbed the Man-Barn's right arm moments before it landed another punch. Elenie, sandwiched in the middle, protected her head with her hands and a cold fury burned in Roman's lungs. They dragged the larger man off her and she rolled to one side as soon as his huge weight was lifted away. With Tyson flat on his back but still swinging wildly, Roman didn't have time to check on her.

A glance to his right told him Milo and Luke had waded in to help Dougie push the Man-Barn back up against the nearest wall. Roman dodged a blow that missed his chin but jarred his shoulder as he grappled with Tyson on the floor. He flipped Dax over onto his stomach in an attempt to subdue him. Flailing furiously, Tyson's hand fell on the jagged neck of a broken bottle. He grabbed it, lunging backward at anything he could reach. Roman placed a none-too-gentle knee on Tyson's back.

"Calm the fuck down!" he grated, pinning Elenie's stepbrother against the floor in a mess of beer and glass.

Dax bucked and swore, lost in a red mist that showed no signs of lifting. As Roman put a little more pressure on Tyson's kidneys, he heard Dougie call the station for backup.

Chapter 41
Elenie

Her chest heaving, hands and clothes sticky with spilled drink, Elenie leaned against the wall. Feeling cold air where she shouldn't, she realized the sleeve of her shirt had ripped at the shoulder and groaned at the loss of another item of clothing. Blood dripped from a shallow cut on the palm of her hand. She'd obviously found some of the broken glass when she'd crawled out from under the pile of bodies. It smarted a little but the bleeding was already slowing.

Sirens wailed in the distance.

Elenie watched Craig slide through the crowd and out the door. Not once did he look for her. And not once did it cross her mind that he would. She stood up slowly, wincing, and moved backward, away from where Tyson continued to twist and fight on the floor in Roman's grip. The huge guy he'd squared up to seemed to have calmed down and was talking to Dougie.

A gentle hand caught hold of her elbow. "You OK?" Thea asked.

Elenie nodded. "I'm fine."

"Want to get out of here?"

"More than I'd like to kick Ty in the balls."

Thea grinned. "Let's go."

They left quickly and quietly, with Thea leaning in to whisper a few words in Caitlyn's ear. She gave them both a thumbs up, rolled her eyes, and went calmly back to sipping her drink. Pulling out of the parking lot in Thea's Prius, they passed a patrol car, lights flashing.

"The cavalry has arrived," Elenie murmured, leaning back against the headrest. She turned to look at Thea out of the corner of her eye. "You getting sick of rescuing me yet?"

Thea's small, lopsided grin reminded Elenie of Roman's half-smile. "Are you kidding? We haven't had this much action around here since my brother was a teenager."

Elenie's dry laugh hurt her freshly bruised ribs. "God damn, Ty. That neanderthal had to pick on someone the size of the Willis Tower, didn't he?"

Thea frowned. "Want to come back to ours? Cait will play taxi driver for the others when they're ready."

"Would you mind dropping me at Roman's? I have his spare key. If you think that'd be OK?" Suddenly unsure, she cursed herself. "Actually, that's probably a stupid idea. Anywhere is fine with me. I can walk home from here."

Thea's lips quirked. "He's spent all evening watching you like a starving man eyeing up a cheesecake and thinking none of us noticed. I've never had the chance to see my brother taken out at the knees by a woman before. I'm pretty sure he'll be happy to come home and find you there."

Elenie gripped her folded arms, so desperate to see Roman, to touch him and have him hold her, that it was impossible to focus on anything else. After Thea had dropped her off and driven away, she dragged herself upstairs, soothing the aches and pains in her bruised body under the warm waterfall of Roman's shower. Elenie let the torrent run over her head and closed her eyes. Inside her chest, her heart drummed an unsteady beat, crying, "Come home, come home," over and over.

It was wonderful to wash away the stickiness but, once she'd toweled herself dry, she eyed the sodden heap of clothing on the bathroom floor and realized her mistake. Even her underwear was soaked with booze. Feeling like a cross between a sneak thief and every female lead in a Hallmark movie, she tentatively opened Roman's wardrobe. His scent hit her and her insides clenched.

For Christ's sake, Elenie. Get a grip.

She pulled a soft denim shirt from its hanger. It hung huge on her shoulders, but she loved the way it felt against her skin—as if Roman himself was wrapped around her. Elenie indulged in a tiny twirl and laughed. She was officially a lost cause. All giddy over a borrowed shirt from the local police chief.

If Frank could see her now.

Padding down the stairs, she threw her clothes into the washing machine. She didn't switch it on; she had a feeling Roman's clothes would be just as filthy as her own. Elenie made herself a warm milk and curled up on the couch. The fuzzy edges of sleep were just beginning to drag at her vision when she heard a key turn in the lock. The front door opened and closed and there were two soft thumps as Roman kicked off his shoes. When he appeared in the doorway, a warm, wonderful smile lifted his lips as he took in her outfit.

"It appears I have been burgled." Rumpled and dirty, jeans patchy and stained, he still took her breath away. Elenie stood, suddenly nervous.

"Can I make you a tea or would you like something stronger?" she offered.

"Tea would be perfect, please." Roman dumped his keys on the counter. He crossed to stand behind her as she filled the kettle from the faucet.

Elenie flushed, her nerve endings tingling. "I hope you don't mind me coming here. Thea thought it would be OK."

As she turned the dial on the stovetop, he slid his arms around her, pulling her against his chest. His mouth next to her ear triggered a sensitive shiver over her skin. "You, in my house, at the end of a very long day, wearing my shirt and smelling like heaven— you are a fucking dream come true."

He drew in a deep breath and her stomach tightened with desire. Elenie's eyelashes fluttered closed. A soft noise came from her lips and she felt him harden against her. "Roman."

"This week has already felt like a month and it isn't even over. I've missed you so much." He rested his chin on the top of her head.

He's not staying. The reminder hit her with the force of a sucker punch.

Roman will get himself steady and he'll leave.

You won't be enough to keep him.

Her mouth trembled. Elenie told herself it was a reaction to the evening's violence. She sagged in the circle of Roman's arms and he held her tighter.

They stood, pressed together, as the kettle began to sing.

Chapter 42
Roman

He'd said he wanted a drink but when it came to it, Roman couldn't let go of her. Everything he'd craved since the gut-churning worry of the handgun and drugs episode was wrapped in the circle of his arms. He forgot the state of his clothes, his desire for a shower, his tiredness. Holding Elenie against him, Roman's need for her eclipsed it all.

She was everything.

His body, already smoldering, began to burn. He lowered his mouth, pressing his lips to her neck just below her ear. Elenie tilted her head for him, wordlessly asking for more. He slid his hands up her thighs, expecting his fingers to find lace, cotton, elastic. Higher and higher they inched, bunching the denim, but there was nothing. Just her satin smooth skin underneath his shirt. She wasn't wearing any underwear.

Roman froze.

"Dear God, Elenie," he rasped. "What are you trying to do to me?"

"Everything was covered in beer—oh!" She broke off as he spun her in his grasp and his mouth fell on her lips, tasting and taking.

Her tongue slid over his. Both demanded, both gave. Her instant heat and her passion sent his own racing higher. There was desperation in the hitch of her breath.

Roman grasped Elenie's hips and lifted her onto the countertop. His hands tugged at the buttons on the shirt she wore.

His shirt. His fucking shirt. He never wanted her to wear anything else.

Scattering kisses against the bare skin he uncovered, his lips followed the path of his fingers. When the denim hung loose from her shoulders, he drew back to take in her naked body with greedy eyes. Her curves, her stomach, the triangle of dark hair between her legs. He needed to touch and taste them all. Run his fingers over every inch of her and read her like Braille. He bent his head to her breasts. Drawing one nipple into his mouth, he teased its tightness with his tongue.

Elenie let out the most delicious breathy moan he'd ever heard and, right there, he lived only to make her do it again. She arched her back, giving him all the access he needed, and he pulled her closer to his mouth. The denim shirt fell from her shoulders into a pool of blue on the countertop. "Oh, yes . . . so good. I love that. Don't stop."

His hardness was a physical pain of the best kind. He pressed against her center, eyes closing when the steel shaft of his erection lodged blissfully between the cushion of her thighs. Roman's mouth traveled blindly to her other nipple, flicking and sucking. One hand fisted in her damp hair while the other, fingers spread across her back, drew her even closer toward him. He reveled in her gasps. So sexy, so enticing.

Pulling back just enough to drag his shirt over his head, Roman threw it onto the floor. His gaze never leaving hers, he reached into his back pocket, pulled out his wallet and took a condom from inside the leather folds. Sliding the wallet onto the counter, Roman scooped Elenie up into his arms—her legs around his waist, her arms around his neck—and carried her to the couch.

"Fuck, I want you. I have wanted you all night." He took her lips again, swallowing her reply, and when he felt the frame bump the back of his calves, he sat down heavily on the couch cushions. Elenie straddled him, knees on either side of his thighs. Roman groaned as she rocked against the hard bulge in his jeans, her warmth surrounding him.

He wondered when he'd be able to take her slowly, play with her body in all the ways he wanted to. The desperation to bury himself inside her grew to an unbearable level but he refused to give in to it.

Taking her mouth, he kissed her again, his hands in her hair tipping Elenie's head to the perfect angle for him to sweep and plunder until they were both breathless. She dragged his lower lip between her teeth and traced it with her tongue. She owned him with her every touch. He worshipped her with his response.

Roman slid a hand between their bodies, dipping past her stomach and inching between her legs. He found her wet and hot around his fingers. Elenie inhaled against his mouth. She rolled over his denim-caged hardness, her chin lifting, eyes closing. He stroked her again and again. Dipping deeper, thumb skating gently across her most sensitive peak. Her thighs clenched and trembled. *His* thighs clenched and trembled. He ached to give her more.

With a hand on either side of her waist, Roman lifted Elenie off his lap. She made a small sound of protest, her eyes glazed, her lips swollen. So fucking tempting.

"Lie back," he growled.

Her eyelashes lowered slowly, hiding her expression. When they rose again, her irises glittered like molten rock. "Why don't *you* lie back?" she suggested.

Roman's breath locked in his throat. Elenie was often so guarded, so careful to fly under the radar, that it was easy to forget she wasn't shy.

Without breaking eye contact, he lay back against the cushions. His heart crashed inside the cage of his ribs when she climbed astride him. He couldn't hold back a graveled grunt as her core settled over his hips. "Fuck—"

Her hands traced the muscles of his abdomen, the planes of his chest. He twitched and jerked beneath her touch, his breath coming harder. Clenching his jaw, Roman fought to lie still enough to let her explore.

"Your body is the most beautiful thing I've ever seen," she murmured and he felt ten feet tall. Elenie lifted dazed eyes. They were deep pools of stormy gray. "Why do I want to sink my teeth into you? I think there must be something wrong with me."

His husky laugh caught in his throat when she leaned forward and flicked her tongue over his nipple. His hips bucked under hers, his hands grabbing at her waist. "Ah, yes . . . That's—"

Her hot little mouth closed over the firm pebble she'd created, sucking him like he'd sucked her. Sparks burst over the surface of his skin. She reached for the button of his jeans, sliding the zipper down with difficulty and releasing the pressure on his aching cock. Elenie's cool fingers slid into his shorts and closed around his hardness. She moved her hand up and down his shaft. Roman's eyes rolled. Every muscle bunched and quivered.

Her touch was magic. Nothing had ever been this good before; never had someone played his body with such mastery.

With every stroke, she kissed him. Teasing brushes of her lips over his nipples, his collarbones, the curve of his biceps. She dragged her teeth up the column of his neck and bit down lightly just beneath his ear, like a racy little vampire. Her bare breasts pressed against his chest and it was all too much.

305

Roman reversed their positions with a growl and surged to his feet. Pushing his jeans and his shorts down in one impatient movement, he kicked them off and left them in a heap on the rug. In seconds, he'd grabbed and ripped open the foil packet of the condom and rolled it over his length.

He locked eyes with Elenie. There was something so intense in her expression but it disappeared before he could examine it. She reached for him, even as he parted his lips to question her.

"I need you," she whispered.

Roman lowered himself over her. "You have me."

Taking most of his weight on one elbow, he threaded the other behind Elenie's knee, opening her up to him. He paused at the entrance to her warmth, dirty words falling like flattery from his lips.

Her eyes fluttered shut as she moaned and pulled him closer. "Yes, Roman. Just there. I . . . ah—" Her words trailed away as he pressed slowly home and slid into her heat. She arched against him.

They moved together, push against push, stroke for stroke. Her softness the perfect fit for his angles. Nothing else mattered. There was nothing but her.

"I want to be so deep," he ground out, rasping the words into her neck. "I can't get close enough. You feel incredible. God, Elenie!"

He tried to remember every traffic violation he'd written up since his return just to distract himself from the way she gripped him as he moved inside her, but it was impossible.

"More, Roman. More." Her breathy gasps drove everything else out of his head.

Elenie closed her teeth on his shoulder and he shuddered, utterly destroyed. She clenched and bowed beneath him, her hips grinding into his as she climaxed. Roman, gripped by the waves that pulled her under, came in surges that wracked his body, emptying himself inside her.

They were both left gasping in the wake of the storm.

Chapter 43
Elenie

"Where did you get this scar? Not Florence again." She ran her finger over a narrow ridge of silver skin on the inside of his forearm.

"I honestly don't remember, but I don't think she was to blame for that one."

She adored the low rumble of Roman's voice when it was a little hoarse from passion. His chest rose and fell underneath her. Elenie rested her chin on her hand and smiled at him. "I like that you have scars. You need a few tiny flaws amongst all that perfection. Makes it less intimidating for the rest of us."

Roman raised one eyebrow. "I'm perfect, am I? Says the woman with skin like velvet and eyes that could lead me into the jaws of hell." He ran teasing fingers over the small of her back and gave her ass a squeeze. "And that's without even mentioning your—"

"We were talking about you!" Elenie batted away his hand.

Roman's deep chuckle tapered off as he traced a darkening bruise on her shoulder. "Is this sore?"

She flexed it. "A little. But that's what you get for being the filling in an idiot sandwich. I think I got in the way of someone's elbow." In truth, she felt a bit like she'd been hit by a wrecking ball. "I mark really easily so I'll probably be covered in bruises by tomorrow, but I've had worse. Tyson's such a jerk."

His arms tightened around her, his eyes pained. Roman turned her palm over to examine the thin, pink scratch that ran across its center. "I hate that I can't stop you from getting hurt. That I can't keep you safe. It makes me want to break things."

Elenie touched the muscle that jumped in his jaw. "Everything in my life is a million times better because of you. I feel safer just by knowing you."

Roman swallowed. He pressed his lips to the palm of her hand. "I was drowning before I met you. You can't even imagine how bad it had gotten. But seeing you battle every single day, seeing your will and your determination—you make me remember that I'm strong, too. I would take on the world for you if I could. It's what you deserve." He pulled her up his body and kissed her with an intensity that fanned the glowing embers in all her nerve endings. "Stay with me tonight?"

Elenie blinked away a hot glaze of tears. She wished she could see herself through his eyes. "For a while, I was so desperate for someone to hold me that I made some really stupid relationship choices. I could pretend nothing else mattered if I closed my eyes and enjoyed the feeling of being held."

Roman expelled a long breath. "Let me hold you tonight." No judgment, just understanding.

She had no defense against his tenderness. "It is very late . . ."

"And your clothes are covered in beer . . ."

"And you seem to have taken back your shirt . . ."

"Well, that's sorted then. I don't want to have to write you up for public indecency."

Elenie could have stared at Roman's teasing half-smile and his strong, tanned features forever. Even though keeping a grip on what they had together felt like cupping a handful of dry sand, somehow he had become the center of her world. It was terrifying.

"Don't." He caught hold of her chin.

"What?"

"You went somewhere else then. And you know I can hear you thinking." There was purpose in his sudden movements as he sat up, then stood. Roman took her hand and pulled her to her feet. "I guess I'll have to distract you."

It was working already. Thinking of anything but the glory of his naked body was a physical impossibility. Elenie ran hungry eyes over him from head to toe and he laughed.

"What an insatiable little thief I have had the fortune to stumble across tonight!" Roman followed the trail of his clothes back to the countertop, scooping up each item as he went. Dumping them all into the washer with Elenie's, he grabbed a laundry capsule from the cupboard and flicked the switch. "Come on, sweetheart." He held out his hand. "Let's get dirty while our clothes get clean?" Roman waggled a dissolute eyebrow, then shook his head ruefully. "That sounded better in my head."

Elenie giggled. "If the good people of Pine Springs could hear you, Chief Martinez, they'd be scandalized!"

He reached for her with a scowl and led her toward the stairs. "If they even think of turning up here before morning, they will have only themselves to blame."

In his bedroom, Roman turned on the small bedside lamp, pulling her down onto the covers. Elenie shivered, goosebumps springing up on her arms. She didn't know if it was from the cool sheets against her skin or the expression on Roman's face. He looked as if he wanted to swallow her whole. She forced herself to stay in the moment. This was too special to spoil with panic about the future.

"Are you cold?" he asked.

"A little." Her eyes fixed on his, her voice husky. "Make me warmer."

He lowered himself to cover her body and his heat surrounded her. It was blissful. His arousal, already hot and heavy against her legs, made her stomach flip. She curled her fingers into his hair, pulling his mouth down to hers, and Roman's tongue parted her lips. Elenie heard herself sigh and he moaned into her mouth.

"The noises you make drive me crazy. I hear them in my dreams." He began kissing a path down her neck, stopping to open his mouth on one of her breasts, stroking her nipple with his tongue. Roman's hand drifted lower, skating over her hip, his thumb drawing circles on her skin.

"I love the way you touch me." Her back arched off the bed, her head falling to one side. "Never stop. Please, never stop."

He laughed against her skin. "Just try and make me. I can't get enough—I want to do it forever."

Forever. That word. It hurt to hear it when it couldn't be true.

But the cramp had no time to take hold on her heart, as Roman's fingers crept between her legs, curling in the dark triangle of hair between her thighs and stroking her already sensitive lips. He caressed her as his mouth switched to her other breast, sucking and pulling. His broad thumb brushed her clit, sweeping backwards and forwards in a movement that tugged at her core. He was so fucking good at that.

Elenie's stomach trembled; her muscles tightened. Her blood was hot, spiked cider, heating her veins and intoxicating her senses. Her body wasn't used to this kind of reverence. She was going to explode.

Roman moved lower, his lips hovering where his fingers traced the moist folds between her thighs, until she tugged on his hair and begged for relief. The flat of his tongue delivered it in strokes that sent her flying. Elenie's fists clenched and the night air turned humid around them. She came with a cry, spiraling over and over as he played her with his clever mouth and agile fingers.

When she could breathe again, he slid up her body and took her mouth, hard and deep, with lips that tasted of her sex. His cock teased her opening, resting heavily against her thighs. "You're my favorite taste. My favorite flavor," he told her huskily.

Elenie tilted her hips in invitation, desperate to feel him inside her again, knowing how perfectly he filled her. Roman sat up in one quick movement, reaching for a foil packet from the drawer beside the bed. She watched him roll the condom over himself— the action, his hands, his bare muscled chest, all so erotic. Just seeing him close his fist around his hard length forced a breathy sound from her lips and his eyes blazed. He guided her legs apart and settled between them.

There was a moment of anticipation so full of need that it twisted her heart. Elenie wanted to pull him to her but it wasn't necessary. She was so wet he slid inside in one exhilarating surge. Roman's eyes closed. He rested his forehead on hers.

"Holy fuck, Elenie. How can it feel this good every time?" He began to move. "I want—I can't . . . ah, yes. Just like that. So damn perfect." The words escaped him through gritted teeth and he pulled her even tighter against his hips with one hand behind the small of her back.

With earthy whispers into her ear and his fingers in her hair, he drove her higher and higher. His control shattered piece by piece, taking Elenie with him as he began to fall apart. She drew him closer, her heart pounding, telling him how unbelievable he felt— how unbelievable *she* felt.

And when they finally broke, they broke together.

* * *

Roman's bedroom was the most heavenly place she had ever woken up in.

They hadn't drawn the curtains, just fallen asleep immediately after the quickest of trips to the bathroom. And now the morning sun was breaking through the trees, casting light and shadow on her face as her eyelids flickered open.

For several long minutes, she watched the treetops bend and dance outside the glass doors, like the most graceful of chorus girls performing in time with each other. A smile curved Elenie's lips—whether it was from the beautiful view, the warm ache between her thighs, or the possessive curve of Roman's arm around her waist, she wasn't sure. She decided she didn't have to choose.

Turning her head just slightly, she found an even better view. Roman looked younger in his sleep. His face lost its hard angles to relaxation, and closed eyelids covered his usual focus and intensity. That he rested so peacefully gave her a fierce jolt of pleasure. He deserved more than undisturbed nights as a reward for all he'd gone through.

His eyes seemed less haunted recently, his posture less strained. If she could ease any of the weight he carried by listening and understanding, she'd do it in a heartbeat. The thought of him struggling hurt Elenie in ways that scared her.

She studied his heavy eyebrows, long eyelashes, and sharp cheekbones with greedy eyes, and that fearful fist pressed down on her chest. Why did it have to happen that the one man she wanted above all others was someone who deserved so much more than she had to offer?

Elenie knew her own value. She'd been told often enough. And she understood to her cost that you could wish all you liked for something but you couldn't make it happen. People like her didn't get that lucky. She swore to herself she would read the signs when the time came for him to move on. And she knew it would.

However painful the memories might be in the future, she'd treasure this pocket of bliss forever.

Roman's lips moved and he sighed. His fingers tightened on her waist. When his dark eyes opened and fixed on her face, Elenie basked in his lazy, sleepy smile.

"Good morning." Rock-star husky, his voice raised the hairs on her arms. "What time is it?"

"Early, I think. I'm not quite sure."

He rolled onto his back and stretched, his body long and lean like a wildcat. So damn sexy, he stole her words. "God, I slept well." Roman's eyes sparkled. "I wonder why." His smile was infectious.

When he reached for her, Elenie slid into his arms. The moon to his sun.

"You are a million degrees," she murmured against his chest. "So hot."

"Why, thank you, ma'am." Roman's laugh rumbled next to her ear. He stretched to lift his phone from the nightstand and squinted at the screen. "You're right—it is early. When are you due at work?"

"Eight."

"Hmmm . . ." He ran his fingers lightly up her arm and she gave an involuntary shiver. "We have plenty of time then."

Roman's hands spanned her waist, dragging her over his body and sitting her astride his hips. When he kicked the quilt down with his feet, Elenie could feel the warmth of his impressive erection spring up against her ass.

"This would seem to be the time for an inappropriate joke about being armed and dangerous." She stumbled over the words, a breathless laugh dying on her lips.

Roman's throat moved as he swallowed and he didn't seem to hear her. Just ran his hands up and down her arms, frowning at the new bruises that had bloomed overnight on her skin. Elenie didn't want to think or talk about them. She leaned down to press her mouth against his neck, glorying in the heat of his skin. His body was huge and solid between her thighs. Tanned muscles jumped beneath her fingers when she stroked him.

"Maybe we could push breakfast back a little," he rasped.

And they did.

* * *

"Tyson will be waking up in the cells this morning."

"Oh?" Elenie raised an eyebrow as she bit into her toast.

"He headbutted Liam Morgan before we could get him into the squad car last night. Add that to pulling a broken bottle on me and he's managed to turn a drunken fistfight into something more serious." Roman watched her over his mug of tea. "If I can throw anything else at him, I will. You could have gotten hurt last night."

"What happened with the other guy?" she asked. "The huge one?"

"Levi Foster. He was pretty apologetic once we took him to one side. Tyson threw the first punch and most of the others too. Foster gave us no trouble at all as soon as we dragged him off you." Roman's face was grim as he recalled the chaos. "We let him go with a caution in the end. But I'll be keeping an eye on him." He stood up to slot another couple of slices of bread into the toaster. "Foster couldn't even tell us what it was all about. He was pretty drunk."

"Just trash talk, I think. Ty was knocking them back too and it doesn't take much to make him flip out." She watched Roman's face as she spoke. He grunted but said nothing.

One of these times, her repellent family would color this fragile thing between them. He wouldn't be able to help himself from tarring her with the brush she'd been trying to avoid her whole life. It was guaranteed. And no amount of sexual pull would be able to stop it.

Elenie put down her toast, her appetite disappearing, as Roman came back to the table.

"So the handgun has gone off for analysis with the DEA. Dorsey was pretty understanding about it coming via me. And they're looking into the Saginaw address you gave her as well. I've also had a couple of interesting emails from June Reed Sanders. You did well to get her on board. The information she's forwarded from Craig is illuminating." Roman frowned at the butter as if that might be next under the spotlight. "The balls are lining up over the pockets, Elenie. One of them will fall soon. When it does, we'll be ready."

His words sounded like a promise. It was one that she needed to be true so badly it hurt. No matter what came with it.

"I'm heading into Detroit tomorrow. Milo has to make a work trip—he's got meetings through the afternoon and evening—so I'm going to grab the chance to share the ride and go with him. There's some business I need to take care of."

Elenie wondered if she was imagining the way he avoided her eyes. Roman swept some crumbs from the table into his hand and brushed them onto his empty plate. For a moment, his face looked stormy, as if old memories were biting at the thought of returning to the city. She reached out to curl her fingers around his wrist. His mouth softened immediately.

"I'm staying overnight but I'll be back first thing Sunday." He gave her a devastating smile which had her stomach jumping, her skin tingling. Damn, but she loved that smile.

"OK." Elenie didn't miss the flicker of relief that crossed his face.

She wanted to trust Roman would tell her if there was something she needed to know, but trust didn't come easy. She opened her mouth to question him. Closed it again when she realized how many things she might not want to hear.

Chapter 44
Elenie

Though her muscles ached from where she'd taken a battering between Ty and Levi Foster, the discomfort faded to the back of her mind as Elenie completed her shift. Her body still hummed with the ghost sensations of everything she and Roman had done last night—and again this morning.

Special Agent Dorsey might not have raised any issues about the handgun being in Roman's possession, but Elenie had held back from telling him about the blistering message she'd received from Booth. He was less than impressed.

She'd been right to take the more expendable phone with her to Saginaw. Better by far that Frank had gotten his hands on that one. But the chief deputy was deaf to her reasoning, pushing for more information, better results, and making sure she knew how little faith he had in her.

Elenie's feet paused on the driveway as she approached the house after work. On impulse, she headed out back to the garage and found the doors ajar, the chunky chain lying in a heap on the ground. Opportunity for a look inside shone like the high bay lights Frank had hung from the roof beams. She hesitated only slightly, before crossing the scrubby grass and sliding into the outbuilding.

"Hi."

Frank paused in the process of hefting one blue plastic drum on top of another in the corner of the garage. "Yes?"

"Is Mom in the house?"

"I don't know, Ellie. I'm in the garage. Did you look for her?" He rolled an old tire out through the doorway and let it fall onto the grass.

"Yes," she said, although she hadn't, digging around for a way to extend the conversation but coming up short. She could never think of anything to say to Frank. "What are you doing?"

"Tidying."

"Why?"

It didn't look so much like tidying. There was little or no order to how the garage was organized. A workbench, piled high with discarded car parts, random bolts and half-used bottles of oil, screen wash, lubricants, and more, was almost hidden behind a stack of tools and fishing equipment. Frank's new baby, a crossover snowmobile he'd picked up last winter, sat beneath a tarp next to Ty and Dean's dirt bikes. She could see nothing that shouldn't be there. Nothing worth reporting.

"Need to clear some space."

Elenie's attention flicked back to Frank. "What for?"

"Fuckin' nosy today, aren't you?" His grouchy grumble was distracted rather than suspicious. "Got a delivery coming in soon. Have you heard about Ty?"

"I was there."

"Fuckin' cops."

"Yeah, fucking cops." She shifted her feet and headed for the door. This wasn't a conversation she wanted to extend. "They still holding him?" Frank grunted, answering without words, and kicked some old overalls underneath the workbench. "Right, well, I need to go and—" Elenie jerked a thumb toward the house. The metallic clangs and dull thuds of Frank's "tidying" continued behind her.

317

Music pumped from Dean's room; the living room lights were off. Elenie wandered through to the kitchen to grab a drink. Reaching for a glass, her hand froze halfway to one of the cabinets on the wall. On the countertop, next to the stove, Frank's cell phone was plugged into a socket and charging.

Her stomach bottomed out.

Oh, crap.

Dare she? What if—

Elenie forced herself to move. This was the only chance she'd had so far; it was too good to miss.

She took the stairs in twos, bolting for her room. Dean's door was shut; her mother's was open but there was no sign of Athena. With shaking fingers, she wrenched open her closet, upended the box of tampons she'd tucked right at the back of the shelf, and grabbed the tiny plug-in recovery device—black and innocuous-looking—from Dorsey's "CI toolkit." Dragging underwear and socks forward to cover everything else, Elenie shoved the doors closed and hurtled back down the stairs.

From the kitchen window, she could still see the garage light and Frank's outline passing back and forth across the half-open door.

Three to five minutes. That's all she needed.

Elenie lifted Frank's cell, pulled the charger out and replaced it with the remote forensic device which would copy and extract his data. His lock screen lit up; the time display read 16:19.

Palms damp, underarms sticky, Elenie swept her hair out of her face with shaky fingers, eyes darting back to the window, back to Frank's shadow. "Stay there. Please, please, stay there." The words were a prayer on her tongue.

She drummed her fingers on the countertop, staring at the phone. Dean's music droned on upstairs, vibrating through the floorboards. She wanted a drink but couldn't swallow, wanted to go to the bathroom but couldn't risk it. The kitchen smelled of burnt pasta. In the sink, a pan held a dirty inch of dishwater and macaroni soup. It almost made her gag.

Elenie jabbed at the button on the side of Frank's phone to light the screen again. 16:21. Never had time crawled as slowly. Her diaphragm cramped. There was a pain stabbing through her chest. Maybe she was having a heart attack. Maybe the stress would kill her before Frank could.

She forced herself to think of Millie Westlake and her family. All the lives Frank had smeared with his filthy fingers, careless of the mess he left behind. All the reasons the Daxes had been shunned so thoroughly in Pine Springs. So many she'd lost count. She could do this.

16:22.

Should she unplug the device or leave it for the full five minutes? Elenie shot another agonized look out of the window. Frank was still there. Still busy. She'd give it one more minute—

"I'll have a coffee if you're making one."

Elenie whirled around, gaping at her mother in the doorway. The blood drained from her face; her stomach plunged like the downward swoop of a rollercoaster. She tried to force her mouth to form actual words but her lips refused to move.

Athena yawned and stretched, planting herself in front of the small mirror on the wall to wipe at the smudges of makeup in the corners of her eyes. Bare, pale feet on the vinyl floor accounted for her silent appearance.

"Where were you?" Elenie's voice was hoarse. She heard the quaver and hoped her mother didn't.

"Fell asleep on the couch."

Elenie's eyes darted to Frank's cell. She didn't dare move toward it. Couldn't unplug the device.

Fuck.

"When did you get in?" Athena asked.

"Just now. I've only been home five minutes or so." Elenie stepped closer to the counter, blocking Frank's phone from view.

Athena wandered over to the back door and peered through the glass. "Better make that three coffees."

"Three?"

"Frank's on his way in."

Elenie's throat closed. She dragged at the neck of her polo shirt. "He'll be pissed if Dean doesn't turn down his music," she croaked.

Athena pursed her lips. "I have a headache, too. That boy has no consideration—" She wandered toward the stairs.

Behind her mother's back, Elenie dived for Frank's phone, whipped the device from the external port and plugged the cell back into the charging cable. Her hands shook so badly it took three tries to connect it properly. She threw the phone back onto the worktop and flung open the cabinet above her head, just as Frank walked in through the back door. In the hallway, her mom was yelling fruitlessly up the stairs against the beat of Dean's tunes.

"Coffee?" The word cracked but Frank only shrugged a bulky shoulder.

"Sure."

Elenie put the kettle on the stove to boil and slid out of the room, data device in the sticky palm of her hand. "Be back in a mo." Heart crashing in her chest, she passed her mom at the bottom of the stairs. "I'll have a word with him. I want to get changed anyway. Keep an eye on the kettle, would you?"

Only her tight grip on the wobbly handrail as she climbed the treads gave her the strength to reach the top, where she sagged against the landing wall in sheer relief, running sweaty hands down the sides of her skirt.

* * *

"Corned beef hash and French toast?"

"No. We asked for two vegetarian omelets." Mrs. Alberty and her friend looked at Elenie as if she had asked them to eat a brace of small children.

"My mistake. Give me one minute." She double-checked the order numbers, took the plates she held to the correct table, and delivered them to Delia's niece, Avery Delgado, and Leo Marsh.

"Sharp as a marble, you are today," Delia groused when she returned to the hatch to collect the omelets. "Any chance you could pretend you didn't bring your brother's brains to work?"

Imagining a world in which her biggest issue was a misremembered breakfast order, Elenie kept her middle fingers under control and her lips zipped. She gave Delia a speculative side-eye.

For once, twenty-four hours out of the bed of Roman Martinez, the graze of his stubble on her skin crystal-clear in her mind—Elenie knew she had something that another person might envy. And, jealous or not, Delia could take her sour-faced, snarky attitude and go screw herself. One day, she could screw the job too.

Elenie had struggled to sleep last night, her mind churning after exchanging texts with Dorsey about the data recovery device. They'd arranged to meet tomorrow to hand it over. As desperate to get rid of it as she had been the gun, she was thankful it was easier to hide. Tucking the tiny object into the toe of a sock, she rolled it with the other in its pair and shoved them into the front pocket of her purse. Better to keep it close.

She longed to spill the story of last night's narrow escape to Roman. Aching for his measured support, the security of his arms, she'd settled instead for a brief text to wish him a successful trip into the city. Craig was also out of town, and Elenie felt some of the pressure in her chest ease because of it. She didn't give a hoot where he was but was grateful for the reprieve.

Diner 43 was pretty dead for once. It didn't happen often and it hadn't helped Delia's crappy mood. Neither did her niece's presence—apparently Delia was no fonder of her family. But Elenie made the most of being able to move slower than usual, noting any low supplies and tidying areas normally neglected. Best of all, she shared her morning break with Otto.

"That damned racoon was back again yesterday, Elenie. I swear he thinks it's more his house than mine. Guess what he took this time!"

"Well, he's had your shoe and your breakfast—what else could he possibly want? Please don't tell me it was your underwear from the washing line."

Otto gave a low, wheezy laugh. "That damn critter unscrewed the lightbulb in my porch. I saw him run away with it along the handrail and over the grass."

"No way! I wonder what he wanted it for. Maybe the cupboard under his stairs?" Elenie snorted into her coffee. That was a story to share with Roman. She'd message him later. "Did you know racoons score nearly as high as monkeys, elephants, and dolphins on intelligence tests? They can even work out how to pick a lock."

"Impressive." Otto raised his bushy eyebrows. "Although, to be fair, that's a tough one for elephants and dolphins, so the blasted racoons aren't competing on a level playing field there."

She had to give him that.

When Summer and Cait came in mid-afternoon, it began to feel more like a day off than the usual hard slog. With only one other table occupied in the diner and the serving area as clean as it had been in a long time, Elenie spent every quiet moment she could hovering near their table, keen to catch up but hyperaware of watching eyes.

Caitlyn shifted uncomfortably on one of the booth benches. She looked incredibly pretty in pale yellow loose-flowing overalls. Her bump was enormous and her eyes were tired.

"If you get any bigger, I'll have to get someone in to unbolt the tables and shift them back a foot," Elenie told her.

Caitlyn sighed. "You won't need to, because if I get any bigger, I'll do myself in."

"Ignore her. She's joking and seriously sleep-deprived." Summer's glance was sympathetic.

Caitlyn rubbed her temples. "Everyone tells you that you'll get no sleep with a newborn—but don't imagine you can stock up in advance. Oh no. It's impossible to find a comfortable position in bed when you're the size of a whale, plus you need to pee every three minutes, night and day."

Elenie winced. "Just think what a pro you'll be at existing on minimal sleep once mini-Milo arrives."

"Please bring me hot chocolate and all the sweet stuff you have." Caitlyn's eyes were pleading.

"Your wish is my command. I'll bring you anything but octopus."

"I'm sorry, what?"

"In Bali, they think eating octopus when you're pregnant will give you a difficult delivery."

A wry smile lifted Caitlyn's face. "If Delia has started using octopus as an ingredient, you've got your own problems to worry about, my friend."

The girls sat and chatted for over an hour. Each time she refilled their drinks, Elenie stayed as long as she dared without risking anyone's attention.

"How bruised are you on a scale of one to ten?" Summer asked. "I can't get over how fast Roman moved when you disappeared into that heap of crazy!"

"Blasted Ty. He could pick a fight with a poodle." Elenie pretended to refill the sugar canister for the third time.

"And he's stupid enough to do it with Levi Foster—the guy with snow shovels for hands." Caitlyn rolled her eyes.

"I swear he has a screw loose." Elenie shook her head. "He'll square up to the wrong person one of these days when there's no one around to break it up. And it won't end well."

Summer gave her a sneaky side-eye. "Where did you disappear to, by the way? One minute you were there and the next you weren't."

Elenie couldn't stop the smile from spreading slowly across her face.

Caitlyn let out a low whistle. "Hot damn, you little snake. There's a story that I need an empty bladder to hear!" Heaving herself up onto her feet and poking a finger in Elenie's direction, she waddled away from the table. "Do not go anywhere. I'll be as swift as these overalls will let me."

Elenie cleared the empty mugs and plates from Summer and Caitlyn's table, unloaded the dishwasher, and began to restack it again. She made milkshakes for a couple of teenagers who wanted takeouts and took coffee to Mrs. Elliott and Ray Parker, who were sitting at a small table in the corner.

It turned out that swift was not that quick at all.

After more than ten minutes had gone by, Summer stood up. A frown pinched at her forehead. "I think I'll just go check—"

She was interrupted by Caitlyn peeping around the edge of the door to the back corridor. Her eyes were a little wild. "Ladies, we appear to have a bit of a situation." They flew to her side and she opened the door wider. The cotton legs of her pants looked like she'd dropped a drink in her lap. Summer's lips parted with a silent intake of breath. "My waters have broken." For a second, no one moved. Then Caitlyn winced and gripped her stomach with both hands. "I've been having some pains, but they're getting stronger."

"And you didn't think to say anything?" Summer squeaked.

"I'm ten days from my due date. I thought they'd go away again. Isn't that what's supposed to happen with first babies?"

Elenie and Summer exchanged looks. Nope, not a clue between them. Delia peered out through the hatch, took in what was happening, and opted right out.

"I'm calling Milo." Summer's voice was decisive. She shot over to the booth to grab her phone from her bag.

"I need to walk," Caitlyn muttered between tight lips. While Summer made the call, Elenie paced slowly with her up and down the center aisle of the diner. "I made a mess in the bathroom." Cait's voice was wobbly. "But I think my socks soaked most of it up. My shoes are kind of squelchy."

"Clearing up messes is my superpower," Elenie soothed. "And I think the contractions will take your mind off your socks."

Summer's face glowed with excitement when she re-joined them, but her voice was calm. "OK, so I caught Milo between meetings. He's heading straight back and will meet us at the hospital. Unless you think you need an ambulance, I've spoken to Dougie and he's on his way to take us in."

Caitlyn nodded, eyes wide, like a small girl being told what to do.

"Let's keep walking while we wait," Elenie suggested. They paced together for the next ten minutes, pausing a couple of times when the contractions came on.

When Dougie burst in, he had a wide grin on his face and was rolling up his shirtsleeves. "Right then, ladies. I hear there's a baby needs delivering and I've washed my hands, so let me at it."

The girls regarded him with varying degrees of eye roll.

"If you think for one minute that your homemade first-aid certificate will give you access between my legs, you're truly delusional," Caitlyn deadpanned.

They helped her waddle outside, where Dougie's truck waited curbside with the passenger door open, a sweatshirt spread out on the seat for Caitlyn to sit on. Sweeping her up in strong arms before she could think of protesting, Dougie lifted her straight in. Summer climbed across from the driver's side to sit in the middle.

Elenie gave Cait a quick hug before she shut the door. "Good luck! I'll be thinking of you." Pulling carefully away, Dougie gave a short blast on the horn and they were gone.

Inside the diner, Mrs. Elliott and Ray Parker had left money on the table to cover their drinks. The place was silent, other than Delia banging about in the small kitchen. Turning the sign on the door to "Closed," Elenie went in search of a bucket.

After mopping the restroom floor, she gave the toilet cubicles and basins the most thorough clean they'd had in a long time. Stretching out weary muscles, she washed her hands, stuck her head into the kitchen to tell Delia she was leaving, and grabbed her purse from the staff area. The others would be at the hospital by now. She wondered how things were going and if Milo would make it in time.

Elenie wrapped her arms around her body. Her uniform and zipped hoodie were thin and it was a chilly afternoon. The sky had turned heavy; the promise of rain hung in the air. She would need to get hold of a coat soon. The weather in Pine Springs around fall could change in an instant.

As she passed the door of Archer and Desai Realty Management, Frank's truck pulled up alongside her, its engine gritty.

Dean pushed open the passenger door and gave her a grin. "Hey, sis. Jump in. Dad's gotten another job for us."

Frank's eyes, dull and impatient, met Elenie's, and an uneasy shiver ran the length of her spine. As she climbed reluctantly into the Dodge, the first light raindrops splattered on the sidewalk.

Chapter 45
Roman

Roman frowned into his Old Fashioned. It felt as if he'd slipped on an obsolete and uncomfortable persona along with his tux and black tie.

The setting was stunning. The deep blue, red and gold of the Monarch Club's interior exuded class and luxury; he couldn't fault it. Even so, he'd give anything to be back in Pine Springs this evening. Either heading to the Rusty Barrel to meet up with his friends or—and he wanted this possibly more than he wanted to take his next breath—relaxing at home, with Elenie in his arms, in his bed. His mouth on hers. His cock deep inside her. Roman suppressed a growl and pushed away from the bar, shifting to reposition himself in his formal pants before anyone noticed.

He cursed himself for not being straight with Elenie. There was no reason at all for keeping this arrangement with Zena from her. Just the simple desire not to taint their limited time together with the manipulations of his ex-fiancée, and the less selfish wish to protect Elenie from any extra stress. She was dealing with enough.

"How are you getting on with those drinks, honey?"

He turned slowly and handed Zena her cocktail. His face was stuck in "fuck this shit" lines, which he didn't know how to wipe away. He'd never mastered the art of appearing invested or interested at functions like this. Roman wondered why everything was easier when Elenie was near him. She made him laugh and relax. Around her, he could be exactly who he felt like inside.

Instead, he was standing somewhere he didn't want to be, with a date he didn't respect, talking to people who didn't interest him, drinking a cocktail he didn't like. And he was hating every minute of it.

"I don't think you've met Penelope St. John, Mark Levison, and Ryan Pullman from St. John Associates, have you? Our firm assisted them with a buyout. It completed last month." Zena rested a proprietorial hand on his upper arm. "This is my partner and Pine Springs' Chief of Police, Roman Martinez."

Roman nodded, twisted his mouth into a smile, and shook hands around the small group.

"Police chief and lawyer? Not a couple to be messed with, then." Levison's grin was friendly, his handshake warm.

"It's why we don't have any friends and don't get asked out much," Roman replied, his face deliberately straight.

Zena gave him the stink eye. She wore an aqua blue satin evening dress held up with spaghetti straps. Her long hair was twisted and pulled neatly into a pleat at the back of her neck. She looked elegant, delicate, and unattainable, all at the same time. Which was fine with him because he felt no desire whatsoever to put his hands on her.

He'd forgotten how boring this sort of event was. Introducing yourself over and over again, playing the game of "Who has the most impressive job title?" He had no patience for it.

Roman reached into his pocket for his phone, checking for any messages from home. There was nothing new. Just the earlier text he'd had from Milo on his way to the Monarch Club.

Milo:

Cait's in labor and I'm heading to the hospital. Sorry to leave you without a ride. Give Zena a middle finger from me and wish us luck!

He was excited for them; he really was. There was even a pang of jealousy mixed in there somewhere. But, more than anything, he wanted to be in the car with Milo, heading for Pine Springs and back to Elenie. His need to be with her was far greater than his willpower to get through this evening.

Home. He wanted to go home. And his home wasn't in Detroit anymore.

Zena's fingers pulled at his sleeve. "Honey, you're being rude. Penelope asked you a question."

Roman slipped his phone into the inside pocket of his jacket and turned to the lady in question. Trying to fix a charming smile on his face, he wondered why the hell she had drawn her eyebrows in so very dark and so very triangular. "I'm sorry. What did I miss?"

"Well, that was my question really." Penelope gave him a flirty look. "Swapping the city for a small town—there must be a lot to miss. I know I would."

Zena laughed. "That's an understatement. Pine Springs is homely but a little backward. A lovely place to decompress for a while as long as you don't mind drive-in movies being the cutting edge of sophistication."

He clamped down on a rolling surge of irritation. "Fortunately, I have simple tastes. And it saves me having to get my tux dry-cleaned very often."

Zena made their excuses and dragged him away. "Like you actually have a dry cleaner in the Ass End of Nowhereville," she

329

hissed under her breath. "For God's sake, Roman. Do you have to make it so clear you don't want to be here? We had a deal."

He extracted himself from her grip. "And I'm keeping my side of it. You can't complain about my attitude when you've blackmailed me into lying for you."

"Zena."

They both turned at the same time.

"Philippa. Ben." Zena air-kissed an eerily similar-looking blonde. Roman held back a smile. He'd forgotten how closely Zena and Philippa Barrett resembled each other. It seemed Ben had a type, and his type was Professional Barbie. "Roman, you remember Philippa and Ben Barrett? I believe you met briefly at the Commerce Leadership Awards a couple of years ago."

"I do indeed." He shook hands with the couple. His eyes ran over them both, assessing them as they assessed him.

"Lovely to see you here together." There was a definite undercurrent to Philippa's words.

"We've been a little like ships passing in the night since Roman's secondment. I'm fortunate he's managed to make it tonight." Zena kept her voice light, unruffled, a soft smile on her lips. Her shoulders were straight, her chin up.

Roman felt a moment of deep disgust at the ease with which she could stand in front of a woman she was betraying in the worst way possible. None of his thoughts showed on his face.

"It's been a busy few months," he said simply.

A waiter paused on the edge of their group with a selection of canapés. Ben took a couple, everyone else declined. Roman craved pizza, eaten on the couch with friends; he could almost smell it.

Zena slid her arm around his waist, lifting her other hand to rest on his chest. "I'm hoping we'll manage more weekends together now Roman's more settled in his new role."

He saw Barrett's eyes drift to the drape of blue satin that lay across Zena's chest. The form-hugging fit of her dress was aimed to entice and it seemed to be doing its job. Damn, this was painful. He despised emotional game-playing; this was turning his stomach.

Uncomfortably hot, Roman unbuttoned his jacket and shrugged it off his shoulders. Zena was forced to step away.

"So, you were part of the Detroit PD Homicide Unit?" Ben Barrett wore his tuxedo in the casual manner someone else might wear jeans, his shoes polished to perfection. There was more than a hint of fake tan. Roman fought an instant mistrust of any man who paid that much attention to his own grooming and tipped his chin in reply. "I'm surprised you've stepped away. Did it wear you down?" The question was meant to needle.

"It's a tough job." Roman gave a bland answer.

"I guess the hardboiled detective with an iron grip on his emotions is more of a fictional concept than I realized." Ben wasn't going to drop it.

Roman took a long swig of his drink. "Thankfully, these days there's a variety of stress-coping strategies available. But back-to-back murder investigations take a toll over time." He waited for the tension to hit him, braced and expecting the worst. It was a pleasant surprise when the flashbacks, the memories, stayed at bay.

"Especially the cases you never solve, I'd imagine."

Zena must have told him. The guy was being a dick. And even his wife seemed to notice.

"It must be incredibly challenging to stare man's inhumanity to man right in the face." Philippa gave him a searching look. "I have huge admiration for the people who deal with that day after day."

Ben cut in again. "When nine out of ten women murdered in the US are killed by men they know, it must make it a lot easier to narrow down your suspects." He raised a casually careless eyebrow. "Handy in some ways that misogyny is such a key factor in homicide."

"You are mistaken." Roman's eyes were as cold as Alaska, his voice lethal. "The key factor in homicide is death. Death, in many gratuitous forms and for a staggering number of reasons. None pleasant, none simple, and not a single one of them handy."

Ignoring Zena's glare and Barrett's tightened lips, he let his gaze wander around the room and swore there'd be no rerun of this purgatory.

Chapter 46
Elenie

"I'll do the talking. Dean's the eyes and you're the ears." Frank pulled up in front of a single-story building.

The drive had taken them just shy of two hours, most of it spent in silence, tension slowly building as the rain began to hammer on the windshield. After winding through the outskirts of Flint, they entered an abandoned industrial area, bumping along roads that were rough and unfinished. Puddles already formed in the worn-down dips. Derelict and neglected units lay on either side of the track.

How unexpected to find herself just an hour away from Roman in Detroit, when she'd had no idea this job was in the offing the last time they spoke. Elenie hoped his evening was a cut above hers in the fun stakes.

She gazed past Frank and Dean to squint through the rain at the nearest building. Blinds, hanging at an angle, covered the windows of what looked like an old office. Three lockups extended to one side. Roller shutters were pulled down on two; the third was open. "What am I listening for?"

"You speak other languages. Just let me know if you hear anything I should be worried about."

"I don't speak *all* the languages. Just a few useless bits and pieces. Who are we meeting and where do they come from?" Frank didn't answer. "What the fuck?" Elenie mouthed at Dean, who just shrugged.

She'd be lucky to hear anything through the driving rain anyway.

She pulled her hood up over her head as they all climbed out of the truck. Within seconds, it was soaked through. Rivulets of icy water ran down the side of her neck. A stocky guy emerged from the depths of the open lockup, wheeling a dolly stacked high with boxes and protected by a clear plastic sheet. He had a mustache that looked like it had been bought online.

Frank stepped inside, out of the rain, and two more men appeared. They all gathered around the dolly. Frank lifted the plastic, picked up one of the boxes and opened it. Hanging back with Dean by the cab of the truck, Elenie craned her neck but couldn't see any better.

Was Frank collecting something? Buying something? Checking something out?

The mini digital recorder Dorsey had given her sat uselessly in her drawer at home. It wouldn't have been much good even if she'd had it to hand, as the pounding rain on the lockup roof drowned out much of the conversation. Tense and wet through, Elenie tried to take in and remember as much as she possibly could, even as she wished she was anywhere but here.

"How many?" Frank asked.

"Two hundred and fifty." Although the taller of the two men spoke with a heavy accent—maybe Turkish, maybe not—there was clearly no need for a translator. He wore a bright orange and black North Face jacket which looked enviably warm. Frank grunted. They both took out their phones; blunt fingers tapped for a few seconds. Then they waited. The silence wasn't a comfortable one, the atmosphere oppressive. Dean fidgeted. Elenie, sweaty and frozen at the same time, watched the rain soak through her sneakers as the puddles around her feet grew.

"Done," said Frank.

North Face nodded, his eyes still on the phone in his hand. Another minute went by. "OK," he said finally, and pocketed his cell.

At a signal from Frank, Dean climbed into the Dodge and backed it up to the open lockup. Frank unclipped and folded back the tarp covering the cargo bed. "Get over here," he growled at Elenie.

When she stepped forward, she felt the gaze of all three men turn to her. Six eyes, flat and blank like a trio of dead fish, ran over her from face to feet. Frank shoved an armful of boxes into her hands. They were all identical—white, new and glossy, images of games console controllers on the outsides.

Dean climbed up onto the back of the truck and reached toward her. She passed the boxes to him and he began to stack them. There would clearly be no help offered from the other men. They moved swiftly, trying to get everything under cover and out of the rain as soon as possible. Between Frank and Elenie, the dolly was empty within a quarter of an hour. Dean jumped down and began to fix the tarp on all sides.

"Yilmaz can reach you on the usual number?" North Face asked. Frank nodded. "He'll be in touch about distribution. You hold the stock until then."

"My cut will be higher if I'm expected to cross state lines." There was a tense stare-down for ten seconds or so, before North Face gave an infinitesimal shrug of questionable agreement. Frank seemed happy to take it at face value.

One of the other men said something Elenie couldn't hear. The water was dripping from her chin now. More nodding, no further conversation, and apparently they were done. Frank climbed into the truck, so much dryer than either Dean or herself. They were going to steam up the cab before they reached the end of the road.

As they pulled away, Elenie twisted to look over her shoulder. The guy with the mustache was reaching for the mechanism to bring down the roller shutter. There were no visible numbers on the lockups; they all looked the same. It wouldn't make it easy to pinpoint the location for Dorsey.

Suddenly all hell broke loose.

"Fuck!" Frank hit the brakes so hard Elenie's seat belt bit into her shoulder as she whipped her eyes back to the windshield. She threw out a hand to brace herself on the dash. Dean choked on an inhale beside her.

A swarm of cars—eight, nine?—appeared out of nowhere, some marked, some not. Menacing in their number, chilling in their velocity, they skidded to a halt, blocking the truck on all sides. Water sprayed from sliding tires.

Police officers spilled out, each of them heavily armed. Everyone was shouting something different—commands, instructions, warnings. The noise, even over the pouring rain, was deafening.

Frank was dragged from the driver's seat, Dean from the passenger side. Then someone grabbed Elenie's arm.

It was almost impossible to make out individual words as officers shouted across officers. Rough hands pushed Elenie to the ground in a puddle of surface water, the concrete grating on her bare knees, wet gravel against skin. Stones bit into her shins. Exhaust fumes and confusion hung heavy in the air.

Someone yelled, "Put your hands on your head!" so close to her temple that it rang in her ears and she instinctively cowered.

Her lungs forgot how to do their job, short, strangled gasps escaping from her lips. Dean caught her eye, his face blanched, mouth slack. She couldn't see Frank on the other side of the Dodge.

North Face and his two companions, all on their knees, were surrounded by more officers.

Behind each car crouched policemen with weapons, covering their colleagues. Elenie was staring into the business end of firearms on all sides. Black, sinister, terrifying. Her eyes darted from one vehicle to the next; she recognized no one. There was no sign of Dorsey. Even Booth's mistrustful face would have been a comfort amid the sea of chaotic intimidation churning around her.

Two men in plainclothes climbed onto the back of Frank's truck. One unfastened a corner of the tarp and they both crouched down out of sight. The ratchet of steel around Elenie's right wrist sent a wash of pre-emptive claustrophobia through her. Then both hands were wrenched down behind her back and her wrists were cuffed together. She swayed, off-balance, light-headed and trembling with cold, confusion, and terror.

This couldn't be down to her. Dorsey had made no mention of a raid in their brief conversation last night, and Frank had sprung this collection of his on Elenie without warning. The data from Frank's cell was still on the device in its sock hideaway, inside her bag. She didn't have her DEA phone with her, but she did have the one Roman had given her the other day.

Keep steady, stay strong, she told herself. *This can all be sorted out.* But the full-body tremors that gripped her muscles refused to listen.

There was one thing Elenie knew beyond a shadow of a doubt. Games console controllers didn't demand this kind of police interest.

She fixed her eyes on the blue emergency light mounted on the roof of an unremarkable black sedan and let all the crazy wash over her.

* * *

Hours passed before she was allowed to make a call.

Separated from Frank and Dean immediately, they'd been transported to the police station in different cars and she hadn't seen either of them since. Elenie asked to speak to someone in charge but was told they'd get to her in due course. And due course hadn't happened yet.

She'd been searched, processed, led to the cells, and left there until the custody officer came to tell her she had the right to inform someone of her detention. Stripped of her saturated hoodie, Elenie had wrapped the thin blanket from her cell around her shoulders instead.

She dialed Roman's cell number on the phone in the interview room, her fingers shaking uncontrollably. Panic froze the cords in her throat. The custody officer clattered away on a keyboard at his desk as the ring tone sounded in her ear.

Please pick up.

The cold had seeped right into her bones; her feet were still wet. Without her purse and her phone, she had no idea of the time. She should have asked someone. Her teeth chattered.

"Hello?"

Elenie's fingers fumbled the receiver.

"Who is this?" But, dear God, if she didn't know already.

"It's Zena. If you're after Roman, he's not available right now."

There was music, conversation, and laughter in the background. It sounded like a party. The pain in her chest was indescribable.

"Um, this is Elenie Dax. We met at the gala dinner. I need—"

"Look, we're busy tonight but I'll give you some quick advice." Zena's voice softened. Somehow the sympathy cut deeper than her acerbity. Elenie couldn't string any words together. She thought she might throw up. "Keep your contact to his on-duty hours. I'm prepared to turn a blind eye here and there, but you can't offer him what I can. Roman is meant for greater things than policing small-town squabbles, and he will be coming home soon. To me." Her words drifted away slightly, as if she'd turned her head from the phone. "I'll tell him you called, Melanie."

"It's Elenie," she corrected in a whisper, but Zena had hung up.

"You done?" the custody officer asked.

Elenie lowered the handset and nodded. Tugging the blanket tighter around her shoulders, she rubbed at her arms. An overhead light buzzed and blinked.

Forcing herself to think, her brain fuzzy, she trudged through her options. This felt nothing like the days when Chief Roberts would pull her in for questioning. The absence of Roman was huge. So much worse for having had his support and losing it than when she'd only had herself to rely on. She ached for reassurance, a friendly voice, someone on her side. But Dougie, Summer, and especially Caitlyn and Milo all had more important things to concentrate on right now.

Elenie drew on her last vestiges of grit and squared her shoulders. Crumbling was not an option. "I need someone to reach either Special Agent Faith Dorsey from the DEA or Chief Deputy Shawn Booth. You can tell whoever's in charge that I'm asking for them and it's urgent."

The custody officer noted down the names without any change of expression. He opened the door and gestured. "This way."

Each minute of the walk back to her cell felt like a soul-destroying shift at Diner 43. Elenie locked the jumbled tangle of misery down tight and turned her back on it. If Zena was right, there would be endless time for a pity party in the future.

She'd managed alone before. She would manage again now. With or without the help of Roman Martinez.

Chapter 47
Roman

When Roman came back from the bathroom, Zena pushed another drink into his hand. She was still talking to Ben and Philippa. He didn't know how she had the nerve.

Another couple joined them. He proved to be a stuffy stereotype of every middle-aged, white lawyer across the country. His wife had clearly given up on having an opinion. For the next half an hour, they all talked shop. Roman was so fucking bored he could have set fire to the soft furnishings.

He wouldn't miss any of this if he stayed in Pine Springs.

Without even realizing it, he'd built a life he loved. The desperate, high-octane chase for promotion held no appeal anymore. He was finding far more satisfaction in the immediate and visible effect he could have on his own tight community. He wanted to keep doing it. He wanted to stay.

"The law is the law," the Pompous Ass declared as if he were making a groundbreaking announcement. "People need to accept it's there to protect them for a reason, whether they're smart enough to understand that reason or not."

It was the perfect setup for one of Elenie's curveball conversation pieces. Roman's lips twitched. He couldn't resist. "Dueling is still legal in Paraguay as long as those taking part are registered blood donors. So, does that protect the duelers or only the recipients of their blood?"

Silence settled over the group. Roman almost checked for tumbleweed. Only Philippa looked even the slightest bit amused.

"My brother-in-law was born in Madrid and he assures me it's illegal to drive in a thong in Spain," she countered.

"I guess the law really does protect everyone," Roman grimaced. The first genuine smile of the evening tugged at his lips. "Not easy to enforce though. Unless he means it's illegal to drive in *just* a thong."

Philippa laughed. Zena shot him a withering look, blatantly torn between pulling him up for being stupid and not wanting to antagonize her boss.

"I need another drink. Anyone else?" Barrett tipped his head in the direction of the bar. The Pompous Ass turned his shoulder deliberately on Roman and asked for a refill. His wife held out her glass but Philippa passed.

"I'm good." Glacially dismissive, Roman looked away. He wanted nothing from that dick.

Zena drained the last of her drink. "Let me help you." Bright and artless, one work colleague to another. He watched them impassively as they walked to the bar.

Wondering if Milo had sent him an update, Roman looked around for his jacket. He spotted it draped over the back of a chair behind Philippa. She'd started a conversation with someone he didn't recognize so, unwilling to interrupt, he stood and brooded. If his scowl put people off talking to him, then all the better.

Raised voices by the bar made them all turn around, a shocked silence cutting suddenly through the babble of noise.

A woman with knockout curves encased in a black bodycon dress was fronting up to Zena and Barrett—another blonde,

Roman noted with a flicker of his eyebrow. She radiated fury, an empty cocktail glass held aloft in each hand. Zena's mouth hung open, a colored, sticky stain spreading from her chest down the front of her dress. She plucked two ice cubes from her cleavage and dropped them onto the floor. Barrett's hair was plastered to his head, with what appeared to be an olive stuck in its styled sweep.

Roman's eyes whipped around to Philippa, who had frozen with her own drink halfway to her mouth.

"It's on me that I bought your pitiful 'my wife doesn't understand me' crap." Each word the blonde threw at Barrett echoed through the bar. "But it's on you, you lying sack of shit, that I'm not your only side piece!" Barrett's flinch dislodged the olive. It rolled off his head and down the side of his nose. The woman aimed a seething smile in his direction. "Apologies for the dramatics—please do enjoy the rest of your evening. But, before that, go fuck yourself."

And with that impressive mic drop, she slammed both glasses down onto the bar and swept out, her head high.

Roman fought an urge to applaud. He took a stride toward Philippa, closing a gentle hand around her elbow. "Why don't we share a cab?" he suggested.

"You knew?" she asked him.

"I did."

"Me too," she muttered, eyes flashing.

Reaching behind her to snag his jacket from the back of the chair, he took the drink from her hand and placed it on the nearest table. He didn't spare so much as a glance in Zena's direction. As they left the club, Roman leaned down to murmur quietly in Philippa's ear. "In Hong Kong, a wife is legally allowed to kill her husband if he cheats on her as long as she does it with her bare hands."

"Don't fucking tempt me," she answered through tight lips.

* * *

There was complete radio silence from both Elenie and Milo. It didn't concern him as Elenie was often unable to text and Roman guessed Milo was still at the hospital with his cell switched off. He considered calling Dougie just to check in, but it was heading for midnight when he got back to his hotel room. There was nothing that couldn't wait until morning.

He messaged Elenie once he'd stretched out in bed.

Hey. You there?

He waited for five minutes but there was no answer. The message stayed delivered but unread. Roman hesitated, then began to type.

Missing you, sweetheart. Been a hell of a day but I'll fill you in when I'm home. I assume you've heard Caitlyn's in labor. Milo dumped me to go to the hospital so I'll hire a car and head back first thing tomorrow. I hope your day's gone well. Can't wait to see you.

He ran a finger over the words on his screen. The simple sentences were a poor excuse for what he really wanted to say, and he couldn't even send them.

This evening had opened his eyes to everything he'd suspected. Brimming with plans, determination, and fervor for the first time in months, he knew without a shadow of a doubt that he wanted to stay in Pine Springs. Everything was different now, and being away from Elenie was as painful as hell; he didn't plan on making a habit of it. For someone so swamped in drama and difficulty, she was the easiest company he'd ever kept. She held his heart in her slim hands and Roman had no desire to ask for it back.

Desperate for the connection, he stared at his phone, willing the typing bubble to appear on the screen. But Elenie didn't reply to his text.

Deleting his second message without sending it, Roman turned out the light. He made plans to be up early and get on the road as soon as possible.

His phone woke him before the alarm.

"Yes." Roman's voice was pure gravel from last night's drinking and the early hour.

"Thank fuck!"

He sat up, dragging a hand through his hair. Dougie's words chased the last bit of sleep from his mind. "What's up?"

"Elenie's been arrested. So have Frank and Dean. They're being held by Flint PD's Special Investigative Unit. It wasn't a DEA hit but they've jumped on board now." Dougie sounded harassed. "I've come straight to the station from the hospital. Forsberg and Morgan brought in Athena Dax overnight when the DEA sent in a team to raid the house. She's being transferred to Flint later today."

"Shit!" Roman was out of bed and pulling on his pants as he listened, his jaw tight, heart pumping. Flint was only an hour away. "Why hasn't she called me?"

"Don't know, Chief. We heard nothing either."

"I've got to go, Dougie. I'll call you back once I'm driving. Keep me updated." He grabbed his clothes, throwing them roughly into his bag, and his cell rang again.

"Am I talking to Chief Martinez?" Both the voice and the number were unfamiliar.

"You are. Who's this?"

"I'm Detective Niall Belltower, Flint Police Department. We need to talk."

Chapter 48
Elenie

Elenie was past hunger but she couldn't eat anything. Her eyes, gritty from exhaustion, begged to close but she couldn't sleep either. Shivers wracked her body. And she was pretty sure she stank.

To hold it together, she thought about Caitlyn and the baby, who must have been born by now. *Girl or boy?* She hoped they'd have a girl with just as much sass as her mother. She wanted to see her new friends so much. And Roman even more. But it didn't look as if he was coming.

Elenie rubbed at her chest. Her heart hurt like it had been scooped out with an apple corer.

She tried to have faith. Roman would come through for her in a professional capacity, one way or another. That was the kind of person he was. Sleeping with him gave her no automatic rights to keep tabs on his every move. There was probably a good reason for him to have been with Zena. As she had pointed out, Zena was a better fit for him in every way. And they had history.

Neither Dorsey nor Booth had shown up yet either, but the custody officer had done his job and passed on her message. In a small side room, a Detective Belltower listened carefully as she told him about the CI deal, the data recovery device in her bag, and, with some hesitation, her connection to Roman.

Eyebrows more animated than the rest of his face, Belltower gave nothing away and said little. He made copious notes, brought her a chocolate bar and a coffee that tasted like ditchwater but was at least warm. Then he took her back to her cell, told her to sit tight—like she had other options—and promised he would be back.

Elenie counted the blue tiles that ran in a band, two deep, halfway up the wall. There were twelve across the longest walls and eight along the shortest one. The rest of the tiles were white. She counted the number of rows from floor to ceiling and spent a while estimating how many tiles there were in total. It helped to focus on something so methodical.

She imagined the nearest Zena would ever get to the same experience would be counting ceiling tiles at the beauty salon while she got her bikini line waxed.

The sliding hatch in the cell door clattered across. The custody officer met her eyes through the gap before fitting his keys into the lock on the outside of the door. He pulled it open and stood back.

"This way, please."

Elenie followed him out into the corridor. Her pulse hammered. The constant wash and backwash of adrenalin was exhausting. She didn't know whether she felt ready to fight an army or sleep for a week. A sign saying "Consultation Room" was fixed to the door the officer pulled open and her heart leaped into her throat.

Inside the room, radiating frustration and with a scowl as deep as she'd ever seen, was Roman.

Huge, fierce, and furious, like a dark avenging angel, both hands were shoved deep into the pockets of his jeans, the sleeves of his black shirt rolled up and forearms tight with tension. Her knees threatened to buckle. Never had he looked more attractive. And never had Elenie felt less worthy or more pathetic.

"Detective Belltower says you can have fifteen minutes." The custody officer closed the door and locked it behind him. A CCTV camera blinked in the corner of the room.

Roman's eyes raked over her tangled hair, her sodden clothes, her filthy legs and shoes, and a muscle rippled along his jawline. When he closed the gap between them, Elenie took a step backward, afraid to contaminate him. She'd been in the same clothes for more than twenty-four hours and hadn't brushed her teeth. She felt disgusting.

"I'm sorry I didn't get here sooner." His voice vibrated in her chest. "Why didn't you call me?"

Elenie glanced away. "I did."

Roman's eyebrows knitted together. "I didn't have a missed call."

"I spoke to Zena. She said you were busy."

He cursed explosively, eyes blazing. "You've got to be fucking kidding me." He looked like he wanted to punch something. She felt dangerously near to breaking down. She didn't know the rules for needing someone so intensely it made your thighs shake. Being that weak could only end badly for her. "I didn't know you'd called. Believe me, I would have come immediately."

"OK." Elenie gave a small nod and a tiny shrug, as if it didn't matter.

"I think there was a perfect storm of missed communication." Roman sounded seriously pissed. "I was tied up during the evening, and Dougie and Summer stayed at the hospital all night. His phone was off and so was Milo's. Dougie only caught up on things this morning when he got to the station." Roman's eyes burned into hers. "I should have been here."

She chewed on her lip. "How is Caitlyn? Has she had the baby?"

He nodded. "A little girl. They're both doing well."

"I called it," Elenie murmured to herself.

Roman tugged at his ear, jangled his car keys. The awkwardness between them an unwelcome blast from the past. She hadn't known what to make of him when they first met, and she wondered if she really knew him any better now. It had never occurred to her that his plans in the city might involve Zena.

347

"Elenie—" He broke off, muttered a curse under his breath and tried again. "Look, I've spoken with the detective in charge to clarify the situation and Booth's just turned up, too. Flint PD had the guys Frank was doing business with under surveillance and they moved on them, not knowing the wider picture. Dorsey's on her way now. She should have fucking been here already but the DEA were caught on the hop as well and she had to head up a coordinated search on your house. You shouldn't have been held all night without support but all the multiple police jurisdictions muddied the water."

"I get it."

"Detective Belltower wants to conduct a formal interview once Dorsey gets here. They'll let me be there in a professional capacity so I'll be able to ask questions but not answer any of them. They'll use digital equipment that will audibly and visually record everything for evidential purposes. Are you OK with that?"

"Sure." Elenie nodded, automatically.

Every bit of him was calm and decisive now. "My advice would be to let the on-call public defender support you initially and, if it turns out you need more specialist legal representation, then I'll give a signal and we'll call a halt to regroup. But I don't think it'll come to that." She nodded again. "Any questions?"

"Yes." His piercing eyes met hers and Elenie swallowed. "What time is it, please? I've lost track a bit."

Roman moved closer, his huge hands encircling her upper arms. Heat flooded from them, warming her chilled skin. Elenie held herself rigidly in his grip. Exhaustion threatened her shaky control. For a moment she thought he might pull her into his arms, and she closed her eyes, praying for him to do it.

Instead, he hesitated and his hands fell away. "It's just before eleven a.m."

She wondered if he found her as repulsive as she felt.

Chapter 49
Roman

Even with regular breaks, Roman could tell Elenie was hanging on by a thread, though she looked composed on the surface. The unreadable expression that masked her thoughts was back in place. He admired it as much as he loathed it.

It took the best part of the day to get all the details on record.

She sat upright and still as Detective Belltower and Special Agent Dorsey grilled her over and over on the movements, connections, and business dealings of each Dax family member. She gave a detailed description of the transaction at the Flint lockup and a stabbing pain jabbed through Roman's temple at the danger she'd been in without him knowing.

Dorsey disclosed that the firearm Elenie had given Roman had been positively linked to multiple crimes involving the same suspect—a dealer in the Saginaw area. The data recovery device was being examined. Elenie focused on their words with absolute concentration, the public defender chipping in to explain anything she was unsure of. Belltower was thorough, kind, and respectful, Dorsey calm and professional beside him. Roman knew neither of them had missed the faint tremors in Elenie's hands or the fatigue darkening her eyes to charcoal.

She kept those eyes mainly on either the detective or the special agent. Yes, she flicked them briefly to Roman each time he interjected a question, but mostly she avoided looking his way at all. Elenie had put up some sky-high walls around herself and he hated every single inch of them.

Dorsey finally brought the interview to an end. "Frank Dax and Dean Dax have been charged with possession and distribution of illegal narcotics and will be remanded in custody. Further charges will likely follow relating to the firearm."

Elenie looked dazed. "And Ty?"

Roman took that one. "Unclear at the moment. He's still being held in Pine Springs, but we'll know more later."

Belltower sat back in his chair. "I'm sorry it took us this much time to coordinate our facts. I know the special agent will be adding her thanks separately but I would like to express my appreciation for the information you've provided so far that will help us with this case. Every division of my police department is committed to targeting the drivers of crime within our community. It's often dangerous work, but they have chosen this line of policing and are dedicated to getting results. You, however, have made a difficult choice with the same goal in mind. I don't underestimate how hard that must have been."

He offered her a genuine smile and Elenie gave a small, contained nod in acknowledgment.

Dorsey straightened her notepad. "While we've been conducting this interview, your mother has been brought into the precinct for questioning. I can authorize five minutes under supervision if you'd like to see her."

Elenie wavered. She looked both fragile and yet immensely strong. Roman ached for her. "Yes, please. I'd appreciate just a few minutes," she said finally.

The public defender exchanged some quiet words with Elenie, gave her shoulder a squeeze and left.

"I'll see you when you're done," Dorsey said, gathering up her paperwork.

Belltower led them to the holding cells. Guy-rope taut, Roman followed in Elenie's footsteps. Desperate to touch her, everything in him wanted to grasp Elenie's fingers in his own, professionalism be damned, but her arms were folded tightly around her body and she didn't give so much as a glance over her shoulder.

The custody officer handed over his keys to the detective. Unlocking one of the cell doors, Belltower gestured to Elenie and Roman to step inside, giving them a little respectful distance.

Athena perched on a bunk, her back against the wall, watchful eyes swiveled to the door. In skin-tight jeans and a chunky knit sweater, she looked disconcertingly mall-ready but the tendons in her neck were taut and her fingers twitched, drumming on the mattress.

"Mom." Elenie's voice cracked slightly on the single word and Roman felt the echo in his chest. She was shaking so hard, the hem of her skirt juddered against the backs of her knees.

"Are we getting out of here?" Athena dropped both feet to the floor, ignoring Roman and the detective completely. Her nostrils flared and she plucked at her sleeves.

"I—" Elenie stuttered on her reply. "I'm not sure they're done with you yet."

Athena's pupils darted over Elenie's face, her brows arcing, and Roman saw the moment of reckoning hit her like a storm burst. "You've done this. I don't know how, but you have." Her lips clamped so firmly they drained of color. Something fearful crawled across her expression. "You need to undo it," she hissed.

"Even if I could, I wouldn't." Elenie shook her head.

"Get. My. Husband. Out. Of. Jail."

"No."

Roman saw Elenie swallow. Athena curled her fingers so tightly into her palms that her nails would have punctured the skin if she hadn't bitten them all short.

"I need him," she said.

"We can manage without Frank. I'll help you. We can do it together."

It was agony to hear Elenie beg.

Athena studied her with wild eyes and she let out a burst of panic-roughened laughter. "You can't help me—you can't give me any of the things he does. I don't need you. I need Frank!"

"Mom—"

Athena reared back, a fleck of spit bubbling at the corner of her mouth. "I don't want to hear it! I can't believe you would do this to us."

"*I* didn't do this to us."

Her mother wasn't listening. All reasoning had fled. "I gave up everything for you! You've been a burden to me from the day you were born. All I wanted was the chance to live my own goddamn life."

"You can live your own life now. Start again. Tell them what you know about Frank and wipe the slate clean."

Athena scoffed. "I love him. You don't turn on people you love."

Elenie flinched. "What about me, Mom? Where do we go from here?"

Roman cataloged the array of expressions that chased each other across Athena's face. Fear, fury, confusion, dread. She was on the edge, near a meltdown, far weaker than her daughter. There was a moment when she wavered. Then her eyes hardened, her mouth twisted, and she stepped away.

"You are nothing to me." Each word was a bullet. "I'm done with you."

"You don't mean that." Elenie's voice was a whisper.

Athena lifted her chin. "I do."

Elenie searched her mother's face during the silent standoff that followed. Time dragged its feet through the tangible hostility. Eventually, she nodded.

"I'm done too." Her dignity sent splinters through Roman's heart. "Goodbye, Mom." In the doorway, Belltower stepped aside. She walked past him and out of the door without looking back.

Roman took a few long strides further into the cell. Fury pounding in his bloodstream, he itched to wrap his hands around Athena's scrawny neck.

"You've made the wrong choice. I don't care where you go or what you do now, but don't even think of trying to have any further contact with Elenie. You've screwed with her enough. Unless she reaches out to you, you will leave her alone. Or I swear you'll regret it." The words were low and deadly, danger radiating from him like a forcefield.

Athena broke eye contact first. Roman turned away, finding grim satisfaction in the sound of the cell door closing behind him as he left. Belltower turned the key. Grateful for the support the detective had shown Elenie in his own absence, Roman offered him a handshake.

He paced outside while waiting for Elenie to be processed and released. Self-disgust blistered his throat at having let her down so badly, pain for her pain twisted his insides. The presence of Deputy Chief Shawn Booth in the parking lot, leaning against the hood of Dorsey's car, had Roman grinding his teeth even as he crossed the asphalt.

Booth took a leisurely sip from a takeout coffee cup and lifted a cavalier shoulder. "She came good in the end, eh? I had my doubts for a while. The data extracted from Dax's phone is pure gold."

A red mist spread through Roman's chest, the image of Elenie— shattered, frozen, and alone in the cell—branded on his mind.

He stalked closer. "You left her in the system all night. Where were your flags? Her backup? We trusted you had it under control." His eyes blazed from Booth to Dorsey and back again.

"Christ, Martinez, if I cut my shuteye short every time a CI got locked up, I'd never get my eight hours in." The chief deputy actually smirked.

Dorsey's lips curled with distaste, though she didn't speak.

Composure shredding, Roman clenched his fists. "I had to hear she'd been arrested from my own fucking deputy. Neither of you called me."

"We don't answer to you," Booth bit back. Dorsey tried to speak, but the chief deputy talked over her. "And Elenie Dax isn't new to spending time in police custody. It's practically ingrained in her DNA."

He couldn't have picked a more inflammatory comment to make. Roman, his rage begging for an outlet, had him pinned against the car before he'd finished speaking. Knuckles bone white, Roman was seconds from plowing his fist into the chief deputy's face.

"You hit me and I'll fucking bury you," snarled Booth.

"No, you won't," Dorsey snapped. "You are out of order." She turned to Roman. "Elenie did well. I know what it cost her."

"She's a fucking star." His voice was a deadly growl.

He loomed over Booth for another minute, before unpeeling his fingers from the chief deputy's shirtfront with reluctance. Booth swiped a hand over the sheen on his top lip.

Dorsey's eyes flicked over Roman's shoulder. "Someone needs you."

He turned. Elenie stood on the steps of the police precinct, looking a little lost and smaller than he'd ever seen her.

His fucking star.

"I'll be in touch," Dorsey said.

Roman didn't hear her. He was already walking away. He forgot Booth. Nothing else was important.

Only Elenie mattered.

Chapter 50
Elenie

Huddled in the soft navy hoodie Roman had given her from his overnight bag, it took half an hour before Elenie could control the shudders that shook her body.

She was aware of him glancing her way with ravaged black eyes, concern written deep into his forehead. He tried a few times to start a conversation but she struggled to produce more than one-word answers, punch-drunk with emotional overload. Elenie was grateful when he fell quiet and let her watch the miles go by in silence. Night had fallen before they hit the Pine Springs limits, the rain long gone, the sky a vivid indigo awash with stars. Roman guided the rental car along the sandy track, winding through the familiar pine trees, and pulled up in front of his house.

"Maybe I should just go home?" She curled her hands inside the cuffs of his sweatshirt. Everything inside her churned. She felt absolutely trashed, lack of sleep jumbling her thoughts.

"That's not a great idea tonight." Roman studied her face. "The DEA search was a thorough one. I asked Dougie to get a locksmith out this afternoon to repair the front door but it's a mess inside. Best to face that tomorrow."

He flicked the light switch by the front door, and the cabin, so snug and cozy, glowed softly around her as Elenie stumbled inside. The heating must have come on with a timer; the whole house seemed to wrap her up in its warmth. Blinking gritty eyes, she kicked off her filthy sneakers and hugged the hoodie around her, the scent of Roman in her nose. Comfort and torture in one hit. Her stomach was so empty she wouldn't have been surprised to look down and find a hole right through her middle. Part of it was hunger—although she wasn't sure she could eat a thing—but most of it was loss and loneliness, corroding her insides and leaving her hollow.

Roman opened the oven, gave a low huff of approval, and turned the temperature dial on. "Ma made us lasagna. Thea brought it round. Shouldn't take long to warm up."

The corner of his mouth lifted in the half-smile that did so much damage to her heart. Elenie couldn't bear to look at it.

She wandered to the window, wishing she could see the trees. It was so dark outside, so light inside, that the view was mainly a reflection of the room behind her. Roman watched, his hands in his pockets, deceptively relaxed.

Elenie wasn't sure why it had hit her this hard. She'd known what they were working toward, the events and the results she had deliberately helped to bring about. And, fuck, if her mother hadn't said a million similar things to her before now. But it hurt so much more for being the last time and the last words.

She'd wanted to plead. *Choose me, Mom. Please, choose me this once.* As if begging for love was the only way she could ever expect to receive it. And now, the tattered, desperate threads of hope were no longer enough to power the life support keeping her relationship with her mother alive. The sound of the flatline rang inside Elenie's head.

She should feel free. Instead, she felt completely adrift. And utterly worthless.

"I need to tell you why Zena answered my phone." Roman stepped closer and a reactive shiver moonwalked across the surface of her skin. "Come and sit on the couch, Elenie. Please."

"I've got such a headache. I don't think I want to eat anything—I just need a shower and some sleep."

Not looking at him was the answer. If she could avoid his inimitable face, she might stand a chance of keeping the frenzied volcano of feelings inside where they belonged. She might be able to hold it together just a little longer.

Roman rubbed a hand over the back of his neck. Elenie could feel him studying her. "Go on up," he said finally. "I'll sort a few things out down here and I'll join you soon."

Her feet were leaden as she climbed the stairs. In the bathroom, she stripped with shaky hands, goosebumps on top of goosebumps raising the hairs on her arms. The steaming water in the shower was blissful. Elenie washed the grime from her body and her hair, then lifted her face and closed her eyes. Motionless, she let multiple one-last-minutes go by before she could bring herself to shut off the flow. When she stepped out, she was so exhausted she could barely stand.

Crawling under the covers in a t-shirt from Roman's dresser, she settled carefully at the furthest edge of the mattress. Her eyes were closing already, her mind wonderfully blank. Elenie was asleep within seconds.

She didn't hear Roman come up the stairs. She was unaware of the long moments when he crouched next to her, eyebrows drawn together as he watched her sleep. When he slid into bed behind her and gently drew her body against his, she sighed without waking and curled instinctively into his warmth. His heart thumped steadily against her back throughout the night. If his arms felt like a shield of devotion and protection as she slept, Elenie knew the sensation was conjured only by her dreams.

Chapter 51
Roman

Roman woke early in his bed without her. The sheets on Elenie's side were cold. He didn't know how long she'd been gone. Fear settled low in his stomach. Making a quick call to Dougie, he drove across town and up the hill, parking in front of the Dax house next to the 2010 Camaro he knew belonged to Tyson.

He had no doubt at all that he'd find her here.

The front door was shut and locked. Whoever Dougie had called to mend the damage from the raid had done a good job. Walking around the side of the house, Roman crossed the shabby backyard and ducked under an empty clothesline. The handle on the back door turned easily in his grip and he let himself into the kitchen.

Something tacky on the old floor tiles pulled at the soles of his shoes. Looking beyond the mess the DEA team had caused in their search, Roman took in the cabinet doors hanging off their hinges and the pile of dirty pans on the counter. Even before the cutlery drawer had been upended on the floor, this room wouldn't have won any awards for cleanliness.

On impulse, he pulled open the door of the fridge. Eight beers, two cans of cider, a tub of butter, and three bottles of nail polish.

Roman walked into the hall. He considered calling out but the contents of the fridge had stolen his voice and he couldn't get Elenie's name past the lump in his throat. He paused in the doorway of the living room. The cushions had been dragged from an enormous couch and ripped apart, the same done to an armchair. Empty cans, broken glasses, newspapers, overturned ashtrays, and random pieces of clothing were littered across a mud-colored carpet that had seen better days. A huge television stood upright and undamaged on a black glass stand, presiding over the chaos around it. The weak morning light, streaming in through the window, illuminated the room in all its bleakness. A stale smell of cigarettes, weed, and body odor hung in the air, clinging to the curtains and soft furnishings.

Roman's eye twitched.

Crossing the dingy hallway, he began to climb the stairs. The landing was small, with two bedrooms on one side and two on the other. All the doors were open. Mattresses had been tossed, pillows cut open, drawers pulled out and the contents dumped on the floor.

The sound of movement drew him to the doorway of a compact bedroom. Inside, Elenie tugged at a thin, single mattress which leaned on its longest side against the wall. She wrestled it back onto the bedframe. Someone had taken a knife to the material and long slashes ran across its width, exposing the coils of metal inside. An open closet held nothing but hangers. She bent over to pick up some clothes from the floor.

Roman shifted in the doorway and Elenie shot him a sideways glance. The hollow expression on her face cut him to ribbons. So pale this morning she was almost translucent, she'd pulled on fresh jeans and a sweater. There was something purposeful about her movements.

"I'm sorry about the mess." His words fell like stones into murky water.

"Not my first raid. And you did warn me." Elenie folded a t-shirt in her hands and laid it on the bed, gathering up a few more pieces from the floor. Roman watched her add her denim jacket, a hairbrush, and a few items of makeup to the small pile of clothes.

"What are you doing?" His voice sounded rough even to his own ears.

"I want my things. There's not much. And I'm not coming back here." She kept moving, kept folding, and a vise clamped around Roman's chest.

She was going to leave.

"Let me explain about Zena." He was dangerously close to pleading. "I went to a work function with her because she threatened to blow your cover if I didn't. And I couldn't risk it. I should have told you but I thought I could save you from dealing with another complication."

"It's OK. I get it." The smile brushing Elenie's lips was empty. "Your relationship with Zena is none of my business. You don't need to feel responsible for me anymore. You've already done so much. More than anyone else ever has. I'll be fine."

Her bravery crucified him, even as his fingernails bit into his palms. She was ripping his heart out with both hands, leaving him hollow and bloody. "What about me?" His voice broke on the question.

"What do you mean?"

"What if I won't be fine?" Roman pushed away from the doorframe.

Elenie wouldn't look at him. "Of course you'll be fine. This was just a small setback for you. The rest of your secondment will fly by. You'll head back to Detroit stronger than ever."

He closed his eyes. Even now, she believed in him.

"I'm not going back to Detroit. I don't want my old job. And I don't want Zena."

That stopped her folding clothes.

His senses on overdrive, synapses vibrating, Roman was hyperaware of the scent of his own shampoo in Elenie's hair, the rhythm of her breath, the tremor of her hands.

360

She turned to face him, her reply choppy. "Zena is the perfect partner for you."

He shook his head. "Nothing about Zena is perfect for me. She's self-centered and egotistical and she wanted me for what I gave her, never who I was. I felt pressured into proposing at a time when I was struggling. I wasn't thinking clearly then, but I am now." Roman never took his eyes off Elenie's face. "There's been a space in my life exactly your size, just waiting for you. Now you've filled it, you've ruined me for anyone else."

Elenie clasped a dress to her chest. It was the one she'd worn for their fake date at the Barrel. "You deserve more. I'm just a complication you're better off without. I need to make a fresh start somewhere I'm not hated for my surname."

Roman took one long stride into the tiny room. The fuck he'd let her leave. "I don't know if you've checked your phone at all, but mine has blown up with everyone asking about you. I haven't even had time to answer the messages. My mom and dad, Thea, Flo, Summer, Dougie, Otto—even Caitlyn called from the hospital. You have so many more friends than you realize." His fists clenched and released, clenched and released. "And you're so far from a complication it isn't even funny. You are my calm. My place of peace. You saved me. Being able to share what I went through saved me. I'm coming to terms with my ghosts because of you and I'm managing to let them go because of you. There's nothing I want in Detroit anymore. My home is here. Because of you."

She opened her mouth but Roman couldn't stop the torrent of words he'd been kicking himself for not saying last night.

"I was there yesterday. I heard your mother, so I know what you're thinking. But Athena was wrong, Elenie. She's selfish and desperate and she's completely wrong. You are so much more than nothing. You're everything to me."

She sagged against the wall, searching his face. "My family—"

"I don't give a damn about your family. And I couldn't give less of a shit if anyone else has an opinion about us. You have more strength and courage than anyone I've ever met. I'll support you and protect you in any way I can if you let me. I like the person I am when I'm with you. Everything I am and everything I have belongs to you. It has from the minute we kissed at the gala dinner." Roman lifted his hands to grip her arms, his fingers shaking, heart hammering inside his rib cage like a concrete breaker. "Feel it, Elenie, and believe it. Take it. I'm all yours."

He bent his head to taste her chilled lips. She sucked in a pained breath, like someone being shocked back to life.

"I love you, Elenie." Roman murmured the words against her mouth, pulling her closer into his body. "I love you and I love your beautiful face and your sexy body and your incredible facts and your odd sense of humor. I want to buy you new underwear and eat cotton candy and too much pizza and see your wonderful smile every single day." He kissed her again, his tongue dipping between her lips with a growl. "I want to share my family and my friends with you because they all love you, too. There's only half of me left when I'm not with you."

Elenie's eyes filled. She pulled his head back down and pressed her mouth to his, fingers curling through his hair. A sound—part sob, part laugh, part sigh—bubbled from her throat.

"I think I love you, too." Her voice rasped around the words he suspected she'd never said before.

"I'll take that." Roman clamped her to his chest, blocking out the trashed and soulless bedroom, this house with its miserable memories and Athena's damning words. She wasn't alone anymore. "Stay in Pine Springs with me, Elenie."

"OK." She whispered the word into his shirt, and Roman's throat burned with relief as he swallowed.

"Let's get out of here, sweetheart. I want to take you home."

Elenie's smile was sunshine and flowers, heat and joy.

"I'm ready when you are," she told him.

362

Chapter 52
Elenie

"I guess he was lucky there was no umbrella in the cocktail or he could have lost an eye." Milo continued to find the story of Ben and Zena's public humiliation utterly hilarious. It might just have been that he was sleep-deprived or high on the excitement of becoming a father. Either way, he'd laughed himself sick.

Elenie paid little attention—not to Milo, not to Dougie and Summer who had pulled up chairs to join them, nor to the general hum in Diner 43 going on around her.

Roman, chatting now in a low voice to Otto on the other side of the table, had told her in detail about the events of his evening in the city. She had no further interest in Zena or her misguided affair, because five-day-old Annie Walker, on her first proper outing, was fast asleep in her arms. Wrapped in the softest pink blanket, knitted by Summer in the color of flamingo feathers, the baby's fingers flexed and twitched as she dreamed.

"She's so beautiful, Caitlyn," Elenie whispered.

"I know. How the hell did I make something so perfect?" They leaned closer together on the bench seat of the booth, shoulders touching as they smiled at Caitlyn's daughter.

Delia slapped a tray down in front of them and Annie startled in her sleep. "Five coffees, one hot chocolate, and a tea." Glaring full-on machetes rather than just daggers, the diner owner clattered the cups noisily onto the Formica. "I need you back at work, Elenie—I'm up to my ass in alligators! I've had to pay out for a relief chef this week just so I can wait on tables."

Elenie blinked at her impassively. *Welcome to my world.*

"I'll be back in on Monday, like I told you." Losing her job held less fear for her now. The baby pulled a frowny face, pursed her lips, and settled again in Elenie's arms.

"Those alligators are braver than I am." Dougie's muttered aside followed Delia as she stormed away, short legs going like the clappers.

"I'll let her get back over to the serving hatch before I remind her about my maple swirl." Otto stirred his coffee, slowly and deliberately, a devilish smile playing on his lined face.

He'd immediately offered Elenie a place to live when he heard about the raids and her arrest. Since she didn't have to worry about reprisals anymore, it was the perfect solution for now. Although Roman's cabin had become her favorite place on earth, she desperately needed time to assimilate all that had happened. Otto would be the perfect landlord while she found her feet.

"Any sign of Craig Perry?" asked Milo.

Roman shook his head. "Seems to have gone to ground."

Elenie knew he'd taken great satisfaction in pointing the US Securities and Exchange Commission in Craig's direction. The emails and recorded phone calls that June Reed Sanders had sent Roman were damning. It looked likely that Perry would soon be under investigation for fraud, false accounting, and tax evasion.

"It'll be fun to catch up with him when he's back in town." There was both threat and promise in the smile Milo shared with Roman.

"Chief Martinez?" Seven heads turned at the hesitant inquiry. Millie Westlake shuffled her feet. Her cheeks flushed slowly from white to pink, but her chin was high and her face held more than a flash of her old confidence. She directed her words to Roman, her eyes on Elenie all the while. "I've been calling the helpline—it's made a big difference and I think I've gotten my head straight now. I'd like to make a statement, if it's not too late."

"It's never too late, Millie." Warmth coated Roman's reassurance and Elenie fell a little more in love with him. "Can you come into the station this afternoon with your parents?" The teenager nodded, exhaling a tremulous breath. "Let's say two o'clock, and I'll see you then."

Elenie loaded all the gratitude and admiration she could into the look she exchanged with Millie before the younger girl turned and walked away.

"I'm really sorry we weren't there to bust you out of jail." Summer bumped her gently.

Caitlyn sighed. "The likelihood of me ever being a getaway driver is looking slimmer all the time."

"Inexcusable, I'm afraid." Elenie tucked Annie's tiny hands back inside the blanket. "It's not even as if you were doing anything important."

"That kid's got a lot to answer for," said Caitlyn. "I'll give her some chores to do as soon as we get home. She needn't think she'll get away with stuff just because she's cute."

"Don't you listen." Elenie pressed her lips to the baby's fluffy hair. "She doesn't mean it and I forgive you. Your mom is a superstar. If I ever need a getaway driver, she'll be my go-to. Summer will paint your toenails and I'll warn you about boys and teach you how to swear at people in languages they don't understand."

"Hey, boys aren't all bad," Milo protested, no heat in his complaint.

Elenie glanced over at Roman. His rangy frame took up much of the space on the other side of the booth. Elbows resting on the table, he watched her holding the baby, his face soft and relaxed. Catching her eye, he gave her the sexiest wink and a grin that was fire and temptation all rolled into one.

This man who had never judged her, who was honest to his core, actually loved her. She had no reason not to believe him.

It had been four days since he'd held her so tightly she could barely breathe—warm, firm, familiar, and offering everything she'd ever wanted. He'd given her the tools to save herself, the incentive to demand more. And then he'd opened his arms and offered himself. Roman might say that she'd saved him. But he'd saved her right back. They'd come out of the storm together.

A smile, as luminous as fall leaves in the Michigan sunshine, spread over Elenie's face. Her heart shone in her eyes, laughter lilting her voice.

"You're right," she conceded. "Some of them are pretty special."

Epilogue

The Following Year

Pine Springs Observer

PINE SPRINGS, WELLER'S LAKE &
SURROUNDING AREAS

JUNE 13, 2024

LOCAL DEALERS SENTENCED AFTER FLINT DRUG BUST

POLICE RAID BRINGS A HALT TO ILLICIT FAMILY-RUN OPERATION

Frank Dax, 58, of Pine Springs, was arrested following an undercover bust last year and charged with possession and intent to distribute narcotics, including meth, cocaine, and nearly 1,400 counterfeit oxycodone pills laced with fentanyl. The drugs and $80,000 in cash were concealed inside a shipment of electrical gaming equipment. At his trial last month, Dax asked for additional firearms and arson charges to be taken into account and was sentenced to 15 years in jail.

Tyson Dax, 25, received a mandatory minimum sentence of 20 years for assault, two counts of arson and the distribution and selling of fentanyl, in one case resulting in the death of a young man in Jackson.

Dean Dax, 23, was jailed for 5 years, with the possibility of parole, for his part in the family operation.

Three further men from Detroit will be sentenced shortly.

Flint PD received information that Class A drugs were being sold by a criminal network in the Central/Mid Michigan area and officers, working closely with the DEA, launched an undercover investigation.

"This satisfactory result shows the unwavering commitment by the County Sheriff's Office and our law enforcement partners to relentlessly pursue those who conspire to distribute harmful drugs in our communities," said Chief Deputy Shawn Booth.

Roman

As expected, plans for the new business center had come to nothing and the business guild gala dinner was held once more at the Elite Lodge Hotel. Progress moved slowly in Pine Springs in some areas. Not so slowly in others.

No one at their table gave any consideration to the tired décor this year. They were all talking over each other or laughing too hard. Milo and Caitlyn, with a babysitter booked for only the second time since Annie was born, were determined to enjoy every minute of a precious night out. Luke and Thea had given them a ride, along with Dougie and Summer. New to the group were Owen and June Reed Sanders. Roman had a lot of time for the couple and they were getting on like a house on fire with the others. The fact that they were firm Elenie fans was good enough for him.

"So, if I start up a town baseball team, you're all in, right? We're not wasting this guy now we have him back for good." Dougie leaned over in his chair to punch Roman on the shoulder. "Liam Morgan's up for it, too. Kristina's a maybe."

"I haven't played in a while. I'll be rusty," Roman warned.

"Don't listen to him. He's a natural. We're both in." Milo grinned. "And I know a couple more guys we can ask. Let's put our heads together this week."

Roman liked the idea. It would be fun.

There was a lot more fun these days. With Elenie.

As always, the moment she entered his mind, he found himself reaching for her. Roman caught hold of her hand under the table and her fingers curled immediately around his. The jolt to his heart was something he still wasn't used to. He pulled her a little closer.

"You OK?" she asked, lifting gray eyes as warm as a summer storm to his face.

"More than OK. Just wondering if you might like to dance with me?" He raised an eyebrow in invitation. And yes, maybe just a little because she'd told him she thought it was hot. She grinned and Roman knew he was busted. Laughing, they stood and pushed their chairs back from the table. "Excuse us for a moment, please. I'm just taking my lady to the dance floor."

"Ooo, us too! Come on, Milo." Caitlyn jumped up, tugging on her husband's hand. Summer and Dougie were quick to follow.

"So tempted," drawled Luke, heavy with insincerity.

June and Thea, who'd both kicked off their heels beneath the table, waved them away, and Owen just raised his glass. "We'll look after the drinks."

Pulling Elenie into his arms, Roman was hit by a flashback of Craig Perry, on this same dance floor, mauling the girl he wanted so badly.

"Craig was lucky I didn't rip his fucking arms off last year," he growled in Elenie's ear. "You have no idea how hard I had to struggle to keep some control."

"And there was me thinking your manly clenched jaw was all because of my stripper dress." She fluttered her eyelashes at him, mock flirting, so happy and confident she glowed.

He tugged her closer, his body tightening like it always did when she was in his arms. And quite often when she wasn't. "I told you then, it had nothing to do with what you were wearing. It was all you. It always is."

Tonight, her velvet dress, in deep forest green, was the color of the pine trees that dwarfed his house. The tactile material hugged her chest and her hips, both a little fuller these days. His hands reveled in the luxury of following those curves, stroking the soft material and the even softer skin exposed on her back. He gave a rumble of appreciation.

He'd bought the A-frame cabin because they both loved it, and Elenie had moved in with him in early spring after renting a room at Otto's for the longest four months of Roman's life. In the end, they'd quickly realized all they wanted was to come home to each other. Finally having her close, under the same roof, was heaven. He bought her flowers because he loved the way her face lit up when he gave them to her. If he treated her to something she picked up and put down again in a shop, it surprised her every time and made him want to do it even more. She had all the underwear she needed—and then some. A pleasure for them both, he liked to think. Spoiling Elenie had become his favorite thing to do. He'd never tire of making her feel special.

She leaned into his chest. "Craig had so little of my attention that night. There was this other man at my table I couldn't keep my eyes off. He wore his suit like an absolute boss and all I could think about was how much I wanted to kiss him."

"You and me both, sweetheart." Roman pressed his lips to her hair. "I was nearly insane with jealousy. If it hadn't been for the badge, I'd have killed Perry and disposed of his body in so many tiny pieces the SEC would need magnifying glasses to find them."

Elenie stifled a laugh against the front of his shirt, looking up at him with eyes that danced. "Instead, it seems payback comes in many different forms."

He suppressed a chuckle. "I couldn't possibly comment."

"How much do you wish you'd seen Craig's face when his porch steps disappeared overnight?"

The corner of Roman's mouth twitched. "More than breathing," he admitted.

"Kind of whoever did it to replace them with a kid's slide though. Super fun. You'd need a carpenter for a job like that, I'm guessing. Someone with skills like Luke, maybe."

"The snowman that blocked his front doorway just after Christmas was majestic."

Elenie snorted. "And almost as creative as plastic-wrapping his car—which Milo seemed to find exceptionally funny."

"Strange," murmured Roman. *And childish. But so, so satisfying.*

A more no-nonsense serving of revenge had come when Otto hit Perry smack in the face with the door at the general store, giving him a bloody nose and a split lip. The older man had made sure he was effusive with his apologies.

Roman grinned. His own behavior may have to be faultlessly above the line, but his friends would always have his back. He tightened his arms around Elenie's waist.

Long before the twelve-month secondment was up, he'd put in a request to make his position as chief of police in Pine Springs permanent. With the success of the Drug and Alcohol Helpline, a schedule of regular high school visits and a proposed Police Explorer program aimed at encouraging high school graduates into law enforcement, Roman had the full support of the town council. The conviction of the Daxes—although he couldn't take credit for that—was the icing on the cake for local residents. When he'd received confirmation that the role was his for good, Pine Springs threw their returning Golden Boy a party.

Roman was publicly flattered and privately humbled.

He'd also reached out to an old work colleague, who put him in touch with a counselor specializing in PTSD within the force. Regular sessions, conducted online in the peace of his own home, were helping him deal with the trauma that had played such havoc with his inner strength. It'd never leave entirely; it was part of his fabric now. But Roman wasn't afraid to talk about the memories when they surfaced. And his sleep was mostly restful again with Elenie in his arms. Always close, always tempting. His reason and his security.

At home, locked in the same drawer where he stored his gun, was the small burgundy box he'd picked up from the jewelers ten days ago. Inside, an emerald-cut peach sapphire sparkled on a white gold band. Soon, he'd ask Elenie to marry him. Not in front of anyone else, nowhere flashy, nothing rehearsed. Just the two of them, together. Quiet, meaningful, and magic. He couldn't wait. The thought of sliding the delicate engagement ring onto her finger stole the breath from his chest. Nerves ran like an army of ants beneath his skin. He wanted what his parents had, what Thea had found with Luke, and what Milo was building with Caitlyn and their baby.

"What a difference a year makes," Roman murmured into her hair, breathing Elenie in with a crooked smile on his lips. "I can't wait for the next one. And the next. I want to share all the ordinary and celebrate the successes with you. Turns out you're my favorite person in all the world."

Elenie

His words still floored her. When Elenie finally managed to answer, her voice was husky, her heart turning joyous handsprings behind her ribs.

"Well, it was a close call, but I think you've just tipped the balance. This date is definitely better than last year's gala dinner." Pressing closer, she inhaled the scent that was one hundred percent masculine and totally him. She rested her cheek against Roman's chest. "I think I could pick you out of a line up by your smell alone."

His laugh rumbled against her ear. "You are so strange sometimes but I love you."

"It's not strange at all. It's true. Smell is as distinct as fingerprints, apparently."

"Well, you can sniff me all you like, but I'll stick with taking prints at work, if that's OK with you."

She lived for the smile in his voice. Life with Roman was heavenly. His house, their home, was a happy one. So unlike the place where she'd grown up.

In the end, Frank had tried to turn on some of his criminal fraternity in exchange for a lighter sentence, but there had been others just as quick to turn on him. Millie Westlake had kept her resolve and finally identified Tyson as the dealer who'd sold her the pills she'd taken at the Masons' party. Scared and not smart enough to think of an alternative strategy, Dean had done himself the biggest favor of all and told the truth. He gave the DEA enough details to tie up Frank and Tyson's convictions and lighten his own sentence, his evidence adding weight to Elenie's. It was likely he'd be out of prison in under five years. Whether he chose to turn his life around then would be up to him. Elenie wrote Dean regular letters and visited once a month. She knew from experience that it only took one person to believe in you to make all the difference.

Her mother had moved briefly back into the Dax house, packed up her things, and then disappeared. Elenie didn't know where she'd gone. She hadn't seen her again and she didn't want to.

She had all the family she needed now; she was starting over and creating something afresh. It was painful, but cathartic.

Rewarding and wonderful. Otto spoiled her like Elenie imagined a grandparent might. Living with him had given her a chance to catch her breath and think about what she wanted to do with her life. She hadn't joined the circus and she had yet to ride a horse, but she had applied for a position at the local library when Josephine Alberty approached her out of the blue. After an interview where they bonded over shared passions for crime fiction and Butterfingers, Elenie was offered the job.

Now, she only visited Diner 43 as a customer, in the company of her friends.

"When you lose yourself in a book, you discover a whole new reality which you can visit for as long as you like, as often as you like, no matter what's happening in your everyday life," she told groups of children on their regular school visits. "And that magic begins again with every new book you pick up."

It had kept her sane during the worst of times. Roman got it, just like he got her. Thirsty to gain more experience and bursting with ideas and suggestions, she finally had prospects. And the future was exciting.

"You still with me?" Roman's lips dipped to touch her temple. "I lost you there for a minute."

"You'll never lose me. You're stuck with me for good now."

"Dammit." His contented drawl made her stomach flip.

"All my dreams are about us. And I would go through everything again to end up here, with you." Elenie looked up at him—her strength, her love, her everything. "*Mi media naranja.*⁶"

Roman closed his eyes and cleared his throat. "Ditto to that, sweetheart."

---

6   Mi media naranja (my soulmate / my better half / literally: my half-orange)—Spanish

He pressed a kiss to her hair, his stubble grazing her skin. The warmth of him, his closeness, filled her nostrils. Filled her heart. Long fingers tracing the zipper running down the center of her back, he smoothed his hands gently over her ass.

"I can't wait to undo this when we get home, and watch your dress slide to the floor. Starting and ending every day together is never going to get old." A shiver of desire snaked down her spine and she reached up to brush her mouth against his, running her tongue over his lower lip. Roman's groin tightened against her stomach. "Stop that or we'll end up in the storage room again." The deep rumble of his voice was the sexiest sound she'd ever hear.

Elenie lifted herself on tiptoes to whisper in his ear. "Promises, promises."

ACKNOWLEDGMENTS

This mad journey properly began when an email from Tanera Simons made me squeal in a National Trust café. I couldn't believe then that she was prepared to give my characters a chance and, to be honest, I'm still getting my head around it now. Thank you, Tanera. I'll be forever grateful to you and Laura Heathfield for your initial interest and advice.

Huge thanks to my lovely agent, Rebeka Finch, who inherited me soon afterwards and is the perfect person to have in my corner, and to the rights team for their solid support. I'm thrilled to be a part of the wider Darley Anderson family.

Thank you to Victoria Pepe and Victoria Oundjian for your kind and enthusiastic expertise and navigational guidance through these unfamiliar waters. And to everyone else at Montlake Romance and Amazon Publishing, including Allyse Karam and the design team for your work on the stunning cover of *More Than Nothing*.

Thank you to Fischer Verlag in Germany for your early interest in this book and for the heavenly sprayed edges—author goal unlocked!

Thank you to the writing friends I've made along the way— Malika Nekhla and Elaine Hastings, I'm talking about you. It means so much to be able to share the craziness (and all the waiting!!) with you both, and your input, advice and moral support continues to be invaluable. I'm so grateful you answered my tragic plea for a writing buddy, Malika. And Elaine, should we thank Asteroid Guy for bringing us together or did we just bond over a mutual loathing for question time? I don't remember. Either way, I had no idea then how much fun our group WhatsApp would turn out to be. Let's hope it never gets hacked.

Thank you to Madison Myers and Kaymie Wuerfel for sharing your beautiful books with me and for reading and enthusing over *MTN*! (I particularly love the 'I'MMM SCREAMINGGGGG' messages I get—they make me happier than I can express.)

The immensely talented Courtney from Romance and Rosemary is another newfound joy in my life. She continually manages to pluck the essence of my characters out of my head and produce them in perfect art form. The world is not ready for the Roman she has created—right down to his mug of hot tea. You are phenomenal, babe.

Thank you to Cherise Watson, who read a copy of *More Than Nothing* way too early and was still kind enough to say nice things.

Thank you to my wonderful Ma, who let me lie inside the tent and read on many a family holiday without moaning too much about me missing out on the wonders of rural Wales/France, and to Dan and Minnie for kindly sharing the humorous genes which make us all so very, extremely funny. I love you all. My dad always wanted to read anything I wrote and I wish he was still here so I could show him this book. I know he'd be extremely proud. But it's also a relief not to have to redact an entire copy just to be able to look him in the eye come Christmas. "Yeah, it was just kissing in Chapter 37, Dad. A lot of kissing."

A special mention to my gorgeous girls, who are beautiful, kind and crack me up every single day. My proudest achievement is being your mum. Second proudest achievement, maybe, now I've written this book. Thank you, Mads, Erin and Martha, for reading

MTN and being so cool about it. Thank you, Ims, for not. Perhaps now you're officially an adult it might be OK. But probably best not to risk it.

It wouldn't be fair not to mention here the many, many 'classic thats' which Martha made me take out of earlier drafts and her witty and incisive edit notes such as '#startedreadingithadabreakdownbonappetit' and 'Reading this part felt like I was being kicked in the throat whilst also being serenaded by puppies.' Thank you, MJ, for making me laugh until I cried. Cake or a scone at Nymans?

Finally, thank you times a million to my fantastic husband, Trevor, who made *MTN* the first work of fiction he's read since leaving school. He's not a fan of 'made-up shit' usually (that's a direct quote), but he made an exception for me and, honestly, who could ask for more? He's my media naranja and the voice of wholehearted encouragement in everything I do, even if a lot of the talking is a bit early in the morning for me. He always believed I could do this and so I did.

I really did.

I wrote a book!

Yay, me.

If you enjoyed *More Than Nothing*, read the next book in the Pine Spring series, *Every Reason Why*!

Chapter 1
Leah

Never flirt at a funeral. As far as life lessons go, it was right up there at the top.

There had been a tightness in Leah's throat, a prickle behind her eyes, right up until he walked to the front of the chapel and started speaking with a voice like honey-coated gravel. She'd have put money on her tears falling when the beautiful words began to echo in the still and airless room. Instead, she was hooked.

He was enormously tall. A mountain of a man in a charcoal three-piece which made Leah's mouth water. Without referring to any notes, he recited the Leo Marks poem "The Life That I Have" which Esther had requested—the same poem the old lady had read herself at her late husband's funeral. His deep voice was steady, a frown pinching his eyebrows. His gaze swept over the small gathering of mourners as he spoke, a laser beam scanning the room, scalding a path through the chapel. Dark hair curled just above the collar of his shirt, a little longer than average and less sleekly groomed than the rest of him, attitude in every strand.

Tense and shuttered, nothing about his face was friendly. His shoulders were rigid. Posture as arrogant as an NFL linebacker, the tilt of his chin had superiority written all over it. And yet Leah felt the impact, the click, an indefinable *something* that whispered, *There you are.* A soft, thrumming soul-voice calling to her, invisible fingers tugging on her sleeve. In the plain and stifling room, he was a star of zinc sulfide, luminescent and mesmerizing. When their eyes connected, Leah's heart went into freefall like an elevator in a disaster movie.

Despite the occasion and all the distress of the past couple of months, she smiled at him.

You've got this, Leah told him, mind to mind.

Great job.

I love your suit.

You're gorgeous.

Without the slightest flicker, his arctic blue eyes slid impassively from her face, passing to Hazel on her right (Esther's friend and neighbor), to Gerry and Marjorie (from the general store), Ailsa (Esther's gardener), and across the aisle to three of the ladies from their book club. He spared them each as much attention as he'd given her. And moved on to the next row.

Mortification formed a messy knot in her chest. Leah had never been more grateful she wasn't a violent blusher. When would she learn a little restraint?

Sending an apology skyward to Esther, she focused on her hands as the oblivious object of her attention finished speaking and stepped back to his seat at the front. It was quite an introduction to Esther's grandson, Jackson Hale. The only person listed on the heavy, cream-colored order of service other than the funeral officiant who'd already addressed the gathering. Even if his name hadn't been there in black on buff, she'd have known who he was from the many times she'd discussed him with Esther. And her own personal Google searches.

Jackson sat beside a pretty blonde with a blunt-cut bob and exquisite makeup. Flanking him on his other side were his parents.

His father, who Leah also recognized thanks to a stiff corporate headshot from their company website, was Esther's son. None of them had visited Esther in the two years Leah had lived with her, and she would be lying if the reminder of that didn't stick a big, fat needle into the balloon of momentary attraction.

All four were dressed head to toe in immaculate black, the girlfriend sporting a fascinator which bobbed and quivered each time she moved. Leah curled her fingers into the tatty cuffs of her black sweater dress, feeling like a small and scruffy eighth grader, the sodden mess of emotions in her chest growing weightier by the minute.

Matt would have sneered at the Hales. He'd have told Leah to toughen up, rolled his eyes at her stricken face. For all his easygoing outward chill, her ex-boyfriend had been hard through and through—as warm and supportive as concrete pantyhose. Well, Matt wasn't here. Matt could fuck off.

The first chords of "Amazing Grace" rippled through the air and everyone rose to their feet. They stumbled through the verses in a painful display of too few voices and little musical talent, made bearable only by a loud and enthusiastic contribution from the officiant. Leah's voice grew tighter and tighter, stuttering entirely on the word "home" in the third verse. A vortex of panic swirled in her stomach, turning her hands clammy.

Home.

Was she always to be stuck in this holding pattern, one slip of a foot away from couch surfing and begging favors? Memories of homelessness rolled and swelled, huge and monstrous. It was impossible to sing anymore. A tear ran into the corner of her mouth, hot against her lips, and she made it vanish with the tip of her tongue, furiously ashamed to be crying for herself at Esther's funeral. By her side, Hazel reached for Leah's hand and held it firmly in her own as the hymn lumbered to an end.

She had to believe it would be OK. At the very least, she had Esther's approval to remain at Amity Court until the house was sold. There was still time to concoct a plan, build allegiances, win people over if necessary. Be friendly, appealing, undemanding—helpful, even. She'd done it before, a dozen times. She could do it again if it meant keeping a roof over her head until she found somewhere else to go.

As piped music swelled to mark the end of the service, Esther's family stood first and slowly left the chapel through a door at the front. None of them looked at the coffin. Jackson Hale rested a broad hand between his girlfriend's shoulders. How comforting to have that kind of support.

"Short but sweet. Just how she wanted it." Hazel sighed as she stood, stretching knees that had likely stiffened while she sat. The old lady's face was drawn. "Are you alright, sweetheart?"

Leah nodded, scraped raw, suddenly exhausted. She tucked her hand beneath Hazel's elbow. "I'm fine."

By the time they'd made their way to the main doors, edging carefully past the tasteful floral display of white roses, baby's breath, and eucalyptus stems, the Hales had climbed into a black Tesla and were already pulling away from the parking lot. Leah watched the car until it disappeared toward the highway, heading in the opposite direction from Esther's home on the edge of Pine Springs.

They exchanged hugs and goodbyes with the other book club ladies. Cassidy, mom of professional hockey player Tanner Stone, gave them both a kiss on the cheek and paused for a chat with Hazel, while Ava and Florence Martinez, mother and daughter, dragged Leah in for a tight hug. It was a testament to her love of Esther to see Ava in muted colors when her natural exuberance usually spilled over into an array of bright clothing.

"She'd have been very happy with a simple send-off like that," Ava murmured into her ear. "Surrounded by family and friends. That's all any of us can ask for."

"I know you're having a hard time with this, but we're here for you, babe." Florence's reassurance did nothing to dispel the lump in Leah's throat, so she just nodded in response and forced a smile.

The remains of a late flurry of snow lay on the ground and a bitter wind lifted Leah's hair, blowing it into her face, but there was a faint promise of the Michigan springtime in the fresh air. She lifted her head, blinking slowly, and savored the glow of weak sunshine on her closed eyelids.

There should be a rule against holding funerals in March. March was for new beginnings, not endings.

"Anyone for an Oreo mini?" Marjorie asked as Gerry popped the locks on their Honda Fit. "I think I have some in the glovebox. Funerals always make me hungry."

"Why would you keep my least favorite snack in your car?" grumbled Hazel. "Oreo minis are worse than no cookies at all."

"I bet the Hales have Crumbl cookies in their glovebox. They look like boxed-snack kind of people." Gerry cleaned his glasses with the end of his tie.

"Boxed snacks, maybe. Cookies in the glovebox, I'd doubt it." Hazel sank onto the back seat with a relieved huff.

Leah, climbing in beside her, thought of Jackson Hale's girlfriend and her flawless appearance. "Blinis in the conservatory. That's the kind of people they are." She wrapped her arms around her body for warmth and gazed out of the window at the sign that read "Sandy Grove Funeral Home and Cremation Center." The letters blurred, the conversation around her faded out.

She was alone. Again. She'd lost someone she loved. Again. And the feeling of isolation that clawed at her chest was worse than grief, worse than fear, worse even than the prospect of having nowhere to live.

* * *

Leah did her best to bury herself in work for the rest of the week; Esther had left plenty to get on with. Fragile rays of sun eased through the smeared study window, pooling in dappled patches on the wooden floor and playing on the desktop as Leah shifted through some papers. The verse of a song had snagged in her mind and she hummed the lyrics on repeat as she busied herself, searching for what she needed.

"Come on, Esther. Give it up—" It should be here somewhere.

She was transcribing Esther's last manuscript—the conclusion to a crime series—which Leah had helped the old lady complete in her final months of life. Most of it, plotted before the swift illness had stolen her strength, was written laboriously in longhand on sheaves of white paper, the end dictated breathlessly into a hurriedly purchased Dictaphone. For their own reference some time ago, after struggling to keep things ordered in their minds, they had written out a complicated timeline together, plotting the protagonist's career path, cases and work colleagues over the years. And now Leah couldn't find it.

She spun her pen on the desk, scrubbed at a smear of ink on her forefinger, and stared sightlessly at the fraying drapes framing the window. She knew it was in one of Esther's old notepads. Her gaze wandered the room. She really needed to tidy up soon; it was a mess. But, haphazard though it may be, there was some sense in the order and she knew where most things were.

Definitely not here.

Leah pushed back the chair. Maybe Esther had stored her filled notepads upstairs.

The pulsing silence that enveloped the old house beat even louder in Esther's bedroom, as if this room actively missed and mourned its mistress. How did people just stop being? It still seemed impossible to Leah—that someone could be there one minute, doing everyday things, and gone the next. Not only gone but never to come back again. Not even to pop up and say, "Whoops, sorry! I forgot to say such-and-such."

One hundred percent gone.

She took the lid off a pot of face cream on the vanity and held it to her nose. Honeysuckle sweet, it brought a flicker of a smile to her lips but gave her no sense of the old lady's presence. Esther had been so much more than a scent.

Recapping the pot, Leah replaced it gently in front of the mirror and looked around. Fairly sure the dresser contained only clothes, she tried each drawer in turn regardless, proving herself right. With no closet in the room, there were few other places to store anything. Apart from under the bed.

Leah dropped to her knees and lifted the frilly valance, recoiling at a hidden wasteland populated not so much by dust bunnies as tumbleweed-style balls of debris she'd rather not identify. Plus one storage box and an old suitcase.

She pulled the box out first, grimacing at the thick layer of dust that covered the top. Peeking inside, Leah found it filled with shoes—about eight pairs, some sturdy and practical, some extravagant, obviously expensive and pristine. She wished she'd known the Esther who'd bought and worn the stylish shoes. They were fabulous.

The suitcase was cream in color and scuffed, the hard-shelled lid dipped and creased with age. She heaved at the handle and dragged it out from beneath the bed. Brushing at her dusty knees, Leah flipped the catch and opened it up an inch or two.

Bingo.

A stack of notepads nestled next to a bundle of old photographs, held with an elastic band. On top was a casual shot Leah hadn't seen before of Esther and a small child at the beach—it must be Jackson Hale's father. Tempted to leaf through them, she left the photos where they were. It seemed intrusive to rummage any more than necessary.

There were eleven notepads in total and she stacked them in two piles on the floorboards. Flicking open the top one, she smiled to see Esther's handwriting covering the pages. Green ink. Always green ink. She had no idea why. There were snippets of ideas, diagrams, names, and questions throughout. Some sounded familiar, and Leah linked them to one of Esther's more recent books. Putting the first notebook to one side, she reached for the next.

Before long, she had identified the novel that each notepad related to—there was a new book for each title (*thanks for making this simple, Esther*)—and they rested in chronological order beside her knees. She gave a hum of satisfaction when she came across the one containing the timeline she needed.

A cloud drew across the sun as Leah reached for the last book, the bedroom darkening a little. She debated turning on a lamp but was distracted by the notepad on her lap. Smaller than the others and thin, it had a faded purple cover that looked well-handled, and her fingers brushed the battered edges of an old black-and-white photograph poking from the pages. Leah pulled it free.

The two girls, posing joyfully on a bridge over the Chicago River, were immediately identifiable as youthful versions of Esther and Hazel. Their smiles wide, their arms linked. Their coats, hats, and hunched shoulders told Leah it was wintertime. With unlined faces and dark hair, they looked to be quite a bit younger than her own twenty-seven years. Joy spilled from the image and settled on her own lips as Leah placed the photo to one side.

With casual curiosity, she flicked the book open at the first page and found herself staring at diary entries in a flamboyant hand. They were completed sporadically, a few lines here, a longer paragraph there, not every date given an entry. She ran her gaze over the first few, her smile growing wider.

January 1st, 1972

This is going to be the best year of my life. Lots of firsts already and it's only day one! First New Year's Eve back home with Hazel—fun!! First hangover—not such fun!!! First kiss—better than I ever imagined!!!!!!!!!!!

(Please excuse all the exclamation points.)

January 6th, 1972

Atherton Hale has asked to meet me at the Evanston Library next Wednesday at 2 p.m. I've read and reread his note a dozen times. Hazel says I must go—as if there was any doubt. WHAT DO I WEAR??

January 11th, 1972

Libraries have always been my favorite places and now kissing in the library is my favorite thing to do. How scandalous!

The spine of the diary moved loosely in Leah's hands, front and back covers shifting against the paper within, as if the book wasn't as full as it should be. She leafed through, flipping pages between her fingers, until the entries stopped, abruptly, way sooner than they should have done. The last half of the diary had been ripped from the cover, leaving jagged edges where the paper used to be.

On the final double page, three words—completely at odds with the previous bubbly entries—slashed through the lines over and over again.

I HATE HIM

I HATE HIM

I HATE HIM

I HATE HIM

I HATE HIM

I HATE HIM

I HATE HIM

I HATE HIM

I HATE HIM

The handwriting sprawled with explosive abandon, screaming in painful fury. Pressed deep into the page, the final three words had been underlined with such force it had split the paper.

Leah snapped the diary shut and pulled it against her chest, breath frozen.

What the hell, Esther?

She sat on the bedroom floor for a full ten minutes, fingers running up and down the spine of the book. She'd gone in search of information and unearthed a secret. Like heating Cup Noodles and popping the lid to find oatmeal, it was an unwelcome and disturbing surprise.

ABOUT THE AUTHOR

Sophie Hamilton is a diehard romance devotee. If a lifelong search for her own personal Happy Ever After has taught her anything, it's that the path to true love almost never runs smoothly—but it does make a great story.

A PR journalist for over twenty years, she writes from the Georgian home in West Sussex that she has been renovating with her husband. She is unnaturally obsessed with dinosaurs and quite fond of her children, too.

The second book in the Pine Springs series is *Every Reason Why*.

Follow Sophie on Instagram and TikTok @sophiehamiltonauthor, X @SophieHAuthor, or visit her website: www.sophiehamiltonauthor.com.

Follow the Author on Amazon

If you enjoyed this book, follow Sophie Hamilton on Amazon to be notified when the author releases a new book!
To do this, please follow these instructions:

Desktop:

1) Search for the author's name on Amazon or in the Amazon App.
2) Click on the author's name to arrive on their Amazon page.
3) Click the "Follow" button.

Mobile and Tablet:

1) Search for the author's name on Amazon or in the Amazon App.
2) Click on one of the author's books.
3) Click on the author's name to arrive on their Amazon page.
4) Click the "Follow" button.

Kindle eReader and Kindle App:

If you enjoyed this book on a Kindle eReader or in the Kindle App, you will find the author "Follow" button after the last page.

Printed in Dunstable, United Kingdom